It's Not You

Cara D. Smith

Warning

This is a work of fiction. Names, characters, businesses, places, events, and incidents are either the products of the author's imagination or used in a fictitious manner. Any resemblance to actual persons, living or dead, or actual events is purely coincidental.

The following story contains mature themes, strong language, and sexual situations. It is intended for mature readers.

Dedication

For Isaac and Steven.

One more time, for the people in the back!
The following story contains mature themes, strong language, and sexual
situations. It was written for a mature audience.

Contents

Chapter 1

Ryan

"C'mon, Ry! It's just one class!" Chris rocks back in his office chair and crosses his arms over his chest.

I mimic him, staring him down across his desk as if I can put an end to this argument with sheer force of will. I'm not going to budge here. He should know that. Most of the time, Chris and I work well together. It's effortless. We each have our strengths, and those compensate for the other's weaknesses. But when we don't . . .

"So put them in one of the other classes!" That argument didn't work the first two times, but maybe the third try really *is* a charm. He might be sick of trying to out-stubborn me by now. He didn't ask. He informed me that some stupid magazine—I've already forgotten the name—wants to do a piece on MaxPower. Which sounded great until he told me they wanted to put someone in the class.

The clock on the wall behind him says we've been at this for twenty minutes. His next class starts in fifteen. If we don't come to an agreement now, this will drag into tomorrow, making it a shitty day for both of us.

Chris sighs and shoves his fingers through his curly red hair. "They don't want to do one of the other classes! They want to review MaxPower. This could be good for us—for this program. *Your* program! Think of the business it could bring in. And you and your program could be a household name someday!"

My program. My chest swells with pride. I've worked on developing this program for months, combining years of Chris's data and my training to compile a series of workouts that can be modified to any skill level and deliver results. As long as the students work, it will. *And that student isn't going to work.* Chris has lost his mind.

We've been here before with some blogger friend of Mason's ex. The chick *begged* to be in one of my classes, barely even tried, and then used her platform as a wannabe fitness influencer to bash the hell out of everything from my intelligence to the color of the walls in the studio. This won't be good for the program at all. We'll end up with someone who will coast their way through, then criticize us and our gym when we don't deliver the promised results. And I don't have the patience for it again. Last time, we only lost maybe a dozen members, and they were quick to let us know why. If an *influencer* can cost us a dozen members, how many will a negative review in a widely read magazine lose us?

"But you'll handle the next round! Tell them to wait until the next cycle." If he really wants this, he can deal with them. He is better suited to coaxing people into giving more than their bare minimum. I can be perfectly patient in a one-on-one setting, but when I'm supposed to be helping a full class, I don't have time to hold one person's hand through the whole thing.

There's nothing wrong with being a complete beginner—with having no prior knowledge of *anything* fitness related. Some people come in who have never been to a gym before, who couldn't pick a dumbbell out of a lineup, but woke up one morning and decided they want a six-pack. We make a lot of money off people like that. They come in, they pay for a membership, take a couple of classes, then bail because you actually have to work and sacrifice for that six-pack and they're not ready to do either.

I do enjoy working with the ones who are ready to commit, helping them learn and do everything right. It's a rewarding process to watch them overcome their struggles one by one. But I do not like throwing them in the middle of a class where I've promised my time and assistance to fourteen people.

Chris squints at me and strokes his beard. "What do you have against this?" he finally asks instead of trying yet again to make me see this as a good thing.

My fingers drum restlessly on my thigh. "We both know they're going to send some spaghetti-armed pipe cleaner who has never set foot in a gym. I'll spend all my time babysitting them when I'm supposed to be teaching! I won't be able to help anyone else. They won't put in the work, then they'll roast us for the world to see."

Chris closes his eyes and leans forward, propping one elbow on the desk and resting his head against it while he pinches the bridge of his nose. "But this program is designed for anyone. Even a noob putting in half the work will still see progress. That's why they want to do the article. They want to see if it really works as advertised. It's one class, man. We can pull in one of the other trainers to help, but I promised these guys you'd personally see to whoever they send." His mouth opens like he has more to say, but he closes it.

I grit my teeth. "What else?"

Chris winces, and I drag in a deep breath through my nose, searching for some semblance of calm before he drops another bomb on me. He opens one eye and says, "And five of his friends."

Is he fucking *serious?* A new surge of anger propels me to my feet. I squeeze my fists until my nails dig into my palms, using the pain to remind myself that Chris is my friend and I can't hit him until he agrees with me. No matter how badly I want to sometimes. "That's half the fucking class, Chris!" I manage to say though my jaw is clenched so tightly my teeth are probably in danger of cracking.

He rolls his eyes at me. "Don't exaggerate. It's not quite half."

"Forgive me for not being a glass-half-full kind of guy here," I snap at him. "I know the class is designed to work for beginners, but there are beginners, and there are *beginners.*"

I know he knows what I mean . . . Having *six* of them in one class is a recipe for disaster!

"We'll get Logan to—"

"No," I cut him off. Logan would be a great help, but it's the principle of the thing now. "I'm not doing it!"

Chris's tired smile chips away at my anger. It highlights the dark circles under his eyes and the worry lines around them, making him look much older than our mutual twenty-nine years. *He's got it hard enough, and here I am being an ass. Still . . . what he's asking is ridiculous.* "Well, you kinda are. I already gave them the green light. Think of all the lives you can improve once this piece is published and people see the results, Ryan! We'll get hundreds of new memberships. You might get calls from gyms out of state wanting to pay you to teach their trainers about MaxPower."

I pace to the door before I do or say something stupid. This is *beyond* ridiculous! He's only giving me the illusion of choice, dangling that in front of me when he's already committed me to this. And then he throws that low blow with helping people live their best life. He *knows* that shit is my Achilles' Heel.

I turn around to glare at him some more because it makes me feel better. "I hate you," I growl at him. "I hate this place."

"I'll see you tomorrow," we say together, completing the joke.

He scrubs his face with one hand and leans back in his chair again. "Look, Ry, I know you're not happy about this, but it'll be good in the long run. Just give it a chance. We'll assign Logan to help. Everything will be fine. You've handled worse than six noobs in one class."

He's not wrong there . . . "Wine Wednesday," I whisper, horrified by the mere mention of that colossal catastrophe.

Chris nods. "Exactly. If you can handle a class full of sloshed women every week for three months, you can handle six noobs daily for six weeks."

"Famous last words," I mutter. At least with that women's self-defense class, I had time to blow off steam between sessions. And those women had a point. Defending yourself when you're inebriated *is* different than doing it sober, and they need to know how to do both. But *damn*, a class full of giggling, groping ladies was something else.

This will be its own kind of hell. I'll get one day a week to separate myself from this, and if they don't do the recovery exercises at home like they're supposed to, the next day will be an extra special sort of torture.

A rap on the door has me looking over my shoulder. Logan's blond head is the only visible part of him. "I heard my name?"

"Yeah," Chris says. "You'll be helping with the next round of MaxPower. We're going to have some . . . special students that will require Ryan's undivided attention."

Logan grins. "Sweet! I'm dying to try it!"

"Well, here's your chance. If this goes well, we'll see about getting you set up with your own class," Chris tells him.

Having a third instructor trained and ready *will* take some pressure off me. It will give me some time to plan the next step—a more advanced version for people who've finished the first program. And Logan is a good choice for it. He's got the patience to work with the beginners, but he's fit enough the advanced students will feel comfortable with him. That's the bad thing about this job. If a person can't look at you and immediately see your dedication to fitness, see that you've put in the work, they don't trust you to know what the hell you're doing.

"I'm in!" Logan tells him. "By the way, your spin class is filling up already. Thought you should know."

"Get your ass away from me before I kick it," I growl at Chris, but I grin so he knows I'm messing with him. Yeah, I'm pissed, but Chris has his reasons. He knows what he's doing. I don't have to like it, but he knows. He pushes away from his desk and heaves his heavy ass to his feet, the old chair he refuses to replace groaning in relief. "Go ride your bicycle."

He shoves my shoulder on his way by. "Fuck you."

"Time and place, sweet cheeks. Still waiting for you to name them."

"I fucking hate you." I might believe it if he wasn't laughing.

"Liar."

Sighing, I follow him out and duck into my office. I should work on something, but I'm too restless for paperwork. I get my keys and head home.

Chapter 2
Trista

"*I*'m sorry, you want me to *what?*" I swear I heard my boss say she wants me to do some weightlifting class, but that's ridiculous. No one would want *me* to do something like that—I can barely lift a gallon of milk! We have writers on staff who specialize in such things.

I'm an editor. I edit. I write small, research-based pieces sometimes—nothing that requires me to leave my desk. I have a nice, *safe*, comfortable job. *Just what Mom wanted.*

Exactly what Mom wanted. It was her dream job, after all. Before my dad happened. *Before* I *happened.*

Rachel smiles at me over her coffee cup, amusement dancing in her green eyes. *Even she knows this is ridiculous.* "We want you to do a piece on a workout program called MaxPower."

"Is it April Fool's Day?" I ask, glancing at the date on my computer screen. That has to be the explanation. This is an office-wide joke. But no. It's a random Friday in the middle of July. April is long gone.

"The next class doesn't start until August," Rachel says in a soft tone I'm sure she means to be soothing. "We ask that you don't change anything about your daily life before it starts."

My head spins. Does she not hear me saying I don't want to do this? That they've picked the wrong person? "What do you mean?"

"Don't try to prepare for the class in any way." She sits up a little taller and her eyes rove over me from the desk up. "You don't exercise, do you?"

"No," I answer automatically. I'm used to people speaking for me, but those people tend to listen when I speak for myself. Rachel isn't listening. I don't know what to do here.

She smiles and nods, apparently pleased with my answer. "Good. You were selected for this piece because we want to see if these guys can deliver on the results they promise."

"But Eddie—"

Rachel runs right over my objection without the slightest pause. "What better way to do that than to send someone who doesn't exercise and watch the transformation happen?"

"Rachel—"

She pushes a piece of paper across my desk. "Here are the details. When you get there, ask for Logan. He'll sort everything out. Oh! I almost forgot! I know you're shy, so I worked it out so you can bring friends with you. No more than five."

Well, at least there's that. I open my mouth to try again to make her see reason, but she stands up, sweeps a hand over her skirt, and turns for the door.

"Nice chat, Tris. I've got a meeting in five. Have a good weekend! Ta ta!"

The door closes behind her with a click that sounds a lot like defeat. *What just happened?* How *did this happen?* I was sitting here, minding my own business, and she came sweeping in with two cups of coffee—the "good" stuff, not the stuff from the breakroom that's just okay—and the news that I *get* to do this article.

My desk is already in perfect order, but I compulsively tidy anyway, working around the paper Rachel left until it's the only thing I haven't straightened or dusted. Unable to ignore it any longer, I pull it in front of me and read through the date and the address. That address . . . surely it's not . . . Even if it *is* Ryan and Chris's gym, the note says to ask for Logan, not Ryan.

Of course it doesn't say to ask for Ryan. He's the co-owner. He's way too busy for something like this. Even I can't be unlucky enough to have to work with him. He'll be doing paperwork or working with professionals or something. Most people would rather work with someone they know. Okay, it's me. I'm most people. Not if it means I have to deal with *him*, though. He makes me so nervous!

I'm positive he secretly hates me. He's always so . . . intense. And brooding. He walks around looking like he's half a second from going off on the next person who looks at him sideways. But then something makes him smile, and he's a whole different person for about five seconds. I can never tell if he's actually in a mood or if that's just how he looks.

And God forbid I have to make a decision with him around . . . He stands there watching me like I'm wasting valuable time, but he won't let anyone speak for me, either. That's more pressure I don't need because making decisions is hard enough. What if I make the wrong choice and he's disappointed in me after he's spent all that time waiting for me to make up my mind?

Life would be easier if he avoided me, but then I'd never see him.

But why do I want to see him? It makes no sense at all.

It's not only Ryan, though. I don't want to disappoint anyone, which is why I end up doing a lot of things I don't want to do. I don't know how to say no without causing conflict. And conflict makes me nervous.

My phone screen lights up with a reminder for tonight—drinks at Easy Speak. It's like a light at the end of the tunnel; only I know that heavenly glow is an oncoming train. Mason and Fern will be there. *Because this day isn't bad enough already.* At least there will be booze.

Since I have to do this thing, I may as well get started now. I grab my phone and tap out a text for my besties. I know they'll be in. Tara loves to work out and now that the baby has suddenly decided food is good, she can again. Noel will be there because she knows I need her and because she works out anyway, so we may as well do it together.

Me: I guess I'm doing some workout program for an article. It starts in three weeks. I get to bring five friends. You in?

My thumb hovers over the send button. I really want to invite Jam. But if I invite her, I need to invite Fern. She can probably dead press her own body weight, or whatever the heck it's called. Yet another reminder that she's clearly better than I am. *Stop being bitter.*

She's not better than me, she's just better for him than I am.

But maybe her perfection will distract the trainer, and he won't pay as much attention to me. Yeah. That seems plausible. I can hide behind her, Tara, and Noel.

I tap the appropriate names and add Tara's business partner Madi on a whim. Might as well use all five spaces. And I can use all the moral support I can get.

Answers come in immediately. My phone buzzes so long it's a wonder it doesn't vibrate itself to pieces.

Tara: Heck yes!

Noel: WTF? Did you draw the short straw or something? Yeah, count me in.

Tara: Madi is in too!

Fern: Absolutely! Thanks for the invite. I'm excited!

Jam: You're going to make me get out of bed early aren't you?

Noel: Suck it up! It's good for you. That goes for Tris too.

Me: Thanks ladies.

I put my phone back on its charging cradle and lean back in my chair. A sigh works its way up, but I'm not sure if it's relief or disappointment. I don't want to do this. *Why didn't I just put my foot down and refuse like a normal person?* But that could've got me fired. I might not have picked this line of work for myself, but I do enjoy it. And I'm good at it. I don't want to lose it, so I guess this is a small price to pay.

My phone continues to buzz like a hive of angry bees, but I ignore it and focus on the last hour of work. I can't slack because of this. Rachel would be so disappointed in me. Mom would too, and it'll be further proof that I'm too much of a screw up to take care of myself.

Chapter 3
Trista

The bouncer at the door is one I recognize, but I don't know his name. He nods to Noel and me, and opens the door for us. Since we're technically here with Fern, we get to skip the line. The people waiting complain about it, but the bouncer rolls his eyes and ignores them.

Cringing, I mouth an apology to the closest people before Noel grabs my hand and hauls me through the door of our group's favorite hangout. My mood shifts before the door closes behind me—the day's disappointments washed away in a wave of sound. The music in here is a tangible thing. It's like walking into a wall of sound that quickly surrounds you, pressing in on all sides until every molecule of your body vibrates with it. It's not my kind of music—Mom listens to classical—but I love it anyway. Conversation below a shout is next to impossible, but there's something about this karaoke bar that keeps us coming back.

Noel's slender frame cuts a path through the crowd. People part for her in a way they never do for me, but that's not surprising since most people can look right over my head without trying. With my hand on her shoulder, I make it to the stairs without much trouble other than keeping up with her. That's a chore on a typical day but the heels I'm wearing make it a whole job. There's nothing in the dress code here that says I must wear heels, but I always feel like a little girl playing dress-up if I wear flats.

I dance my way up the stairs since getting swallowed by the crowd isn't a threat anymore, eager to see Tara and the drink I'm sure she has waiting for me since we texted her as soon as we parked. Noel's platinum blond head clears the top of the stairs, and a cheer goes up from our table.

"You came!" Tara cries, greeting us with hugs.

"Yeah, Colton talked me into it," Noel says, plopping down into a vacant seat next to Tara.

Tara huffs out a sigh and rolls her eyes at the mention of her brother.

I squeeze between Gabe's chair and the one behind him and drop into an open seat on the other side of the table, favoring it over the one next to Noel so I can see them both. "Where are the others?" I ask, eyeing the drinks in front of empty seats.

Gabe waves vaguely over his shoulder toward the stairs. "Ryan and Chris texted like fifteen minutes ago to have us order drinks the next time we saw Monique. We did, but they still haven't turned up. Madi is trying to convince her boyfriend to come with her. The others are dancing."

With my back to the dance floor, there's no way to sneak a peek without everyone here knowing exactly what I'm up to. I'm not silly enough to think Gabe doesn't know about my . . . *whatever it is* for Mason. Tara knows, therefore Gabe knows. I'm trying hard to get over it. He's married now; I have no chance. *Not that I ever did.* It's easier said than done, though. Mom likes to remind me that I let him get away every time his name comes up.

Tara tilts her head to the side. "How did you get assigned this article, Tris?"

"Apparently, I'm perfect for it," I tell her with a shrug, hoping to come across as indifferent. I don't want a lecture about standing up for myself tonight. I want to forget all about work until Monday.

"I'm going to guess you didn't jump and down on the spot to volunteer," she says wryly.

I pretend to be distracted by something behind her to give myself time to decide how to answer. "Rachel decided I was the right person for the job."

She nods like she knew I was going to say that. "So you were voluntold."

"Yeah." *Story of my life.* "I tried to tell her she should send someone else, but she wouldn't listen."

Tara drums her fingers on her water glass. "Well, I hate to say it, but for once, I'm kind of glad."

"What?" I ask, certain that I heard her wrong. I expected a lecture about being the grown woman I am and standing up for myself and what I want, not grudging acceptance.

She shrugs and sort of smiles. "Trista, this will be *good* for you. I literally cannot think of a single downside to you doing this."

"Women are supposed to be soft and feminine!" I say, repeating Mom's horrified reaction to the news that a quarter of a semester of weightlifting was compulsory my freshman year of high school. She'll be just as outraged this time.

Tara slaps the table, making me jump. "That's crap. You can be soft and feminine and still be strong as fuck! Look at Fern—wait, bad example," she says with an apologetic wince. I wave away her concern. Fern is not the enemy. It's just easier to blame her, and I don't want to do that anymore. "She's a bad example for more than one reason. Your mother wouldn't consider her soft and feminine at all."

That's accurate. The only softness to Fern is her heart, and even that is stronger than I can fathom.

Tara reaches across the table and grabs my hand to squeeze it. "Trista, this program . . . I think you'll find more than one kind of strength. And I think you need that. I love you, and I'm not saying this to hurt you, but if you ever find yourself in a situation like I was with Gabe not too long ago . . ." She glances at her husband and cringes. "I don't see you leaving."

Gabe stills, but nods. He leans over and kisses the top of her head as if letting her know he doesn't hold what she just said against her.

I don't need his agreement to know she's right. And it sucks that I'm so weak. I could never do what she did. I can't even stand up to my mother, the woman who is supposed to love me unconditionally no matter what. How could I ever muster the strength to walk away from the love of my life if I wasn't happy? *If I just listen to Mom, I'll never be unhappy.* Or I always will, and I'll deal. Perspective . . . But I don't need a man and a bank account to be happy. I just don't know how to make her understand that.

"But this class . . ." she pauses and a small smile tugs up the corners of her mouth. "You'll find inner strength and confidence too."

Tears sting my eyes. It sounds too good to be true. That's a lot to ask of a six-week exercise program. Especially since I'm inclined to believe it'll achieve the opposite. *I can't be any less confident.* "How do you know?"

Her mouth presses into a determined line. "Experience. Do you know where we're going?"

I shake my head, not ready to give voice to my suspicion unless Chris or Ryan brings it up. "Not yet. All Rachel gave me was an address. I'll send it to you tomorrow." I know I should've looked it up already. I'm only delaying the inevitable.

"I'm proud of you for taking it on," she says with a bright smile. "It'll be great for you."

Heat floods my cheeks. My thoughts were too occupied with how wrong I am for this piece to consider how good it might be for me. Maybe when this is over, I'll be able to pour from a gallon of milk one-handed and open jars without the need for gadgets or help from the neighbor. *I hope so.* "Thanks, Tara."

She smiles again. "Your drinks will be here soon."

Noel reaches across the table for the full drink next to me. "Whose is this?"

"Ryan's," Gabe says.

The music hides my groan. I *would* manage to end up next to him. I was hoping for Chris or Austin. Or Mason, but I shouldn't hope for that . . . Better him than Ryan, though. He, at least, doesn't hate me.

"Welp, he's not here," Noel says, picking up the drink. "Shame to let it sit there and get watered down. Ryan drinks the good shit, after all." She tips it back and chugs, seemingly oblivious to our stares. Noel likes to have fun, but this is a little extreme for her.

She slams the glass on the table and looks around. "What?" she asks with a shrug. "That uh . . . conversation with Colt was a little intense."

"Ya don't say," Tara says, shaking her head.

Noel glances at the other drinks on the table and grabs the next one in line, which is likely Chris's. It disappears as quickly as Ryan's. "Relationships suck. Like, why do we do this to ourselves?"

"Sex," Gabe says with a wink for his wife.

My experience is limited, but I can't say sex was ever high on the list of reasons for me to tough it out in my previous relationships. But, of course, I'm not a man. It's different for them. They enjoy it every time.

"Oh yeah," Noel says, nodding as if it all makes sense now. "That."

Or maybe, the men I've been with were doing it wrong? Something to ponder later. Not that it matters. It's probably better that I don't have high expectations. That way, I won't be disappointed in the future.

"That's enough!" Tara cries, holding up her hand to stop Noel. "As long as you're sleeping with my brother, we do *not* talk about sexy times."

"What? You don't want to hear how—"

Tara slaps a hand over Noel's mouth. "No! I don't!"

Movement on the stairs draws my eyes just as Chris and Ryan top the stairs, both decked out in suits that wouldn't look out of place in a movie about the roaring twenties, which is fitting since this bar is a throwback to a Prohibition-era speakeasy and has the dress code to match. I suck in a breath. The other guys do suits for work, but it's always shocking to see these two dressed up. It's hard not to stare, and not just because it's such a change. I shouldn't notice such things about my friends, but *damn* they look *good*.

Tara follows my gaze, looking over her shoulder to watch the guys cross the little balcony to the table reserved for Fern and her friends. Behind them, Austin clears the stairs and turns toward the table with a smile on his face. Jam edges up next to him, and he casually drapes his arm around her waist.

Then Fern stops at the top of the stairs. She turns around and grins at Mason, who is eye level with her, and kisses him.

And I thought this day couldn't get any worse. *I would like to drink now.*

I'm trying. I really am. Realistically, I knew I never had a chance with Mason. I can handle them when they're not all mushy. But things like that are a knife to the heart. The good mood I found upon entering this place evaporates as quickly as it came. *I just want what they have.*

Monique appears behind Mason like an answer to my prayers. She weaves her way around and between the others while they claim their seats, depositing drinks on the table with deft ease. Chris and Ryan split up—Chris taking the long way around and Ryan choosing the same route I did and dropping into the chair beside mine just as Monique places my drink in front of me. My appletini glows in the dim light of the balcony, like some sort of witches' brew. Like a magical potion, it holds a promise. *Drink this and everything will be better . . . For a price.*

Right now, that price doesn't seem so high.

Saliva pools in my mouth in anticipation of my first taste of the sour sweetness in front of me. With the bowl of the glass cradled in both hands, I bring it to my lips and brace myself for the bite and the burn.

The first sip touches my tongue, and my skin erupts into goosebumps. I savor that first little bit before I swallow it. The little voice in the back of my head urges me to be smart, to put my glass down. I know what'll happen if I don't. But I don't want to be smart tonight. I want to make a decision for myself. I want to finish this drink right now and let the stress of the day drown in sour apple and alcohol.

I should know better. Gabe tried to drown his stress in alcohol. When that didn't work, he turned to drugs. I know what stress drinking did to him and to his relationship with Tara. But it's not like I do it all the time . . .

I can let go here, with these people, in a way I can't anywhere else. I don't *have* to be perfect with them, and that's just too appealing an opportunity to pass up. Tara will take my phone so I can't access social media and post something I'll regret, and she'll make sure I get home safely and without waking Mom up. I lower my glass enough to lock eyes with her over the rim. Her eyebrows climb her fore-head, but she gives me a little nod. *At least I thought to ask this time instead of spiraling off the deep end and leaving her to pick up after me.*

Comfortable in the knowledge that I can let go, I raise my glass again and drink until the sourness stops me. Then I hand her my phone before she asks for it.

Ryan

It's always amusing to listen to Austin and Jamaica flirt. Sometimes, they're ridiculously mushy and over the top now, but others I could swear they're a heartbeat away from hating each other. Again. But I'm only half-listening to them bicker while I watch Trista from the corner of my eye.

I'm worried about her. She was drunk when we first met, but after that, it took a whole year for her to drink again. Now, it seems like she's well on her way to wasted every other time I see her. Tara catches my eyes and widens hers, subtly tilting her head toward the tiny woman beside me—as if I wasn't already watching her. I lift my chin just a bit to let her know I understand. We're in for it tonight.

Yes, she does drink more often, but she rarely starts off hitting the booze *this* hard.

But I'm here. Tara thinks I'm only helping her keep an eye on Trista—we've talked about it a lot and she thanks me profusely every time.

What she doesn't know—and never will—is that I'm not doing this for the sake of our friendship.

I look back to Trista without turning my head and watch her throat work as she swallows. Some of her drink drips down her chin, drawing my eye lower to where it lands on her cleavage. My mouth waters. Appletinis aren't my thing, but I think I could like them if I get to lick them off her.

Trista pops to her feet, putting an end to the conversations around us as everyone looks at her. "I'm going to go dance," she says to no one in particular.

Fuck. Me. That dress . . . Tara says it would give Trista's mother a heart attack because it's so short on both ends.

I've got news for Tara; it's not just her mother at risk. She nearly kills me every time she wears it. Death by sexual frustration. Because that is one line I can't cross and my dick is an optimist. Even now, knowing I'll never touch her like that, I'm hard enough to cut diamonds.

"I'll come with you," Tara says.

Next to her, Noel flinches—probably because Tara kicked her—and a flash of light calls attention to her hand. Things must be going well because she wasn't wearing a ring when they finally told us the news. "Yeah, Colton won't mind if I dance. He knows who I'm going to home to," she says quickly.

"Nah!" Trista says, wiggling her fingers at them. "You two relax. You both look tired. I'll be fine. Be back later!" She walks away, ignoring the girls' protests.

The itch of eyes on me turns my head. Austin is smirking at me, practically daring me to chase after her with a look. *Fucker.* I'm not going to give him more evidence to use against me.

Something cold hits me in the neck and falls down into my jacket. "What the fuck?" I cry, jumping to my feet to shake the ice cube out. If anyone else had thrown it, I'd be pissed. But Tara is practically family, so she gets a pass.

"Sorry!" Tara calls, her voice betraying her—she's trying not to laugh. She stands up and grabs Gabe's collar, tugging at it until he stands too. "Will you come with us, Ry?"

There is nothing I'd rather do than follow Trista down those stairs and have a legitimate reason to take her in my arms, her body pressed against mine while we move together, but I don't want to seem too eager. I'm walking a fine line here. "I can keep an eye on her from here."

That, at least, serves as an excuse to turn around and watch.

Chapter 4

Trista

*E*yes shut tightly, I give myself over entirely to the music. Every part of me moves with the beat—even my heart. My head falls back into something soft. I open my eyes and smile at the look of surprise on the guy's face.

He answers with a smile of his own. Hands grasp my waist, and he moves with me. "Hey there, gorgeous. Nice to meet you!" he shouts.

"Hi," I say with another smile, taking in his glasses, the stubble dusting his jaw, his light eyes—the color is impossible to determine on the dance floor—and the blond hair gelled into untidy spikes. He's kind of cute, even if he isn't my type.

This dude's got the height down—not a challenge as short as I am—but something about him reminds me of one of my exes. I'm not sure what my type is, but it's not that. And I prefer brunettes. *Like Ryan.*

Woah. How much did I drink? Not Ryan. He's scary. Sexy, but terrifying. My brain definitely meant Mason.

But none of that matters. It's a dance, not a date. There's no harm in that. Mom would disagree, but she's not here. And I'm not a child anymore. I can make my own decisions.

The song that's playing is only familiar because someone sings it every time we're here. I don't know all the words, but I sing along anyway, making them up as I go. Singing makes me happy. So does dancing. I never want to stop. I'm so happy I can't even remember what I was upset about anymore!

The dude stops before the music. His hands tighten on my hips to the point it's hard for me to dance. *What's going on?* My head falls back against his chest again so I can ask, but I don't need to. The problem is standing next to us with his hand on Dude's shoulder.

"What's your problem?" Dude shouts at Ryan. He's braver than I am. Ryan looks very angry about something, though that is his default setting. He should smile more often. He has a nice smile. It always makes me happy.

Stop that. It's Ryan.

Ryan's lips move but whatever he says doesn't pierce the music to reach my ears. Dude's hands clench tighter in response. Painfully so.

"You're hurting me!" I yell.

He ignores me. *Why does everyone always ignore me?* It's so *frustrating!* And he's scaring me more than Ryan does now. Why won't he just let me go?

Ryan's eyes narrow to a dangerous degree. I'm not sure I've ever witnessed him squint that hard. I don't know what Dude did to make him mad, but he should run. Now.

"Get your hands off her, or I'll do it for you!" Ryan snarls. His intensity surprises me. Why is he so upset? Yeah, Dude is hurting me, and ignoring me, but I'm not sure that justifies threatening him.

"What are you, her keeper? Fuck off!"

Hey now! It's irrational, but I don't like the way he's talking to one of my friends. I just want Ryan to back off and Dude to let me go.

Ryan steps closer, crowding Dude. "You're hurting her!"

Dude looks down at me, blinking rapidly behind his glasses that are probably more for aesthetic than functionality. "Am I hurting you?" He shouts it like an accusation, not like he cares.

If he didn't hear me the first time, he won't hear me now, so I nod instead of speaking. Dancing with him was fine at first, but I don't think I like him very much. He's not nice.

His lips press into a hard line. "Fucking tease! Get caught by your boyfriend and make me out to be the bad guy here!" He shoves me away from him into the thicket of bodies.

Hands grab at me from all sides before I have a chance to get scared, keeping me on my feet. "Thank you!" I shout to no one specific. Without them, I'd probably be on the floor right now.

"I've got her," Ryan's gruff voice calls from behind me. "Thanks, man." A big hand slides into mine. Something settles within me.

He tugs on my hand like I'm some sort of unruly toddler who won't keep up and that sense of peace dissipates. "C'mon, Tris. You need a break."

His comment irritates me. I'd still be happy and dancing if it weren't for him. Everything was fine before he stepped in. I try to yank my hand away, but his fingers tighten around it. Somehow, it doesn't hurt, not like when Dude squeezed my hips. "What is *wrong* with you?" I scream, shoving at him with the hand he isn't holding prisoner. "I was having *fun!*"

Ryan just looks at me with the fraying patience of an adult watching a child throw a tantrum. *That's probably all I am in his eyes—someone to babysit.* And I hate that. I'm a grown woman, not a child. "So much fun you didn't notice him leading you toward the back hall," he says calmly.

"No! He . . ." I stop and look around because I can't honestly finish that sentence. We're a long way from the center of the dance floor now, which is where I was dancing when I bumped into him. And a lot closer to the back hall, and the back door . . . *How'd I get here?*

Ryan's right. The heat of the bodies packed around us doesn't stop the shiver that shakes me from the head down. How did I not notice? *Because you didn't care.* That was the whole point of drinking. I wanted to stop caring. About work. About this assignment. About how mad Mom will be in the morning. About the things I can't control, which is *everything.*

But that's just an excuse. The others won't question it if I blame the alcohol, but I know the truth. Mom's right. I'm too naïve. I let everyone take advantage of me.

"I drank too much," I tell him because I don't want to know what he'll say if I tell him the truth. Either way, the booze or the idiocy, it's on me.

He arches one eyebrow. "Ya think? C'mon. Let's go get some water in you."

"You don't have to babysit me," I mumble, embarrassed that I obviously *need* a babysitter. *And I wonder why he doesn't like me . . .* Dancing has lost its appeal now, though. I think it's better if I just watch.

He steps closer and leans in, putting his mouth directly in my line of sight. *What would it be like to kiss him?* Another shiver of fear works its way through my middle. I shouldn't think things like that. I shouldn't *want* things like that. Not from Ryan. He doesn't think of me that way. But I've always wondered . . .

"What?" he asks, oblivious to my stupid, drunk thoughts.

"I said, you don't have to babysit me!" I shout so loud my throat hurts.

Ryan holds up one finger, telling me to hold on, and turns his head. "What are you looking at?" he asks those nearest.

I follow his stare to the small group of people watching us like we're some sort of Soap Opera. *Not far off, I guess.*

One guy steps closer and holds out his hand to me. "Miss, is everything okay? Is this guy bothering you?"

As hot as I am from dancing, my cheeks get even hotter. Somehow, I forgot the crowd. "No—I mean yes! Everything is fine. He's a friend," I assure him. I might be irritated with Ryan, but I don't want him to get in a fight because of me. I'd feel bad for the people he hurt.

Ryan's a fighter. The way he moves—lightning-quick and smooth as water over glass. It's beautiful. The last time someone pushed him too hard, and things got physical, the other guy went to the hospital. It's been a few years now, but it's not something I'll ever forget. Even if someone else with training stepped in, once the other guys realized Ryan was in trouble, they'd all jump in. *Chaos.*

Time for water.

"I'm going!" I tell Ryan. "I can make it back."

"Right behind ya, Pixie Stix," he says, making a shooing motion with his hand.

Can I slap him hard enough to knock that condescending attitude out of him? Probably not. I'd hurt myself. He probably has a head like a boulder.

It would serve him right if I turned around and walked away. I can't make myself, though. I've already disobeyed too many orders tonight. I got drunk. I danced with a stranger. I listened to music that encourages promiscuity. I lied to my mom about where I am. And look what almost happened because of the first two.

Sighing, I march past him, taking the most direct path even though it'll take longer to cut through the crowd. I can use the time to get my shit together.

I don't feel like dancing on my way up the stairs this time. Not even if Ryan wasn't so close behind me his body heat is warm on my back. What just happened scares me. If not for Ryan . . . At the top of the stairs, I stop and turn to face him. He pulls up short and raises both eyebrows.

"Okay there, Pixie Stix?"

"Yeah . . . I just . . ." I fumble for the words I need to say. Words fail me, though. "Thank you," I tell him. It's inadequate but better than nothing at all.

The perpetually angry glare melts away, and he flashes me a smile. My thighs clench against the onslaught of heat rushing to my core. "You're welcome, Tris. And I know you don't need a babysitter, but I'll always have an eye on you. I do the same for all the other ladies too."

When he puts it that way, it doesn't seem so bad. Impulsively, I lean forward and kiss his stubbly cheek. When I withdraw, the sheer amazement on his face has me biting my tongue to keep from laughing. I never thought I'd see the day that *I* surprised him.

Really, I'm amazed I dared to do it. I'm glad I did, though. His reaction was a rush. Who'da thought I could get to him like that? "I appreciate it."

Good mood restored, I whirl around to dance my way to the table and stop mid-bop. My mood spirals down the drain once more. Mason has Fern in his lap and his lips glued to hers.

Chapter 5
Ryan

*T*rista freezes at the top of the stairs, and I groan on instinct. I have no idea what's got her panties in a twist this time, but it's going to be rough. I thought things were turning around when she kissed my cheek—which I *refuse* to dwell on—but I was obviously wrong. The problem is plain as day over the top of her head. Mase is getting his PDA on. I'm not such a prude that it bothers me, but I know it's destroying her.

I give her a gentle push toward the table, reminding her to move as much as letting her know I've got her back. She stumbles a bit but recovers with a quick assist and marches resolutely toward the table.

I was happy to see her dancing with that douche nozzle—right up until I noticed him guiding her slowly towards the back door. I thought maybe—just maybe—she'd forget about Mase, at least for the night. But that dick had to go and ruin it. I *might've* let her leave with him if she chose to later.

Heavy on the might.

Yeah, I want her to find someone, but she should do it sober. She's not logic-driven when she drinks. Her emotions take the wheel and white-knuckle it down a winding road.

That fuckwad wasn't really giving her a choice in the matter, though. That changed things. He's lucky I didn't have him thrown out. It might still happen if I see him again. And then, I'll follow him out and rearrange his face for being a sneaky little dickweasel.

Tara's not at the table to miss it right now, so I snag her water on my way by and put it down in front of Trista. "Drink."

That spark she found on the dance floor is doused now. I hate it when that happens. I wish things were different so I could kiss her until she smiles again, but I can't.

She picks up the cup without a hint of protest and quickly empties it. There's a pitcher on the table because Monique can't keep up with Tara's and Gabe's water consumption, so I grab it and refill the cup.

"Drink until you can't anymore," I tell her. "Hydration is the key to combating a hangover."

She glares at me, but she grabs the water and drinks.

Trista is sipping on her second refill when Gabe and Tara fall into their chairs, laughing. Tara glances at Tris and does a double-take. A little crease forms between her brows.

"You rode with Noel, right? Do we need to call you an Uber?" Tara asks Tris, shouting to be heard over the thumping music and the pitchy singer on stage.

I love Tara like a damn sister—more than I love my real sisters, actually—but I am not letting her put this tiny, drunk-as-fuck woman in a car with a stranger. I don't care if she should be perfectly safe ridesharing. It's not happening. Not on my watch.

"I'm alright," Trista says. I don't know how she's not slurring her words. I wouldn't trust her to change seats without falling on her ass right now.

Fern pops to her feet. "We'll be back," she announces. "I want to sing."

I'm surprised it's taken her this long to make her way to the stage. She's kind of a big deal to the regulars here. She even has a stage name—Killer Queen. I'm glad they're going, though, for Trista's sake. *Someone needs to tell them* . . . I don't know what the hell I think that would accomplish aside from making things awkward for everyone. It's not like Mason is leading her on.

I nod and watch Tris from the corner of my eye while they walk away. Her chest heaves with a huge sigh.

"It's not fair," she says with her eyes glued to their backs.

I press my lips together to keep from snapping at her for her high school bullshit. Yelling at her is like losing my temper with one of my friends' kids over something stupid, like spilling water or something. It doesn't matter what Trista does wrong. Getting mad at her feels about as horrible as kicking a kitten would. But *fuck*, I'm tired of her mooning over Mason like a lovesick little girl.

And you're a fucking hypocrite.

I'm *not* mooning, damnit. And it's not jealousy. I *want* her to move on and find someone to love. I'm not that someone. I'm the antithesis of everything she wants; otherwise, she wouldn't be so wrapped up in family-man-Mason. That's okay with me, though. My life wasn't meant to have a happily ever after and I'm not taking her down with me.

"Life isn't fair, Tris," Tara says patiently, surprising me with her tough-love approach. She usually coddles Trista—all of them do to some degree—but Mason's marriage must have made her realize that Trista needs to move on sooner rather than later.

"'Life is pain. Anyone who says any different is trying to sell you something.'" Tara continues. *Of course, she has a movie quote for that.* Gabe rolls his eyes but grins to himself. I can't imagine how many times he's suffered through her favorite movie, *The Princess Bride,* with her over the years. It's not horrible, but I'll go to my grave denying that.

I look down to gauge Trista's reaction. Surprisingly, she's smiling along with Gabe.

"They're happy, Tris. Let them be. They deserve it," Tara says.

You've got that right. Those two have been through hell; they've earned some peace.

"No," Tris says, but she nods her head like she agrees with Tara. "You're right. It just hurts."

I take a deep breath and let go of my irritation. Someone needs to be the good cop to Tara's bad here, and I guess it's gonna be me because Gabe isn't helping. In her place, I picture a scared little kitten who might run off and get stuck in a tree if I'm not careful enough. "Going on like this isn't going to help anything, Tris. Don't you want to move on and be happy?"

Tris sighs again, picks up what's left of her appletini, and kills it. "I don't even know what I want anymore."

Oh shit! What have I done? The idea was to get her to stop drinking and maybe go back to dancing. On the floor, not the tables or the bar. "You want to be happy. Everyone just wants to be happy," I say. Everyone else tells her what to do and how to feel without a second thought. I make an effort not to do it *because* everyone else does, but maybe it'll work for me just this once.

She looks my way, and her big, brown eyes zoom across my face like she's reading all my secrets there. "Yeah . . . But it's so hard . . ."

Her eyes stop on mine and delve into my soul. I want to look away from her. I don't want her to see how fucked up I am. Her gaze holds me in place, though. Dusting off the French accent I got from my father, I say, "C'est la vie." *But am I talking to her or to myself?* I clear my throat and slam the door on the dark places in the back of my mind. She's not the person I'm angry with. "There's someone out there for you, but it's not Mason."

She smiles at me, like the sun peeking out from behind the clouds, taking the storm with it. "You're right. But where is he?"

I cock an eyebrow at her. "That is the million-dollar question."

I've heard the term "mercurial moods," and it suits this woman every time she drinks. She's taking it to the extreme tonight, though. She laughs, which makes her seem even more child-like. She's so small she could easily blend in with a fourth-grade class, and her laugh doesn't help matters.

Tara smiles and turns to tell Gabe something. They get up and walk away laughing. I missed the joke; it got lost in the music. It's good to see them happy again, even if I'm irritated with Tara for leaving me with Trista. *No one is making me stay . . .*

I could walk away, and Tara would rush over to watch over Tris. I don't want her to, though. She's right where she needs to be. *Relationships are too fucking much work.* And that's why I don't do them. Well, that and the catastrophe that was my last one. And my parents, of course. They were shittastic role models in the relationship and family department. *Apples don't fall far from trees.*

I am who I am. Mom tried to change me, to make me a "better person" but I'm still the same angry, stubborn, selfish brat I've always been, to her dismay. She warned me that no one would ever want me. Hell, in the end, *she* didn't want me. But I'm not her problem anymore.

Next to me, Tris sighs. I only notice because her whole body moves with it and we're close enough our arms are touching. I should move away, but if it's not bothering her, it's cool with me.

She's watching Gabe and Tara. "Think they'll stick this time?" she asks me, nodding toward the recently remarried pair.

Gabe did Tara bad. Tara isn't entirely blameless, but it's more that she stopped trying to fix what was broken. *Once again, relationships are too fucking much work.* One person can't do it all alone. So it's amazing to me that Tara's girlfriends don't want to shish-kabob Gabe and roast him over an open fire. *I* kind of want to do that, and he's practically a brother to me.

It was hard to watch Gabe and Tara split. They're not blood, but they're family. Only, unlike my actual brothers and sisters, I like them. And they like me. *God only knows why.* It was hell to watch two people that mean so much to me, and to each other, go through that shit.

I shrug. "Just have to wait and see, I guess."

I know the look in Gabe's eyes when Tara is around. It's the same one he's had in her presence since the day they met. He still loves her just as much now as he did then. And I'll do whatever it takes to ensure they continue down the path they're on. Even managing Tara's irritatingly cute friend when she's drunk. No matter the cost to me.

"I hope they do."

It's not what she said, but how she said it that has me doing a double-take. There's so much conviction in those four words. If the two of them need some willpower to make it happen, Tris has some to spare. "Do you now?" I ask.

Tris nods her head so hard I'm afraid she will fall forward, hit her head on the table, and knock herself out. "Yep." She stops and sighs again. "I want to go home."

I don't know if her statement is directed at me or a general announcement, but home is a good place for her right now. I'm not letting her disturb Tara and Gabe. She's not getting near Mason or Fern if I can help it, though either of them would drop everything to take her. Austin and Jamaica would too, but they deserve a night out after all the shit that went down a couple of weeks ago. Chris disappeared on the dance floor, and if *anyone* here needs a night to cut the fuck loose, it's him.

That leaves me.

I'm alright with it, though. I should go before I see that dickweasel again. I don't want to spend the night in lockup, and he's the kind of guy who would press charges.

I grab my phone off the table and tap out a text to Chris, telling him to stay and enjoy himself and that I'll cover his eight o'clock spin class in the morning. *Fucker owes me, though.* I hate spinning. But it's our gym, and I'll take one for the team.

I stand up and hold out a hand to Trista. She blinks at it like she's never seen a hand before. *Oh, sweet little Pixie Stix, you're going to hate yourself in the morning.* She's going to have a hangover from hell. "I'll take you home."

A smile brightens her face. It would be easy to pretend she's happy about leaving with me, but that road only leads to heartache. "Oh! Okay! Thank you!"

She tries to stand without grabbing my hand, loses her balance halfway, and tips forward. Adrenaline rushes through my veins, lending me the speed I need to grab her under both arms in time to stop her from cracking her skull open on the edge of the table. *This isn't going to work.* She'll break her neck going down the stairs, and she'll take me with her. "Damnit, Tris," I mutter under my breath. "Can I carry you to the car?"

"Just do it, man," Gabe says in my ear. Startled, I turn and look into his grey eyes. They must've come up the stairs in time to witness her tumble. "She won't care. She won't even remember in the morning. Not like you're a stranger out to take advantage of her or anything."

"Hey, I don't care if she is a friend. I ain't picking her up without permission." Trista . . . needs to learn to make decisions instead of going along with whatever everyone else wants from or for her. Therefore, I will stand here and wait for her to say what she wants and do exactly that regardless of what I think is best.

"It's okay," she says. "I don't care."

"I'll text you her address," Tara says, already tapping away at her phone screen.

I scoop Trista up like a groom carrying his bride over their threshold. "I'll hurry," I tell her. This is probably as awkward for her as it is for me. Only, for me, it's because it's hard not to enjoy having a reason to hold her a little *too* much. *Don't think about it. Don't think about it.* I'm in a crowded bar, carrying a drunk-to-the-point-of-passing-out Trista. I'm not carrying her to my bed, and there's nothing I can do to hide a boner right now. My body doesn't make that distinction, though. *Why can I just not be attracted to her?* Life would be easier.

Halfway down the stairs, she shouts, "I don't feel good."

"Lay your head down and close your eyes," I tell her. It's not like I can get her to a trashcan or a toilet in a reasonable timeframe from here. There *might* be a trashcan at the bottom of the stairs, but I don't think so. I just hope to hell she doesn't puke on me. *No good deed goes unpunished . . .*

She rests her cheek on my chest. *Fuck my life.* That's nice. My heart takes off like I'm trying to set a personal best mile time. I glance down to make sure her eyes are closed. They're screwed closed so tight, it's probably painful. That will distract her from her nausea, though—I hope. I run down the stairs as fast as I dare, ready to put an end to this awkward situation. The last thing I want is to miss a step and fall. I'd never forgive myself for hurting her. And it's hard to run a gym in casts or on crutches.

Chapter 6

Ryan

"Ryan?" Trista asks in the smallest of voices from the passenger seat of my car. She's hunkered down so far the shoulder strap on the seatbelt isn't going to help if we're in an accident. But she says it helps her stomach.

I grunt and cover the brakes, ready to stop if she needs to hurl. Getting her home as fast as possible takes priority over talking. Stopping if she needs to puke is more important, though.

"Can you drop me off down the block?"

I laugh before I can stop myself. "Trista, you can't walk a step right now. How do you think you're going to walk a block?"

"I'll make it. Please? I don't want to wake Mom up. She'll be so upset. I told her Noel and I were going to the movies because she hates it when I drink."

For fuck's sake. I roll my eyes. I've never met her mother, but I don't like the woman. I might like her less than my own mother, and that's saying something. My parents were absent unless they were teaching us things they wanted us to know or showing us off. *Or chastising me for being me.* My siblings and I were raised by various nannies—not that there's anything wrong with nannies. They were great. But we weren't as lucky as Mason's daughter, Ronni. Mason still parents, even when Fern was Ronni's nanny and not Mason's wife. My parents were just gone.

But Trista's mother . . . she is so far up her daughter's ass, she only sees sunshine when Trista yawns.

"Fine," I growl. "But I'll carry you to the door." I'm not watching her stumble and fall for a block. And I can't drop her off and leave. It's not an option.

"Thank you," she says, barely louder than a whisper.

Silence rules again for a few more blocks.

"Ryan?"

I cover the brake again. "Yeah?"

"I don't have my keys."

Fuck. Guess waking her mom is a moot point now. "Call your mom?"

"Tara has my phone," she says in that pathetic voice.

"Use mine." I remove it from the mount on the dash without taking my eyes off the road, unlock it, and hand it to her.

She takes it and is silent again for a few moments. "Can you just take me to Noel's? I know the code to get in. I told Mom I might just stay there anyway. I do that a lot."

It sounds like a reasonable compromise, but I don't want her to be alone. Not as drunk as she is. Yeah, her mom might be pissed, but she's her mom. She'll take care of her.

Going back for the keys isn't happening. The longer she's in the car, the greater the risk of her puking in it. That leaves me one option . . . With a sigh, I resign myself to a mostly sleepless night. If I'm not worrying about Trista, I'll be thinking about her in my bed. "Go to sleep, Tris. You can take my bed. I'll sleep on the couch."

She reaches over to pat my arm. "Thank you, Ryan. You're a good friend."

***

I kick my front door closed behind me and sigh in relief. We made it. "Wait right here." I help her across the living room and onto the couch. Still half-asleep, she stretches out and gets comfortable. "The bathroom is down the hall, first door on the right if you need it." I don't know why I'm telling her that, though. She'll never make it on her own.

I need to change my sheets before I let her in my room. It hasn't been *that* long, but I do have some manners. And I want to put on the rubber sheet I have for when Chris's son, Keaton, stays over, in case she gets sick.

Two steps into my room, the unmistakable sound of someone hurling stops me in my tracks. *Fuck. My. Life.* "Trista?" I turn on my heel and run back to the front room full tilt to find her passed out on her back, covered in appletini-colored goo. The smell wafts across the room and hits me all at once, nearly knocking me to my knees.

Ignoring it, I quickly turn her onto her side so she doesn't aspirate. I can perform CPR if necessary, but I don't want it to come to that. "Trista?"

She doesn't twitch, but the steady rise and fall of her chest eases me out of panic mode.

Okay. I take a deep breath to calm myself and nearly gag from the smell. Step one . . . where the fuck do I start here? When Keaton is over, I clean him up first if he has an accident, then have him wait on the couch while I make the bed. He's awake, though. And the couch is a safe, clean spot to wait. It's not right now. The chairs? No . . . She might fall off the stupid little things. I can't leave her in the bathtub. She'll freeze if it's empty and she might drown if it's not.

So, step one, make the bed so I have a clean place to put the drunk woman once she's clean. . . . There's no way in hell I'm getting that smell out of my couch. I can't sleep there tonight. *Thank God I have a king-sized bed.* I'll stay on my side. She'll stay on hers. Everything will be fine.

Except Trista will be in my bed, and not because I get to get her naked. Even thinking of her in my bed is enough to wake my dick up. He's in for a whole world of disappointment soon because I'm not even going to look at her once I lay her down. I'm not a creep.

She's passed out, defenseless, and absolutely trusting me to take care of her. That is exactly what I'm going to do. End of story.

Hopefully she's drunk enough to sleep through my nightmares.

***

An ungodly shriek shatters the early morning silence, ripping me from a truly fucked-up dream about a giant donut and a rubber duck named Alfred. The woman in my arms sits bolt upright, violently disentangling our legs, and screams again.

"What the hell?" she shouts. Her hands slap against my arm, and she shoves.

Wide awake and ready to break someone, I sit up and look around for the threat.

"Ryan?"

Oh, fuck. Wincing, I rub the back of my neck. I'd hoped to wake up first and get the hell out of Dodge to avoid this. I knew it would be awkward—in more ways than one. "You might've warned me you're a cuddler," I say, hoping to calm Trista down. I tug at the blankets, hoping she doesn't notice my morning wood or my attempts to hide it.

She doesn't calm down. Her chest heaves as she pants. "How did I get here? Why am I in your bed?" She stops and grabs her head, fisting her hands in her hair. "And why do I feel like I'm going to die?"

I sigh and plop back into my pillow, taking the opportunity to turn onto my side to make it easier to hide. If I'm going to get my ass chewed, I'm going to be comfortable. I tick each event off on my fingers as I list them. "You forgot your keys. Tara had your phone. You didn't want to wake your mom. And you were so drunk I wasn't comfortable leaving you at Noel's by yourself. I was going to sleep on the couch, but you puked all over it. I figured a king-sized bed was big enough for the both of us. I didn't plan on you smothering me all damn night long."

I didn't mind that last one nearly as much I should—not that I'm going to tell her that. I *should* mind because it's going to haunt me later. I'll never look at my bed again without remembering her reaching for me in the dark, her head on my chest and her body draped over mine, and the smell of her hair and skin will linger on the sheets for days. But that's a me problem.

Her cheeks flush bright red. Now that she's not screaming and shoving me, I take a moment to note that she's adorable in the morning with her shoulder-length, dark hair standing up in odd places. *Great, something to torture myself with later . . .*

"So . . . Nothing . . . Happened?" she asks.

Heaven forbid you trust me . . . It's my own fault, though. They all know I frequently indulge in casual hookups. But *not* with one of *"my"* ladies—Tara, Noel, Trista, Fern, Jamaica, or Madi. Yeah, it worked out for Jam and Austin, but it *will not* work for me because I have a better reason for avoiding relationships than he did. He just had to stop being stupid and find someone willing to tolerate him. That's not my problem with relationships. *Finding someone to tolerate my grumpy ass might be a problem too, I suppose.*

"Well, I mean . . . I did get you mostly naked to change your clothes." The blood drains from her face, leaving her cheeks and lips deathly pale. I cringe inwardly for making her uncomfortable. But I would've choked on guilt for not telling her. I rush to reassure her. "But I promise, I didn't look. I even shut the light off." And I was fucking sick with guilt the whole damn time.

She takes a deep breath. Color slowly returns to her lips. "We didn't . . .?"

Does she really think I'm that kind of asshole? Fuck, I hope not. That fucking hurts. I cross my arms over my chest. "You know, I find your lack of faith in me a little insulting. No, we didn't." *And you'd know if we did.*

She drops her chin, hiding her face from me in a curtain of dark hair. "I'm sorry, I just . . ."

Damnit, now I've gone and upset her. And for some stupid reason, I feel bad about it. Never mind that she just upset me. *Women . . . They get you all twisted up without even trying.*

"It's okay," I whisper. *And things are officially awkward.* I clear my throat and speak up because if I'm going to die for running my mouth, I'm not going to have to repeat myself. "Your virginity is important to you."

She shrieks again, and I catch a pillow with my face. *Damn, she's fast when she's mad!* I didn't see her move. I didn't *expect* her to move. She doesn't do things like that. It's . . . refreshing. "I'm not a virgin!"

I fight a smile and lose spectacularly, anticipating the look on her face. "Oh, please! You've never even seen a dick," I say, reviving a joke between us. The day Gabe and Tara got remarried, Trista walked in on me changing at their place before we left for the courthouse. Her reaction was . . . adorable. It was like she'd never seen a naked man, and, of course, I called her on it.

Her face reddens to roughly the shade of a stop sign, just as it did the first time I told her that, as I continue word for word. "Your mother won't allow you to be alone with a man long enough for that to happen!" Never mind that I'm a man and we're alone.

She whacks me with the pillow again, but I block it this time. "I have too!"

"Uh-huh . . . Sure . . ." There's nothing for her to be upset about. We're adults. We're friends. We kept our clothes on. *And would it be so bad if we didn't?*

Yes. Yes, it would.

Austin suspects I have a thing for this woman, and, as much as I hate to admit it, he's right. It's more of a soft spot than anything. In some ways, she reminds me so much of Selene, the one I failed to protect. I don't want anything bad to happen to her, and that's why I look out for her. I'm smart enough to know that *I'm* one of the bad things that could happen to her.

This is why, no matter what, I will never be more than Trista's friend. I will not be the party responsible for her fall from grace.

Dredging up the past kills my abnormally good mood. It's hard to wake up happy after a full night of reliving the worst afternoon of my life. *So why was I so happy this morning?* My blood turns to ice when the reason becomes clear. I didn't have nightmares.

Waves of conflicting emotions crash through me, simultaneously attempting to lift me up and pull me under. It's not the first time I've missed a night in the last nine years. There's no reason to panic. Selene will be back to punish me for failing her tonight. As she should.

The sudden turn of my mood must be catching because Trista's lips pucker into a pout. "Where's my dress?"

I cringe. I forgot about her dress. "Uh, about that . . . I hope it wasn't expensive. I'll buy you a new one." I'm not sure a dry cleaner can save it. That smell is powerful. "You can borrow some of my sweats. And I can drop you off at home on my way to work, or you can hang out here until someone can pick you up."

Her eyes get huge at the mention of her home. "If you don't mind, I'd like to wait here, please," she whispers without the slightest hint of hesitation that indicates she's struggling with a decision. All the fire, all the personality she woke up with bleeds out of her, leaving behind the meek woman I'm familiar with.

Funny enough, the side of her that appeals to me the most is the one I woke up with, not the goody-two-shoes who lives in fear of upsetting her mother. Give me the hot mess who grabs life with both hands, if only for a little while. That's the real Trista White. The other version is a carefully crafted front. And someday, there will be a war between who she *is* and who she wants to be. It'll be interesting to see which side comes out on top. I hope she realizes it's okay to be herself all the time, no matter what her mother says.

"Sure thing. My phone is on the nightstand; code is oh-one-oh-five. You can call someone while I shower. Help yourself to anything in the kitchen. When I get out, I'll make you something for that hangover." I could do it now, but a little suffering might be good for her. I don't take issue with people having a good time, but Tris drinks for the wrong reasons. Yeah, it's the only way I get to spend time with the real her, but she uses it as a crutch—justification for her to be herself. More herself, anyway.

Chapter 7

Trista

My head throbs in time with my heartbeat. Elsewhere in the house, a door closes, followed by the muffled sound of running water. I grab Ryan's phone and unlock it with a little smile. Oh-one-oh-five is his birthday—I can list all of my friends' birthdates from memory. It's something I've done since my very first friend in school.

His background is a picture of his car shining in the sun with a lot of other classics behind it—probably one of the car shows he talks about with Austin. I quickly find his texting app and do my best to ignore the bits and pieces of messages visible on the screen while I find his conversation with Tara. Luckily, it's the top one, and my address is the last message between them.

This is Tris. I'll explain later, but could I trouble you for a ride home?

His phone rings, Tara's name and a photo of her and Gabe take over the screen. I tap the green button. "Hello?"

"Why do you have Ryan's phone?" she asks.

I guess I didn't do a great job of explaining myself in that text, but my brain just wants to be done with today. "I'm at Ryan's house?" I squeeze my eyes shut, embarrassed all over again. She's going to have so many questions.

"Why?"

It could be so much worse. The only thing I have to be embarrassed about is getting too drunk. It's not like I *slept* with him. "Last night is pretty fuzzy, but he says you have my phone and I didn't have my keys. I didn't want to wake Mom, and he wouldn't leave me at Noel's by myself. I think my keys are in Noel's car. Maybe I should've called her . . ."

My car is at home because Noel picked me up and we got ready at her place, but I need my keys more than I need my phone.

"No, you're fine," Tara says quickly. "Noel gave me your keys last night since I have your phone. I have an appointment coming in later, but I'll come get you after."

"Thanks."

"No problem. I'll see you soon." She ends the call, and I put Ryan's phone back on his nightstand.

As weird as it is to be in Ryan's bed, I lay down and pull the blankets up over my head, blocking out the light. I'm out of things to do to put off thinking about *this*. Waking up in his bed—in his *arms*—was confusing. Not only because I can't remember how I got there, but because I didn't hate it. The thought of what might've happened, though . . . That bothers me even now. Sex is important to me. It *means* something to me. I wasn't lying when I told Ryan that I'm not a virgin, but I don't—*won't*—sleep with just anyone. *Because the guys you did it with meant so much to you . . .*

That's not the right way to look at it. The first *did* mean something to me at the time. But Mom was right about him. *In the end, she's always right about everything.* He was only after that one thing. Once he got what he wanted, he was gone along with every penny I had in my college fund, Mom's credit cards, and the cash in her wallet.

The college fund was on me. He convinced me that Mom was abusing me and I should run away with him. The rest was on him. I should've known better, but I was in love and completely convinced that we would be together forever, but only if I left with him. I was *stupid*.

And the sex was *so* was not worth it.

The others . . . I wanted them to mean something to me, but not even sex gave me feelings for them because they never had feelings for me. I was nothing more than a box to check. *Good education? Check. Excellent job? Check. Trophy wife . . .?*

Trophy wife?

We have a runner!

Mom doesn't understand why things didn't work with either of them. They're perfectly adequate as far as she's concerned. Stable, well-paying desk jobs. No bad habits. Acceptable hobbies. How could I possibly resist?

I got tired of listening to them talk about how great they are.

And of their "isn't she cute" attitudes.

And that their idea of crazy was ordering a double shot of espresso, staying up late, and having sex with the light on.

They'd never met, but they were so similar it was eerie. Both were boring. Predictable. They weren't interested in what I had to say unless I was speaking in praise of them. I want more from a relationship than being someone's decoration. I've had enough boring to last me a lifetime.

Maybe I'm asking too much? Mom only wants to see me succeed. But I can succeed without a man in my life, can't I?

No matter what, I can never tell her about this. She'll never believe I didn't have sex with Ryan. I don't even want to think about what would happen then. It would only confirm her belief that I can't be trusted to take care of myself.

I drift off, wondering what it will take to reassure my mother that one bad decision doesn't justify treating me like a child for the rest of my life.

***

"Tris?"

I groan and roll over, away from the cold thing nudging my hand. I feel like death and just want to be left alone. At least I don't know how miserable I am when I'm asleep. "What?"

"Drink this. It'll help."

Something cold and wet touches the back of my neck. Yelping, I scramble upright and away from it. My scream and Ryan's laughter set my head to throbbing again.

"Drink," he says, pushing a cup of brownish *something* into my hand. "You can go back to sleep after if you want."

I bring the straw to my lips without question, even though it looks disgusting, and take a sip. Whatever it is, the flavor of pineapples, strawberries, and bananas brings a smile to my face. "It's good. Thank you."

Smiling, he tips his own glass of goop at me and eases himself down onto the bed at my feet in a patch of sunlight streaming through a gap in the blinds. "You're welcome. He raises his glass to me, then takes another big gulp.

"I got in touch with Tara. I'm not sure when she'll be here, but she's coming."

He nods. "Alright. I need to head out. You up for a quick walk to the living room? I'll show you how everything works in case you get bored waiting on her."

"Uh . . ." I'm not thrilled about walking around in nothing but his shirt and my underwear, but it probably covers enough of me to be respectable. He obviously wants to do this, so whatever. I'll go to make him happy. "Sure."

I slide out of bed and follow him down the short hall. He hands me a couple of remotes, and I listen carefully while he gives me a rundown on how to operate his giant television and the various contraptions hooked up to it. I'll probably forget everything in five minutes, but I try to keep up.

He tells me to make myself at home, and then he leaves, and I'm all alone, stuck in his shirt, in a room that smells like apple puke, waiting on someone else to come save me from the aftermath of my bad decisions.

I'm too hungover for this. I can wallow later. I trudge back to his room, put my cup on the nightstand, and climb into the massive bed.

I suck in a deep breath to sigh. *Crap.* My eyes fly open. The pillowcase smells like mint and something woodsy and something I couldn't have identified before, but I now know to be uniquely Ryan. I'm surrounded by him as completely as I was when I woke up this morning. I freaked out about it then, but the empty expanse of bed leaves me with an odd, hollow ache in my chest.

I scoot to the other side of the bed, away from the pillow that smells like him, only to find that the other one does too. Exasperated with myself for being so ridiculous, I shove both pillows onto the floor and close my eyes. *What is* wrong *with me?* I just need to go to sleep. I'm so tired, and maybe I'll feel better when I wake up.

But sleep abandons me. I lay there tossing and turning until I give up and trudge back to the living room with my cup in hand, dragging the comforter behind me. It might stink out here, but at least I can't smell Ryan.

***

"Oh, honey," Tara coos. "You look like something the cat dragged in."

"Feel like it," I tell her from the nest I made in one of the chairs in the little front room. I can barely stand to be in here with the smell of appletini vomit heavy in the air, but I couldn't stand staying in his bed. It just felt . . . wrong. Too familiar.

It was too much.

I *don't* miss Ryan.

Tara pinches her nose to ward off the smell and looks around. "What the hell happened?"

I duck my head to hide my blush, though Tara knows me well enough to know I'm embarrassed as hell. "He says I threw up on the couch when he went to change the sheets on his bed."

Her eyes snap back to me, roving over every inch of me that isn't hidden beneath the blanket. "Are you alright?"

"Eh," I say, holding up the cup I haven't had the energy to take to the kitchen yet. "He brought me this before he left. It helped."

She nods. "I've had that before." In three quick strides, she crosses the room and takes the cup, then strolls to the kitchen. The tap turns on, and over the noise of her rinsing my cup, she asks, "So . . . Is that where you slept?"

My cheeks sizzle. "No." I clear my throat and try to be an adult about it. There's no reason to be embarrassed. Except I slept next to *Ryan* all night long. We're friends. It's totally normal, right? *She'll find out anyway.* Ryan won't lie about it if she asks. "We both slept in his bed."

The water cuts off. Tara stops in the kitchen door and leans against the frame. "Well," she says, glancing around at the furniture, "it's not like he has a lot of options."

"No," I agree after a quick perusal of my own.

I don't have much experience with typical bachelor pads because my recent exes definitely do *not* fall into that category. Ryan's house is *small,* though—not at all what you'd expect for a self-made millionaire who also happens to come from a family whose wealth is probably well into the billions by now. But every inch of his place is in good repair and utterly spotless. Somehow, I don't think that's normal for a guy living by himself. *He probably pays someone to clean.* I would if I were him. The giant television with every gadget and gizmo known to man is totally in line with what I expect of a bachelor pad, though.

"I guess I owe him a new couch," I say on a sigh. That'll put a dent in my spending money. I'm not hurting by any means—one of the perks of living with Mom. I can easily afford a couch. I hope. How much can one cost, anyway?

Tara's eyes move to the couch, and she frowns. "That's between the two of you, but I'm guessing he'll take care of it."

That doesn't seem right to me. I'm the one who puked all over it. At the very least, I should pay to have it cleaned. But I can take that up with him later. I have his number. I'll text him this evening.

"Do you mind if I hang out at your place for a bit? I don't want to go home until I'm . . ." I trail off, unsure of how to finish that sentence. I'm sober, and the hangover is more or less gone, but the idea of facing Mom in this state makes me shudder. My head still hurts too much to deal with her *alcohol is the root of all evil* lecture right now.

"Normal?"

Is anything *about me normal?* I get what she means, though. "I guess that's as good a word as any."

"Yeah, c'mon."

Groaning, I roll out of the chair and drag his bedspread behind me on my way to his room. Since he changed sheets last night, I'm guessing he'll change them again before he goes to bed. Either way, I'm going to make his bed. It's the least I can do after puking on his couch and scaring the crap out of him this morning.

"I'll be right back," I tell Tara over my shoulder. "I need to tidy up after myself."

Ryan

If I'd known that volunteering to cover Chris's spin class would cheat me out of time with Trista, I wouldn't have done it. I can cover for him anytime, but I don't always have a perfectly innocent reason to hang out with her, and never at my house. There's nothing to be done for it now, though. The class starts in fifteen minutes, and the studio is already filling up.

I don't even know what we'd do together, but it was clear she didn't want to go home.

I hope she's feeling better. I did tell her to make herself at home. The clothes I set out before I woke her up aren't going to come close to fitting her, but I bet she looks adorable in them. And the idea of her in my clothes . . . I can't think about things like that right now. Spinning sucks enough without a hard on.

Is she gone yet? She said she didn't know when Tara would get there. I'm off at one o'clock today. Maybe she'll still be there.

She'll probably be ready to go home by then anyway, not hang out with me . . . But if the alternative is dealing with her mother . . . *Not like I'll ever be her first choice anyway.*

Chapter 8

Trista

Mom opens the front door before I even make it out of the car. Her sharp eyes take me in from head to toe as I make my way up the sidewalk, no doubt noting everything from Tara's clothes to the dark circles under my eyes. Her perpetual frown grows deeper by the second. I have to fight not to cringe. She continues to block the door, forcing me to stop outside and wait while she finishes scrutinizing me. "Oh, dear! How late were you girls up last night? Why didn't you pack a bag? You didn't drink, did you? You know how I feel about alcohol! It's so bad for you! Not only does it impair your judgment, it—"

"Ages you," I say along with her. I can't count the number of times I've heard that line. She steps back, finally allowing me inside now that her lecture is off to a sufficient start and I follow her from the entryway, down the short hall, and into the kitchen.

"I'm fine, Mom. Just tired." I tell her. I forced myself to stay awake for a while after I got to Tara's because I knew I'd get the third degree immediately upon returning home. Having something else to distract her with is better than trying to lie to her. It was nice to catch up with Tara, though. The baby is thriving, and so is her boutique. "I got to feel the baby kick!"

Her frown softens a bit at the mention of the baby, as I hoped it would. "That's marvelous. But, you know, if you'd stayed with Peter, you might have a baby of your own by now. You might know what those little kicks feel like first-hand."

Why does she always *have to bring up Peter?* It's like she delights in rubbing my nose in his success. I turn toward the fridge for a drink before she catches me rolling my eyes at her for bringing up the first guy she set me up with. I grab the orange juice. "Peter and I weren't a good match," I murmur, moving to the cabinet for a glass.

She scoffs at me. "Nonsense. He was perfect for you. You were still hung up on *that boy,* and you didn't give him a fair chance. Peter is an investment banker now. He lives in New York City and makes so much money his wife doesn't *have* to work. She goes to the spa every week and chats with celebrities."

Good for her. That life isn't my scene. And, of course, she has to bring up Tyler again. She *always* has to remind me of my great fuckup. I was over Tyler long before I met Peter, but Mom won't believe it. He's the reason for *everything*. I roll my eyes again and take a drink to give myself time to construct an answer that might distract her. "Well, I'm sure that's nice, but—"

"No 'but's,' Trista. That *is* nice. Your life could've been so easy! Her biggest worry is smudging a nail! Here you are with deadlines to meet and student loans to pay! You're nearly thirty, and you're not married. You don't even have a boyfriend! Not to mention children—are you ever going to give me grandbabies?"

I cringe. I'm not even sure I want kids, but I can never tell her that. She'll disown me, and then where will I be? *Free.* That's not fair of me. Mom is the only family I've got. She isn't *trying* to control me. She's helping me, just like she always has.

The things she worries about are a little outdated at this point. By the time she was my age, I was ten. I've done the things she missed out on. I graduated from college. I got the job she always dreamed of. She doesn't need to worry about me ruining my life anymore. But she does. *Because she loves me and I'm all she has.* As long as we have each other, everything will be fine.

I swat the little voice in the back of my head aside and try to reassure her. I still have plenty of time. "Mom, I—"

She ignores me, rushing on ahead as if I never opened my mouth. "It's not hard, Trista. You don't have to love a man to marry him. You just let him think you do and do what you have to do to make him happy, and he'll take care of everything else!"

I grit my teeth and suppress a shudder to stave off another lecture. That life might work for others, but it's not for me. Maybe I'm foolish, but I know my fairytale prince is out there—my one true love. I just have to find him. I can't tell Mom that, though. Her head would explode.

The only thing Mom ever tells me about her relationship with my father is that it was love at first sight, he was twenty, and he promised they'd get married after she turned eighteen. But she got pregnant, he hopped on his motorcycle and left, and she lost her faith in true love. For her, it's nothing but broken dreams and heartache because her parents kicked her out. She barely graduated high school. College wasn't an option. She had to go to work to support herself. *And she never lets me forget it.*

"I'll find the right guy someday," I whisper, hoping to soothe her.

"Well," she says, a smile in her voice, "I saved you the trouble. You remember me telling you about the new girl at work, Joelle?" There's a slight pause, but she is too excited to wait for me to answer. "She has a son! He's just a bit older than you, thirty-two, but that's not bad at all! He's a *lawyer*, Trista! And good at it! He has political aspirations too! And I got his number for you! You should call him!"

I'm just supposed to call this guy and tell him his mom gave his number to my mom so I could ask him out? I at least *met* the other two at company functions before the moms swooped in and made plans. I turn around to look at her, but she's beaming from ear to ear, clearly oblivious to the insanity of this. "Mom! I can't just call a guy I've never met!"

"Of course you can, sweetie! Joelle was going to tell him you might call. His name is Grant, and his number is on the fridge. Go ahead and give him a call!"

"Not right now, Mom." I cast about for some excuse and decide that the truth is as good as anything."I need some time to wind myself up, or I'll be too nervous to say anything." *Nervous that he'll report me to the police for harassment.*

Besides, if he's so great, why isn't he happily married?

Mom shakes a finger at me. "Don't let this one get away from you, Trista. You'll regret it. Joelle says he's career-driven but that he's finally ready to settle down. This one's a keeper; I just know it."

I try to smile, but my heart isn't in it. "If he's a good guy, I'm sure there won't be a problem."

She registers her opinion with a snort and stomps out of the kitchen. A door slams elsewhere in the house, and I cringe. *That went well . . .*

Fumbling for the opening of the pocket on the oversized sweatpants Tara lent me so I didn't have to explain Ryan's, I find my phone. I need to text Ryan. I may as well do that now before I get sidetracked. I know what happens next. I'll dwell on everything Mom said and start feeling like a horrible daughter. She's already stewing with her words. Before the night is over, she'll apologize for being so harsh and remind me, again, that she only wants what's best for me. We'll hug. We'll cry. We'll binge on ice cream, and chick flicks we've both seen so many times we have them memorized.

Tomorrow, it'll be as if nothing happened.

Me: Thanks for last night. Sorry I freaked out this morning. And about your couch . . . I'll pay to have it cleaned.

I move to pocket my phone again, but the ellipsis that indicates he's typing pops up. So I wait, oddly excited to hear back from him so soon. I figured he was too busy at work to take the time to reply to me right now. If ever. It's not like we're best friends. I'm not sure I've ever sent him a text that wasn't part of a group message before.

Ryan: You're welcome and no worries to both. I'm going to get a new one. I'm probably overdue anyway and I don't think anything will get that smell out.

Biting my lip, I rest my forearms on the counter and lean against it. I appreciate that he's trying to take the high road here instead of getting upset with me over ruining his furniture. However, I *am* the one who ruined it. It's my responsibility to make it right.

Me: I really feel like I should be the one to pay for it.

The ellipsis pops up and disappears several times before his reply finally comes through.

Ryan: If it's what you really want and not that someone is telling you that you have to, alright. I'm picking out a new one today. Pick you up at 3:00? Or do you want to meet me there?

I glance at the time on my screen. That gives me an hour to clean up and deal with Mom. I know beyond a shadow of a doubt that she will *not* like Ryan and will not approve of me going anywhere with him. Or meeting him somewhere.

I've never met my father, but she keeps a picture of the two of them on his motorcycle in her dresser drawer. She never showed it to me. I found it while putting laundry away when I was younger. Ryan doesn't have long hair like Dad did, but Dad had at least one ear pierced, and his arms were nothing but ink. That's close enough for her.

Driving myself would be less of a hassle, but I'd end up lying about where I'm going and who I'm meeting. And why take two vehicles when he's offering to pick me up? A thrill shoots through me at the possibility of riding in his car again. And seeing him again.

I can convince Mom that this is no different than me going shopping with Tara or Noel.

Me: I'll ride with you if you don't mind. But if Mom asks, you asked me to help . . .

If I tell her I'm paying for his new couch, she'll want to know why. It's best she doesn't.

Chapter 9
Ryan

The minute hand on the analog clock on my dashboard rolls over three-fifteen when I turn onto Trista's block. I hate being late but traffic was hectic. I ease my Barracuda into her drive with excessive care. This car is my baby, and she deserves special treatment. I was damn lucky to find her rusting away in a field and even luckier that the old farmer agreed to part with her for a reasonable price.

I reach for the gearshift to put her in neutral. The front door flies open, and Trista's mother comes storming out, letting the screen door slam behind her. *Sonofabitch.* Something tells me she's not coming to let me know Trista is taking too long getting ready or something.

It opens again immediately, and Tris comes scurrying after her mother. Happy as I am to see her upright and walking instead of shuffling along like a zombie, her presence means this shit is probably going to go downhill real fast. I shut my car off and scramble out because, apparently, I finally get to meet . . . Mrs? Ms? Trista's mother. Whether I want to or not. *Yippee.*

I stop in front of my baby and watch them approach, cataloging the similarities and differences between them. It's obvious where Trista got her lack of height now; neither one of them clear five feet. Mrs. White is generously curved, California tan, and her blond hair falls in waves to her hips, whereas Trista is almost painfully thin and Irish pale, with jet black, straight hair that comes to a blunt stop just above her shoulders.

Trista reaches for her mother's arm and misses. "Mom, stop! It's not a date! I'm just going to help him pick out new furniture!"

"I'm not stupid, Trista! Why would a grown man need your help picking his own furniture?" her mom spits over her shoulder. "Since you won't tell me the truth, I'll get it out of him."

Something about the way she says it pisses me off. Why *wouldn't* I want Trista's help? I mean, yeah, I can pick out a couch, but ladies are just better at this. They care more about the fussy little details than most people with a Y chromosome. I don't want something flowery, but otherwise, I don't give two shits about how it looks. But I also do. I don't know why, but I do.

"Because I'm a girl?" Tris asks, stating what I feel is the obvious answer. "And he doesn't want his house to look like a waiting room?"

Yeah. That.

What the fuck have I let myself get dragged into? It's a fucking couch. It's not worth this bullshit. In the future, I'll tell her to meet me down the block or something. *In the future . . .* Chances of me ever picking her up again are nil. I have no reason to.

I don't *hate* parents just because I don't like my own, but I know this woman and I will *not* be friends. Still, I put on my best smile, not even the customer service one I use on new clients at the gym, and stick out my hand when she stops in front of me. "Hello, ma'am. I'm—"

"I know who you are," she snaps, her eyes dropping from the bar in my eyebrow to my arms, more specifically to my tattoos, which she sneers at. "I've seen you in pictures and heard the girls talk about you. What I don't know is what you want from my daughter."

I withdraw my hand, tucking it safely in my pocket so she can't bite me or something if she *really* goes off the deep end. "Uh . . . She's going to help me pick out some furniture? We might grab a bite if it gets late?"

Her small chin, a match to Trista's, juts into the air. In fact, coloring aside, Trista got all of her looks from her mother. They're both beautiful women, even if one of them is looking at me like she'd like to run me through a woodchipper. Smirking, she turns to her daughter, whose face is so red it looks like she passed out in a lawn chair all day long. "I thought you said it's not a date?"

"Mom, it's not! Really. Ryan is just a friend. Friends go shopping and eat out together all the time. You wouldn't be upset if it were Tara!"

"Tara doesn't have a penis!" Mrs. White snaps.

Excellent observational skills, lady. I grit my teeth against the anger bubbling to the surface, hot and thick as tar, and take a deep, slow breath. *Patience, LeDoux. Patience.* "Ma'am, I assure you, I—"

Mrs. White shoves a finger in my face. My left hand balls into a fist on instinct. I force my hand to unclench and lean back a bit, giving myself more space to calm down. "If you get my daughter pregnant, I will sue you for everything you own!"

My mouth opens, but nothing comes out. I don't even know what to say to that. For one thing, I'm pretty sure that's *not* how that works. For another, the implication that I'd abandon my child is insulting. And yet another, *no one* is more cautious about avoiding pregnancy than this guy. I don't want children. Not now. Not later. Not ever.

I don't know the first thing about being a parent because I had shit examples. I love kids, but I'm not going to have one and hope for the best. They're little people, not experiments.

Trista's large eyes scan my face and go impossibly round. She lunges to put herself between her mother and me. One small hand lands on my bicep and squeezes, a gesture I think is supposed to be reassuring. Or maybe she's telling me not to give her mother a piece of my mind. Or my fist. I don't know what she intends, but I'm nearly positive it's *not* to make me hard, but fuck if my jeans aren't too tight in the crotch now. It's a simple touch. It shouldn't be that easy to get my motor revving. And it's Trista. That alone should negate any ideas my body might have. I know it can never happen, but that never curbs my reaction.

"Mom!" she snaps at her mother. "Do you *hear* yourself right now? What is *wrong* with you?"

I flinch at the venom in her voice. Mrs. White's mouth works, opening and closing as if she has something to say, but the words can't find their way out. I've *never* heard Trista talk to *anyone* that way when she's sober. Since she avoids her mother when she drinks, Mrs. White has probably never heard that tone from her at all.

"He is my *friend*. If you can't trust him, trust *me.*"

Mrs. White's face hardens into a nasty glare. "I did trust you once," she spits at her daughter. "You fell in love with a hooligan just like *him,*" she pauses to sneer at me, eyeing me from head to toe like I'm dog shit on the bottom of her shoe, "and look how that turned out."

Oh, shit! The tightness in my pants quickly dissipates. I should *not* be hearing this. For more than one reason. It's none of my business, and now I kind of want to hunt the fuckhead down and make him pay for hurting her. *You can take it out on a bag later.*

Trista tightens her grip on my arm. I can't see her face, but her mother can and something there softens her glare. "I'm only trying to protect you," she whispers, reaching to cup her daughter's cheek.

Trista jerks backward, into my chest and out of her mother's reach. On instinct, I lay my other hand on her shoulder and squeeze, reminding her in case she was too drunk to remember that I've always, *always*, got her back. Even if this is awkward as fuck.

"I was a kid then, mother." Her tone is acidic enough to eat paint off a car. "I'm not anymore. And Ryan is the *last* person on this earth I need you to protect me from. He has gone out of his way to protect me more times than you will ever know. We're leaving. Don't wait up."

Trista pushes away from me and stalks to the passenger door, giving her mother a wide berth on her way by.

"Trista!" her mother cries, reaching and stumbling after her.

Trista's answer is to slam the car door. I'm so proud of her I don't even cringe at the blatant disrespect for my baby. It's about time she stood up for herself. Hell, I'm surprised it didn't happen sooner. A person can only tolerate being babied for so long.

I shift my weight from foot to foot, more uncomfortable with the situation now that Trista has removed herself from it. Some small part of me feels like I should reassure her mother that she's perfectly safe with me—safer than she would be otherwise. But does she really deserve that reassurance? Her daughter is a grown woman, not a toddler. She'd do well to remember that.

I clear my throat. The angry woman whirls around to glare at me as if this is somehow my fault. "You will take care of my daughter!"

I hold up my hands. "Lady, your daughter is a grown-ass woman. She can take care of herself. But I'll make sure she stays out of trouble." Any *real* trouble, that is. It would do Trista some good to live a little. To figure out who she is and learn to be herself all of the time, not just when she's drunk.

I turn around and make it two steps closer to escaping, but a hand on my arm brings me up short. *Are you fucking kidding me right now?* I turn slowly, letting my doneness with this situation harden my face into a glare that intimidates grown men who are trained in the art of physical violence.

Mrs. White doesn't so much as bat an eyelash at me. "Please," she whispers. "She's all I've got."

Her plea softens my anger. *At least she really cares.* Unlike my parents. "Ma'am, if you don't learn to let go a little, you're not going to have her much longer. She's not a child anymore. Sooner or later, you're going to push her away."

Away from you, or down a bad road. Either way, she'll be gone.

Tears well in her blue eyes and she hangs her head. "I just don't want her to hurt. Ever."

"You can't live her life for her. And you can't put her in a bubble and make her watch while life passes by. Someday, she'll break out of that bubble, and you won't like what happens next. I've got places to be." I turn on my heel again and march to my car, determined not to let anything stop me this time.

In silence, I turn the motor over, reverse out of the drive, and burn rubber in my haste to put some distance between Trista and all that nonsense.

A few blocks away, I find an alley and turn in. Once the car is in neutral, I pull the parking brake and shut her down. "Well, that sucked," I say, watching Tris from the corner of my eye.

She nods without looking my way.

I take a deep breath. I need to tell her that I don't blame her for her mother being batshit crazy. She needs reassurance. Encouragement. "I'm sorry it happened, but I'm proud of you for standing up for yourself."

Eyes firmly on her hands, which she's wringing in her lap, she whispers, "Thank you."

"You need to talk?" I'm not eager to prolong the awkwardness, but this isn't about what I want. She needs me to be a friend right now. I'm better at pulling her out of bad situations than talking to her. She needs Tara or Noel, but I'm here. I'll do my best to get her to one of them before this night is over, but she's got me right now. I'll do whatever I have to. *I won't fail again.*

"I don't even know what to feel, let alone what to say," she murmurs.

I shrug and rub the back of my neck. I hate the whole feelings thing, but I can do this. I just have to listen. "You feel what you feel, Trista. It's not right or wrong."

She sucks in a shaky breath and cants her head to smile at me without looking up. "I was sixteen; he was eighteen," she says.

Oh, shit. I did *not* bargain for this. I thought she'd go off about her mother, not give me her life story. Not that I don't want to hear it, it's just not what I expected right now.

She turns her face back to her lap and lets her hair fall forward, hiding behind it. "I was in love, and I thought he was too. He convinced me to run away with him, but we couldn't go without money. I cleaned out my college fund and gave it to him for safe keeping. We were going to meet at the bus station, pay cash, and be out of the state before anyone missed us."

Hunting him down seems like a grand idea. It wouldn't fix anything, but it would make me feel better. Might do the same for her. I'm sure I know where this is going, but I ask anyway to give her the chance to get it out if she needs to. "But?"

"He never showed up at the station. I found out later that he stole a car and it was found in Mexico. And I wasn't the only girl he scammed out of money before he left."

I wait a beat, but she doesn't go on. It doesn't explain her mother's issues, but at least I understand why she puts up with it now. She's scared. I'm sure if I ask her why that's not the answer she'll give, but that's what it boils down to. She trusted him. She loved him. He took her for everything she had and left. "I'm sorry, Trista. Teenage boys are idiots."

She cracks a smile. "Yeah, *teenage* boys." She rolls her eyes, giving me a peek at the sassy woman who woke up in my bed this morning, the side of her that cannot exist in the same space as her mother. "I don't think you can limit it to an age range, Ryan."

She's not exactly wrong. I sit up straight and puff out my chest, feigning indignance. "What are you trying to say?"

Trista giggles, which is all I wanted. "That all boys are idiots, no matter the age."

I pitch forward, clutching my heart as if she shot me. "How *could* you?" Her laughter fills the car. *Perfect.* "You alright?" I ask.

"Yeah," she says through her laughter. "Let's go do this thing."

Smiling to myself, I fire the car up again and navigate out of the alley.

"Hey, Ryan?"

I glance her way to find her serious brown eyes fixed on me. "Yes, Trista?"

We lock eyes, and she smiles shyly. "Thanks."

I return her smile, pleased with myself for earning it. *For helping.* "You bet."

Chapter 10

Trista

Ryan opens the door to the first stop on our furniture hunt and holds it for me. I step inside and stop short, causing him to bump into me. Only his quick reflexes keep me from falling forward. I'm too distracted by the sheer size of the store and the number of people and furnishings they packed in to save myself, but he grabs my shoulders and holds me upright.

"Be right with you, folks," a man calls from a knot of people congregated under a banner proudly announcing their store-wide sale. *Guess that explains the people.*

"We're just looking for now," Ryan tells him with a dismissive wave.

"Whoa," I whisper. This is my first time in a new furniture store. Mom prefers thrift store finds to save money and because she insists that furniture was better made in the '80s.

Behind me, Ryan sighs. "This will take all night," he grumbles.

He's right. There aren't nearly as many couches as it seems, but there are still enough to make it a task. "Good luck," I say, trying not to giggle at the mental image of him flopping down on couch after couch like Goldilocks, trying to find the one that's *just* right.

"What do you mean?" he asks, nudging me onward with a hand on my back.

I lead the way to the appropriate section, already assessing the options from a distance. I know which one *I'd* pick, I think, but I'm not here for me. "You've got your work cut out for you."

He makes a grumpy noise, somewhere between a growl and a grunt. "I think you mean 'we,'" he says.

I stop, and we collide again. *Why is he following so close?* Ignoring it, I turn around and take a step back so we're not chest to . . . well, stomach.

"Really?" I ask, failing to contain the excitement bursting into existence in my chest. Despite the cover story I told Mom about him wanting my help, I didn't believe he'd actually request my input. I'm just here to pay. Never mind the nice words in the car and all of the nice things he's done for me over the years, I know I'm not his favorite person in the world. In fact, most of the time I'm certain he only tolerates me for Tara's sake.

"You did tell your mom you're here to help. Don't want to lie to her now, do we?" he asks, smirking down at me.

I look away so my face doesn't betray my disappointment. I lie to Mom a lot. I have to, or she doesn't give me room to breathe. I don't expect him to let me help just to maintain my cover story. He has to live with what he picks, not me.

Ryan's calloused fingers close around my chin, and he turns my face to his. "What's wrong?"

"I didn't mean—I can just . . . wait here while you find what you want," I whisper, embarrassed that my silly, failed plan to appease my mother made him think I was trying to overstep. I'm here because I puked on his couch and am paying for whatever he picks out. That's it. My disagreement with my mother is not his problem.

Ryan's brows sink over his dark eyes, which is abnormal for him. He usually raises one or the other. "Why?"

"I didn't mean to intrude," I murmur.

Ryan rolls his eyes and drops my chin to grab my hand instead. "You're not intruding. I invited you. Let's go." He takes off, leading me by the hand across the store.

I struggle to keep up. It's not that he's moving too fast for me, but the feel of his skin on mine . . . It makes it hard to focus on anything else. It's only Ryan. He's not even particularly scary right now. There's no reason for my heart to be racing like it is.

He stops at the first couch he comes to and pulls me up next to him. "What do you think?" he asks, releasing me to wave grandly at the furniture.

It's pink and floral and stuffy—the sort of thing that will survive the apocalypse along with the cockroaches. *Exactly* the sort of thing my mother would love.

"It's hideous," I reply immediately, then slap a hand over my mouth. *I can't believe I said that out loud!* Slips like that get me in trouble with Mom when my opinions are diametrically opposed to hers. Those opinions aren't safe in her opinion. Thinking like that is what led me to agree to run away with Tyler. And maybe she's right.

But maybe I don't care anymore . . . It's not like being who she wants me to be makes me happy.

Ryan's face splits into a wide smile. "I agree. Next!" He chuckles under his breath and pulls me along beside him with the hand he's still holding. I fall in step with him, wondering if that was some sort of test. If so, I aced it. But what if I hadn't?

This hand-holding thing should be weird. We're not *together,* together. It's not weird, though. I don't feel the tense urge to yank my hand back and put some distance between us. We're just two friends out shopping. Tara and I will walk arm in arm through the mall on occasion, so why can't Ryan and I do this? There's no reason to overthink it. It doesn't mean anything. Does it?

Walking arm in arm with Tara doesn't give me butterflies, though.

After a few more rejects, whether for aesthetic or comfort reasons, Ryan sighs. "Forget this," he says, glancing around. "From here, which one do you like best?"

My gaze is pulled toward the back of the section, to the black leather couch I noticed almost immediately. It's hard to tell without getting closer, but I think I like it. More importantly, its simple, clean lines are masculine enough they won't look out of place in Ryan's home. But what if we get over there and it's somehow as hideous as the first one? Or if he doesn't like it but says he does to humor me? *This is why I don't like decisions.*

"Lead the way," he says, giving me a little push to get me started. He trails behind while I make my way through the rows of single couches and sets on display to stop in front of my selection. I like it even more up close. It's part of a set. What I thought was a separate chaise lounge is actually attached to it, and there are two matching chairs.

I look up at Ryan to gauge his reaction. The way his lips are straining upwards at the corners gives away the smile he's fighting. After a moment, his eyes swing my way, and he raises one brow. "You like this one?"

His question has me second-guessing my decision, though I can't see what's wrong with it. He's obviously found a flaw . . . "Yes?"

A smile lights up his face. "I do too," he says, unceremoniously flopping down onto the chaise. He pats the space next to him. "Gotta do the job right. Make sure it's comfortable."

I ease myself down and sigh in pure contentment as I sink into the cushion. It's not nearly as firm as it looks, which is a bonus as far as I'm concerned. "I like it."

"Definitely a good pick," he murmurs. I sneak a peek his direction. He's got his head thrown back and his eyes closed.

How can someone so . . . beautiful *be so scary?* I remember the day we met. I could hardly stop staring at him. But Mason showed up a few minutes later, apologizing for his lateness—his daughter didn't want him to leave. It's not that I found him more attractive, but, of the two, Mom would *love* Mason.

He's everything she wants for me. He has a stable, secure job. He makes good money. He's family-oriented. He would *never* abandon someone he loves. He is *exactly* what she's always wanted for me, with a dash of the mischievousness my sixteen-year-old self loved in Tyler. *Is that the only reason I wanted him?*

No. There was more. I know there was. The things that Mom would approve of were just perks. And it doesn't matter anymore, anyway. He's married. I need to move on.

"Do I have something on my face?" Ryan asks, startling me.

Oh, crud! How long have I been sitting here, zoned out, staring at him? How long has he been *watching* me stare at him. I take a deep breath and fight off the wave of embarrassment threatening to turn my cheeks as pink as that first couch.

"No! Sorry, was just thinking! So, is this the one?" I ask, patting the couch.

He smiles, but doesn't bat an eye at the subject change. "I think it is."

Ryan

I hustle Trista out of the store before she realizes what I did. There was no way in hell I was going to let her pay for my new couch. I don't care if she feels obligated or not. Money isn't something I lack. She made it easier to make the switch than I thought she would, though. *She's entirely too trusting.* The silly woman handed me a signed check, explaining that her mom would know the second the charge went through on her card and that it's none of her mother's business, and wandered off to browse while I paid and made delivery arrangements. Now that I know about the fuckwad who took advantage of her before, that trust is priceless, though.

So why did I invite her along? I could've told her no from the start. There was no reason to play along, knowing it would come to a standoff at the register. And I didn't really *need* her help picking. We both liked the same one, so much so that I bought the whole set.

I don't want to answer that question.

"Gabe is coming over to help me move the old couch out," I tell her on the walk across the parking lot. Chris would be my go-to for a task like this. I don't like to put Gabe in a position that might bother his old soccer injury. However, Tara will come with him, and Trista needs Tara.

Trista's steps slow and stop. "Oh . . . Okay . . ." I stop and turn in time to watch her reach into the little bag slung across her body and pull out her phone. "I'll get an Uber."

I ignore the surge of disappointment at the mention of her leaving. Time with Trista always comes with some sort of disappointment if I'm doing it right.

"Why? Would you rather go home?" There's no reason for her to think she needs an Uber unless she thinks I'm ditching her here now that she's upheld her end of the bargain—or so she believes. *She must think I'm the biggest dick on the planet . . .* Yeah, I can come across a little rough, but I don't think I've ever done anything to give her cause to believe I'd do something like this. I hope I haven't, anyway.

I saw the way she looked at me the day we met. I knew from the beginning that I needed to be careful to avoid giving her any ideas about *us.* Maybe I push a little too hard at times? It was easier before, when she was only Tara's friend. Before I developed this soft spot.

"N-no. I thought you were . . ." She stops and looks up at me, but doesn't finish her thought. She finally shakes her head. "I don't really know."

"Let's try this again. Gabe is coming over to help me dispose of the old couch. If you'd like to ride along, you're welcome to. I'll take you home later. If not, I'll take you home now."

Her eyes flare wide, then she ducks her head. If she were anyone else, I'd think she's flirting. Trista doesn't flirt, though. At least, she doesn't flirt with any of us. "I'd like to go, please."

Perfect. Not that I *want* to spend more time with her. That's not it at all. It's good that she's going so she can have time with Tara. She needs more support than I can give after her fight with her mother.

Chapter 11
Trista

*I*t took no time at all for Ryan and Gabe to load the furniture into Ryan's truck. The hardest part was navigating it out the door. Of course, it was all easy for Tara and me because we watched from the comfort of the floor in the living room while they worked to carry it out and stack it into the back of the truck like an overgrown game of Tetris.

Tara barely waited for the rumble of the truck's big motor to fade away before she turned on me.

"How's your mom?" I snort and roll my eyes, to which she raises her eyebrows. "That . . . sounds ominous. Everything okay?"

"Ryan met her today . . . That was a mess." We look at each other and laugh because it's the understatement of the century. "Oh! And she's trying to set me up with someone new."

Tara giggles. "I don't know who to feel more sorry for, your mom or Ryan."

I look at her, waiting for her to decide. I already know the answer. "Ryan," we say at the same time.

"So, a new guy, huh?" She leans over and bumps my shoulder with hers.

"Yeah, he's a lawyer. He has political aspirations. I shouldn't *let* this one get away."

Tara winces. "Does your mom realize we're living in the twenty-first century?"

Sometimes I wonder . . . "She just wants to see me settled. Doesn't want me to suffer what she did," I say, parroting the lines I've heard since . . . forever.

"Yeah, but you're not a kid anymore, Tris. Sure, it would suck if you got knocked up and the baby daddy bailed, but it wouldn't be as hard for you now as it was for her. She was a teenager, and your grandparents suck."

"Tell her that," I mutter. I can't agree or disagree with the part about my grandparents sucking since I've never met them. That used to bother me, but I stopped caring a long time ago. Mom tried to get them to be part of my life. They declined. The rest is accurate, though.

She smiles just a little. "Maybe you should."

I think about it, picturing her face if I said that, and shudder. "I like breathing."

"Hey, you forgot to send me the address for the gym," she says, changing the subject.

I cringe. "Oh, yeah." I forgot in all of the drama with Mom. "I'll do that when I get home."

The front door opens, admitting Gabe and Ryan, effectively killing the conversation. "That was fast," Tara says.

"Didn't have far to go," Ryan answers. "I donated it all to a charity of sorts."

I guess some good will come of my fuck up at least. I duck my head to hide the residual embarrassment.

Tara beams at him. "That was nice of you." She clambers to her feet. Gabe swoops in and helps her.

I eye them, trying not to wish it had taken longer. Or that they were staying longer. I don't want to leave yet, but I have no reason to linger.

"We can give you a ride home, Tris," Tara tells me.

I smile, hoping to hide my irrational disappointment. Before I can answer, Ryan says, "I don't mind if you hang out here. I'm going out to the shop to work on my project car, but you're welcome to stay. I could actually use a hand with something."

Surprise delays my reply. I can't believe he's volunteering to spend more time with me. It's the last thing I expected from him. He's always there when I need him, but this is the first time we've ever hung out without the rest of our friends. "I'd like that, thank you."

"Yep. I'm gonna go get changed." He shoves off the door frame and strides across the living room.

"We're heading out then," Gabe calls after him. "Mom is coming over."

"Tell her hi for me, yeah?" Ryan says over his shoulder. "And thanks man. Appreciate it."

"You got it."

"Are you sure, Tris?" Tara asks softly.

"Yeah. I'll be alright. I'm not going to puke on anything this time." I mean it to be funny, but it falls flat. I stand up so she doesn't have to bend over to hug me. "Thanks, Tara," I whisper in her ear.

"For?"

"Believing in me."

***

Ryan comes back to the living room and tosses me a shirt. "You're not gonna want to wear that out there," he says, his eyes on my top.

I really don't care—I don't even like this shirt—but I pull his on over it. He tries to turn around to hide his smile, but he's not quick enough. I know I look ridiculous. The hem hits me just above my knees. I quickly gather the excess material to tie it into a knot behind me, out of the way.

"You surprised me today at the furniture store," he says while my hands work.

"How so?" I ask, breathing a sigh of relief that we're not going to talk about what happened with Mom anymore.

"I figured you'd pick something white or tan. Something fussy."

"Why would you think that?" I ask. It's a fair assessment. Anyone who saw me before I put his shirt on would assume I adore pink and unicorns and all things girly. That's what Mom wants for me. But I don't really care for pink. Or most things girly, glitter aside. I've never worked out how to tell Mom that. I've never worked out how to tell *anyone* that. Even myself. It's easier to go along with Mom's preconceived notions of what I should or shouldn't like. At least, it was . . . Until recently.

I'm not sure what happened to change that.

And that bothers me.

Why do I find it so hard to go with the flow now? Why am I lying to her and sneaking around behind her back again? I can't blame it on a desire to see Mason anymore. That was what I used to tell myself to make it all better. The answer to my questions scares me. I don't want to think about it right now.

I look up at him, and he shrugs. "Because you strike me as the type to like that first couch—the pink flowery one."

This is my chance to set the record straight, so why am I not jumping at it? *I've made it this long; why change now?* It's safer; I won't make another mistake like I did with Tyler.

"Some floral can be okay," I murmur, though I've never found a floral pattern I like, "but that was a little much."

Ryan's eyes narrow, focusing on my mouth. He frowns a little and sweeps his gaze up to my eyes. "You just lied to me, didn't you?"

My pulse races, pounding in my ears. "What? No! Why would I lie about that?"

"Why indeed? But you did . . . So what's the truth?"

Defending myself is only lying more. "Can I tell you a secret?"

His mouth stretches into a smile that sends my pulse racing again. "I'm good with secrets."

"I don't like floral," I whisper. "At all. Or pink."

Oh, my God. I'm broken. Where are these thoughts coming from? Why are they surfacing now? I've existed in a bubble of pink flowers since birth despite my misgivings.

It must be the argument we had today. I'm still not over it and looking to lash out. That's all this is; a mild case of rebellion. Everything will be back to normal tomorrow. I'll feel like myself in the pastels and florals Mom picks for me.

No, I won't.

Shut up, me. Yes, I will. Just go with it.

"Really now?" he asks, his eyes on his shirt like he can see through it to the one I wore today—white dotted liberally with pink roses. "But your mom does?"

"Yeah," I whisper. Some little part of me dies, but I can't determine if it's *me* or *her*—the good daughter.

Ryan sighs and reaches for me. He pulls me close and wraps both arms around me and squeezes uncomfortably tight, but I don't mind. I could stay here for hours. "It's okay to like what *you* like, Tris," he whispers. "You don't have to let her dictate every detail of your life."

"I . . . She's only trying to protect me; give me a good life," I whisper, crumbling under the weight of my disappointment in myself.

"Let me tell you something," he says, his voice a soothing rumble under my ear. "Something I learned the hard way. Life isn't easy when you're not you. You can try to be her version of perfect all you want, but in the end, you'll hate yourself, and you'll hate her, and no one will be happy."

I look up, intending to ask for an explanation, but the hard anger in his eyes kills the words before they make it to my tongue. I clear my throat instead and change the subject. "So, what did you need help with?"

He smiles a little and drops his arms so he can lead the way. I follow him out the back door into the hot July night. I noticed the giant metal building behind his house earlier today, but I assumed it was a business or belonged to a neighbor. He opens a normal, person-sized door and steps inside, flicking a switch before I follow him in.

I stop and stare. It's massive! His whole house could fit comfortably inside it if not for the hunk of rusted metal that looks like it might've been a car once upon a time taking up the middle of the space. A metallic squeal makes me look around. Ryan is working quickly, his big arms flexing, straining the sleeves of his shirt while he pulls a chain hand over hand, raising the big bay door.

"What *is* that thing?" I ask when he's done, jerking a thumb toward the car-like thing. There's no hood on it, but I notice an appropriately shaped—and equally rusty—slab of metal leaning against the wall.

He looks past me and laughs. "It's a '68 Chevy Camaro. A cat was hiding in this thing when it was brought in," he says, giving the car an affectionate pat. "It's somewhere in the shop, I hear it crying every now and then, but I can't find it. Maybe you'll have better luck."

My heart melts into a giant pile of goo. The kitty has to be terrified. "Awwww! Poor baby! I'll find her."

He grins at me. "That would be great. I'm already tired of cleaning up cat shit."

He's clearly not a cat person. Or maybe it's just that he's tired of the messes she's leaving for him, and he's secretly a softy and plans to keep her? "What happens when I find her?"

He shrugs. "If we can get her in a box, I'll take her to a shelter. If not, I'll settle for out of my shop." He walks over to a workbench and grabs something, turning to hand me a bag of cat food. "I bought this hoping to tempt her out, but it obviously isn't working for me."

"There's nothing breakable out here, right?" I ask. The last thing I need is to break something expensive. I just bought the man a new couch.

His head falls back with his laughter. "Only you, Pixie Stix."

"Alright."

He kicks a long, cushioned thing with wheels on it and squats to sit on it. "I'll be under the car if you need me." He lays back on the thing and rolls, disappearing under the hunk of rust.

"Okay," I murmur, already distracted with the kitty problem. *If I were a cat, where would I hide?*

***

"Pix, everything okay?" Ryan asks, shattering the silence otherwise only broken by the sound of the tool he's using and me moving bits and pieces of things to look behind them.

I've lost track of time. It's hot in here. I'm sweating more than I ever have in my life. Everything is dirty and dusty, and all of that grime is sticking to my sweat and my clothes. But I *will* find the kitty. "Yeah," I call back.

"Just checking. You're kinda quiet."

"I'm trying not to scare the kitty." If she, or he, I really shouldn't assume, is feral, calling might scare them. And they won't know the sound of a food bag shaking. It'll be scary too.

I drop to my hands and knees to look under a long table thing. A soft hiss comes from near my hand. "There you are," I whisper, struggling not to shout in my excitement. *I did it!* The filth on the floor doesn't matter. I drop to my belly and press my cheek to the ground to see better. A kitten hisses and growls at me. Its black and tan patches blend well with the shadows under the table. An expert on cats I am not, but since its eyes aren't blue anymore, I think that means it's at least eight weeks old. "Oh, Ryan! It's just a baby!"

"I figured. You found her?"

"Yeah. Poor little baby is terrified."

"Probably hungry too. Hold tight." The rolling thingy he's laying on squeaks. "I'll bring you some gloves. You're more likely to get a hand on her than I am."

I keep my eyes fixed on the kitty and track Ryan by his footsteps, so I'm not surprised when he crouches down behind me and holds a pair of gloves that will be huge on me in my line of sight. I slip them on, ignoring Ryan's soft chuckle.

"Hey kitty, kitty. It's okay," I say quietly. "Are you hungry? Come here, and we'll get you some food, okay?"

The kitten hisses at me again as I reach for it, but it doesn't back down. "Poor baby, you must be too tired and hungry to run. How long have you been here, hmm?"

"Car came in on Tuesday," Ryan murmurs.

The baby backs away from my hand, but not fast enough. The hissing becomes snarling and growling, but I hold fast and carefully pull her out. I want so badly to snuggle it to my chest and shower her with the love she needs, but I don't want to get close to the business end of those claws. "Oh, you poor thing. Four days without your mama or any food?"

Ryan grabs the loose skin on the back of its neck with one hand. "Hey, I'm not a heartless bastard. I put food out every night. I was hoping she was tame enough it would get her used to me." He stands up and holds out his other hand to help me up. "Good catch, by the way."

"Thank you," I tell him while doing my best to brush the worst of the dirt off my clothes.

"I don't think she's wild at all," he says. "Just scared to death."

I glance up and almost lose my balance and fall on my face. Ryan, big, bad, angry, growly *Ryan*, cradles the little kitty against his chest with one arm, scratching its ears with his free hand. *Would it be weird if I took a picture?* I've never seen something so . . . I don't even have words. My brain is malfunctioning.

"You okay?" he asks, watching me like I'm the unpredictable wild animal in the shop.

I shake my head sharply. "Yeah. Just . . . surprised that the kitty isn't ripping you to shreds."

His eyes narrow. "Lie."

"How do you *do* that?"

The kitty must dig its claws in because he cringes a bit and looks down at it. "I don't know, something about the way you talk. You talk faster when you're lying," he says without looking up from the ball of fluff."

"Fine!" I huff. "I was surprised to see you snuggling a kitty. It's cute." Cute is an understatement, but I don't want to make this weird. "Happy?"

"Yep," he says, grinning broadly. "You wanna hold her?"

"How do you know it's a her?"

"Good point," he murmurs. "Easy there, baby." He slowly moves the kitty away from his chest, turns it around, and raises its tail.

"How rude," I tease.

He smirks, his eyes darting my way. "Girl. Need to see for yourself?"

I shake my head. "I'll take your word for it. Wouldn't know what to look for, and her privacy has been invaded enough for one day anyway."

"Here," he says, holding her out to me. "I'll go get a box and some food and water."

I take her, delighted by her soft, fluffy fur, and snuggle her close like he did. Her little claws pierce my shirt, but I think she's only holding on, not trying to hurt me. "I wish I could keep you," I murmur to her.

"So keep her," Ryan says.

My head jerks up. I thought he was already gone or I wouldn't have said anything. "I can't," I whisper, my eyes dropping to the floor to avoid the anger in his eyes when I explain. "Mom won't let me."

"I'll make sure she has a good home, Tris." He whispers it, but somehow even that manages to be gruff.

"Maybe Ronni? Or Keaton?" If one of them takes her, I'll see her again at least.

"I can ask. I promise I'll find her a home, Pixie Stix."

"Thanks, Ry." He really is a softy. Who knew?

***

The kitchen light is on when Ryan pulls up to the house to drop me off. I sink into the seat, wishing it would swallow me. I didn't want to leave Ryan's. I was perfectly happy sitting in the shop, petting the kitten and listening to him growl and grumble and cuss while he worked. It was . . . peaceful.

But I can't hide forever. Ryan is probably sick of me, even if I did my best to stay out of his way.

"You good, Pix?" he asks, eyeing the front door like he's afraid Mom will come flying out any second. His hand tightens on the gearshift, ready to throw it in gear and drive.

"Yeah." I cuddle the kitten close one last time and put her in the box between my feet.

He releases the gearshift to get out, no doubt to get my door because it's something all five of my guy friends do, but I open the door and tumble out of the car before he can. I don't want to risk another scene with Mom.

"Thanks for letting me hang out for a while," I tell him, ignoring his little frown. "I'll see you later."

"Anytime," he says, but . . . there's pain in his eyes. *Maybe I offended him by not letting him get the door? Or maybe he's just ready to get away from me?* "Thanks for helping with the furball."

"Happy to help." I close the door between us and run to the door, stopping to turn and wave before I open it. He waits until I'm inside to leave, though.

"Trista?" Mom calls as I pass the kitchen door. Cringing, I stop short and turn around. She's seated at the table, a mug of tea and a book in front of her. "Did you have a good evening?"

"Um, yeah," I say, bracing myself for her anger.

She takes a deep breath and folds her hands on the tabletop. "I apologize for before," she says, looking me square in the eye. "I've done a lot of thinking this evening, and I realize that we both could've handled it better. And, going forward,

I hope we can avoid more misunderstandings like that one. But it will take both of us. We have to learn to trust each other. I will try to be more . . . open-minded, but you have to stop lying to me."

"I don't lie to you because I want to," I tell her softly. Every muscle in my body is tense, waiting for the other shoe to drop. She's never apologized to me before.

"I know," she says, holding up her hand to ask for silence. "Let's just . . . put all of that behind us and start over, alright? Talk to me. What's going on in your life?"

Alarm bells sound in the back of my head, but I pull out a chair and sit. The lies I tell her aren't big, and I could argue that it's really none of her business, but they weigh on me. She's my mother. I love her. I don't want to hide things from her. All of my girlfriends are close with their mothers and I've always wanted that. Maybe this is where it starts.

So I tell her about my weekend, starting with Rachel walking into my office and giving me that stupid assignment. I downplay waking up at Ryan's, never specifically saying we slept in the same bed, but otherwise, I tell her everything, and she listens in silence with tears in her eyes.

Ryan

I turn into the Supercenter's parking lot with twenty minutes to go until closing. *I'll have to haul ass.* Being a small business owner myself, I'd prefer to support a local pet store, but concessions must be made for the time. I don't know what the hell I'm going to do with this damned kitten, though. I wouldn't leave her in my Barracuda even if it wasn't hotter than Satan's asshole outside.

Maybe I can sneak her in . . .

I lean across the console to peer into the box riding bitch. "Alright, fuzzass, here's how it's going to be. Trista isn't here to spoil you while I go in, so you're going to have to be quiet because I'm not leaving you out here to shit all over my car."

I reach behind me and snag the tech hoodie that basically lives in my back seat, then pull it over my head. The front pocket is big enough for a small, four-footed passenger. She doesn't fight when I put her in, but she pops her head out the other side and shakes it hard enough to make her ears flap.

"Gotta stay hidden," I tell her. *I can't believe I'm doing this.* Not just smuggling a cat into Walmart, but *keeping* her. Trista had a point; Fern and Mason would probably let Ronni have a kitten. But after listening to Trista fuss over the little beast all evening, I can't bring myself to get rid of her. I can't have Trista, but keeping the kitten is almost like having part of her.

I stuff both hands in the pocket with the kitten and do my best to not look threatening since I'm wearing long sleeves in the middle of summer. I don't want security thinking I'm here to rob the place. Since I was here earlier in the week to buy cat food, I don't have to wander around to find it. The kitten seems content, her little throat vibrating under my finger while I scratch her chin to keep her quiet. *I'm going to pull this off.*

I turn down the correct aisle and swallow a curse. There's a woman and a little girl browsing the cat food options. The little girl looks at me and moves closer to her mom—not an uncommon reaction to me. There was a time in my life when I would've been jealous as hell of that closeness, but I've outgrown it. I smile at her and sincerely hope she has a happy home life.

I slip one hand from my pocket and grab a litter pan. *So far, so good.* Now for litter and we can split. Anything else I need, I can come back for tomorrow without my tiny stowaway.

I give her one last scratch and slip my other hand from my pocket to grab a bucket of litter. She wiggles, but doesn't make a peep. *Good girl.*

Now to pay. I ease past the mother-daughter duo, smiling at the little girl again when I catch her watching me. The traitorous little beast chooses that moment to poke her head out of my pocket, which is roughly eye level with the girl, and *meow*.

The little girl's face breaks into the same delighted smile Trista wore all evening. "Kitty!" she cries.

"Shhh!" I shift the litter pan in my hand so I can press a finger to my lips, but I'm not sure if I'm talking to the cat or the kid.

"Can I see?" she whispers.

"Molly, don't talk to strangers," her mother scolds without looking away from the cat food.

"But he has a kitty! What's her name?"

That gets the mother's attention. She turns around, gets a good look at me, and grabs her daughter by the shoulder.

Uhh . . . Shit. "Chevy," I tell her because it's the first thing that pops into my head. The cat came to me in a Chevy Camaro. It seems fitting.

"Molly, leave the nice man alone," her mother says, but she's looking at the cat and me the same way Trista did earlier.

"It's alright, ma'am." I put the litter bucket down, glance around for wandering workers, and pull Chevy out of my pocket. "I couldn't leave her in the car. Too hot and she might make a mess, so I had to smuggle her inside."

"She's so cute!" Molly whispers. "Is she yours?"

"I guess she is." I thought of it more as keeping her for Trista, but that's the same thing as mine. "I have a friend who wanted her very much, but she can't have pets. So I'm keeping her."

"Aww, that's so sweet," Molly coos. "Now when your friend comes over, she can see the kitty too, and she'll be so happy."

"Yeah, she will." *Unless Tara tells her, she'll never know.* It's not like Trista hangs out at my place frequently. But it's something to look forward to if she ever does come by with Tara sometime.

Chapter 12

Trista

Anxiety eats at me, making my stomach churn and turn as the GPS on my phone guides me through the last few turns to the gym. *That was the shortest three weeks of my life.* The sweat beading on my forehead has nothing to do with the midsummer heat my air conditioner car barely hold at bay. It's all nerves.

"Your destination is on the right," the overly chipper female voice announces.

The Bar is an odd name for a gym, but I'm not surprised. It's definitely something Chris and Ryan would pick. The sun is just bright enough to cast a dim glow on my surroundings, making it easier to find the entrance to the gym's parking lot. *The one time I wouldn't mind getting lost* . . . With a shaking hand, I reach for the turn signal and give it a flick.

"You can do this," I tell myself softly, hoping to instill some sort of confidence by talking to myself. "Ryan won't be here, and if he is he won't know *you're* here." After spending so much time with him a few weeks ago I'm not nearly as intimidated by him as I used to be, but I don't want him to see me fall flat on my face. "There's nothing to be scared of. No one is going to laugh. You just have to try your best. And you won't be alone."

I navigate my car into a parking space as far from the building as I can get. Hopefully, the walk will help me calm my nerves. Moving on autopilot, I climb out of the car, close the door, and lock it. And I stand there in the early morning heat, staring at my car and the safety of familiarity it represents.

"Tris?" Tara calls from closer to the torture chamber awaiting us. "What are you doing way over there?"

"Trying not to freak out," I call back. I check my reflection in the window and cringe. I barely recognize myself in the form-fitting athletic clothes Noel helped me pick out, and my hair pulled back in a high, tight ponytail. Other women look strong and capable in such outfits . . . Whatever the opposite is, that's me. These clothes only amplify everything I try to hide with oversized, billowy tops and maxi dresses—that I haven't grown an inch *anywhere* since sixth grade.

Thank God I was out the door before Mom got up. This outfit would give her a heart attack.

"There's nothing to freak out about," Tara calls back. "We've got your back!"

I turn and look her way. She wasn't using the royal we. The others are all here already, waiting for me to join them. Even from a distance, I can tell Jamaica is *not* happy about being awake this early, not that I expected her to be. She is the antithesis of a morning person. Noel is hardly better but at least seems mildly alert. Madi and Tara are used to waking up early, so they're good to go. And Fern is practically vibrating with the energy of a toddler on a five-day espresso bender. *Just peachy . . .*

The flaw in my plan to hide behind her becomes painfully apparent. Yes, I'm certain she'll excel at this, but instead of overshadowing my ineptitude, she'll highlight it. *Too late now.* There's nothing to be done for it.

My heart thudding against my ribs like it's trying to punch its way out, I make my way across the parking lot to join them. Instead of calming me, each step closer to the gym raises my anxiety levels until I can scarcely breathe, and my brain is screaming at me to run away and hide.

Eddie should be on this piece, not me. They might as well call me Jon Snow because I know *nothing* about any of this. What's Eddie doing that's so important he can't be here? I know the reasons Rachel listed, but *seriously!* This *has* to be someone's idea of a sick joke. I'm going to walk in, and they're all going to be standing there laughing at my expense.

"Oh, my God," Noel groans as I approach, letting her head fall back. The sun turns her long, white-blond hair to pure gold. "You look like you're marching to the gallows, woman. It won't be *that* bad."

"Oh, I dunno," Jamaica says, her words still sleep-slurred. "It's too early for this. Now, if we could come back after lunch . . ." I stop in front of them and offer her an apologetic smile, which she answers with a slow, sleepy blink. "Austin is probably still laughing at me. He was too happy about waking me up."

Noel shakes her head, rolling her eyes skyward. "You two are impossible," she grumbles under her breath. She grabs Jamaica and me by the arm and hauls us toward the door. "This'll be great. I'm sure there will be . . . perks to this."

Behind us, Madi giggles, distracting me from deciphering Noel's odd pause. "Yeah, pecs—I mean perks. Honest mistake."

The others laugh, but I can't figure out why. I mean, yeah, there will definitely be an upside if this program actually works, but why is that funny? "I don't get it."

Tara snorts. "Oh, you will . . ."

I'm not sure that I want to now.

Fern hurries forward to open the door for us. We all murmur our thanks as we pass and I make a point to smile at her. Facing forward again, my smile slips. It takes actual effort to keep my jaw from dropping and drool from trailing down my chin. *Pecs . . . I get it . . .*

The blond man leaning against the front desk fiddling with his phone missed his calling in life. He should be gracing the cover of magazines the world over, not hiding in them. I was prepared for a gloomy, one-room cave, but this place is actually bright and airy. And since there's not a single piece of workout equipment in sight, definitely bigger than one room. It's almost impossible to keep my eyes off the hunk who hasn't looked up yet. His bright blue tank top clings to his muscular torso in such a way I find myself wondering if it's possible for him to remove it without help. Or scissors.

Each of us falls silent in the face of such awe-inspiring masculine beauty.

"Pecs," Madi whispers, making us all giggle again.

That gets his attention. He looks up and smiles, and it's more perfect than the rest of him. And it does *nothing* for me. Not like . . . No, I refuse to think about Ryan's smile today.

"Hello, ladies. I'm Logan. Does one of you happen to be Trista White?"

Someone shoves me forward, but Noel is still holding onto my arm, so I don't make it far, but I don't fall on my face either. "Um . . . That's me," I stammer, too shy to meet his eyes. He steps closer and, through my lashes, I note that his eyes are almost as blue as Mason's.

The silence behind me takes on a tense edge, but I don't have time to analyze.

Logan smiles again and extends his hand to me. "Nice to meet you," he says, taking care not to crush my hand when I give it to him. "If there are no last-minute changes to the paperwork you sent in, we're ready to get started. The rest of the class is here."

"I—I think we're ready," I stammer on what little air remains in my lungs. Something isn't quite right here, and it's only adding to my anxiety. But Ryan is nowhere in sight! That's a definite bonus. I was right.

Logan directs us to the women's locker room to store our belongings, then leads the way, taking on the role of tour guide. I cringe the moment we step out of the foyer and into the gym proper, if that's what it's even called. It's a wide-open space, much like I imagined it would be, full of different machines. And people. Which means we'll be doing this class in front of *everyone* who happens to come in.

"Alright, ladies, some of you aren't technically members, but the boss said he doesn't mind if you make use of our other facilities for the next few weeks. So, the door on your left is where spin classes are held every . . ."

Logan keeps talking, but I stop listening. If there's a room just for spin classes, does that mean we'll be shut away in a room as well? *Oh, gosh, I hope so.* This will be a little less embarrassing with fewer witnesses. And less of a chance that Ryan might wander by and see me.

"And this is where we'll be," he says, dragging my attention back to him and the door he's leading us to. He opens it and steps back to let me pass.

Movement catches my eye, drawing my attention to the tall, dark, and angry individual prowling around the room like a caged panther. His head jerks up and swings my way. Familiar dark eyes meet mine. *Oh, shit.*

Ryan

I suck in a deep, steadying breath, letting the familiar smell of stale sweat, rubber, and metal ease my anger. It works, but barely. The inconsiderate fuckers this fucking magazine sent are fucking *late*. It's only a couple of minutes so far, but they're wasting my valuable time and that of everyone here. Calling it unacceptable is an understatement. The other students are handling it well, though. A lot better than I am.

They're all regulars. Most of them have taken this class before, so they know what to expect. They're congregated in the middle of the room, chatting like they haven't seen each other in ten years while I pace. That negates some of my concerns about this project. Between Logan and me, we should be able to pull this off without a hitch. Maybe Chris really did know what he was doing, and this won't be the disaster I feared.

The door *finally* opens. Logan shoots me a crooked smile and steps back to admit . . . *"Trista?"*

Oh, no. No, no, no, no, no. This has to be a joke. Any minute, they're all going to laugh. This is worse than I imagined. Not only is she a beginner, she's a shy, insecure beginner. She'll need extra attention.

But this will be so fucking good *for her!*

And *I* get to help her.

I also have a legit reason to see her six days a week. In those tiny little shorts. *What was the downside here?*

"Ryan?" she says in precisely the same disbelieving tone of voice I used. Tara steps up behind her and guides her into the room, shaking with silent laughter. Fern, Noel, Jamaica, and Madi file in after them, all displaying various levels of amusement.

"Pay up!" Tara says, extending her hands, palm up, to Noel and Fern. "I *told* you he had no idea!"

"Why didn't you *tell* me?" Trista and I say at the same time. *How did Trista not know?* She had to have known this was my gym. Why is she so surprised to see me? And why did she react like it's a bad thing?

Tara looks at me and grins. "I assumed you would figure it out because of the paperwork," she says to me. "But we haven't all spent a lot of time together since it happened. Gabe said you were still salty about it a few days ago and I couldn't decide if calling to tell you would make things better or worse, so I left it to fate. However, these two," she jerks a thumb toward Noel and Fern, "were certain you'd figure it out before we got here."

"Logan and Chris handled the paperwork," I tell her. I had a bad attitude about the whole thing and wanted nothing to do with it. Now, I wish I'd at least peeked if only to be better prepared. I can't believe Chris knew all this time and didn't tell me!

Tara's grin becomes a smile. She looks at Trista and shrugs. "I just figured you knew when you let me know where we were going. What did you expect?"

Trista glances at me, then at Logan. "My boss said to ask for Logan, so figured we'd be working with him." She looks at me and spreads her hands, then quickly looks away. "I mean, you own the place. I figured you had better things to do."

I shake my head. "This is my better thing to do. It's what I love." I watch her, hoping she'll look at me again so I can . . . I have no idea. She doesn't, though.

"I take it you all know each other?" Logan asks, looking between the ladies and me.

"Yes," I say without offering more of an explanation. I glance at my watch and frown. This isn't a social hour. We're here to work, and we're fifteen minutes behind. I'm ready for this to be over so I can talk to Trista and make sure we're alright. Maybe I said something?

"Alright, let's get moving. Logan, we're going to need some lighter weights. You might have to raid Michelle's room for twos," I say, naming the woman who rents space from us to teach Pilates three days a week. "She won't mind this once. I'll make sure we have our own tomorrow. Everyone else, huddle up."

I know people don't like the whole introduction part of *anything,* but we're all going to work together for the next six weeks. It's best to start building a good group rapport on day one, especially with three of the team being novices. *Face it, you're worried about Trista.* I can alleviate some of the awkwardness since I know everyone here, though.

"Alright, you all know me," I begin.

"Unfortunately," one of the guys—Bryce—pipes up with a grin, making the others laugh.

"Asshole in Chief!" Dalton yells.

"Yeah, yeah," I tell him, swinging my towel his way. "You've all met Logan. He's a trainer here. We're teaching him to do this program so he can organize his own classes in the future."

That gets a round of cheers from the die-hards.

"So, ladies first. Trista, front and center." Best get her out of the way now so she has less time to dread being in the spotlight. She stumbles through the huddle to stand in front of me, her big eyes wide and anxious. I turn her around to face the crowd, leaving my hands on her narrow shoulders in case she passes out or something.

"Trista here is a friend of mine. And if you're thinking this is the last place you'd expect to see someone like her, you're correct. She's an editor for *Great Life Magazine* and is here because they're doing a piece on MaxPower. They want to know if our claims are true, so they sent Tris to get some hands-on experience."

"So everyone be nice to Trista!" Dalton jokes from the back.

"That's right. Everyone be nice to Trista." *Or I'll kick your ass.* "Tara?"

I lift my hands and let Trista melt back into the crowd, head ducked to avoid meeting anyone's eyes as the guys she passes pat her on the back and tell her she'll do great. I appreciate the sentiment, but I kind of want to break their fingers for touching her. I'm used to fighting that battle, but it's harder than it used to be. I'll go an extra round with the bag later to chill my ass out. Tara bounces forward and greets me with her customary hug.

"Tara here," I say loudly to make myself heard, then wait for the noise to die down, "is Trista's guest, as well as my sister from another mister. And, if you can't tell, she's pregnant."

Eight pairs of eyes drop to her stomach.

"I trust her doctor has cleared her to exercise, and she's not new to lifting, but I'm obviously going to keep an eye on her to make sure she's not overworking herself. If you notice something, please do speak up."

One by one, I call everyone to the front and introduce them, even the repeat offenders, because the girls don't know them, while Logan scrambles to find some lighter weights for Trista, Jamaica, and Madi. I'm not so worried about the other three.

I clap my hands once to get their attention and pace around a bit, anxious to get started. I have a good feeling about this, even if Tris is less certain. "Alright. Now that we've all forgotten each other's names, let's do this thing. Grab a mat and your weights. Ladies, you'll want three or four sets, light, medium, and heavy. Remember, this is about challenging yourself. Don't be afraid to go heavy. You can always drop weight if you need to. No shame in going lighter to maintain proper form!"

The huddle breaks up. I move toward the front of the room to compare notes with Logan. I'm sure he knew we had a pregnant team member before I did, which is no one's fault but my own, but I want to make sure.

I notice Trista before I make it to Logan and can't help but smile. A set of two-pounders in hand, she hurries across the room, making a beeline for the back. *Nope.*

I rush to intercept her, grabbing her arm and using her momentum to turn her. "Oh no, ya don't. You, Jam, and Madi are working up front. You'll be able to see demonstrations better that way."

And if one of the others notices that she's doing something that might hurt her, they'll let me know. Telling her that will only increase her anxiety, though. I don't want that. I want her to be comfortable here. I want her to enjoy this program. To look forward to coming every day.

I want her to learn to turn to a pair of dumbbells instead of a bottle when she's frustrated with her mother—or life in general.

Chapter 13
Trista

"Great job, everyone! Drop those weights!" Ryan shouts loudly enough to rock the walls. He wades through the rows of people, passing out fist bumps and high fives like they're candy.

Gratefully, I crouch down and force my fingers to uncurl from around the handles of the five-pound dumbbells I surprised myself by being able to use. Sides heaving, chest burning, legs wobbly to the point I'm afraid they're going to fail and dump me on my face, I turn around just in time to catch Tara engulfing Ryan in a sweaty hug. He gripes and groans like it's the most disgusting thing in the world, but he hugs her and carefully pats on her back, telling her how proud of her he is. It all seems like it's happening around me, like I'm not a part of it at all. I'm watching from the eye of the storm. Even the sound is muted.

Then, Ryan reaches me. He sticks out his hand, and I take it on reflex. Instead of shaking, he uses it to tug me closer, into a hug that lifts my feet from the ground. The protective bubble around me pops, and sound rushes in. "I'm so *proud* of you!" he cries as he spins me in a circle. "You killed it!"

"*You* killed *me!*" I whine. So I'm being dramatic. Sue me. The prospect of walking back to the locker room, let alone my *car*, is daunting. *And they said leg day would be easy . . .*

"I know it was hard, but if it doesn't challenge you, it doesn't change you." He lowers my feet back to the ground and steps back.

"Don't let me go!" I cry, reaching out and fisting my hands in his shirt like I'm actually strong enough to hold him here. "I'm going to fall if you do!"

Chuckling, he steps back into my space to steady me with a reassuring hand on my shoulder. "No, you won't. But I know that feeling. It means you—"

"Did the work!" several of the guys in the class shout in tandem, the onslaught of noise making me flinch. *That must be like a class motto or something, or maybe just a Ryan thing.* I knew they could all hear, but I didn't know anyone was paying that much attention to what we said.

"Cuddle puddle!" a man shouts. I'm supposed to know their names, but my brain doesn't know anything but exhaustion and pain right now. And an odd sense of euphoria. I *actually* did it! Okay, so I had to modify every move to make it easier, and I never touched the eight-pound weights I optimistically brought to my workspace, but I did every rep of every exercise.

"No! Do—" Ryan's protest is cut short by a cheer. He quickly pulls me to his chest, wrapping his big arms around me while a bunch of the others crowd around us.

So that *is a cuddle puddle.* A big, sweaty, smelly, dogpile of hugs. Cringing, I curl in on myself, trying to lessen the damage if this group hug turns into a real dogpile.

Ryan bows forward as everyone presses closer like he's trying to bodily shield me from the others. "So, uh, Dalton likes hugs," he groans in my ear.

"The sweatier, the better!" someone, presumably Dalton, shouts enthusiastically from my left side. "Oh, shit . . . Uh, I forgot to make sure everyone here is cool with hugs," he adds, a distinct note of guilt in his voice. In my head, that tone projects the image of a puppy caught doing something naughty. The weight around me lessens as the people back off.

I open my mouth to automatically reassure Dalton that it's fine. Everything is fine. It wasn't making me cringe. Surprisingly enough, it's mostly the truth. I *don't* mind. It's kind of nice—disgusting, but encouraging, like I'm actually part of something. "It's alright," I tell him. "But, maybe, a little more warning next time."

"No shit," Ryan gripes. He makes sure I'm steady on my feet and backs away. "You're going to break her if you throw out surprise hugs like confetti."

Dalton flashes a contrite smile. "Sorry man, didn't mean to break your girl."

Ryan's cheeks turn red, and if my face weren't already hotter than the surface of the sun, I'm sure it would too. We both edge away from each other a little more.

Ryan clears his throat. "She's, uh, just a friend."

For the first time, I don't doubt that Ryan considers me a friend instead of someone to tolerate. But why is he acting like it's a bad thing?

Dalton holds up his hands. "My bad. Just thought—"

"It's alright," Ryan says, waving away his explanation.

"Time for cooldown!" Logan calls from the back of the room.

I turn to watch Logan's demonstration, but Ryan puts a hand on my arm and stops me.

"Tris?" he asks, his voice pitched low enough to keep the others from hearing. "Are you okay—are *we* okay?"

Why wouldn't we be? He's the one acting funny. I smile up at him, and the little groove between his brows smoothes out. "Yeah, why?"

He shrugs. "I was just worried. You didn't seem happy to see me here today."

I bite my lip. I hate to admit it, especially now that the first class is over and was nothing like I expected it to be, but I don't want him to keep worrying. "I was afraid to work with you because I thought I'd be bad and you'd be frustrated."

His face goes slack, and he sighs. "Damnit, Tris. C'mere." He pulls me into another quick hug that ignites something warm and tingly in my chest. "I'm so impressed with the effort you put in today. And I'm glad I'm here to help you," he says when he lets me go.

"Thanks," I whisper. That tingle quickly spreads, banishing the pain and exhaustion weighing me down.

A smile brightens his face. "Now, stretch, or you'll hate me tomorrow."

***

A full day of work is *last* thing I want to do, but it's Monday. I can't go curl up in a ball and sleep for three hours, even if my body is begging for it after that workout. The warm tingles didn't last long once I left the studio. It's odd; I've never been so physically exhausted but mentally alert in my life.

I could swear someone replaced my legs with lead weights as I trudge to my office, but that keeps my mind off the whole 'just a friend' thing. Each step takes as much effort as the entire forty-minute workout, but I finally make it to my little office. It's a glorified cubicle, but it has a door and a window, and it's mine. And, most importantly, it has a *chair*.

"So, how was it?" Rachel's question sends me into orbit in the middle of my office.

I drop my purse, but not my coffee, and clutch my heart with my now free hand. "Don't *do* that!" I cry, wheeling around to face her. "You're already trying to kill me with this article. Don't give me a heart attack on top of that!"

Rachel blinks at me. Her mouth opens, then closes, and she smiles. "I don't think I've ever heard you talk like that."

My head drops to hide the way embarrassment heats my face with a blush. "Sorry," I murmur to my shoes.

"Why? I scared you. You reacted. It's not like you told me to go . . ." She looks behind her and lowers her voice to a whisper, "To go have intimate relations with myself."

"But you're my boss," I say. I'm supposed to respect her. Tara, Noel, the others, *they* react like that. But that's them. They're all strong—badasses in their own rights. It's not *me*. I don't know where it came from. But . . . it felt good.

She waves a hand at me and closes the door. Sauntering across the room, she passes me and drops into the chair I keep for visitors. "So, how was it?" she asks again.

"Well, I lived." I sigh and turn back toward my desk to—finally—sit down. It's such a relief to get off my feet. "It was leg day. They assured me legs are easiest. I assure *you*, they're lying. There was nothing easy about that. My legs are *dead.*"

Rachel's smile transforms her face in a way I've never witnessed before. There's a new depth to it—an understanding—we've never shared. "That's how this usually works. Just wait for tomorrow."

I sigh and sit forward to rest my elbows on the desk and prop my chin in my hands. "Yeah, they've already warned me. I'm trying hard to pretend I'll be fine in the morning."

She reaches across the desk to pat my arm. "Stretch. A *lot.* When you think you've stretched enough, do it again. And you *might* be able to walk tomorrow. So, two things. This is your piece, and you can handle it however you want, but I'd suggest keeping a workout journal so you have notes to draw from. And you can work from home tomorrow. Maybe the next day too. We'll see how you feel."

I breath a little sigh of relief even as apprehension twists my stomach into a pretzel. Am I really going to hurt so badly tomorrow? *Guess I'll find out soon enough.* "Thank you, Rachel. That helps."

"I know this isn't easy for you. And I know I didn't give you an option. I'll do what I can to help."

"You could take over," I suggest with little hope of her taking me up on it. If she *wanted* to be the one, she would be.

"Nope, this is all you. You really are the best person we could send. Eddie *can* do it, but no one wants to read about someone who is already in peak physical condition getting better. People want to see results from someone like you, someone they can relate to."

I hate to admit it, but I understand. It's what I would want to read if I were interested in such things. Even though I'm not, there's still a chance I'd read an article about it if I somehow identified with the person writing it.

"We should do weekly progress photos." The words take me by surprise, but even more shocking is that *I'm* the one who said them. I would expect something like that from Rachel. It will be good for the article, which will be good for the magazine. But that was all me.

If I'm going to do the damn thing, I might as well do it right. Don't I owe it to myself?

Rachel smiles. "We've already thought of that, but I didn't want to spring it on you yet. I know you don't like pictures. I hoped you'd get there on your own, so thanks for that. Someone will be up before lunch."

"Yay," I cheer without any real enthusiasm.

Ryan

Between Chris's class schedule and mine, it's noon before I catch up with him to give him a piece of my mind. He's in the breakroom at the microwave, his back to the door when I walk in.

"Alright, dick," I snap at him, laying the anger on thick because I know he knows this is coming. He has to. I'm really not mad at him, not anymore, but it's more fun to pretend I am.

His shoulders shake, giving away the laughter he's trying to hold back. He turns around and holds up his hands, his face arranged in a mask of wide-eyed innocence, but his mouth twitches at the corners, trying to stretch into a smile. "What the hell?"

I cross my arms over my chest. "You *knew* who they were sending, didn't you?"

His smile gets a little bigger, but he's still fighting to hold it back. "Maybe."

"When we were talking that day?"

He shakes his head. "No. I knew she worked there, of course, but I thought they'd send someone else."

"So why didn't you tell me once you *did* know?"

The smile wins the fight. "Because if you weren't such a diva about it all, you wouldn't have needed me to tell you."

A diva? I kind of was, I guess. "Man, fuck you!" I ruin it by laughing, though. He got me good.

He looks me up and down. "Eh, you're not my type," he says, chuckling along with me. "So, how did it go?"

I hook my foot around a chair leg and pull it away from the table. "Great," I tell him as I sit. "I mean, my argument still stands. It would've been hell with a whole bunch of beginners. But half of them know what they're doing, and the other three catch on quick."

He gives me a knowing smile that irritates the fuck out of me and joins me at the table. "I won't say I told you so, mostly because you're right. It could've been worse. But I knew you could do it either way."

It's nice to know he believes in me, even if I don't like his methods of showing it. "Thanks, I think. But I still can't believe you didn't tell me."

His fork stops halfway to his mouth. "Serves you right for being a hardheaded dick."

"Yeah, yeah. I'm sorry I was a dick about it."

"No, you're not," he says around a mouthful of food.

I smile because he knows me so well. "You're right. Sort of." If I'd known then who it would be, I wouldn't have argued against it.

Chapter 14
Trista

It will get better. That seems to be my mantra. I wake up, I say it. I get to the gym, I say it. I *move,* I say it. It's becoming as much of a part of my routine as waking up early to meet the girls at the gym. As much as I hurt, I do enjoy it—the camaraderie, the sense of accomplishment, and the absolute focus required. There's no room in my head for anything else during the forty minutes we're working. But I'm looking forward to the day when I can get out of my car without wanting to cry.

I have no measurable proof that I'm stronger, but I *feel* like I am. Every morning before I walk out, Ryan tells me I am. What he said this morning is still rattling around in my head because it hit a little harder than he maybe intended. *'I know it's hell, but every day, you get up, you show up, and you walk out of here a stronger person in more ways than one. And I'm so proud of you."*

It's hard not to feel better about yourself when someone like Ryan says something like that with so much conviction.

But closing a car door shouldn't hurt quite so much.

I turn toward the little café Tara, Madi, and I agreed upon for lunch and wince, eyeing the distance while I lock my doors. This was the closest spot I could find, though. *Better get moving, or I'll be late.*

"Trista!" Tara stands and waves when I walk in. I bypass the hostess with a nod and weave my way between tables to get to her.

There's a box wrapped in silver foil paper in front of one of the two empty seats, so I take the other while I mull over who else they invited. It's no one's birthday that I know of, no special occasion. It could be a baby gift from Madi, but why wouldn't she just give that to Tara at their boutique?

I sling my purse over the back of my chair, and the box is in front of me when I face forward again. "We got you something," Tara announces, bouncing in her seat in her excitement.

"We?" I ask, shifting uncomfortably. I love getting presents, but they always make me feel weird. Like, what did I do to deserve this? And was I supposed to get them something?

"All of us chipped in, even Ryan and Chris," Madi says. She bites her bottom lip and watches me expectantly. *Ryan too?* I don't know why it matters, but that makes me happy.

"Go ahead!" Tara urges.

Too curious to deny them, I slide my finger under a flap of paper and tug. "But why?"

"Because we're all proud of you!" Tara says with another little bounce. "You're working so hard."

The paper falls away in one big sheet, revealing a black box sporting the logo for a popular fitness tracker. I swallow hard to force the grapefruit-sized lump in my throat down. "You guys," I whisper.

Tara and Fern have these. They're constantly comparing notes on steps and calories burnt, easily measuring their progress. I never thought about getting one for myself.

"It was Fern's idea," Madi gushes. "She noticed that you get frustrated when you feel like you aren't making progress and thought this might help so you can actually track what you're doing!"

"I love it," I whisper.

"We'll help you figure out what all the numbers mean," Tara tells me.

"Thank you so much. I don't even know what to say."

Tara grabs my arm and squeezes. "You've said enough." I reach to hug her, but my phone rings. "That's probably Fern now," she laughs.

I get my phone, but the number isn't one I know. I'm inclined to ignore it, but what if something happened to Mom? "Excuse me," I murmur, pushing my chair back. I answer the phone on my way to the door. "Hello?"

A man clears his throat on the other end of the call. "Uh, hi. I'm looking for Trista White?"

"This is she." I push the door open and step out onto the sidewalk, mouthing *sorry* to passing pedestrians for getting in their way.

"Sorry, this is . . . Awkward. My name is Grant Malcolm."

Grant . . . Why is that name familiar?

"My mother works with yours . . ." he continues.

Oh, no. My stomach does flips, threatening to send the remnants of my breakfast back. I try to say *something*, but no words come out. I don't know what *to* say. This is . . . mortifying, and exactly why I didn't call him. *Is this really happening? Maybe I'm dreaming?*

He's wrong. This is beyond awkward. "Oh! Yes, Grant. Hi," I finally manage.

"Hi," he says again. This time his tone conveys a smile. I'm not sure that it's possible to *sound* attractive, but his deep, clear voice does. It makes no sense and does nothing to help make this any less weird. "Like I said, yeah, awkward. I told my mom I can't just call random women because she says it's okay, but . . . Moms."

"Moms," I agree, smiling because he used the same argument I did. He probably doesn't want to be doing this, either. Which probably means he won't ask me out; he's just calling so he can tell his mother he tried, and we'll both go on with life. *Thank goodness.*

"Well, I wasn't going to call you—Mom says you're the shy type—but she wouldn't quit badgering me about it," he says, seeming more comfortable now that we've established some common ground. "Even sent me a picture of you last night. So, I decided I'd at least call and say hello so I can tell her I did. And, I was wondering if maybe you'd like to get brunch on Sunday?"

My free hand balls into a fist. *A picture? Seriously?* I don't know why I'm surprised. I should probably be thankful Mom stopped at passing along a picture and didn't call him herself to arrange a date. That doesn't make it right, though. I take a deep breath and let it out. I'm mad at Mom, not Grant. I can't take it out on him.

As tempting as it would be to turn him down to spite Mom for the picture, she will be *livid* if she finds out. And we're doing a lot better lately. I don't want to ruin that progress just to get back at her. And really, going can't hurt anything. Maybe this guy will be different. "Uh . . . Brunch, sure! That sounds nice. I'm sorry, this is just—" I wince, not wanting to say it again.

"Awkward," he finishes for me, clearly amused.

"Yes! I mean no! It's not, but yeah, I'm shy, so . . . I'm glad you called, though." *It takes the pressure off me.* Now I can tell Mom we're going out. It'll work out or it won't. Either way, she can't say I didn't try, and I'm off the hook.

"Me, too. What do you say I name the time, you name the place?"

I like that. I can pick somewhere I'm comfortable this way. *I wonder if he did that on purpose?* "Sure! There's a diner near the U that has a really good brunch."

"I know that place! Excellent! Ten-thirty?"

"Perfect."

"Perfect," he repeats. "I'll see you then."

"See you then." For some reason, I'm actually not dreading it already.

"Who was that?" Tara asks as soon as my butt hits my chair. "I ordered your favorite, by the way."

"Thanks. Um, *the guy*," I tell her, bracing for a lecture about standing up for myself and what I want. But, really, I don't feel like I agreed to go along with what Mom wants. Yeah, she pushed for it, but in the end, I made the decision to say yes.

Tara only groans, though. Madi's head tips to one side and she regards me with mild curiosity.

"My mom and her co-workers like to play matchmaker." I follow up with the stories of Peter and my other ex, Nick. I give her the short, slightly less depressing version, so I finish up just before our food makes it out.

The Ceasar salad here is phenomenal, but I don't have the heart to tell Tara it isn't my favorite. I only ever ordered it because that's what Mom expected of me. It's no surprise when that's what the waitress plunks down in front of me, though. *It's what I would've ended up ordering anyway.* Menus always overwhelm me—too many options. Trying something new is scary. What if I don't like it? Then, I'm stuck eating something I don't enjoy. Or paying for something I don't eat.

It's just better to stick to what I've always ordered. Even if it's boring.

Chapter 15

Trista

"Alright, everyone, listen up!" Ryan pauses and waits for the team to settle into silence. It doesn't take long. *Damnit.* "Gents, you know what we're in for. Ladies . . . Don't hate me. Day six is another total body day."

"What?" I cry to the general amusement of the team. "You're joking, right?"

He shoots me a smile. "Nope. Sorry, Tris. There is good news, though! It's all plyo."

Everyone groans. Even Fern. That gives me chills. She hasn't complained about *anything.*

"Do what now?" I ask. He says this is good news, but the team's reaction says otherwise.

"Plyometrics," he says like adding two syllables explains it all. "They're exercises designed to increase speed and strength. You'll start with bodyweight."

That doesn't sound so bad. So why is everyone acting like he just announced his dog died?

Behind me, Fern murmurs, "Doing them after yesterday's workout will be hell."

Ryan must hear her because he grins again and points at her. "Yes. Maybe not so much for those of you who exercise daily, but for you newbies, this is going to hurt. I'm not asking you to do anything you can't do, though. Today, you're going at your own pace. Some of you might get ten reps of an exercise done in the given work time. Some might only get three. That's perfectly fine as long as you're committing every last ounce of effort. Let's get started."

It still doesn't sound horrible. Logan leads us through our warmup. It's familiar enough after five days that I know what's coming next. Blessedly, the dull ache in my muscles fades. And I'm not quite as breathless by the end as I was on day one. *I am getting better!* My fancy watch doesn't have enough data to back it up yet, but I *know* I did more squats today than I did yesterday. I counted.

I want to shout it for the whole team to hear, but I don't want to draw that much attention to myself, either. I'm more comfortable with them all than I was on day one, but I still don't want all eyes on me.

The euphoria fades as I absorb Ryan's demonstration of the next set of workouts.

He's trying to kill me.

***

"Don't forget, pool party at my place!" Fern announces after our cooldown. She mentioned it a few days ago, but the weatherman started talking about rain.

"Yes!" Dalton cries. "That's what I'm talkin' 'bout! Where's your place?"

"You mean it?" Ryan asks, cutting her off before she has a chance to answer.

"Yep. Mase and I spent all week planning it with our fingers crossed. We weren't sure the weather was going to cooperate, but it did! Grand opening of the pool!"

Ryan looks at her and pointedly raises a brow. "But, *everyone?*"

"Yep!" she says, bouncing on the balls of her feet. "The more, the merrier!"

Ryan rolls his eyes skyward. "I'll text everyone her address."

"Do I get to push Ryan in the pool?" I ask quietly.

She turns my way, grinning widely. "*I* won't stop you. Her eyes flick upwards, focusing over my head. "*He* might, though."

I whirl around and find myself nose to pecs with Ryan himself. "Bring it on," he growls. "I'll take you down with me if I go in at all."

I cross my arms over my chest, matching his stance, and glare up at him. "I'm not scared of you," I lie. The very idea terrifies me, but I *would* like to push him into the pool to get even for the last week of hell. "I'm faster than you are."

The hard set of his mouth softens, and he *almost* smiles. "Bet."

"Bet."

His smile breaks free, wiping the menace right off his face. "Just remember that when you end up in the pool."

"Just remember that when I *don't*." I stick my tongue out at him because I'm mature like that.

"Someone is feeling very confident."

"Revenge is very motivational."

He chuckles. "Revenge, huh?"

I lift my chin a bit. "Yes. You've tried to kill me every day this week."

"Oh, sweet little Pixie Stix, if I wanted you dead . . ."

It's not a threat, but I shudder. He doesn't have to elaborate. How many times have I put my life in his hands? Letting him drive me home. Trusting him to keep an eye out for me when I drink. He's never anything but gentle with me. Something about that is . . . appealing.

He's so strong he could hurt me without trying, but he's held me in his arms as carefully as I'd hold something fragile and precious to me.

Someone clears their throat, and we both look toward the sound. "Yeah. Just friends," Dalton says pointedly.

I don't move. There's no voice in the back of my mind urging me to. I have nothing to hide because we *are* friends.

Ryan takes a step back, though. "Yep. Just friends."

For some reason, hearing him say it this time doesn't make me as happy.

***

With shaking hands, I shove the tiny bikini Noel convinced me to buy last summer into the bottom of my bag. Mom is doing a *lot* better about accepting my decisions, but I haven't pushed her too hard since that night at the table. She definitely won't approve of the bikini—not that she'll approve of the cutoffs and the cami I'm wearing, either. Neither have so much as a flower to redeem them in her eyes. But, baby steps.

I bury it under a fluffy, *flowery,* pink beach towel. Just to be safe, I add a Mom-approved floral one-piece swimming suit as a decoy.

But it's so *frustrating.* I shouldn't have to sneak. I shouldn't have to *hide* things. I'm not a child anymore. I know we're making progress, but it's not fast enough for me.

One last peek in the mirror to ensure my butt really is covered in these shorts, and I scurry to my door.

"Mom, I'm going out! Don't wait up."

Her bedroom door flies open. "Where are you going? I thought we were— *What are you wearing?*"

I cringe, then recover and give her a look.

"Sorry," she says, holding up both hands.

"I'm wearing clothes, Mom," I say with more patience than I'm really feeling. "And I'm going to Fern's for a pool party."

"Oh . . . Fern's," she says faintly, her eyes roving over my tiny top. "Wait, I thought you didn't like Fern?"

I smile a little. "You're right. I didn't."

"But you're going to her house?"

"I've gotten to know her better." In truth, it's almost impossible to *not* like Fern. She's a little quiet around people she doesn't know well, and I mistook her shyness for bitchiness. In truth, she's the biggest sweetheart on the planet unless you piss her off. "I misjudged her, and I blamed her for something she had no control over."

Mom nods. "She married that man you were in love with, right?"

I pause, trying to find the right words to answer that question. I've come to realize a few things since they got together—no matter how hard they are to accept. Ironically, it was Mom calling me out about Tyler in front of Ryan that really drove the point home. "She married Mason, but I only thought I was in love with him."

Because he was the answer to everything. You can't love someone when you don't know them. I was obsessed with him because, in my mind, he was everything I needed to be happy in life. A man my mother would approve of who wasn't self-absorbed and boring. I was doing to Mason what my exes did to me, and I kind of hate myself for it. He checked all the boxes, and that was good enough.

Mom's lips stretch into something that she probably means to be a smile but reads more like a grimace. "Well, at least I know you're not a homewrecker. But if you're not wearing this . . . outfit to impress him, who are you wearing it for?"

Why do I have to be wearing it for someone? Nearly everyone who will be there has seen me in workout clothes. This is nothing to any of them. I shrug one shoulder. "For myself. It's hot out."

"Wouldn't you be more comfortable in a nice sundress?"

Probably. It's not about comfort, though. It's me making my own decisions. "Not really. I'll see you in the morning."

Mom latches onto my arm, stopping me in my tracks. "Why are you punishing me like this?"

"Punishing you?" *How did she reach that conclusion?* It makes no sense. If I wanted to punish her, I'd . . . I don't even know.

"Yes!" Her eyes are fixed on my clothes again. "Why else would you even consider walking out the door dressed like you're bound for a *street corner?*"

I bite my lip. *Am* I punishing her? I'm tired of her rules. I'm tired of feeling like I can't be myself—like she won't love me for *me* if I don't do exactly what she wants. Is that the only reason I'm wearing this? Or is it because I really want to? "I'm not punishing you, Mom," I say, but even I detect the doubt in my voice.

"Then go change into something appropriate! You look like a floozie! You don't want the kind of attention clothing like this attracts."

Maybe I did go a little overboard. I probably have longer shorts. And a shirt that isn't so tight.

"I just don't want my baby to walk out of this house looking like a whore!"

She's doing it again. We're right back where we started; she disagrees, so it must be wrong. And it hurts all the worse because I should've known it was too good to be true. "I'm not a little girl anymore, Mom!" I snap. I'm so sick of her treating me like a child.

I yank my arm from her grasp and run to the door, my flip-flops *thwacking* ridiculously with every step like mocking laughter.

Ryan

"This is a nice setup, man," I tell Mason, admiring his backyard from the giant picnic table on the patio.

The space has undergone a radical change from this time last year when it was nothing but a few chairs, a poor excuse for a firepit, and a playset for Ronni. He never entertained outside because his ex was a pampered city princess to the bone. Now, Ronni's playset is a treehouse that's nicer than my home. There's an outdoor kitchen, a bar, a firepit that will hold more than a couple logs, an in-ground pool, a hot tub, and an area just for outdoor games. Every time I show up, there's something new to check out.

"Thank you," he says, reaching across the table to touch his beer bottle to mine. It's an odd sight to see—Mason with a beer bottle instead of Scotch—but sometimes, you just can't beat an ice-cold beer after a long day of sweating your ass off in the sun. "And thanks for helping."

"No problem." What kind of friend would I be if I sat on the sidelines and watched him complete his last few honey-dos? Mason's willingness to be hands-on is something I've always admired about him. The man has more money than God, but he's not above doing the menial shit. Like hanging up a bunch of fake wasp nests to repel the little monsters because he's highly allergic to them. I'm glad I showed up in time to take that one over.

The back door opens, and a bunch of people spill out into the yard. I scan the group, hoping to see Trista, but she's not among them.

"Here we go," he murmurs.

I cock an eyebrow at him. "I thought this was partly your idea."

"Oh, it was," he says with a rueful half-smile. "I'm just tired. And hot."

"Go jump in the pool. Or, I could push you," I suggest, smiling for more than one reason. I can't help but think back to Trista threatening to shove me into the pool to get even with me. *I can't believe how much she's come out of her shell already.*

One of my professors in college said that a lot of people find themselves at a bar, and he wasn't talking about the alcoholic kind. There's something about good, honest effort and a lot of sweat that makes a person come to terms with who they are. There's no room in your head for pretense when you're focusing every fiber of your being on a lift. It's cathartic.

It's exactly what she needs.

I'm so glad she's finally where she needs to be. And that I'm the one who gets to help her. But the extra time with her is making it hard to remember that I *can't* be with her.

Tara and Noel collapse at the picnic table on either side of me, Tara in a pair of cutoffs and a tank top that hugs her belly, and Noel in a dress over her bikini. "Whew, this heat . . ." Tara says, fanning herself with her hand.

"Want me to shove you in the pool too?" I ask. Not that I would—right now. I might hurt the baby or something.

"I think I'll take the ladder," she says dryly. "Who are you planning to push into the pool, aside from Tris?"

"Mason," I tell her, tipping my beer bottle his way. "He said he was hot, tired, and crabby. I offered to shove him in to fix at least one of those problems."

"He's too good to me," Mason mutters.

Tara giggles, reaching over to squeeze my shoulder. "Isn't he, though? Such a sweetheart."

I lift my bottle in salute. "I live to serve."

"What would we do without you?" she asks.

I start to answer, but stop short when the back door opens again because Trista stomps out like the ground did something to offend her. She marches straight up to Noel snatches up her lowball.

I'm on my feet so fast it's amazing I don't tip the table. "Nope," I tell Trista, snagging the glass from her hand before she gets it to her lips.

"Hey!" she protests, reaching for the drink again. I hold it over my head to stop her.

"What the hell?" Noel cries. She stands up and takes her glass out of my hand, keeping it well out of Trista's reach. "You should thank him. You'd be pouring yourself into bed in about five minutes. That's straight whiskey."

"I don't care," Trista mutters.

Stealing Noel's drink isn't the only odd thing about her this evening. "What are you *wearing?*" I blurt out. *You dumb fuck.* If I could kick my own ass, I would. But she looks . . . *good.* Good enough to surprise me into saying stupid shit, obviously. I clear my throat and sit while everyone is too distracted by Trista to notice my boner.

I've seen her in tiny dresses that didn't affect me the way those cut-offs and that cropped cami are.

She gives me the stink eye, proving that I was right. Calling her out on her outfit was not a good idea. "Clothes," she snaps.

"I think you look great!" Tara tells her.

"I'm not arguing that," I say. "It's just a shock."

Noel wiggles her glass. "I'm assuming you had words with your mother about your outfit?"

Trista's eyes slide from the glass to the beer bottle dangling from my hand. "Yeah," she says, her voice tight as tears pool in her eyes. I fucking *hate* it when something makes one of my ladies cry, but having someone pat her on the back and tell her it'll be okay isn't what Trista needs right now. But I know what she does need.

Her tears are a great fix for my problem. I stand up and hand Noel what's left of my beer. It's no comparison to the top-shelf whiskey in her glass, but she'll drink it. "Come with me," I tell Trista, grabbing her hand. I'll drag her if I have to. Over my shoulder, I tell Mason, "We're borrowing your basement."

"But the beds are upstairs," Noel shouts back, loudly enough to interrupt every other conversation taking place in the yard. "Unless there's something we don't know about the basement . . ."

Dalton wolf whistles. "'Just friends' my ass," he shouts after us. I glance at Tris to gauge her reaction, but her head is hung low.

"Ha ha," I call back, hoping to fix any damage they might've done. "Tris needs to hit something before she gets herself blackout drunk." *Though, Noel's suggestion would be good, too.* That's never gonna happen, though. At least, not with me.

The door opens from within as I reach for the handle and Ronni blinks up at me. "Is everything okay, Uncle Ryan?" she asks, looking uncertainly between Trista and me.

"Yeah, we're just going to borrow your dad's heavy bag. Hey, you don't happen to have gloves, do you?" Her hands can't be much smaller than Trista's.

She shakes her head. "I use Mom's."

"Use my what?" Fern calls from elsewhere in the kitchen.

Ronni steps aside and allows us to enter. Fern, Jamaica, and Austin are at the counter wrapping little smokies in bacon and skewering them with toothpicks. My stomach gives a hopeful little rumble. *Please let that be what I think it is.* Even if it isn't, anything Fern makes will be fantastic.

"I want to teach Trista the joy of beating the shit out of a heavy bag when you're pissed. Can she use your gloves?"

Fern grins because she knows exactly what I'm talking about. She shares my love for hitting things when she's angry. "Sure. Ronni, can you go? My hands are gross."

"Yep," the little girl answers, but her eyes are fixed on Trista's hand in mine until she turns around to lead the way.

I drop Tris's hand like it fucking bit me. She's following me. I don't need to force her. Don't need to drag her. Don't need to torment myself with her skin on mine.

We follow Ronni down the stairs and into Mason's home gym. It seems like a lifetime ago that he gave Chris and I carte blanche to plan it for him. Very little has changed since the day it was completed.

"Here ya go," Ronni says, handing Trista a pair of well-worn gloves from a shelf by the door.

"Thanks, Ronni," I tell her, edging by to get better access to the shelf. I grab the scissors and a roll of tape. "I know my way around. You can go back up to the party."

She takes a step toward the door and hesitates. "Can I watch?" she asks, turning around to face me.

"I don't care," I tell her with a shrug while I cut a length of tape. I'm just going to teach Trista the basics, how to stand, how to pivot, not to tuck her thumb into her fist. Nothing exciting.

"Why are you doing this?" Trista asks me from where she lingers in the doorway.

So you don't end up like Selene. I grab a roll of gauze cut a couple lengths to wrap her hands with. "Because this is a much more constructive outlet for your anger than drinking it," I tell her, beckoning her into the room.

Another time, I will teach her how to do this for herself. Today, it just needs to be done before she decides to walk away. "Hold out your hand. Keep it flat, and your fingers spread."

"Why do you care?" she asks softly.

Ain't that the million-dollar question? No, it's really not. I care because she's my friend. Full stop. End of fucking story. She's my friend, and I don't want to see something bad happen to her because she makes reckless decisions when she's mad. A heavy bag isn't likely to land her in a coma. Or a coffin.

I look up from my work to find her eyes on mine. They pull me in like magnets. I'm petrified of what she might see looking back at her, but I cannot look away, and she doesn't. "Because punching your feelings out is better than drinking 'til you puke."

Tiny lines mar the smooth skin around her eyes. "Maybe I'd rather drink until I puke? I'm not strong enough for this, Ryan. This is *me* we're talking about. I'm weak. I'm pathetic. I dress like a wh—" Her eyes cut towards Ronni. "Never mind."

The world around me flashes red with anger at her mother for putting those thoughts in her head, but instead of hitting something, I want to kiss her until she stops spouting that nonsense. I can't do that, though. Instead, I put the scissors down on the shelf, freeing my hands to cradle her face.

"Now you listen to me. I will not force you to do this, but you *are* strong enough; you only need to believe in yourself. Until you learn to do that, I'm here to do it for you. You are not weak. You are not pathetic. And no one here is running to your mother for fashion advice." My hands slip down the smooth skin of her arms to her hands, and I curl them into fists before holding them up at her eye level. "Let it go, Trista. Take it all out on that damn punching bag. It can't feel it. You might be a little sore tomorrow, but it'll be a *lot* better than a hangover."

Her eyes squeeze shut. One tear leaks out and rolls down her cheek, fueling my anger, but she nods.

"Alright, let's get that other hand wrapped."

I help her glove up and walk her through the basics. She's tentative at first, like she's afraid she'll hurt the damn bag, but after a few solid punches and some encouragement from Ronni, she unleashes on it.

"That's it!" I cheer, clapping when she lands a particularly savage right hook. *I didn't teach her that one.* Her form was beautiful, though.

She doesn't last long, but I didn't expect her to. It only looks easy. After a couple minutes, her punches slow. Her breathing becomes labored, but I expected that. She's still building her endurance. It doesn't matter as long as it was enough for her.

Trista lands one last weak punch and turns to me, her whole body sagging to a such degree I step forward to catch her if she begins to fall. "Alright?" I ask.

Ronni scurries forward and presses cup of water into Trista's hands, helping her figure out how to grip it with the gloves on.

"Yeah," she pants. "That was . . . Amazing. Thank you. Thank you both," she adds with a shy smile for Ronni.

"Any time." I mean that more than she realizes. I'd rather meet her at the gym at two in the morning to let her work out her frustrations than visit her in the hospital. Or worse, attend her funeral. Just the thought of something happening to her is more than I can bear. "I mean that, you know," I whisper around the fucking softball suddenly wedged in my throat. "I'm always a phone call away."

Chapter 16

Trista

This was a horrible idea. The tiny bikini seemed like a great idea from the safety of my bedroom. The house is mercifully deserted, but the backyard is swarming with people. It wouldn't be so bad if it were just the girls and me. But there are a lot of other people out there.

You're joking, right? Ryan's reaction to my clothes when I got here proves that wrong. My whole body feels hot just thinking about the look on his face. *The way I used to feel with Tyler.* I felt like Mom was right, like I should be on a corner. It was so . . . embarrassing.

My hand shakes visibly when I reach for the handle on the back door. *I can do this.* It's just a swimming suit. It probably covers a lot more than Noel's. *No one will look at me.*

I open the door and creep out into the yard, telling myself that the sweat beading on my forehead and the small of my back is from the heat, not embarrassment.

"Who are you and what have you done with Trista?" Noel asks, shouting across the yard once again. Some people glance her way, but none of them pay me any mind.

I need a drink. No, I don't. Ryan was right—drinking my feelings is not a sustainable plan. I could use the confidence boost right now, though.

"Hush," Tara says, swatting Noel into silence. "I like it."

I shuffle across the patio to join them at the picnic table. At least there, I'm not as obvious. *Maybe I'll just hide here until everyone is busy eating.*

"Well duh, I picked it out," Noel says. I sit next to her, hoping she'll deflect attention, and she thumps me on the back. "I didn't think you'd ever wear it when I bullied you into buying it, though."

I have to clear my throat to get the words out. "Neither did I."

"It looks good on you, Tris. It's just . . . different," Tara assures me.

"You can say that again," Gabe mutters from her other side. She elbows him. "Ow! I didn't say it was a *bad* thing!"

"No one asked you," she growls at him. She smiles at me and asks, "So, did you and Ryan have a good time in the basement?"

Noel chuckles softly. "If Ryan is taking me to a basement, there'd better be a different sort of playroom."

"Hey!" Tara snaps, reaching across me to swat Noel on the shoulder. "You're married to my brother!"

Noel shrugs. "Just sayin'! I'm taken, not dead!"

I cringe when I catch on to what she's talking about. I know she's only joking, but Ryan isn't interested in me that way. We're just friends. "Can you two just . . . not? That's not even funny. He taught me how to hit the heavy bag."

"And?" Tara asks.

I flex my hand at my side, stretching out the little tendons that are still slightly protesting the abuse. I shouldn't have clenched my fist the *whole* time, but I was angry. "And . . . I liked it. I feel better."

"You're also not dancing on the bar drunk on whiskey," Noel points out.

There isn't much on the table to mess with, but I busy myself tidying so I don't have to look at them. Telling them is embarrassing enough without seeing the pity in their eyes. "Yeah, well . . . My mother told me I was dressed like a whore. I needed a drink, alright?"

Noel pops to her feet. "The fuck! She did *not* say that to you!" She turns around and searches the yard like Mom might magically appear for a beatdown.

"Yep. And she said I was only wearing those clothes to punish her."

Tara grabs my hand and squeezes. "I'm proud of you for standing your ground."

I bite my lip and search the table for something else to fidget with. "Well," I say, hesitant to disappoint them with the truth. Mom *almost* had me convinced, after all. "I was actually going to change, but then she like snapped or something and told me that she didn't want her baby girl to leave her house dressed like a whore. And I got mad."

"As you should," Noel huffs. She plops back onto the bench and mutters something low enough I can't catch what she's saying.

Tara squeezes my hand again. "Still, you didn't back down. There's nothing wrong with the clothes you had on before. There's nothing wrong with your bikini. Hell, I'd wear that if I weren't six months pregnant."

"It would still look good on you," Gabe assures her.

"Good answer," Tara tells him.

He winks at her. "But if it's on you, Princess, it'll look better on the floor."

"Ewww!" Noel and I cry together like a couple of kids listening to their parents flirt.

"If you don't like it, go away," Gabe says. He grabs Tara to kiss her, but she's laughing too hard. He throws his hands up in a gesture of defeat. "Fine. I know when I'm not welcome," he says, playing up a pout. He clambers off the bench and slouches for a few steps. Then, he straightens up and looks over his shoulder to smile and wink at his wife. He holds up his water. "I'm getting another. Need a refill?"

"Please," she calls.

"Still sober?" Noel asks, reading my mind.

Gabe's only been out of rehab for eight months. They've only been married again for four of those. I still worry that he'll slip again. Quitting his job seemed to do wonders for him overall, though. He's a much happier person now, and he insists that he doesn't want any of us to change for him. *If I can't trust myself around booze, I want to find out around people who care enough to stop me.*

"Yes," Tara says, tracking him across the yard with a pleased smile turning up the corners of her mouth. "He had a glass of champagne at Fern and Mason's wedding because he wanted to test himself, and he didn't finish it. He's perfectly in control now. No more drinking to cope."

I look away in case my disappointment in myself shows on my face. I used to wonder how Gabe got as bad as he did, but I get it now. I owe Ryan for stopping me today, and for helping me realize that my occasional drink to cope with a bad day was becoming a problem.

"Good," Noel says with a decisive nod. "I'd hate to have to knee him in the junk in front of all these people."

Tara blows a raspberry. "No, you wouldn't! Don't lie to me!"

Noel's gorgeous face splits into a smile. "Okay, you got me. I would totally knee him in the junk anytime he deserves it, regardless of where we happen to be."

"I appreciate the sentiment, but I don't think that'll be necessary," Tara says through a little grin. "Oh!" she gasps, pressing a hand to her abdomen. "Either she doesn't like the idea of Auntie Noel hurting Daddy, or she's practicing to help."

"Clearly the latter, because she's brilliant already," Noel says, her head held high.

"Can I feel?" I ask shyly. I don't want to be one of those crazy people who paws at Tara's belly constantly, but Mom's little stab about babies a few weeks ago haunts me. What *would* it feel like to be the one being kicked? Feeling it second-hand is probably the closest I'll ever get. I can't decide if I'm alright with that or not. It's something I always expected, but because Mom expected it for me, not because it was a decision I made. I'm not sure I care either way . . .

Tara grabs my wrist and places my hand on her belly. "Of course! Noel?"

She shakes her head hard, making her hair fly. "Nope. I'm good. It might be contagious. Be sure to wash your hands when you're done, Trista."

"Did no one ever tell you where babies come from?" Ryan asks, startling a little jump out of me. I was too distracted by Tara and the baby to notice him approach.

I look up and straight into his eyes, which flare wide for a fraction of a second, and my belly does a little flip. It happened so fast, I'm not sure I didn't imagine it. He takes a small step back, then another. "How are you feeling?" he asks me.

"Fine?" It comes out as a question because he's acting like someone should be asking that of *him*. I'm happy for the distraction, though, because I'm not the only one who changed. His swim shorts sit low on his hips, and he must've forgotten his shirt because all his hard work is on full display from those stupid little V thingies to his broad shoulders. Of course, he's not the only one. There are ridiculously cut men all over Mason's backyard. But I don't feel like someone dropped me on the surface of the sun when I look at them. "My hand is a little stiff, but that's probably my own fault."

He smiles. "Between that and today's workout, you're going to hurt like hell tomorrow."

I give him an annoyed look I've practiced behind Mom's back most of my life. "Gee, thanks."

His smile brightens, and he inches forward a bit. "You're welcome." He turns his attention to Tara. "Did I miss all the kicks, T?"

"Nope," she says, holding her hand out for his. She places it on her belly so close to mine our hands brush, and I'm hyper-aware of every inch of my skin touching his.

He crouches in front of her and smiles at her belly like it's the most wonderful thing in the world. "I still can't believe you're not going to find out what you're having," he murmurs to her.

"Oh, trust me, Gabe wants to. It's killing him. But I like it this way. We can't pick a name until we meet our baby, so there's nothing to argue about."

I don't think I could do that. Even if I did decide to wait, I'd still have lists of names prepared. But I'm glad they're not arguing. They don't need that.

"It's a boy," Gabe insists, finally reappearing with Tara's water. "Sorry, got to talking to Fern about the vineyard."

Noel gasps. "She's not selling it, is she?"

I can see how Noel would jump to that conclusion since Gabe is a realtor, but the vineyard is thousands of miles from here. Surely, if Fern were going to sell it, she'd hire someone closer to it. But what do I know?

Gabe chuckles. "No, though she's had some interested parties approach her about it. I was just curious how it's working out. And if she has a friends and family rate."

"No way!" Tara cries.

He shrugs. "You said you wanted a getaway, just you and me, before the baby comes."

"Not gonna lie, I kinda hate you right now," Noel grumbles, but she ruins it by smiling at Tara. This is a *huge* change from the old Gabe. "Okay, I don't. But I'd *love* to go."

"I'm sure that can be arranged," Gabe tells her. "Fern said her suite is private and we're welcome to use it. She'd probably let you and Colton too."

"Or, since our friends own the damn place, maybe we can all go and support their business sometime?" Ryan suggests.

"I like that idea." It sounds like a lot of fun. It would also be an obvious show of support. And I owe her that after being so jealous.

Supporting Ryan and Chris is as easy as paying for a membership—something I now have even though I didn't need it for the class. Obviously, if any of us are in the market for property, we'll call Gabe. If we need clothes for special occasions, Tara and Madi are our first stop. It's harder to support Mason and Austin, other than binge shopping online since they own a shipping company. Yeah, we can buy the wine that comes from her vineyard, but this would be better.

Gabe squirms in his seat until Ryan rolls his eyes and says, "I'm not saying you shouldn't take her up on the offer of a free room. I'm just saying we could all go sometime. Make a trip of it. Take the whole place over."

Gabe taps his chin. "That's a good idea," he murmurs. "I'll talk to them next week and get a list of dates. A week, you think?"

Ryan grunts his assent. "Chris and I can swing it with the gym with enough warning."

My heart begins to race. A whole week without having to go home and face the Wrath of Mom? To not have my every decision scrutinized to ensure it meets her exacting standards. Our . . . argument before I left was a huge setback. *Rome wasn't built in a day.* Be that as it may, I can't keep living like this.

Gabe took himself out of the situation that stressed him out. Maybe it's time I do the same? I just have to stop being afraid of failing at life.

"Where's Chris?" Gabe asks Ryan, jerking me out of my daydream of a life where I can wear what I want without being raked over the coals.

"Couldn't find a sitter for Keat," Ryan tells him.

"So?" I ask without really meaning to. The question just sort of hit my brain and rolled on out. Ronni is here, after all. There's no reason Keaton can't come.

Ryan lifts his beer bottle in a salute. "That's what I said."

"Where's my phone?" Tara asks, patting her pockets. "I'm calling his ass. We don't care if he brings Keaton."

"I told him that," Ryan says softly. "He said that he hates feeling like he's foisting his kid off on other people who are there to have a good time just so he can."

Tara growls wordlessly. "That's ridiculous! *Mason* was a single dad. If anyone here can relate, it's him. He's not going to care if they come. Fern won't, either. Absolutely no one here will mind." She finds her phone and taps at the screen, then puts it to her ear.

"Good luck." Ryan raises his bottle to his lips. He takes a long pull of his beer while watching her wait for Chris to pick up his phone. "He seems to be more sensitive about the whole situation with Keaton since he kicked Becca to the curb," he says, naming Chris's recent ex. They were together in May, at Mason's wedding, but I never heard what happened between them. She just sort of disappeared.

"Wait, what happened with Becca?" I ask.

Ryan cocks an eyebrow at me and says, "Becca contacted Keaton's mother behind Chris's back and tried to get her to sue for custody. She didn't want the packaged deal thing Chris has going on."

That's terrible! How dare she! If she were here right now, I'd . . . What *would* I do, punch her? I'm me. Fern can get by with that, not me. *Then I'll tell Fern to punch her.*

"Yeah," he says, nodding at me.

My face must tell him exactly how horrible I find the whole situation because I know I didn't say any of that out loud. He finishes his beer and drifts away to toss the bottle in the recycling bin. My eyes follow him there, then across the yard to the pool. *The pool . . .*

"Excuse me for a minute," I whisper since Tara is still technically on the phone, even though Chris isn't answering. I have a promise to keep.

I kick off my flip-flops and creep across the yard. Ryan is standing next to the deep end of the pool with his back to me, talking to some of my MaxPower teammates who are enjoying the water. One of them glances my way, and his lips twitch like he's fighting a smile. I raise one finger to my lips, asking him not to warn Ryan. The team might not have heard my threat, but they did catch the rest of the conversation. They know what's going on. The man—Bryce—says nothing. His eyes dart from me to Ryan, and he doesn't look my way again.

To pull this off, I'm going to need a running start. I stop some distance away and steel myself. This is so unlike me . . . But it's *fun!* And it's *Ryan.* I just have to. I can't explain it. There's no way I'm backing out, though. I'll never get a better opportunity.

Decision made, I break into an all-out sprint. *I'm going to do it! I'm actually going to pull this off!* I'm so giddy I can scarcely breathe.

I stick my hands out in front of me, ready to give him a shove as soon as I make contact with his back. Eyes locked on my target, I barrel forward full steam ahead. A split second before collision, Ryan whirls around. We collide, and he wraps one arm around me. Instead of standing safely next to the pool, watching him fall in, I'm falling with him.

"No!" I shriek.

Ryan laughs. His body breaks the water, sheltering me from the sting of impact I know too well from childhood summers spent being picked on by bigger kids— not older, just bigger. I suck in a breath and squeeze my eyes shut before he drags me under with him.

I expect him to let me go and let me find my own way to the surface, but that's not Ryan. He's a protector until the bitter end, even when I brought this upon myself. He holds me tight to his chest and does all of the work, dragging me to the surface along with him.

"How did you know?" I ask as soon as my head breaks the surface. Even treading water, he holds onto me, helping me keep my head above water, though it can't be easy for him. It's a good thing too because my brain is struggling to function properly for some reason. He's so warm! And his arm around me . . .

Ryan laughs, letting his head fall back like that's the funniest question he's ever heard. "I didn't really. I thought I was being paranoid."

"Damnit!" I thought I was really going to get him. I should've paid more attention. "So you basically let me do that?"

His head bobs from side to side. "By the time I turned, it was too late to stop you without hurting you. I'd rather let you take me down than hurt you. Besides," he adds with a careless shrug, "it's not like you were out to hurt me. You clearly stated your intentions today. It's on me for putting myself in a position to allow you the opportunity."

"Well, thanks for sucking all the fun out of it for me!"

His smile, which hasn't faded since he turned and saw me, somehow gets a little brighter. *Why does that make me happy?* "I'm proud of you."

Somehow, that statement hits differently from when Tara said it earlier. The only thing keeping my head above water is Ryan's arm around me, because I just stop. "For what?"

He cocks his head to the side. "A year ago, you wouldn't have dreamt of tackling me into the water. Not just me, *anyone.*"

"No," I agree. He's right. A year ago, I would've sat meekly on the sidelines, or maybe hung out in the shallows, watching the fun happen around me.

Someone clears their throat obnoxiously loud. Dalton is standing in the shallow end of the pool, smirking at us like he knows something we don't know. I can *hear* that smirk, and it's saying *uh-huh, just friends.*

I roll my eyes, but Ryan's arm vanishes like it just fell off and sank to the bottom of the pool. I can tread water, but I've never been great at it. *Maybe he's worried about embarrassing me.* Dalton is a little over the top with his teasing sometimes, but he doesn't know us collectively. He's never seen the silly shit this group will get up to, like when Fern threw Ryan over her shoulder at her and Mason's joint bachelor party.

Not only that, I've seen the girls Ryan goes home with. I'm so far from their league I might as well be on a different planet. Whatever Dalton thinks he sees, he's wrong.

Chapter 17
Ryan

You're slipping. If others are noticing that I have any sort of softness toward Trista, I definitely need to get my shit together. But should I talk to Dalton? Tell him he's reading it all wrong? And that he needs to back off or he'll make her uncomfortable? Or will that only make things worse?

"Are you always this crazy?" Trista asks Dalton, sputtering between every other word to clear the water from her mouth. She's keeping her head above water without my help, but only just.

Motherfucker. If Dalton had just kept his mouth shut . . . No, fuck that. I can't watch her struggle like that. I hold my arm out, Dalton be damned, offering to help her again if she wants it. She swims a little closer and sighs in relief when keeping her head above water becomes less of a chore for her. Instead of going for the ladder, I make for the shallow end. She can decide if she wants to get out or not.

"It's only crazy until you realize I'm right," he calls back in a singsong voice. "Kinda like conspiracy theories."

I let her go, and she wades toward dry land. "Or, it's just plain crazy either way you look at it," she says as she goes.

I follow her, watching him over her head. "What's it to you anyway, Dalton?" Maybe directly calling him out will get him to stop. "You hoping to make a move?"

Dalton eyes her up and down, causing my temper to flare, and bobs his head side to side. "She's cute, but nah." He winks at her. "No offense."

Trista snorts as she grabs a towel off the nearest stack Fern scattered around the pool. "None taken." He walks away, ginning, and she mumbles, "Don't want someone who calls me cute anyway. I'm not eight."

My laugh is loud enough it startles her. Her cheeks flame. "You weren't supposed to hear that," she mutters, throwing a towel at me. She walks away, making for a lounge chair in a patch of sunshine.

That sass surprises me too. I don't know if I have alcohol to thank or if this is another example of her finding herself. Either way, I count it a good thing. "Did you get Noel's drink after all?" I ask, stretching out in the chair next to hers to soak up some sun.

She scowls at me. "No. Why?"

I wave in her general direction. "You're you."

Her eyebrows draw together. "I'm sorry, you were expecting the Queen of England?"

I can only blink at her, completely caught off guard by her reply. *Is she* sassier *than normal?* "No, I mean . . . Never mind."

She moves to cross her arms over her chest but seems to think better of it because she stops and lets them rest on the arms of the chair again. "No. Explain . . . Please."

"You're *you* when you drink," I explain, hoping I can find a way to make her understand. "When you're completely sober, you're . . . different."

Every trace of personality bleeds out of her face, leaving it as blank as a mannequin's. "I'm who Mom wants me to be."

"Yeah," I whisper. That's probably the best way to describe it, and it breaks my heart. But all I can do is help her find the confidence she needs to break free of the fear that shackles her.

I can't tell if a tear rolls down her cheek, or if it's pool water dripping from her hair, but I squash the urge to reach out and brush it away. "That's not me. I don't know who that is, but it's not me."

You don't know who you *are.* She knows exactly who the other person is; it's who she really is that is foreign to her. And that's dangerous. Most people have their entire childhood to learn who they are, what they like, what they dislike, every little thing that makes them a person. *Even if their parents don't like it.*

Trista didn't get that. Her mom was worse than mine. I was at least given freedom to make choices—even if I always made the "wrong" ones. She was told what she likes and doesn't like. She's lived in that box all this time, but she's starting to realize that it's too small for her to live in happily. If she figures things out bit by bit, she'll be okay. It's if she jumps out of that box and dives into life with the plan to try everything all at once it might destroy her. *Like it did Selene.*

"Hey, you're Trista." I stretch my leg across the space between our chairs and nudge hers with my foot. "You're my friend. You dance on the bar when you drink too much. You have one helluva right hook. You were terrified when you walked into my gym Monday, but you absolutely fucking killed that workout and every other one this week."

I pause to rack my brain for more positive things that I know to be facts, not things I think might be the truth because I don't want to be another voice in her head telling her who to be. She smiles at me before I come up with something else. "Thanks, Ryan. I don't deserve a friend like you."

I freeze. It's eerily similar to the last thing Selene ever said to me before she overdosed. *Why are you so good to me? I don't deserve it. I'm a terrible person. I never should've left home.*

"Why do you say that?" I barely manage to whisper.

She ducks her head like the answer embarrasses her or something. "You're always doing stuff for me, but you get nothing in return."

"Real friends don't expect anything in return." The words roll off my tongue before I fully think them through, but I wouldn't take them back for all the money in the world. I don't *think* Tara and Noel are using her, but I can't swear it. She's too easy to manipulate. They could do it without meaning to, but it's not like she has anything they couldn't buy themselves.

Tris rolls her eyes. "I know that. But . . . it feels unequal. Friendship *is* a give and take in a way. When I need something, my friends are there to help. When my friends need something, they can call me. But what do I ever do for you? What *could* I ever do for you?"

I have a few ideas . . . I mentally slap myself to keep my mind from taking a hard left down the gutter. "I'm a simple guy, Tris. There's not a lot I need. You wanna pay me back? Be happy. That's all I need, for my friends to be happy people."

Her smile fades. "I'm trying."

I know you are. I wish I could hug her, but it would only set Dalton off again. "That all any of us can do. But remember, you don't have to do it alone."

She ducks her head. "Um, this probably sounds a little crazy, but can I give you a hug?"

Yes, please. "Only if you don't mind if Dalton starts squawking about 'just friends' again."

She blows a raspberry, but rolls off her chair to stand. "What does he know?"

Too much, apparently. I stand up and lean down so she can thread her arms around my neck. The anger that's always raging in the back of my mind like a fire waiting to break loose and consume the world recedes into embers, dormant until something fans them to a flame again. I could stand here forever and bask in the simple peace of hugging her. *If only* . . .

Too soon, she lets go, murmuring about needing a water before she slips away. It's good that she let go when she did, though. Not even the shittiest memories could distract me from all that skin pressed against me. That little bikini she's wearing should be illegal. I dive into the deep end of the pool to hide until my brain decides it needs my blood back from my dick and it's safe to get out.

There aren't many people in the pool, so I swim laps in hopes of encouraging the redistribution of blood. I force myself to think of anything but that little bikini, but I don't like the direction my thoughts take. They don't stray far from Trista.

I didn't figure out her problem soon enough. I thought she was one of those people who can't get over their shyness without liquid courage. The first time I saw her drunk, she danced on a bar and did a fucking trust fall off of it. I thought she was a free spirit, if only when she was drunk, and I admired that about her.

I hoped that someday, she would find the confidence to embrace that side of herself fully so she could be free all of the time. The world needs more of her light. *Knowing the truth from the start wouldn't have changed anything.* Maybe I would've protected myself a little better, made sure I didn't develop anything close to feelings for another ticking time bomb. But I'd still be right here, ready to save her from herself if she needed me. I wouldn't care any less.

Because Selene was wrong. She was worth the effort, and so is Trista.

***

"Hey, Ryan?" Austin asks on his way back to the hot tub. The yard is quiet now. The guests from the gym have gone home. Chris finally turned up. Ronni and Keaton are asleep on the couch. The sun has set. It's just the usual suspects hanging out in Mason's yard, so Austin doesn't have to shout. But he does. "You got a text from Amanda. She asks 'your place or mine?'"

Motherfucking shit-stirrer. That's what little brothers do, though. Mason's just happens to make it an art.

"Thanks," I growl, uncomfortably conscious of the eyes on me. It wasn't so bad before, when Gabe was the only one in a relationship that wasn't going down like the Hindenburg. *Or so we thought.* Now, Chris and I are the odd ones out, and there are a lot more women hanging around.

Don't shit yourself; you only care what one of them thinks. I'm careful to keep my eyes away from that one face because I don't need to see her judging eyes.

"Here ya go!" He holds out my phone. "I'd hate for you to miss your booty call."

"This was more fun when I could give you shit too," I tell him, waking up my phone. But he's committed now. No more random hookups to tease him about. Sure enough, I've missed a call and two texts from Amanda, the sexy massage therapist who has a thing for being tied up.

As fun as she is, I'm not interested. I'd rather stay here and shoot the shit. Drink a few beers. Go home alone . . . *Said no one ever.* But it's the truth.

I send a one-word reply because it's all that's expected of me. "Well, this has been fun, but I've got a hot date."

"Doesn't a date imply at least dinner first?" Austin asks just to goad me.

"Oh, I'll be eating," I tell him as I climb out of the hot tub, lying my ass off so he doesn't have something else to tease me about. The only thing long and hard where I'm going will be the conversation Amanda and I have. She's gotten too clingy, and she's not taking the hint, so it's time to spell that shit out for her. "So will she. Thanks for dinner, Fern. Mason. Night."

I dry off as best I can in wet shorts and wrap the towel around my waist while my friends call their goodnights after me. It's hard, but I make it to the house without looking back at the little dark-haired woman I'd rather be running off to mess around with. But she will never be an option.

Trista

Something ugly ties my insides into knots as Ryan walks to the house. I struggle to keep my face blank and my hands at my sides instead of fidgeting with the tab on my soda can. It didn't take a genius to figure out what he's leaving for, but it's no business of mine.

I've never cared before and I shouldn't now. We're only friends.

Chapter 18

Trista

The house is dark when I pull into my spot in the driveway. *Thank goodness.* My next breath isn't a struggle against the bands of anxiety wrapped around my chest. I just *knew* Mom would be awake, waiting to lecture me for the way I left. *I should've taken Fern up on her offer of a guestroom.*

There's a chance Mom will have realized that she overreacted. Again. But I'm not banking on that. It's best to accept that the coming lecture is inevitable. I may as well get it out of the way first thing in the morning.

I take care not to close my car door too forcefully. It's already past midnight. Mom will be that much more upset if I wake her now. I slip off my flip-flops so there's no chance the silly things will make too much noise and tiptoe up the walk. Gabe taught me how to oil hinges *years* ago, so the door opens and closes silently. I lean against it and thank my lucky stars.

Now, if I can wash my face and brush my teeth without waking her.

"So—"

I start so violently my feet leave the ground and scream like a little girl with a June Bug in her hair.

"You finally decided to grace me with your presence."

Clutching my heart to make sure it doesn't actually beat its way out of my chest, I slide down the door and land roughly on my ass. *That's settled, then. Ass chewing it is.*

"Mom! I—"

"I should call the cops and have you arrested for driving under the influence!" she shouts over me.

"But I'm not—"

"Don't *lie* to me, Trista! I know you think you have me fooled, but I'm not stupid. Every time, *every time*, you go out with *those* people, you come home drunk!"

And you tell me not to lie. There are plenty of times I go out with the others that I don't drink. Or, don't drink that much. It just seems to happen more often than not lately. "Fine! Call the cops! Tell them to come and do a breathalyzer. I don't care. I'm. Not. Drunk. Not even a little bit."

I didn't have a drop of alcohol all night. Ryan was right; the heavy bag did help. I only wish I could've beat on it longer.

"Watch your tone with me, young lady!"

I scramble to my feet because sitting on the floor while she yells at me makes my stomach ache. "Mom! I'm twenty-seven! I'm not a child anymore."

Her chair legs protest loudly, and she shoves to her feet. "But I'm your mother, and you will not talk to me that way!"

"But it's okay for you to treat me like I'm ten?"

"Yes, it is! You're my daughter! And it's increasingly clear that you *are* still a child!"

"What's that supposed to mean!"

She holds up a fist and raises a finger for each charge she lays at my feet. "Lying. Drinking. Sneaking around! I tried to give you room to come clean about sneaking around to have sex with *that man* a few weeks ago, but you left that out when you were confessing all the other irresponsible things you did. I hope you're still taking your birth control!"

What is she talking *about?* There was nothing to tell!

"You want me to treat you like an adult; you should act like one! You could start with telling me the truth about where you were and what you were doing tonight."

"I am!" I shout back at her. "And if you weren't so fucking crazy, I wouldn't ever have to lie about anything!"

The silence fills my ears in a way the shouting didn't. *I can't do this.* I run to my room and slam the door before she can stop me or accuse me of more bullshit. With that barrier between us, I empty my bag and shove a change of clothes and my pajamas into it. I'm not staying here tonight.

All that progress I thought we were making was obviously a farce. I told her the truth, but she doesn't believe me. She hasn't believed anything I've said since she came to pick me up at that bus station.

"Trista?" Mom calls softly from the hallway.

Damnit. I need my toothbrush and my cleanser. I can't get them without facing her again. I should've grabbed them on my way by. Whatever. I can live one night without them.

I stare at the door. She's waiting on the other side for me; I just know it. When I open this door, she'll smile, maybe apologize, tell me how hard it is to watch children grow up and how she only wants to protect me from all the bad things in the world. And she'll promise to stop worrying so much.

I've fallen for it so many times it's laughable. *So why not this time?* Maybe a better question would be, why did it take me so long to stop?

Because she's my *mother*. She's supposed to be right.

But she isn't.

I can't go to a hotel. Mom will know as soon as the charge hits my card and come beat my door down. But Noel made it clear that she was going home to rock Colt's world. There's no way I'll call her right now. I don't want to call Tara and worry her. She'll fuss and that's not what I need. They'll *all* fuss or want to talk. So who do I call?

I pull my phone from my pocket and dial Ryan.

"Yeah?" he answers, breathlessly, after the fourth ring, and the awkwardness of him leaving Mason's for a booty call comes rushing back. *He's not alone.*

My cheeks flush boiling hot. "I'm sorry. I forgot!" I hiss into the mic.

I lower the phone, thumb reaching to end the call.

"Trista?" I barely hear him call my name before I press the button and back up until my legs collide with my bed so I can sit and regroup. *How could I forget?* Watching him leave tonight was . . . strange. For some reason, it was hard to sit still. I had to force myself not to squirm in my seat.

My phone screen lights up a split second before it vibrates and Ryan's name appears on the screen. I quickly tap the button to ignore the call. Just because I'm having a bad night doesn't mean he has to.

It rings again immediately.

He's not going to stop. I should just answer and tell him not to worry, to go back to bed. I'm a big girl. I'll be alright. I tap the green button and raise the phone to my ear.

"What's wrong?" he asks before I can say a word.

"I'm sorry I called," I whisper so Mom can't hear. "I forgot you . . . are entertaining. Don't worry about it. It's nothing."

"Trista, it's after one in the morning. You're sober, so I know it's not a drunk dial. What is it?"

"No—"

He cuts me off. "If you say 'nothing' again, I'm coming over there."

I sigh and give in to the inevitable because it's the only way to get him off the phone and back to his . . . friend. "Mom and I had a fight," I whisper.

"I'm sorry, Tris," he says softly.

"Don't worry about it."

I'm about hang up again when he asks, "Were you calling to talk?"

I shake my head before I remember he can't see it. "No. I . . .." I don't want to tell him because he'll feel obligated to help and I feel like a burden. He's Ryan. It's what he does. But he won't leave me alone unless I do, so I may as well get it over with and try to convince him that I've got somewhere else to go. "I was calling to ask if I could borrow your couch. Don't—"

"Always."

"Worry—what?"

"Come on over, Tris."

That ugly feeling in my chest urges me to say yes, but I ignore it. I've bothered him enough tonight. "I don't want to interr—"

"Do I need to come get you?"

"No! Ryan, look, just . . . go back to bed." *Why is it so hard to tell him that?* "I can—"

"You can get your ass in your car and drive over here. I'll be watching for you." The call ends before I can argue.

I am a horrible person. If I don't go, Ryan will come looking for me; I just know it. Maybe I can change his mind once I'm there? He can call her and tell her . . . What? I'm sorry I kicked you out for my trainwreck of a friend?

Yeah, that ship has sailed. I guess I may as well go so he didn't piss her off for nothing.

Mom is waiting in the hallway when I open the door. "Tris, I'm—"

"I don't want to hear it anymore," I tell her, ducking under her outstretched arm and into the bathroom. I slam the door in her face and lock it. I only need two seconds to grab my things, but that'll be easier without her in here crowding me.

I shove what I need in the bag and yank the door open again, startling her. That gives me the opening I need to get past her. She follows me, spewing more apologies, laying it on thick, and begging me to listen, but I've listened to her long enough.

At the door, she grabs my arm to stop me." Where are you going?"

"Away." I open the door and yank my arm out of her grasp, then run for my car before she can stop me again.

I pull into the same alley Ryan stopped in all those weeks ago and park because I'm not going to make it to his place in time. Hot, fat tears of anger and pain run down my cheeks and I heave huge, shuddering sobs that wrack my body. But each tear and each sob leaves me a little lighter until I'm crying happy tears because I. Fucking. Did it. I stood up to my mother. I hate that it had to happen, but I feel so much better.

Ryan

The car coming up the road slows. I didn't need that to tell me it's Trista, though. This neighborhood is usually quiet after ten o'clock, even on the weekends. I'm one of the few people on this street who doesn't subscribe to the old adage "nothing good happens after midnight." She slows down and parks in the street instead of taking a spot in my driveway, likely worried about blocking me in because she feels she's already a nuisance.

She's dead wrong about what I was doing when she called. Amanda left hours ago after calling me every name under the sun, throwing a remote at me, kicking my Barracuda, and screaming in pain loudly enough that the neighbor ran out to see what the hell was going on.

I wasn't in bed, balls deep in a redhead. I was in the garage, taking my frustrations out on a bag.

I wait for Trista on the porch. She doesn't want someone to make a thing of this, or she would've called Tara. It's best I let her come to me. She takes her time about it, but I'm not in a hurry. She lets herself in the gate, still wearing the cami and shorts she had on at Mason's, and crosses my yard one little step at a time, head hung lower than usual and her shoulders hunched—the picture of defeat. Odd, considering I count this a win.

Trista stops at the base of the stairs and peeks up at me, her eyes all red and puffy from tears. Her mouth opens, but nothing comes out. I doubt more words are what she really needs right now, not if her mom gave her an earful, so I open my arms. She inhales sharply and runs up the three stairs to throw herself at me.

I bite my lip to hold back a groan. I wish my body would get with the program and stop reacting like I'm a hormonal teenager again. The enthusiasm I lacked when Amanda texted me is no problem now. I angle my hips away from Trista so she doesn't notice, not that she'd say anything. Or think it's because of her. She'll think I'm still hard because she interrupted.

"Need to talk about it?" I whisper, smoothing her hair, which is still snarled from the pool.

She shakes her head. "I just want to sleep and forget about it."

"Sleep, yes," I tell her. I let her go and step aside. She doesn't need to forget; she needs to learn. "Forgetting about it won't help, though. C'mon. You can take my bed."

She shakes her head frantically. "No! I-I'll be alright on the couch."

I roll my eyes. "I changed the sheets." I could tell her the truth but letting her believe this lie serves her well. It's another barrier between us.

The darkness doesn't hide her blush. "No, it's not that. I just . . . don't want to put you out even more. I promise the couch is fine."

"Alright," I say, relenting though I don't think that's the whole story. It makes no difference to me where she sleeps, but there was *something* about watching her sleep in my bed a few weeks back. I was only being nice, trying to make her comfortable in an unfamiliar place since she's not drunk enough to pass out this time. I nod toward the bag hanging from her shoulder. "You got everything you need?"

"Um . . ." She ducks her head, looking down at the bag. "Mostly, but Mom tried to stop me from leaving, so I might've forgotten something."

Feminine hygiene products aside, I should have anything she might need, and I don't mind sharing. I gesture toward the door, waving her inside. "Make yourself at home. There are towels in the cabinet if you want to shower before bed."

"Thanks, Ry. I really am sorry."

"I'm not."

The tinkling of a little bell distracts her from whatever she opened her mouth to say. "What was that?"

More tinkling heralds the arrival of the little beast who owns my ass now instead of it being the other way around.

Chevy prances out of the hall, spots Trista, and breaks into a run. "You *kept* her?" Trista hits her knees and scoops the little ball of fluff into her arms, her face the picture of delight.

I shrug and rub at the back of my neck like I can rub off my embarrassment. "I promised you she'd have a good home."

The look she gives me hits me right in the chest. It's *almost* as good as the orgasm I passed up tonight.

Chapter 19

Ryan

"Ryan? Ryan!"

My name echoes through the absolute darkness surrounding me. Gotta hurry. I can still save Selene; I only have to find her.

"Ryan!"

She needs me. She has to be here somewhere.

"Wake up!"

Trista's voice cuts through my nightmare, pulling me back to consciousness. The familiar twin stabs of disappointment and loss pierce my heart again. "Tris?" I rasp. There's just enough light to make out her silhouette next to my bed. I probably scared the everloving shit out of her.

"I'm here," she whispers. One of her hands finds mine, and she squeezes tightly. "You were yelling. A lot."

Fuck. I hate that she witnessed that. "Sorry. I should've warned you. I have nightmares." I can never decide which is worse, the one where I'm searching for Selene in the darkness or the one where I relive finding her body. They both leave me wrung out and angry, though.

Trista squeezes my hand again, and it goes a long way toward alleviating that anger. "It's alright. D-d'you need to talk about it?"

"I *don't* talk about it," I snap, wincing immediately for my needless harshness. "Sorry. Sore subject."

"It's alright," she says again. Her thumb lightly skims the back of my hand, back and forth, trailing fire that slowly sinks into my skin and burns its way to my heart, chasing away the coldness of my dreams. "You didn't have nightmares last time I was here."

"No." I don't have an explanation for that. Usually, the only time I don't have nightmares is when I take the pills my doctor prescribes to knock me out cold. They work a little too well, though. I'll sleep twelve hours minimum and wake up practically hungover, so I rarely take them. But occasionally, I sleep deeply enough they don't happen. So maybe not having one when she was here before was a fluke.

Her hand slips out of mine. The loss of that contact hits me as hard as my nightmare did. "Tris?" She's moved away from the window, so there's no light to find her by. *Come back. I won't snap again. Please.*

"I'm here," she says from the other side of my bed.

I swallow hard. I've had dreams that start like this, too. They're not much happier than my nightmares of Selene because it'll only ever be a dream. "What are you doing?" I must be a glutton for punishment because my dick snaps to attention.

"Well, you didn't have nightmares last time I was here. So . . . maybe you won't if I . . . never mind. It didn't sound so stupid in my head."

What if she's right? Hell, I don't care if she's wrong. I'll take any excuse to have her curled up next to me again. *Glutton for punishment, indeed.* "Come on in," I tell her, patting the space next to me. "Just don't scream this time."

"I won't," she whispers. The bed barely dips under her weight. She moves just close enough that our hands brush and sighs tiredly. The bell on Chevy's collar tinkles, announcing her arrival. She probably left when I started yelling. I listen as she jumps as high as she can, catches her claws in my comforter, climbs the rest of the way up, and claims her spot on my pillow. She's shredding the fuck out of my bedding, but I enjoy waking up to the little fuzzball curled up next to my head. I didn't realize how lonely I was before she moved in.

The silence that settles between us isn't uncomfortable, but I don't like it. I have this overwhelming urge to fill it with words. To tell Trista things that I don't tell anyone else because, here, in my bed, wrapped in darkness and blankets, friendship and trust, it feels like I *can.*

"I lost a . . . someone to a drug overdose in college," I whisper slowly, carefully testing each word in my head before speaking it. It's been a long time since I broke down over losing Selene, but I don't know what talking about her will do to me.

There's no reason for me to hide that she was my girlfriend from Trista, but acknowledging what we were is hard. Probably because, like Trista, she was a friend first. After she died, our last fight made me realize that I *can't* be a good partner in a relationship. Friends, business partners, all that I can do. But I'm too selfish to be someone's someone.

Trista wiggles a little closer and covers my hand with hers. "I'm so sorry."

I can't resist the comfort of her touch right now. I'm not strong enough. I turn my hand over and lace our fingers together, clinging to her like she's my last tether to life. "Please, don't tell anyone. I meant it when I said I don't talk about it. Chris knows, but I never told the others."

They didn't even know I was seeing someone. It wasn't like high school where we saw each other every day. Yeah, we stayed close and hung out a lot, but we had our own lives. Chris only knew because Selene would text me while we were working. I was waiting for her to settle some before I introduced her to them; otherwise, they all would've worried about me.

"I won't tell anyone," she promises, and I don't doubt her at all. Trista can probably keep a secret better than anyone I've ever met.

Now that I've started, the words won't stop. "Her name was Selene. You remind me of her a bit."

"Oh?"

I wince. I didn't really mean to tell her that part. She'll probably think it's weird because the two of them have very little in common. It's too late to take it back, though, so I want her to understand. "Yeah. She was very sheltered before college too. Only, when she got her first taste of freedom, she went apeshit. Parties, dancing, drinking, drugs, you name it, she tried it. I thought I was helping her by letting her experience life, but I was just an enabler. I didn't want to accept how bad things were getting. I just . . . ignored it and hoped it would go away. Told myself it was just a phase; she'd get tired of it. But she didn't. She overdosed and . . ." A lump in my throat strangles the rest of that sentence.

Into the silence that has stretched on too long, Trista whispers, "You found her, didn't you?"

I force my eyes open wide, staring at the ceiling in the dark. If I close them, even to blink, I'll see her again. "Yeah," I breathe, hating myself for how weak I sound. "I had a key to her apartment. I let myself in and found her on the bathroom floor." It's weird to say it so matter-of-factly, like it didn't nearly break me at the time. I knew she was gone as soon as I found her, but my heart refused to accept it. I can still hear the blood pounding in my ears, drowning out my voice as I screamed for help until the neighbors came.

"You can't blame yourself for that, Ryan."

The fire of my anger flares hot. She wasn't there! She doesn't know! "The hell I can't. There were so many things I could've done differently. I could've got her help like we did for Gabe. I could've kept her away from the wrong kind of people. I could've told Chris I couldn't do lunch that day and got there sooner."

That one kills me. If I'd gone straight there that day, would she be here now? Would a few minutes have been enough to save her, or was she gone before I even got out of class that day? I never found out an official time of death. I didn't need another reason to be angry with myself and knowing I maybe could've saved her would give me one.

Trista rolls onto her side and hugs our joined hands to her chest instead of shoving me away and telling me off for snapping at her like she should. *I am such a dick.* I open my mouth to apologize, but she doesn't let me. "Ryan, I hear that.

All of it. And I'm not going to tell you that you're wrong. But she made her own decisions. You didn't buy the stuff for her and force her to use it, did you?"

I squeeze her hand, grateful beyond words that she's not upset with me for lashing out. I don't know if I could handle it right now if she pulled away from me. What she's saying is nothing I haven't heard before, though. Chris tried the same logic. It didn't help.

". . . No. I took her to the party where she tried pot for the first time, though." The question I've asked myself millions of times runs through my head yet again. *Was that decision the one that lead to her death?*

"You didn't hold her down and force her to smoke it, Ryan."

I can't argue with that. I didn't, and I didn't encourage her to try it. It was all her. That doesn't make it better, though. "No . . . I tried to convince her she didn't want to try. But not hard enough."

"You couldn't stop her. She would've found a way if that's what she wanted to do, with or without you."

If only I could believe that. But I can't because I'll never know for sure. "Yeah, the thing is, logically, I know that. But my heart says otherwise. If I'd loved her more or something, maybe—"

Trista moves closer and presses her lips to my cheek, her aim perfect in the dark. She might not mean it the way I'd like her to, but it still goes straight to my heart, easing some of the pain and the anger. "You loved her enough. *She* didn't love herself enough."

That doesn't even make sense. She wasn't suicidal. She didn't *want* to die. "What do you mean?"

"Well," she says slowly, "there's a difference between loving yourself—I think—and loving who you are. If there's something about either of them you don't love, the rest suffers while you try to fix it. It sounds like there were things Selene didn't like about who she was, and she neglected herself trying to fix that."

That . . . actually makes a lot of sense. Selene didn't like feeling like a small-town bumpkin in the big city. She didn't like that her parents kept her on such a short leash her whole life. Instead of approaching the freedom of adulthood logically and carefully exploring what that freedom meant, she abused herself to try to "fit in."

I still should've stopped her.

But with Trista's explanation rattling around my skull, it's harder carry all of the blame. "You're pretty smart, ya know?"

She squirms beside me, but doesn't acknowledge what I said. "You said I remind you of her . . . Is that why you're so . . ."

"Yes." I don't need her to finish that sentence, though the word she's probably looking for is overbearing. I hold my breath and brace myself for the tirade I probably deserve.

"Ryan, I'm not going to do drugs if that's what you're worried about," she whispers, squeezing my hand again.

I roll to face her, studying her profile in what little light is coming in through the window. She's close enough to kiss, but just thinking about it tears me up after revisiting what happened with Selene. "I worry about everything," I tell her, reaching to brush back a lock of hair that's resting on her cheek.

My feelings for Trista aren't because of the similarities I see between her and Selene. That has nothing to do with it, but it's one more good reason for me to keep my distance for both our sakes. "I don't want to lose someone else. I know you're not the same person. I know you're not going to make the mistakes she did. I just worry that your mistakes might have a similar outcome." *Even if this is as close as I ever come to being with you, it's better than losing you.*

"But you don't stop me from living my life."

I shake my head. It's her life to live, but I don't enable her, either. At least not in any negative aspect. *I hope.* "No, but I'll always be here for you if you get in over your head."

"Why can't Mom love me like you do?" She gasps. "Sorry, I didn't mean . . . That wasn't . . . I'm not implying—"

That one little word makes my heart pound, but I take a deep breath and force myself to relax because there's no way she knows how close to right she is. "Tris," I cut her off, chuckling at her awkward attempts to make things less awkward. It's all on her end, though. "I get it." *What would she think if I tell her that the feelings I have for her aren't strictly friendly?* It doesn't matter. I can never tell her because I will never do anything about it. It wouldn't be fair to either of us for me to put her in that position.

That doesn't stop my imagination from running to a world where I could kiss her right now. Roll over and cover her body with mine. Strip her clothes off and sink myself inside her. *That's not creepy or anything, you asshole.* She's doing something nice for me, and here I am, fantasizing about fucking her senseless. Some friend I am.

"I just wish she could have my back like that instead of making me feel like she won't love me if I don't do what she wants."

This is where I should tell her that parents always love their children, no matter what. I can't do that, though. It's not always the truth. *It wasn't true for me.* I don't want to say that and later be proved wrong. She might hold it against me and never want to see me again. Maybe I'm being ridiculous, but it's a risk I'm not willing to take. "At some point, you're going to have to decide if it's more important for you to love all of yourself, or to have her conditional love."

"Yeah," she whispers. "It's just . . . Hard. I shouldn't have to choose."

Been there, done that. "I know."

Chapter 20

Trista

Sunshine wakes me up. It's my first reminder that I'm not at home in my bed, because the sun doesn't shine through my window in the morning. My other clue is the steady rise and fall of Ryan's chest—my pillow—in time with the *whoosh* of his breath, the slight rasp of the occasional snore. The top of my head is too warm. It can't be from him breathing on me, though. That warmth moves a bit, and a sustained rumbling reaches my ears. Chevy.

Ryan! Oh, my God. The poor guy. I didn't think I would ever get him to wake up. It was breaking my heart. I wanted so badly to hug him, but I was afraid of what might happen. For all I knew, he was dreaming of being chased by an axe murderer, and I might've ended up with broken bones for my troubles.

But the truth is almost worse. *How long has he carried this guilt?* He said in college . . . He was in his third year when I met him. Did it happen before then? Why doesn't he tell anyone? It's something he and Mason could bond over, as they both lost girlfriends in college . . . *What if that's* why *he doesn't tell anyone?* It could've happened around the same time Mason's girlfriend died in childbirth. I can see Ryan deciding that his friend needed all the support he could get at that time and keeping his troubles to himself.

The time to ask about it has passed. If he wanted me to know, he would've told me. I should respect his privacy.

I wiggle until the sunshine isn't on my eyes anymore and open them. Ryan was right the last time I was here; I *am* a cuddler. That's the only explanation since I'm plastered to his side again, my head on his chest, his arm around me, hand on my hip. It's kind of nice. Last time aside, I've never woken up with someone. *What would it be like to do this* every *morning?*

I just want to stay here a while. Especially since the alternative is going home and dealing with my mother. *On second thought, I'll just go back to sleep.* I could. Easily. I'm warm and comfy, and Ryan smells good.

Stop that. I can't think of him as a . . . man. *That sounds so stupid.* He *is* a man. A man who is my friend, which means such things will never happen. But that feeling when he looked at me yesterday . . . It wasn't embarrassment.

After Tyler ran off, I was embarrassed that I ever wanted to be with him. Between that and Mom constantly lecturing me for being so stupid, I associated what it really was—lust—with shame. I don't remember feeling this way for my exes, which is probably why I didn't recognize it for what it was. It's been a long time since I *wanted* someone. *I guess that should've been my first clue with Peter and Nick.* But Ryan understands me in a way those two never did. There's just something about being *seen*.

It's also been a long time since someone last put their hands on me, and my body is beginning to realize there's a gorgeous man close enough to help me out with that. It doesn't care about stupid things like friendship.

Bzzzt . . . Bzzzt . . . Bzzzt.

My phone vibrates on the nightstand behind me, causing Ryan to twitch and start. I quickly roll out of his arms, across the massive frozen tundra that the other side of his bed has become, and snatch up my phone as quickly as possible in hopes that he'll sleep on. He needs it after that nightmare.

I blindly send the call to voicemail, then notice the name on the screen. *Oh, crap.* It's Grant. And it's Sunday. I keep on rolling until my feet hit the floor and bolt from the room as fast as I can without being noisy. In the kitchen, I bring up his number and call him back, pacing back and forth, torn between wondering if he's calling to cancel and grateful he did before my stupid body did more than notice that Ryan has a dick.

"Hello?"

"Grant? It's Trista, sorry about that."

"Did I wake you?" he asks.

"Nope!"

"Is everything alright? You sound breathless."

Like Ryan did when I called last night. Fortunately, Grant can't see me blush through the phone. "Yep, I'm good. I stayed with a friend last night, and they're still passed out. I ran to another room so I didn't wake them when I called you back."

"Ah, I'm sorry. I wanted to make sure we're still on for brunch."

I glance back toward the hallway and Ryan's room, then mentally boot myself in the butt for it. I have no reason to want to crawl back into bed with Ryan. For all I know, Grant is my dream guy. I should be thrilled with this opportunity. "Absolutely!"

"Excellent. I'll see you soon then."

"Everything okay?" Ryan's voice is all deep and rumbly from sleep. Any other time, I could listen all day. *Stop that!* I'm not happy about hearing it now, though.

I look out the door to find him stalking down the hall, rubbing sleep from his eyes, and hope my face doesn't betray my guilt. "Who was that?" Grant asks in my ear, a note of suspicion creeping into his voice.

I wince. This isn't going to be good, but I won't lie about it. If Grant can't handle me being friends with Ryan and the other guys, it's better to know beforehand. "My friend . . . Ryan."

"You stayed with a guy last night?" *Definitely not happy.* His hurt is almost tangible, and he's not even in the room.

I have nothing to feel guilty about, but I really hope he'll let me explain before he runs off and tells his mom, who will tell my mom, which will only make an already crappy situation worse. "It's not what you think," I tell him quickly.

"What is it then?"

"Exactly what I said. He's my friend." Ryan stops in the doorway to the kitchen and leans against the frame, watching intently. Chevy prances into the room, sits primly next to her food dish, and looks expectantly at Ryan. As cute as that is, I can't find a smile. I don't want to have this talk in front of him. I'm not afraid of saying anything he won't like, but I am worried he might take my phone and yell at Grant for being a bonehead. "I'll explain at brunch, alright?"

Grant hesitates but finally agrees and says goodbye.

I suck in a deep breath and blow it out slowly, letting my cheeks puff out. "Your timing sucks," I tell Ryan.

He steps into the kitchen and leans against the counter across from where I came to a stop. "Who was that?"

"Grant Malcolm."

His pierced eyebrow lifts. "That name supposed to mean something to me?"

I shake my head. "Probably not. You asked, though."

"You're having brunch with him?" He pronounces brunch like it's a foreign— and possibly highly offensive—word.

"Yes." Although I'm anxious about it now. How am I going to explain to him that one of my best friends is a guy? Or make him believe that nothing happened, because I'm sure he'll ask. *Better question, why do I care if he does?*

Maybe I don't . . . I'll have to wait and see.

His head tips to the side a bit. "So, it's not a date then?"

"Beg pardon?" I bite my tongue to keep from laughing. It's really not funny, but I asked myself the same thing.

His upper lip curls into a sneer. "I dunno, it just doesn't scream date to me."

Since when are you the leading expert on dates? To my knowledge, he's never had one. I don't pretend to know everything about him, though. I mean, obviously, he has before; he had a girlfriend. Maybe he's really private about his private life. "Well, since we're meeting for the first time, I think brunch and a not-date are probably appropriate."

All trace of expression vanishes from his face. "You've never met this asshole?"

That's not very nice. "How do you know he's an asshole?" It's a very unfair assessment. Grant sounds perfectly nice.

"He got defensive when he found out you crashed on my couch, and he invited you to *brunch*. He's not just an asshole; he's a pretentious asshole!"

"Or," I begin, holding up a finger to stop him from finishing that tirade if he wasn't done, "he recognizes that I was more likely to agree to brunch because I *don't* know him and it's not a date." I don't point out the obvious. I didn't pass the whole night on his couch, but it shouldn't matter because *nothing happened.*

Apparently, he can't find a flaw in that logic because he asks, "So how'd you find this asshole?"

I have to put effort into holding back a sigh. This won't go over well with him, either. "Our mothers."

Both eyebrows rocket upwards. "Your *mom* hooked you up with him? Hope you like sweater vests with those funky little triangles on them and weird hats."

A laugh works its way up from my belly. I slap my hand over my mouth to contain it, but it's no use. I don't, as a matter of fact, but I'm not the one wearing them, so . . .

Ryan crosses his arms over his chest. "What?"

"You just described my ex." My explanation is muffled because I'm still pretending I can hide my smile from him.

He smirks. "Your mom hooked you up with him too, right?"

"Yeah."

Shaking his head, he turns around and pushes a button on his coffee maker. "I need caffeine for this shit. How do you like your coffee?"

"I don't." The confession takes me by surprise. I didn't mean to say it. I've never told *anyone* that I don't like coffee. When it's offered, I doctor it up with as much cream and sugar as I can get by with and smile gratefully while I choke it down.

"Huh?" he grunts, turning to look at me again.

"I don't like coffee," I whisper the words because if I'm not careful, I might shout them. Speaking the truth to someone without fear is a heady experience.

Ryan scowls at me and, possibly for the first time ever, I don't so much as flinch. "Bullshit. I know I've seen you drink it."

"Doesn't mean I like it."

He leans against the counter again and eyes me skeptically. "Okay, we're going to ignore the whole how do you *not* like coffee thing for now and address what might be the more important issue. If you don't like coffee, why do you drink it?"

I shrug because I don't have a good answer. "Seemed like something I was supposed to do. Learn to drive. Drink coffee. Graduate high school. Go to college. You know . . ."

He mutters something under his breath—I think it might be French—and shakes his head. "So, you secretly hate coffee, but you drink it because you think you're supposed to?"

That basically sums up my life. Wow, I'm pathetic. But I'm working on it. "I guess? I mean, Mom put a cup in front of me one morning when I was tired from studying for a test and said, 'drink this.' So I drank it. And I guess she thought I liked it because every morning after that she put another cup of it in front of me."

Ryan's eyes close. He takes a deep breath and lets it out. I can almost hear him praying for patience. "Do you ever say no?"

"Yes?" Of course, I do. Most people just ignore it. He knows that, though.

"When? Near as I can tell, you go along with whatever someone wants for or from you without question. Did you ever consider telling that asshole you don't want to go out with him? Or telling your mom that? It seems like anyone with a fat bank account and a dick is eligible in her eyes."

By that logic, he's eligible too. Probably best not to point that out, though. I don't answer because he's right, more or less. I *did* entertain the idea of turning Grant down. Brunch seemed like such a little thing at the time, though, almost like an olive branch between Mom and me. And I don't regret agreeing to it, even if I'd rather stay here right now.

Ryan pushes off the counter and crosses the space between us in one step.

"What are you doing?" I don't shrink from him, but it takes conscious effort to hold my ground. He's so close. Close enough to kiss, but that's . . . That's not going to happen. *But I wouldn't be mad if it did.*

His voice drops an octave and picks up some gravel that grates on *all* of my nerves in a very good way. "Tell me no, Trista."

I swallow hard and hope he can't tell that my panties are drenched. *Deep breath, Trista. Don't react. Don't let him see that you don't want him to stop.* Whatever he's doing, it's not what it looks like. "Um, no?" I squeak, cringing at how small my voice sounds.

Quicker than I can follow, his hands are on my hips, and he has me backed up against the refrigerator, holding me there with his body while his hands move to my face. *Yes, please.* He leans in until our foreheads touch. It's unexpected and exciting, and I should be terrified, but I've never felt safer in my life. Or more turned on.

What if he *doesn't* stop? My mind runs away with me, filled with images of his lips on mine, and on my neck. His hands holding me tightly, pulling me closer.

"What if that asshole does this?" he growls, snapping me out of my daydream. "What are you going to do? Are you going to tell him no and make it stick, or are you going to let him get by with it because it's easier to say yes?"

"Uh," I squeak. It's impossible to think like this because my mind is yelling, 'what the fuck?' and my body is begging him to come closer. My eyes drink in the small details of his face—the long, thick lashes women would do crazy things for, the gold flecks softening the dark chocolate color of his eyes, the lines between his eyes because he frowns too much, and the lines around them etched by smiles.

His pupils dilate. As suddenly as he charged in, he backs off and lets me go. The fridge is the only thing that keeps me on my feet because the sudden absence of his hands, his *heat*, leaves me lightheaded. "If he puts his hands on you, you use him as a punching bag, you hear me?"

"Yeah," I whisper. *Could I really?* Yes, I think I could. *Unless he makes me feel like that . . .*

He turns around, but looks back and says, "And you're not going alone."

"No, Tara, Madi, and Noel are going separately." *Get it together, Trista. It's Ryan.* He was proving a point. There's no way a god of a man like him would want *me*.

Ryan nods. "Good. Since you don't like coffee, how about tea?"

I grab onto the subject change gladly. "Sure! You don't strike me as a tea drinker, though."

He smiles over his shoulder while opening a cabinet, revealing a collection of mugs. The one in front reads 'Asshole In Chief.' *Dalton.* "I'm not. Tara left it here when Gabe was helping me in the shop last month. I'll make tea. You go get dressed for your . . . What's the opposite of a hot date?"

I roll my eyes, but he's not looking at me anymore. "How do you know he's not hot?"

"How old is he?"

"Thirty-two."

Ryan nods like that explains it all. "That, plus he's single, plus your mom approves."

"That's it?" Really? He's basing this assumption on the fact that he's over thirty and single? And Mom's approval, of course . . . His logic is seriously flawed, because it could cut both ways here. One could argue that Ryan isn't hot because he's pushing thirty himself.

"Yep. Want me to Google him and prove it?"

No. Looks aren't everything. I don't need someone with a body like a Greek god to be happy. I just need someone who sees me. *Ryan does . . . but that's never going to happen.* "I'm going to go get dressed."

"You know I'm right," he calls after me.

Chapter 21

Trista

So Grant doesn't have biceps as big as my face, and I probably couldn't do laundry on his abs, but that's not what's important. I'm not exactly a ten myself, after all. He has a pleasant face and kind eyes. He's quick to laugh, his table manners aren't atrocious, and there's not an argyle sweater vest in sight. *Shove it, Ryan.*

"I must admit, I was concerned when you said your friend was a man," he says, finally bringing the conversation around to that awkward subject after the obligatory get-to-know-you questions that got us through the meal. "It felt like you were hiding something."

I firmly squash a flicker of guilt and fold my hands on top of the table to curb the urge to compulsively organize my silverware, glass, the salt and pepper shakers, my straw wrapper, and used napkins. The plates are long gone, at least. "Well, I knew how it would sound to anyone but the people who know us," I reply. "Ryan and I are just friends. He's very protective of his female friends."

Grant leans back in his seat, making himself comfortable in the booth. "If you have girlfriends you could stay with, why him?"

My face flushes, but I don't try to hide it. I did nothing wrong to be embarrassed about it, but I know how it looks. Actually, I'm happy I was there. I was able to do something for Ryan. "Usually, I would call one of the girls. Last night was a . . . special circumstance." Grant's mouth presses into a hard line. Too late, I realize how that might sound. "I'm the only single girl in our group right now," I try to explain. "And the others were uh . . . busy last night, if you get my meaning."

His eyes widen, and he laughs loudly, and the tension between us evaporates. "Oh! I can see how that would create issues."

"Yeah," I tell him with a grin. I take a deep breath and relax fully for the first time since I sat down. "I didn't want to interrupt." *You interrupted Ryan.* "So I called Ryan." I probably shouldn't mention that he kicked his bedwarmer out for me. That'll come across wrong too. Ryan would've kicked her out for any of us. I think. I grab my glass and take a big gulp of orange juice to cover my uncertainty.

"So, the two of you aren't friends with benefits?" he asks, watching me closely.

I nearly spit my orange juice. "No! Not at—" To his left, the door opens, and Ryan stalks in. My head and my heart go to war; one happy to see him, the other wondering what the *fuck* he's doing here. *Did he not trust me to handle myself?*

Grant follows my errant gaze and turns around in the booth. He quickly turns around again and rolls his eyes. "Yeah, he looks good, but he's probably a giant asshole," he says, obviously assuming I'm distracted by the muscles. And they *are* very distracting. But that has nothing to do with it.

Damnit. I should explain. Awkwardness aside, he's a nice guy. If this goes somewhere, I don't want him to think I'm shallow and thirsting after other guys all the time. "That's Ryan." From the corner of my eye, I watch as he pulls out a chair at the table across from us where Tara, Noel, and Madi are seated.

Grant's eyes go wide and he sits up straighter. "*That's* the guy you stayed with last night?"

"Yep," I say on a sigh. He looks over at my friends, not even trying to hide his interest. "And the girls are Tara, Noel and Madi. They came to make sure you weren't a serial killer or something."

I don't know if he hears that last part, because right as I say it, Ryan looks over. He locks eyes with Grant, grins, and winks. *I'm gonna* murder *him!*

Grant turns his attention back to me, dialing in on my face with laser focus, but I don't think he heard a word I said after my confirmation. "How many tattoos does he have?"

How should I know? I shrug again. "Dunno. I mean, I've probably heard him say before, but it's not like I've ever counted them." Is he a tattoo aficionado or something? Ryan gets stopped and asked about his art a lot when we're all out together, and it's on display, but no one has ever asked me about it. Why would he think . . . "Wait, are you testing me?"

Grant leans forward, propping his elbows on the table. "Yes. I don't buy it. Look, just tell me the truth. I don't care if you've had a bit of fun with him. It's not like I'm a saint. But before we discuss seeing each other again, I have a right to know if you can't give him up or if you're only here to get your mother off your back."

I guess he has a point, even if he is way off the mark. I shake my head. At this point, Mom isn't even a factor in my presence here. If I was only doing this to pacify her, I wouldn't see him again. "I'm here because I want to be. I've never slept with Ryan. I'm not going to beg you to believe me. You either do, or you don't."

Grant holds up both hands. "Alright, alright." He lets his hands fall to the table and cocks his head to one side. "You know, you're very different than I expected."

"How's that?" I ask, though I'm not sure I care. I'm tired of trying to live up to someone else's vision of who I should be.

His fingers drum on the tabletop. "Mom said that you're very demure. I expected someone quiet. Maybe a little eager to please. Compliant."

I roll my eyes. I've never met his mother, I don't think, but that sounds exactly like what Mom would tell someone about me. Because that's what she wanted me to be. "Sorry to disappoint you." *You met me too late.*

Watching me closely, he smiles slowly. There's something unhappy about it, though. "On the contrary. Demure is boring. You are anything but, and I'd really like to see you again. Friday maybe? Dinner?"

Hopefully, my smile doesn't look as forced as it feels or as unhappy as his. While this was a perfectly enjoyable brunch, Ryan aside, I can't imagine ever seeing him as anything other than a friend. *I'm not giving him a fair chance.* Everything could be different next time. I'll never know unless I try. "I'd like that. I get off work at five."

"Seven o'clock then?" He slides out of the booth and offers me a hand to help me up.

I take it, noting the absence of any sort of thrills or flutters or tingles when we touch, and allow him to pull me to my feet. "Sure."

"Need some time to decide on a place?"

"Yes, please. I'll text you?"

"That would be great." *How do you tell someone goodbye after a sort-of date? A handshake?*

Grant solves that dilemma for me by opening his arms for a hug. I step into his embrace, but my heart sinks. It's not that I'm not giving him a fair chance; I am not attracted to him at all. *"It's not hard, Trista. You don't have to love a man to marry him. You just let him think you do and do what you have to do to make him happy, and he'll take care of everything else!"*

"Can I walk you to your car?" he asks, offering me his arm.

"I appreciate it, but I've got plans with my friends now." It's not strictly the truth, but I need some girl time.

His lip curls and he looks over, but Ryan is already gone. That curl becomes a smile. "Have a great time, Trista. I'll see you Friday."

The girls are on me before he makes it to the door. "Well?" Tara asks.

I want to ask her why the hell Ryan was here, but I'll save that anger for him. "We're going out again Friday."

She starts to smile, but it quickly melts away. "What's wrong, Tris?" she asks, studying my face.

I fall back into the booth, and she squeezes in next to me while Madi and Noel take the adjacent seats. "Mom and I had a fight last night," I tell them.

"But I thought—" Tara begins.

"Yeah, so did I." I tell them everything, from Mom waiting at the table to interrupting Ryan's booty call. I don't cry again. I got all of my tears out of my system before I got to Ryan's, but I do figure some things out while I talk.

"Now what?" Madi asks when I run out of steam.

"I'm going to start looking for a place of my own," I tell her. It's a decision I just made, but it feels right. I'm ready. Fear was the only thing holding me back, but I'm more afraid of what will happen if nothing changes.

Tara gasps. "Oh, honey. It's about time. You can stay with me in the meantime."

I shake my head. "Thank you, but no. I don't want to leave angry." Telling them about running out of the house while she tried to stop me made that decision for me. I'll go home and make an attempt to patch things up, but as soon as I find a place I like, I'm out.

"Better idea," Noel says quietly. We all look at her, but her eyes are focused on her hands on the table. "Why don't you just take over my lease? I'll need time get my things out, but I'll leave the furniture and all that. Colton has everything we need."

"Are you sure?" I ask, not daring to get my hopes up yet. Her apartment is her refuge when things with Colton get a little too overwhelming for her. "I don't want to—"

Her lips curve up into a little smile. "Yeah. I'm sure. I'm ready to go all in."

"That's perfect then," I say, hardly able to sit still because of the excitement thrumming through me. "Thank you so much!"

Chapter 22
Ryan

I shouldn't have done that. Normally, beating the shit out of a bag leaves no room in my head for thinking. It's not working for me today, though. Between each jab and cross, my brain manages to berate me for my moment of weakness.

Finding Trista was an easy matter. She told me Tara would be there to watch her back. Tara had no reason to deflect when I asked her what she was up to. I should've left well enough alone, but I had to see the guy.

I can keep my feelings to myself, even knowing that she would not have stopped me this morning. I can watch her get married and start a family as long as she's happy. None of that bothers me at all because it's what is best for her. As long as the guy isn't some fuckhead who will dictate her life like her mother does. That's where I draw the line.

What the hell do you think you're going to do about it? Ask her out?

"Where is he?" Trista's shout carries back to me at the heavy bag on the gym floor. The gym is busy for a Sunday. I don't look up, but I know every person on the floor is staring at me. Their eyes are burning holes in my back.

"Uh, could you be more specific?" Logan asks, his voice conveying appropriate levels of concern.

Sober Trista doesn't shout. *She's come so far in a week.* I can't take all of the credit. She was already making progress before she started MaxPower. The class is just giving her a shove in the right direction. Her confidence is skyrocketing, and it's beautiful to watch. One day at a time, she's learning to be a person she can love instead of a mouthpiece for her mother. I'm so fucking proud of her.

"Ryan." She packs enough venom in one syllable to make my name sound like the filthiest curse word in any language. Smiling probably isn't the appropriate response, but I do while I continue to rain punches on the bag.

"Uh . . ." The panic in Logan's voice turns my smile into a chuckle. "I had no idea he was here. He must've come in while I was on break. If he's not in his office, check the bags. And please remember that this is a place of business. I'm sure yelling at him is justified, but take it outside, please."

Fuck you, ya little runt. He's not wrong, though. It is justified. And we do need to take it outside. But, as ever, I let her come to me. She can dictate how this is going to go down within reason. I won't stand here and let her chew my ass in front of members, even if I do have it coming, but she can yell to her heart's content in private.

With half of my attention focused on Trista, my punches slow. I never stop while I wait for her, though. But after a few minutes, I get antsy. There's no way she missed me. So where is she?

Chest heaving from the effort of a prolonged session, sweat pouring everywhere, I drop my hands and turn around to look for her. She's stopped in the open double doors that lead to the foyer, backlit by the sun shining through the windows behind her, watching me with a hungry sort of look on her face I've never seen before. *She definitely didn't look at that douche that way.*

If she were mine, that look would be a one-way ticket straight to my bed. Or the back of my car. My desk. The locker room. I'm not particular right now. But she's not mine. She never will be. And she doesn't want to be. *So why the look?*

"Someone tape a sign to my back or something?" I ask her.

She visibly starts, and her face flashes through a range of pinks before settling on a burning red. "Sorry. I forgot how beautiful you are when you're violent."

She gasps and slaps a hand over her mouth, but it's too late to take it back, and I don't want her to. I can't remember the last time a woman who isn't Tara paid me a compliment that wasn't related to my performance in the bedroom. I like it, even though it makes me laugh.

"That came out wrong," she says over my laughter. "I didn't mean to make it sound like violence is appealing, just—"

"I get it, Tris. No worries," I say, waving off her explanation. No one needs to explain that to me. Violence is ugly every time, but there's beauty in the fluid grace of a body moving through the motions. "I don't think you came here to ogle my form, though."

Her eyes harden at the reminder of why she's here. "No."

I jerk a thumb over my shoulder. "Let's take this to my office. I'd prefer not to have my ass handed to me in front of paying members."

Soft laughter ripples around the room, telling me what I already knew. Everyone is paying attention, even if it seems like they're wholly focused on what they're doing. I nod toward my office while I pull off my gloves, inviting her to join me there.

"I'm sorry," I say as soon as the door is shut. I lean against it, not blocking her in but making sure everyone else stays out.

"You had no right to—"

"I know."

"So why did—"

I look up at the ceiling because I don't trust my face to hide how much I care. "I wanted to make sure he was good enough for you."

"It was—What?"

"Really, I didn't think you'd even notice me. I thought I'd slip in and have coffee with T-Bird, Noel, and Madi. I wanted to make sure you weren't miserable and that he isn't some controlling asswipe who will try to dictate your every breath." The *like your mother* is unspoken, but it hangs in the air between us. I finally look down, giving her the attention she deserves. The fire in her eyes is stunning. I might've misjudged here—I just thought I was ready to face her. I hate that her anger is directed at me.

She anchors her fists to her hips and stares me down. "And?"

The way she's looking at me, I swear she can see straight into my soul. Like all of the things I try to hide are on full display for her. My insecurities, made worse by my mother's mental abuse because I wasn't the golden child my brothers were, my fears, my feelings for her. I cross my arms over my chest as if doing so will somehow shield me. "I dunno. You could do better."

Her eyebrows arch toward her hairline. "You got that from sitting across the room, smirking at him?"

"Yeah."

"How?"

I shrug. I'm always going to think she could do better. Even if she had ended up with Mason and he would've treated her like a fucking queen. But I set the bar high enough God hits his head on it because that's what she deserves. "I just did."

"Ryan," she sighs.

I have to work not to let that sigh go straight to my dick. It's not so difficult, though. I just have to imagine that asshole Grant putting his hands on her.

"Are you going to turn up every time I go out with someone new?" she asks, her voice so soft it barely reaches my ears.

I shrug again. It sounds like a good idea to me. If my mere presence in the background can scare off assholes who aren't right for her, I'm in. "I dunno. Probably. Are you going to see him again?"

Her eyes squeeze shut, and all of the fire goes out of her. "Yes."

Why? I saw enough in the five minutes I was there to know that she's not into him. I clench my fists, wishing like hell that action could crush my anger. It hurts to know that she's wasting time with someone who doesn't set her soul on fire. "You don't sound happy about that."

"Oh! I-I am!" That slight stutter betrays her. I don't call her on it, though. She knows. "It's just that we left things a little awkward and—"

"Because of me?" I'll do it again if it'll keep her from making this mistake. If she isn't happy about seeing him again, she will never be happy with him.

She bites her bottom lip while she considers her answer. "Because he wouldn't believe me when I told him we've never had sex."

"Oh." *Don't think about it.* There's no way in hell I can hide a hard on in these shorts. I'll be pitching a tent. "And that was a problem for him? He afraid he won't measure up?" *I know he won't, Pix.* He looks like he spends more time riding his desk than anything.

Trista rolls her eyes at me. "No. He's afraid it's an ongoing arrangement, and that's a deal-breaker for him."

"You talk like you're already together. It was one *brunch.*" *Please tell me you're not settling for this guy because you don't have a better offer.* The very idea is fuel for my anger, which doesn't need any help to begin with. She's so close to being free of her mother and actually *being* happy. How can she throw it away like that?

She shrugs. "I can't blame him. I would hate to spend the time getting to know someone only to find out that when he's not with me, he's off fucking some girl I could never hope to measure up to."

A thrill surges through me. *She thinks he wouldn't measure up to me?* Not that she has first-hand experience, but does she imagine—nope. *Nope, nope, nope. Not going there.* Not going to torture myself. I do that enough.

She carries on, oblivious to my wandering thoughts. "I'd feel like he's settling and that the chances of him cheating are high. He's just . . . weeding out the bullshit."

"No man would be settling for you, Trista." The words are out before I can stop myself. *I could kick my own ass for that.* It's the truth, but it's too close to revealing how much I want to be hers. But she can do so much better than me too.

She rolls her eyes at me again. "Oh, please. You don't have to lie to try to make me feel better about myself, Ryan. I know what people see when they look at me. I'm just lucky I haven't had to fight off some guy with a fetish for little girls."

She's got me cornered with that last one. She *does* look like jailbait. "That doesn't mean a guy has to settle for you. But you don't look like a kid when you're here for class."

She smiles. "Nice try."

"No, I'm serious. You look like a badass when you're here. No reason you can't all the time." *Damn, does she ever look good in class.* It's forty minutes of strengthening my willpower, six days a week. Personally, I think all the flowers and pink are her problem, not that those can't be badass. They just don't work out that way for her. But that's for her to decide. I don't want to make a suggestion and have her latch onto it.

"Thanks for trying. And Ryan?"

"Hmm?"

Her smile is long gone, replaced by a blankness that speaks of exhaustion. And, I suppose, in a way, she is exhausted. Trying to be two people all of the time must be hell. "I do appreciate that you're looking out for me, but please, don't try to scare my dates away. I don't want to be alone forever."

Like me. There's no way in hell she's implying that, but I don't need her to. It's the truth. But I don't like the idea that she's tying her happiness to her relationship status. It's not healthy. She doesn't *need* someone to be happy; she only thinks she does because of her mother. "So you're just going to take the first guy who makes you an offer?"

If that's the case, then wouldn't I be as good as any? At least I know I don't deserve her. But I don't know that I'll treat her right always, which is why it's not worth the risk. Mom made a point to let me know what a horrible, selfish, insufferable asshole I am. I work hard to keep that side of me tamped down, but you can't hide your true self from your partner, and I don't want Trista to see that side of me.

"I . . . I don't know," she says, her voice choked with tears that twist my heart into knots. And I can't do anything about it because it's Trista and she's pissed at me. "But it's my choice."

"Not really." *Motherfucker.* Will I ever learn? *Mom was right.*

She glares at me, the exhaustion burning away. "What do you mean?"

"If it were your choice, you'd pick the guys you date. Not your mom."

My stupid mouth douses that fire in her eyes again. "That's one area where Mom is probably right, like it or not. I . . . tend to gravitate toward guys who are unavailable in some way."

"Like Mason?" I ask softly. *Just shut up, you bastard.* There's no need to rub salt in that wound, but I'm not asking to be an asshole. I want to understand why she's settling for a guy her mom chose because he looks good on paper when just talking about it makes her cry.

She nods. "And Tyler. And . . ." She stops suddenly, her eyes flaring wide in surprise, or maybe panic. Either way, it makes me want to hug her. That's a bad idea for multiple reasons, though.

And? Has she finally moved on from Mason, or was there someone before him? "And?"

"Never mind. I'll let you get back to whatever you should be doing."

I step aside so she can leave, holding the door to stop myself from reaching for her. *You'd only ruin her life. You can't make her happy, either.*

Chapter 23

Trista

I don't know what to do with myself, but I have five minutes to figure it out before Rachel runs me out of my office. Telling Mom about brunch with Grant and our plans for Friday went a long way toward smoothing things over with her, but things are still a little tense. Especially since she caught me sneaking some boxes inside to pack into. It won't take long; I don't have much I care to take.

On a whim, I grab my phone and text Ryan, asking him what he's doing. I actually enjoy spending time with him when he isn't interrupting my dates. Things are simple with Ryan. I don't have to think about the right thing to say or do. I can be myself without reservation, whoever I am.

He said this morning that he's off work this afternoon. Maybe he's working on that old hunk of junk or something, and there's a job I can help with. His reply comes much sooner than I expected.

Ryan: Working in the shop.

Trista: Need a hand?

The ellipsis pops up and disappears almost instantly.

Ryan: Sure?

I can almost see him scowling at his phone, wondering why the heck I'm suddenly interested in helping, but he's too nice to tell me no without good reason. He'll see right through me if I tell him I enjoy hanging out in his shop. It's the truth, but he'll know I have ulterior motives, so I cut to the chase.

Trista: Mom's still upset. Don't want to be home longer than necessary.

Ryan: Wear old clothes.

Trista: See you soon.

I can get home, change, and be gone again before Mom makes it home. *Maybe I'll pack a bag . . .* I might stay with Tara tonight or at Noel's if Colton doesn't stay with her. I can't take another night of Mom's pointed comments about Saturday night.

***

It takes me forty-five minutes, but I manage it. Ryan doesn't answer the door, so I walk around the house to the shop. The big bay door is up, lights are on, and there's music coming from somewhere—if you can call it that. It's mostly loud guitars and yelling. Ryan isn't on the ground under the car this time, though. The car isn't even in one piece anymore.

"Ryan?" I call, warning him that I'm here as much as trying to find him in the mess.

"Yeah?" he calls back.

"Did the car explode?" He isn't groaning in pain or screaming for help, so I assume this mess was by design.

He chuckles, but I still haven't found him. "No. Just part of the restoration process."

"Alright, I'll take your word for it. What've you got for me?" *Process indeed.* My hands itch to tidy, but they'll be busy soon enough, I hope.

Ryan steps out of his hiding place, wiping his filthy hands on a rag that's probably leaving behind more grime than it's removing. "Ever used an impact wrench?"

"A what?" That doesn't even *sound* safe, and he wants me to use it?

He laughs again. "That's my answer. Doesn't matter anyway. I'm going to have you removing some rust."

I sigh my relief. "Okay?"

"We'll start you off with something simple for practice." He motions for me to follow him and winds his way through the scattered car parts.

"Um, Ryan?" I ask, picking my way after him.

"Yeah?"

"The *whole car* was rusty."

Another laugh. "Yeah, but somewhere under all that rust is the real beauty. We've just gotta strip it all away and find her."

He's clearly more optimistic about this than I am; however, he's done this before. Who am I to argue?

He takes me to a workbench and shows me a bucket full of sandwich baggies, each containing little metal bits and pieces. "I *can* replace them if need be, but I'm sentimental and like to retain as many original parts as possible," he explains, showing me the contents of one bag.

Great. No pressure. If I mess this up, it'll cost him money and be less original. Maybe this was a bad idea . . .

Next to the baggies is a plastic tub full of water bottles, a roll of masking tape, a marker, a funnel, and gallons upon gallons of Apple Cider Vinegar. "Lable the bottle to match the bag. Empty the bag into the bottle, pour in some vinegar, cap it, give it a shake, and repeat."

I look up at him, waiting for the rest of the instructions. He just looks at me, a smile crinkling the corners of his eyes, until I ask, "That's it?"

"That's it for this job. We'll shake them again every so often, but the vinegar will eat away most of the rust without damaging the good metal underneath. And the neighbors don't complain too much about the smell this way."

"So, I can't mess this up?" The excitement in my voice is ridiculous, but I don't want him to regret letting me help.

He grins. "You can't mess this up, Pixie Stix. Just make sure to label the bottles. You good here?"

"Yeah." This I can do. It's almost *too* easy.

He nods, just a quick jerk of his chin. "Alright. Let me get you some earplugs. I'll be using air tools since the neighbors aren't sleeping. They get a little loud."

He comes back with a little plastic baggie with a pair of pink and yellow foam earplugs inside. "Thank you."

"You bet," he calls over his shoulder, already halfway back to whatever he was doing when I got here.

"Hey, Ryan?" I call after him.

He turns to walk backward. "Yeah?"

"Thanks."

"No, thank you," he says, laughing. "I hate that part of a restore. So fucking tedious."

I spread my hands. I asked to help, not to have fun. "Probably, but I'd rather be here doing this than home getting the Mom treatment."

His smile is bright enough it should blast all the rust off the car. "Always happy to give you the shit jobs, Tris."

We work in silence, sort of. He's right; his air tools *are* noisy. I'm very appreciative of the earplugs but glad they don't completely block the sound. He sings while he works. I didn't know Ryan could sing, but he has a nice voice, and I'm a little bummed I only get little snippets when the tools aren't going. The job isn't that bad, though. I'm cleaning and organizing—two things I enjoy.

A quick thirty minutes later, I'm done. Ryan is busy with the air tool and can't hear when I call for him, so I wait patiently for him to finish up and give me a new job. I don't mean to stare, but all of this is kind of fascinating to me. Somehow, he's going to turn this heap of rust into something beautiful that someone will treasure someday. It's like the ultimate cleaning job.

My attention is quickly pulled from the car, though, attracted by the flex of the muscles in his arms. It wanders from there to where his sweat-soaked shirt clings to his back, showing off more muscle. And down to his butt, which always looks good in his jeans. I *try* not to notice, but it's hard. Somewhere along the way, the flicker of fear I used to get when I look at Ryan turned into butterflies. *Or maybe it was always butterflies, and I was in denial.*

"See something you like?"

Busted! Somehow, despite the heat in the shop, my face manages to get hotter. I am *not* supposed to be checking out my friend. How the hell did I miss the silence? Was I *that* deep in thought? "J-j-just imaging what the car will look like when you're finished!" I say, spitting out the first thing that comes to mind that *isn't* the truth for a change, unlike a few days ago at the gym when I told him he's beautiful.

"Mmmhmm. Sure." He winks at me. "Done with the, uh . . . nuts and bolts?"

"Yes!" Thank God for the subject change. I do *not* want to go into detail about what I was really thinking about—not even with myself. He's made it clear that we're just friends. That line of thinking will go nowhere.

He lays down the gun thing he's holding and shucks off his gloves. "Alright. Hungry?"

My stomach rumbles, taking me by surprise. I was too distracted by work and by Ryan to realize how hungry I am. "Starving, actually."

He smirks, eyes fixed on my middle. "Pizza? Thai? Chinese? Suggestions?"

"Uh, whatever." Peanut butter and jelly sandwiches are closer to what I expected. Maybe some cold cuts. Something quick and easy so he can get right back to work.

He frowns at me. "Trista . . ."

I'm not sure what to tell him. I really don't have an opinion when it comes to eating out. Mom never lets me choose, and when I go out with friends I go along with whatever sounds good to them. Ryan won't accept that, though. He'll want an answer. "I've never had Thai. Had Chinese once. I wasn't impressed."

His eyes narrow. "You're doing it wrong then. May I?"

Did he just volunteer to make a decision for me? Ryan just doesn't do that. I swear, he delights in watching me sweat over making up my mind. "Sure?"

"I don't consider this making up your mind for you. I consider this introducing you to something new," he says, correctly interpreting the question in my reply.

"Okay?"

"There's a difference. One can't expect you to make an informed decision when you lack information. Like Chinese is *fucking good.* Do you like spicy food?"

"Yes." That one is easy enough to answer. It's one thing I do know I like, and not because Mom wanted me to.

"Sweet. Leave it to me." That smile of his makes an appearance, conveying how happy he is about this situation. His excitement makes no sense to me, but I suppose it doesn't have to.

"Want me to sweep up while you do that?" I ask.

His eyes drop to the flecks of rust coating the floor. "That would be great, but you don't have to. It'll just happen again."

I shrug. It's not like it's hard. Cleaning as you go is never a waste of time. "Less to clean up later."

"Alright. After that, I've got some more bolts ready for bottles." He jerks his chin toward a pile of baggies stacked on top of a piece of the car.

***

"Yo, Ryan?"

Ryan stops singing. My head swivels toward the door to find a lanky teen with a plastic bag looped over one arm. He shakes his head to get his too-long bangs out of his eyes. Somehow, I'm not surprised that Ryan is on a first-name basis with a delivery driver. "What you working on this time, man? Looks like a Chevy Rust-bucket Special."

Laughing, Ryan lays down his torque wrench. He has an agreement with the neighbors—no air tools after six P.M. It slows him down, but he insists it's better than stopping. And I like it because I can ask him questions, like "what the heck is that thing?" which is how I know it's called a torque wrench.

"Hey, Matt," he says, snagging a relatively clean shop towel to wipe his hands. "You're right on the Chevy part," he tells the kid while he gets his wallet and pulls out cash for a tip. "Somewhere under all that rust is a Camaro."

"Uh-huh," Matt mutters, his attention no longer on the car. With his free hand, he smoothes back his shaggy hair, and he smiles at me. "That your sister? You gonna introduce me?"

Ryan looks back at me. His smile hardens into something sharp and dangerous before he turns back to the delivery boy. "You wouldn't catch either of my sisters dead in a place like this. That's Trista." His tone says more than his words, clearly conveying that it's time to change the subject.

I offer the poor kid a smile. It's not his fault Ryan doesn't like to talk about his family. "Hi, Matt. Nice to meet you."

"You too." Matt's lips twitch into a quick smile before he turns his focus back to Ryan. "So, can I see this thing when it's done? What are you doing with this one?"

Clearly dismissed, I return to the task at hand—shaking the bottles of vinegar—with one ear on their conversation.

"Sure thing. I'll call you. I don't know what will happen with this one yet. I thought about keeping her. A '68 Camaro is one of my dream cars, but I don't *need* her. Just have to see how attached I get before she's done."

"Well, if you keep her, I want a ride!"

"We can probably make that happen. If I keep her."

"Alright, man. I gotta get back. Have a good one."

"Thanks, Matt. See ya next time." Plastic rustles behind me, closer than it should be, so I look over my shoulder. "Let's eat, Pixie Stix."

I look at my hands, which are orange from the rust, and wrinkle my nose.

Ryan laughs at me. "We can go inside. Clean up, cool off a bit, get a drink, all that good stuff. Chevy will be happy to see you."

He had me at 'clean up,' but seeing Chevy really sells it for me. "Lead the way!"

Inside, Ryan quickly clears the other half of the tiny, two-person table in his dine-in kitchen while I wash my hands. The table is not untidy or unorganized—because nothing in his house is—but it's clear that's where he does his paperwork. It's also clear that he doesn't have many people over to eat.

Chevy comes running and skids to a stop on the linoleum floor. Meowing nonstop, she winds herself around my ankles, begging to be picked up. Or trying to kill me. I pick her up before she manages to trip me and cuddle her to my chest, scratching her little ears until she purrs. I never tire of that sound. It's so soothing.

"Little runt is louder than a big block," Ryan grumbles without looking up from plating the food. I have no idea what that means, but he smiles while he complains, so it mustn't be a bad thing. "You gotta watch her or she'll try to get on the table while we eat."

He puts our plates on the table along with a couple glasses of water, then turns to take the kitten from me. "C'mon, Chevy. Let's get your dinner." He opens a cabinet, revealing an entire shelf of canned cat food. Opening a can one-handed doesn't present a problem for him, not even while holding the wriggling kitten. Chevy knows what he's doing, and she wants her food now. It's clear this is a routine for them. And, oh, my God, it's the cutest thing *ever*.

Ryan catches me watching and smirks. "If I put her down, the little hellion climbs my pant leg." Chevy meows loudly and bats at his mouth with her paw as if to say less talking, more feeding. Chuckling, he carries her and the can to her food bowl and dumps the contents of the can into her bowl before putting her down next to it. "Bon appétit."

With Chevy situated, he turns and steps around the table, moving to the side that was previously covered in paperwork, and pulls out the chair. "Madame."

Grinning at his silliness, I take the offered seat, squeezing past him in the narrow space. This close, the air is perfumed with him plus a dash of grease that somehow makes it even better. I have to hold my breath so I don't do something crazy like stop to sniff him.

He helps me with my chair, then takes his and watches me expectantly. With a roll of my eyes, I spear a piece of what I believe is chicken coated in a reddish-brown sauce with my fork and pop it into my mouth. It doesn't matter if I like it or not, I'll eat it to be polite. I've done it my whole life.

Whatever else that sauce is, it's amazing. Sweet and spicy and tangy and savory, all of the good things rolled into one. My face must say what my mouth isn't because Ryan smiles and digs into his dinner.

The comfortable silence from the shop doesn't continue through our meal. Ryan asks about work. After answering, I return the favor. We trade questions and answers—inconsequential stuff. Where he got the car. Exactly what I do for a living. What made him and Chris decide to buy a gym. But eventually, he brings up Dad.

"So, what's the deal with your dad?"

The question, as harmless as it is, prods at a wound long healed. It doesn't hurt, but I know it's there. I shrug because I don't really have an answer. As far as

Mom is concerned, he died before I was born. "I've never met him. I'd like to, but I don't even know his name. According to Mom, she told him she was pregnant, and he hopped on his motorcycle and left."

Ryan winces sympathetically, but it doesn't bother me. You can't miss someone you've never known. Can't love them, either. "I wasn't allowed to ask questions, but she keeps a picture of them in her dresser. I assume it's him, anyway. It's of her and a guy on a motorcycle, so . . . She doesn't know I found it. I don't know how they met. I don't know what the heck my *mother* was doing with a guy with more ink on his arms than you have, long hair, a pierced ear, and a motorcycle to begin with. He's like . . . her polar opposite. I could see her calling the cops on him for disturbing the peace before agreeing to a date with him, much less getting *pregnant* by him at seventeen."

"Just because that's true now doesn't mean it always was," Ryan murmurs.

My shoulders slump. Thinking about that always bums me out. "I know; it's just so hard to imagine her any differently. Especially since she made a huge fuss over me doing the same thing she did, minus the pregnancy. It's so . . ."

"Hypocritical?" he offers.

"Yeah, that!" I hate to think badly of my mother. She worked so hard to give me a good life growing up, and she still does. But why is it okay for her to censure me for making the same mistakes she did? "Instead of helping me through what happened, she yelled at me for hours and grounded me to my room for a month. Every day, she'd stand at my door and lecture me some more. I was grounded for another month after that, but at least I was allowed to visit somewhere in the house other than the bathroom. Sadly, I know she has a point; that's why it's so hard to break away from all of the things she wants for me."

Ryan reaches across the table to squeeze my hand. "You can be yourself and not end up in the situations she wants you to avoid, Pixie Stix."

His touch sends a surge of warmth through me, melting away tension I wasn't aware of. I don't mean to, but I look up, and our eyes lock. There's something in his gaze that I don't want to try to name because it doesn't make sense. Whatever it is, it leaves me a little dazed.

Somehow, I have the presence of mind to look away. I clear my throat to rid myself of the lump trying to choke me. "Thanks, Ry. She wasn't always this bad, you know? Not even after what happened with Tyler. It's like she realized she can't force me to do the things she wants me to, and instead of backing off and letting me be me, she's pushing harder."

I risk a peek, but he's not looking at me anymore. "But you've realized *you* are in charge of your life, and that's the important part."

We've talked about my drama enough. I came here to get away from that, so I cast about for a question to ask him. "Where did you learn French?" I ask. Yes, the phrase he used earlier is common, but his accent is too on point to be something he picked up in a class in high school.

His top lip curls into a snarl, but it's not directed at me, so I don't backpedal and apologize. "My father *is* French. He took a job here right out of university," he explains, answering my next question before I ask. He must decide to show me that I'm not the only person with mama drama because he doesn't stop there, though he becomes increasingly angry with each word. "He met my mother. They were young and in heat and decided they should get married. My mother's parents tried to talk them out of it but gave up in the end as long as Dad agreed to sign a prenup. Fast forward a few months, the honeymoon was over, and they hated each other."

I make a face at my plate. That must've been hard a hard situation to grow up in. "They must not hate each other too much. You have siblings."

He nods, pushing the last little bit of rice on his plate around with his fork instead of looking at me. "I'm the baby, actually. That's the only thing they *don't* hate about each other. But they don't particularly care for their kids, either. Mom always says we remind her of Dad. Dad says we're too much like Mom."

"Well," I say slowly, searching for a way to put a positive spin on it for him. "At least they gave us you." It's not much, but I don't have a lot to work with. It must do the trick, because a ghost of a smile teases the corners of his mouth.

He waits in silence for me to finish eating. While we work together to wash dishes, the clinks of plates and silverware, and Chevy's purring and tinkling bell while she washes her face and paws, are the only sounds. With nothing left to do, we walk back out to the shop, and Ryan teaches me how to remove rust from the Camaro's bumper.

We work late, though the only conversations we have revolve around the car and him teaching me what I need to do. It leaves me with a lot of time to think. It's hard to fault Mom for doing the best she could with what she had and for wanting to ensure I have the kind of life she wanted for herself. But that doesn't mean I have to have *the life* she wishes she'd had. Ryan was right; I can be me and still make her proud to call me her daughter. I just have to make her see that. It's time for me to live a life that makes *me* happy.

Chapter 24

Trista

My stomach does cartwheels each time I glance at the time on my watch. If I had a superpower, I would want it to be the ability to control time right now. I'd love to pause and give myself more time to prepare, or maybe fast forward until this date is over. It's ridiculous. I've known this was coming all week, but now it's Friday, I'm at the restaurant, and Grant should be here any second.

We've been texting all week, so I feel like I know him a little better now. I should be excited, not anxious, but what happens if I was wrong and he shows up, and I still can't picture him ever being more than a friend? Do I tell him and apologize for wasting our time? Or do I go along? I don't know what I want.

That's a lie, but I can't have what I want. I wasn't lying when I told Ryan that I have a habit of falling for unavailable men and I've gone and done it again. *Why do I do that to myself?*

It's too late for whys. It happened. It sucks, but I have to get over it. And this date with Grant is a good start.

The Chinese buffet I chose isn't exactly romantic, but that's part of why I chose it. If I *do* maybe feel a spark of something towards Grant, I don't want to wonder if I'm being influenced by the atmosphere. And since it's a buffet, there's no waiting to place orders or anything like that to drag things out if this is awkward. And Noel said the food here is good.

"Trista?" I turn at the sound of Grant's voice, and a smile comes easily to my lips. *At least we're off to a good start.*

"Hey!"

He opens his arms for a hug. "Good to see you again," he says as I step into the embrace.

"Good to see you too." I try to stop it, but a sad little sigh fights its way out. There's no spark when he hugs me. No rush of happiness at being in his arms. I'm not sure if I'm relieved or not.

My smile is still fixed in place when I step back, but that's not hard for me, either. I have lots of practice. "So, I've never been here before, but my friend says the food is good."

Grant's smile doesn't fade; it vanishes. He watches me closely and asks, "Would that friend be Ryan?"

I sigh again, exasperated with his suspicion. "No, my friend Noel."

The corners of his mouth tilt upwards, and he lifts his chin. "Ah. Well, shall we?" He waves toward the door and offers me his arm. I bite my tongue, swallow my misgivings, and slip my hand into the crook of his arm.

Why did I want to do this?

That question nags at me while the hostess shows us to our table and takes our drink orders. Since it's a buffet, we don't wait around. I'm thankful for that. But filling my plate only gives me more time to stew. If my friendship with Ryan is going to be a problem, this isn't going to work.

I might be naïve, but I know Ryan will never reciprocate these feelings I've developed. It's not as cool as controlling time, but shoving thoughts and feelings into a box and pretending they don't exist is my superpower, and that's exactly what I'm going to do with that mess. Like I did when we met, and I knew there was no way Mom would approve of him. It won't interfere with my friendship with Ryan or the possibility of a relationship with Grant.

But Grant's inability to accept that I have friends who are guys will definitely interfere because I'm not giving up my friends for anyone.

He beats me back to the table because I struggle to decide what to put on my plate. That's the downside to a buffet. There are *so many options,* and I have no idea what I like. I grabbed anything that looked like it might be the stuff I had with Ryan.

Grant smiles when I sit, and it eases the nagging suspicion that this date is going to bomb. "May I be blunt?"

Or not. His question catches me off guard, so it takes me a moment to answer. "Sure?" What else am I supposed to say? Lie to me? Or tiptoe around whatever you have to say because I'm too fragile to handle it?

He presses his fingertips together and rests his chin on them, ignoring his plate. "Excellent. I know nothing about this situation is typical."

You can say that again. But where is he going with this? I grab the edges of my chair and squeeze to keep my hands still and do my best to keep my attention on him instead of cataloging the things on the table I could tidy.

"And to be honest, I never thought I'd find myself in it."

"How do you mean?" I ask, hoping to prompt him to cut to the chase. He asked if he could be blunt. I expected him to get to the point. He's making me nervous by dancing around it.

He takes a deep breath and lets it out slowly, watching me the whole time. "My high school sweetheart dumped me for my college roommate. I came back from class and found them going at it in my bed. She planned it. That's how she broke up with me. Said I deserved it because if I'd paid more attention to her and less attention to my coursework, I would've known she wasn't happy."

Whoa. That is both extremely fucked up and a lot to throw on someone you've known less than a week. But I don't interrupt because he's on a roll.

"So I threw myself into my studies. I figured there would be time for a relationship later. But later never came. I've worked hard, and now I'm ready to enjoy life, and I want someone to enjoy it with while I'm still young. And I think, maybe, you understand."

I think you're wrong. What am I supposed to understand? That he had a shitty experience with relationships in college—I mean, who didn't? But that has nothing to do with me? "I'm not sure what you mean."

He speaks slowly, like he's carefully choosing each word before he says it. "I mean, I'm more interested in companionship than love."

I guess I can understand why he might feel that way, but I sort of feel sorry for him. Why have so many people in my life given up on the possibility of love? Even one is too many, but this is the third if you count Ryan. And I do because he has in his own way. "And what makes you think I share that view?"

He smirks. "A couple things, actually. First, that your mother is so insistent on finding you a date. And second, I saw the way you looked at your friend last weekend, yet you're here with me instead of out with him. For whatever reason, you're at least interested in seeing what happens with me."

I swallow hard and glance away, afraid of what he'll see in my eyes if he looks too closely. The only reason I wouldn't rather be out with Ryan is that I need some time away from him to get a handle on things. I haven't seen him outside of the gym since Monday, and it's sucked, but distance helps.

He carries on without comment, though. "At first, I thought you were trying to make him jealous, but you weren't happy to see him there Sunday, and you were very upfront about everything. That made me think that maybe love hasn't worked out so well for you, either."

No . . . It really hasn't . . . I'm not going to say that the feelings I have for Ryan are love. I'm not even sure I know what love feels like. I thought it was what I felt for Mason, but now I know better. And I don't trust what I felt for Tyler because everything about that situation was a lie. Maybe Grant has the right of it. As much as it hurts to even think it, maybe I wasn't meant to find love. I know I'm not that old, but at what point do I put practicality ahead of the fanciful notion that there's some guy out there waiting to sweep me off my feet? Especially since I keep looking in the wrong places.

When I don't respond, he continues, "I'm not suggesting we run off and get married right away. We can keep doing what we're doing for a while. Make sure we're compatible. Do you like to travel?"

"I don't know," I answer, responding automatically to the part that makes sense to me. "I've never been anywhere."

His eyes light up. Clearly, it's something he loves, and he's anxious to share it with someone. "We can fix that. I'll take you anywhere you want to go."

I hold up a hand to stop him before he goes any further. My head is already spinning with what he's thrown at me. "I'm sorry, I just . . . This is a lot to process."

He nods. "Of course. I apologize if I maybe read you wrong."

"No. I mean, yes, kind of. Nothing is going on between Ryan and me. I wasn't lying. We're only friends, and I was upset that he took it upon himself to show up. I'm . . . struggling to accept that you might be right about the rest of it."

"It's hard to give up on the idea of love," he says softly, and his eyes betray what this decision cost him. I wonder if there's more to the story he isn't sharing, but I don't feel right asking. Not yet.

"Can I think about it?" He hasn't exactly asked me to commit to anything yet, but if he wanted to drag out the dating process, he wouldn't have said anything. If I'm not up for the future he has in mind, a relationship free of the complications of emotions, he's moving on to the next option.

"Of course," he says with a smile that doesn't quite reach his eyes.

As much as it hurts to know that I've once again developed feelings for the wrong guy, I'm not sure that I'm ready to give up yet. I need to do something first. Something for myself.

I need to see Ryan.

I want to jump up and run out the door, but I force myself to sit and finish my meal and chat with Grant. It's a date, after all.

As soon as I'm in my car, though, I turn toward Ryan's before I can change my mind. I only hope he's home.

Chapter 25
Ryan

My doorbell rings, startling me out of a doze. It's a rare Friday night when I'm not out with friends or in the shop working on a car, and I'm kind of pissed that someone is intruding on my downtime. Chevy meows in protest when I move her so I can roll off the couch and stomp to the door, hoping to work out some of the anger before I have to do the people thing.

I stoop to look out the peephole just to be safe. I don't have any enemies or anything like that, but sometimes people do stupid things for the sake of doing stupid things. But the redhead on my porch is possibly more unwelcome than a would-be robber or someone trying to help me find Jesus after eight o'clock on a Friday evening.

I open the door just enough to peer out, hoping that gets the message across. "Amanda. What are you doing here?"

She smiles and flutters her eyelashes at me like looking cute will make me less of an asshole. "Well, you told me to lose your number, but you didn't say anything about your address."

"Lose it too," I growl at her. I tried to do this the nice way and apparently failed, because she's here again. I won't be so nice this time. I don't want to encourage her to keep this shit up or be accused of leading her on later.

Her eyes narrow. "Why are you doing this? I know you aren't hooking up with someone else, so don't even lie."

"How do you know?" I ask. I wasn't going to try that tactic—I'm not afraid to tell her the truth—but I'm very interested in knowing how she's reached that conclusion.

She shrugs one shoulder. "I've kept an eye on you."

"You're *watching* me?" Does she even hear how sketchy that sounds? I'm not scared of her, but fuck, that's creepy. Is she looking in the windows, or sitting across the street in her car watching the place?

Her top is already struggling to contain her tits, but she crosses her arms under them, pushing them up and straining the fabric even more. She has a fantastic rack, but I have more discipline than that. *Otherwise, I would've made a pass at Trista years ago.* "You blew me off for months, then you got my hopes up only to kick me out with no real explanation and no orgasm, Ryan. I wanted to know why."

No explanation? I told her we had different ideas of what our arrangement should be. That was an explanation. I keep my mouth shut, though, because I don't think that's all she has to say. If I give her a chance, she'll probably give me enough rope to hang her with.

"I know you didn't fuck that little brunette that keeps showing up here. You've been home every night this week, and no one but her has come over. So I figured, since it's been so long, maybe you're as tense as I am and want to make last weekend up to me? I brought my table . . ."

Fuck, that would be good, but I'm not falling for that. That's how this all started. She came here one evening a week after work because I couldn't find anywhere open when I could get in. It took about a month for us to escalate from flirting to fucking. Neither of us wanted anything serious. We were in it for the fun and the release, nothing more.

But I suspected that wasn't true for her anymore. It's not a suspicion anymore. Letting her in tonight will only make things worse. "Look, this arrangement was great, but I think it means more to you than it does to me. We're done."

Her flirty smile vanishes. The glare that replaces it might intimidate Chevy, but it's not working on me. "You're kidding yourself if you think you don't care about me."

She's right, but not in the way she thinks. I care about her general wellbeing. That's different than what she wants it to be. She's not going to make that distinction, though. "I *do* care about you, and that's why I'm telling you we're not doing this anymore. I told you from the start I wasn't looking for something serious. You were okay with that then. I don't know what's changed for you, but nothing has for me. It won't. There's nothing here for you, Amanda, and I don't want to hurt you."

She slaps a palm against the door, trying to push it open, but she never had a chance. "You *are* hurting me! What the hell is wrong with you? I love you!"

Really? She's going to try that? Is she going to cry pregnant next? I swallow my anger and manage to scrape together some patience. *Maybe I'm not such an asshole after all.* "No, you don't. You love my dick. You don't know me."

Austin was on to something. He never took a girl home with him because there was a fifty-fifty chance she'd be crazy. Amanda isn't crazy, just confused. The results are the same, though. Behind her, a car pulls up along the curb. I know who it is without looking by the knock in the motor and the squeal of a slipping belt. *I need to convince her to let me fix that before it leaves her stranded.* Actually, she needs to throw the whole car out and start over. But what the hell is Trista doing here?

Amanda throws herself against the door. It almost works because I wasn't expecting it, but she doesn't weigh enough to move me. "Damnit, woman, stop this shit! Why are you fighting so hard for someone who doesn't want you to? Do you see how crazy that is? Look, I'm a shit boyfriend, okay? I'm a selfish asshole. I don't want to ruin relationships for anyone else. Do yourself a favor and forget me."

That's the part of the story I didn't tell Tris. Things start out great, but once the new wears off, I turn into my dad. I work too much, I play too hard, and I forget to take time for the little things that make girlfriends happy. It's why Mom hates Dad. It's why Selene was pissed at me the day before she died; because I worked through some party she wanted me to attend with her. She forgave me for not showing and begged me to forgive her for overreacting. We made up. The next day, she OD'd.

It was one stupid party. Chris would've understood if I called it a night early. It wasn't do or die then, just a project we were doing to see if we could. But I was focused, and I didn't want to stop. Maybe if I had, she'd still be alive.

Tears drip down Amanda's cheeks, but I don't react. I can't let it affect me. I can't show weakness now, even if I hate seeing a woman cry. "You're just saying that to get rid of me," she hiccups.

I glance over her shoulder at Trista, who somehow managed to exit her vehicle without Amanda noticing and is halfway up the path. She seems to sense that something isn't quite right here and stops. I can't tell her to wait, or to come on in, without letting Amanda know she's there, which might make this situation worse if she decides Trista is getting something she's not. *Fuck this shit.*

Trista needs me, or she wouldn't be here. I need to hurry up convince Amanda to give up this picture she has of an us. I haven't been part of an us that isn't platonic in a long time, and if I ever decide to change that, it won't be with her. "Mandy, baby, I'm really not. Think about it. I'm young, I'm not bad-looking, and I have money. Why the hell else would I be single if I weren't a horrible boyfriend?"

She steps back and blinks at me. "You really believe that, don't you?"

"I know it." The apple didn't fall far from the tree here. Or maybe mommy just didn't love me enough to counteract the childhood trauma of growing up in a broken home that was perfect from the outside looking in. Who the hell knows? Gabe keeps trying to talk me into therapy, but I don't think you can fix problems that started in the cradle.

"You're lying," she says with another hiccup. "It's that little brunette bitch, isn't it?" *Guess you forgot you already told me you know it's not her.*

"Nope," I reply quickly, hoping like hell she doesn't look around. "She's a dear friend who knows my door is always open *for her* when life gets too complicated." I throw that in as much for Trista as I do for Amanda. I don't want her to think I'm running Amanda off for her—again, since she doesn't know she had nothing to do with it last time. "Seriously, Amanda. You're smart, you're funny, you're gorgeous. There's a guy out there who will be very lucky to have you. That guy is not me. We've had our fun, but that's over now. Go be happy, sweetheart."

Finally, she nods. "You're wrong, you know." She sniffles softly. "You're a good guy. I don't know what the hell happened to make you think otherwise, but it was a fucking crime."

That doesn't just touch a nerve; it fucking sucker punches it. *What I wouldn't give to be wrong.* "The crime would be me letting you prove yourself wrong."

She shakes her head but turns to go only to freeze mid-stride when she catches sight of Trista. Amanda cuts a nasty glare at me over her shoulder but walks on with her head held high.

"Don't you have a hot date tonight?" I ask Trista.

"Yeah," she answers. Something in her voice tips me off that things didn't go so well. So I step back and open the door all the way to let her pass when I'd rather go find the little dickweasel and grind him into the pavement. I told her that I'm always here for her and I will keep that promise. I can take care of him later if I need to.

"How much of that did you hear?" I ask as she passes, anxious for her to answer with next to nothing. The anxiety makes it easy to keep my eyes somewhere appropriate, not on her little ass in the tight skirt that is not something she'd normally wear. Even her dresses for Easy Speak aren't that fitted. She's definitely dressed for a date. *Lucky bastard.*

"All of it. So I wasn't interrupting last week?"

The fuck? There's no way. There are parts of that I didn't want her to hear. "No, but how? You haven't been here that long."

She holds up her phone. "You pocket dialed me."

Something interesting happens in my chest. My heart tries to sink and soar at the same time. I didn't *want* to interrupt her date, but I'm asshole enough to be happy if I did. It doesn't add up, though. There's no way she managed to get here from wherever she was in the short time since Amanda arrived. "You didn't leave your date for me, did you?" I ask, hoping to come across concerned, even casual, not like the happy selfish bastard I am.

"No." She inhales quickly like she's got more to say, but she hesitates.

"Make yourself at home," I tell her just as I do every time she's here, and will until she walks in and does it automatically. She's already proven I'm doing something right by the number of times she's turned up when she needs a place to go.

Trista doesn't sit, though. She paces back and forth in my living room.

"What's on your mind, Pixie Stix?" That name suits her more now than it did when I gave it to her—a lot of sweetness, a little tartness, in a dainty package. I lean against the wall and wait, too amped up after dealing with Amanda to sit.

She doesn't answer, just continues pacing, wringing her hands in front of her.

Now she's freaking me out. Something is definitely seven different kinds of fucked up if she's acting like this. She hasn't even acknowledged Chevy, who is waiting patiently on the couch for one of her favorite humans to love her. "Trista. Stop spazzing and talk to me. What can I do to help? Did you kill him? I know how to hide a body."

She stops and turns on her heel to gape at me wide-eyed. "You'd do that f-for me?"

Oh, fuck. Squeezing my eyes closed, I take a deep breath and prepare for whatever this night brings because something is *wrong* here. "Okay, first, please tell me you didn't really kill him. Second, yeah, but if that ever needs to happen, I'd like to be part of the actual murder so we can make the disposal thing easier, okay?"

Her mouth snaps shut, but the intensity in her eyes doesn't change. "He's alive."

"Then what's wrong?" If he's alive, it can't be that bad. *I hope.*

She presses the heels of her hands to her eyes and shakes her head. "God, this is crazy!"

"What is?" I ask, clinging to the fraying edges of my patience. I need her to tell me what she needs me to fix before I jump to more conclusions.

"I can't believe I'm actually considering this!"

I shove off the wall and go to her. Whatever the hell is up, she's got me beyond nervous. And angry because it probably has something to do with that asshole. *If he hurt her . . .* I grab her wrists and carefully move her hands, ready to stop the second she so much as twitches. A tear slips down her cheek, followed quickly by two more.

Aw, fuck. Those tears hit me like bullets to the chest and make me want to do stupid things, like hold her. If I get her in my arms right now, I might never let go. Instead, I cup her face in my hands and brush the tears away with my thumbs, one by one, until she opens her eyes.

"Trista, I just offered to help you commit murder. Whatever this is, it can't be any crazier than that, can it?"

That earns me a watery smile and a laugh. "Please tell me you were only joking."

"Mostly." Chances are, if she needs someone dead, I'll have it done before she reaches that conclusion. But I'm not in a hurry to go to prison, so it would take something extraordinary. "What do you need?"

"You," she whispers.

My heart does this weird little flip. *Oh, my God. Am I having a heart attack?* I'm too fucking young for a heart attack! It stops before I worry too much. I'm reading way too much into what she just said, giving it the meaning I want it to have. She just needs a friend. That's all. "I'm right here."

"No, you don't understand." She tries to look down, but I don't let her. We're not going to get anything figured out if she keeps stalling.

"So explain it." My patience is still tenuous at best. I need to act, to do something to make things right for her.

She sighs. Her eyes rove, trying to look anywhere but at me. "Okay, look, I've always believed that I'd find my one true love like some fairy tale princess. I don't want someone who only wants me because I meet his preconceived notion of what a perfect wife should be. I want someone who loves me so fiercely it echoes in every atom of their being. I want what Mason had with his first love. I thought he could have that with me, but now he has it with Fern."

I have no idea what that has to do with me, but I'm following, so I make a noise to let her know I'm keeping up.

"Well, I've come to realize that it was just that—a fairy tale. If my true love is out there somewhere, he's not riding to my rescue, and I'm going to end up married to the boring duke who is a politically advantageous match. I mean, he's a good guy, but he's not *the* guy, you know? There's no reason I can't be happy with this duke, though."

"I *think* I'm following?" I don't like it, though. She's acknowledging what we talked about last Sunday—that she's settling for someone. After our dinner conversation Monday night, I didn't think she'd do that. I swallow the questions that spring to my lips and tamp down my anger because it won't help anything. I can try to talk some sense into her after we figure out whatever is going on right now. "But what does that have to do with me?"

She swallows hard. My eyes drop to her throat, tracking the movement and mapping all the places I'd like to kiss if things were different. Her chest expands as she sucks in a deep breath. "I know this is insane, and I don't care if you get drunk, turn out the lights, and pretend I'm someone else, but last weekend, I kind of got the impression that you maybe wanted to . . . not stop what you started in the kitchen to prove a point. Maybe I read that wrong, but I came here hoping that maybe we could do . . . that."

The fuck did she just ask me? My dick doesn't have a problem keeping up. It thickens instantly, straining against the jeans I'm suddenly happy I haven't changed out of yet. My brain is another matter entirely. *This isn't right. I should tell her to go.* If she wants to get laid, I'm sure Grant would be happy to help her out. The list of things I wouldn't do for Trista is short, but this—whatever it is to her—is on it.

She reaches up and wraps her little hands around my wrists, holding my hands to her face as if she can sense my reluctance. Another tear rolls down her cheek, and I wipe it away reflexively.

"Grant is a good guy. We've been texting all week. He's funny and charming. He's tired of being alone and wants someone like-minded to share his life with. If I can't have the love I want, that's not a bad alternative. And, who knows, maybe we'll learn to love each other eventually? But before things go any farther with him, I want one night to remember with someone I'm actually attracted to so I can remember what it's supposed to be. I swear I'll never tell the others. It doesn't have to change anything between us. I just want a memory in case he's another guy who couldn't get me off if I came with instructions."

She's attracted to me? My brain finally engages, and I find my voice. "Trista! Stop!"

This has to be the universe's idea of a joke. She has no idea what she's asking of me, and it breaks my heart. I can't give her what she wants. It might not mean anything to her, but that's not true of me. It would be *everything* for me.

Her chest heaves and tears fall so fast I can't keep up. "I'm sorry. It's stupid. I knew I was reading too much into what happened." She releases my wrists. "I'll go. I'm sorry to bother you. Just forget it. Please."

No, you weren't. I knew that would come back to bite me in the ass. I came so close to losing control. She was *right there,* and that wasn't fear in her eyes. I slip one hand around to cradle the back of her head instead, holding her in place. "You're not going anywhere yet."

"I shouldn't have come here," she whispers.

You came to exactly the right place. I hate every second of this. I'm selfish enough to want to do what she's asking and give her a night she'll never forget. But one night wouldn't be enough for me. I don't know if I can handle watching her walk away in the morning, knowing she's off to settle because she thinks she has to.

I grit my teeth. "Better here than the bar to go home with the next Jeffrey Dahmer!" At least I can talk some fucking sense into her. *Or fuck her senseless.* "Jesus, Trista! Do you *hear* yourself? Why are you even considering marrying someone if you aren't at least a little attracted to them? And I'm not necessarily talking about Grant, just anyone." It's amazing his name doesn't burn my tongue, but now isn't the time for my petty, jealous digs at him.

"Because it's the smart thing to do!" she shouts. *Good, get angry!* She should be angry. That's the most ridiculous thing I've ever heard in my life.

"Says who?"

She doesn't even think about it. The words just roll out of her mouth like she has them memorized. "It's what comes next, okay? I graduated high school and college. I got a good job. It's the next step in the plan. And Grant . . ." She sighs and looks away. "He's safe and reliable. I'll never have to worry about a man like that leaving me like my dad left Mom. And I know what you're going to say, that I shouldn't let Mom decide who I date. But you're wrong. I'm not doing it because it's what Mom wants; I'm doing it for myself. I made this decision."

So she's going to marry someone in the running for least interesting man in the world so she has a safety net? That's some bullshit right there. He's *more* likely to leave because he'll eventually figure out that she's only going through the motions.

My hands fall away from her face, and I tuck them in my pockets so I can't try to shake a little sense into her. "I've got news for you, Pixie Stix, those guys you described? The boring ones? You can't count on them to stick around just because they're as vanilla as it gets. Some of them are the perfectly respectable people you're making them out to be, but not all. They can leave too. You shouldn't settle for boring because you think it's safe."

She rolls her eyes. "Because bad boys are so much less risky. That's not the point, though. I'm tired of being alone. I can't wait forever for someone who might not be out there."

She's got me there. This is no laughing matter, but I can't help it. "You're *ignoring* the point. Relationships are risky. Period. A man who loves you—truly loves you—isn't going to leave. Love doesn't do that. Look at Tara and Gabe. Things got bad, and they tried to go their separate ways, but love pulled them right back together. Love is glue, Trista. Find someone you love, who loves you. Not someone you think is safe. But the first thing you have to do is throw these stupid ideas about what life is supposed to be out the window and stop being this person your mother decided you should be. Whoever that person is, it's not you."

I grit my teeth and wait. Getting that off my chest was amazing, but she won't be happy to hear it. She needs to, though, before she runs off and throws her happiness down the toilet. She says he wants companionship; I say he wants someone he can control.

Instead of snapping at me that it's none of my business, she steps past me, and I turn with her. She drops onto the couch, scooping Chevy into her lap to scratch her ears. "Maybe it's not just about a night to remember?" she murmurs. "Maybe it's about figuring out who I am too? I'm not doing any of this for Mom. I realized the other night that I can't keep living my life for her."

It's a good thing she didn't lead with that angle because turning her down would've been a lot harder. "Trista, I'm happy to help you figure out who you are and what you want from life, but that's no way to go about it. It's not fair to either of us."

What she wants would ruin me. Yeah, I could probably act like it never happened. Our friends would never know. But I would. And it would kill me to know I can never do it again.

She tucks her chin to her chest. Her hair falls forward, hiding her face. "I'm sorry," she whispers.

"Don't be." No matter how much it hurts, I'm glad she came here. To me. For me. *She wants me like I want her.* Fuck, if only things were different. If I were a better man. *What if that's not what she needs?*

What if . . . I can give her the happiness she's looking for, even if only for a little while? At least she would know it exists. That might make her think twice before settling for someone she feels nothing for because she thinks it's the best course of action.

What if, by refusing to try, I'm depriving her of a choice? I always assumed that keeping my distance was best for her, but maybe I was wrong. What right do I have to make that decision for her? Would she even choose me if she could? Probably not. She heard me talking to Amanda. *I'll never know unless I try.*

Yeah, she could shoot me down. She *should.* It'll hurt for a while, but that's not so different from hiding what I feel. I just have to lay it all out for her and let her decide. And then I'll know.

She looks up at me through her eyelashes. "Can I stay here and pet Chevy for a bit, please? I'll take her outside if you want to be alone."

"You can. Or . . . It's still early. We could . . ." *Shit. I should've thought this through more.* What the hell do people do on dates? Dancing? Movies? Fuck it, she can pick. "I don't know, go do something?"

Her hair hides her face again. "I think I've bothered you enough tonight."

Fuck. I don't have time to tiptoe around this. It's do or die. "Trista, I'm asking you out."

That gets her attention. Her face quickly turns toward mine, her pretty, plump lips forming a perfect O. "What?"

I drop onto the couch next to her and reach to lay my hand on her cheek. She watches me, her lips still parted, as I lean in. My heart hammers in my chest. I can hardly breathe. I've wanted this for so long I'm afraid to close my eyes. When they open again, she might disappear. This might all be a dream.

"Tell me no, Trista," I whisper, just like last weekend in my kitchen. It's okay if she doesn't want this. She doesn't owe me anything. I'm not going to force myself on her. She only has to say the word, and I'm gone, and everything that happened from the time she walked through my door *never* happened.

Her mouth snaps shut, which is all the answer I need. I move slowly, giving her time to change her mind. Just before our lips touch, her eyes drift closed. *This can't be real.* But it is. I'm finally kissing Trista, and her lips are softer than I ever dreamed.

Trista moans softly. It spreads through my body like a drug, lighting up every nerve ending it touches. She brings her hands to my face but stops, letting them hover inches from my cheeks like she's afraid to touch me. I ease back and tilt my head, pressing my cheek into her palm. "I've wanted to do that for a long time," I whisper against her lips.

Her reply is to grab my face and kiss me again. My heart hammers against my ribs and my whole body throbs with need. It would take nothing to pick her up and carry her to my bed, but that's not how this night is going down. I don't want to be a momentary lapse in judgment that she'll regret later. I will not give myself to her unless she wants all of me.

Chapter 26

Trista

"Okay, back up." I mean that figuratively because Ryan is already on the other end of the couch. *Damnit.* Everything was going great, and then it wasn't anymore. He was suddenly way over there, breathing like I do after MaxPower, babbling something in French. Occasionally, some English would slip out in the form of 'I can't do this yet.' "*How* long have you wanted to do that?"

I've known him for five years. That's a long time. *And I thought he hated me most of it.*

"Honestly?" he asks his hands, which are clenched between his knees. "Since the night I met you."

"No way." There's no way in hell someone like Ryan liked the good daughter version of me, and that's all I was back then. I think that night was the first time I'd ever drank and I hated myself for like a week. Not because I felt crappy, but because I did it.

Most of that night is a little blurry for me. We were at a bar, celebrating finals. After a point, the only thing I really remember is being held aloft by a *lot* of hands. But I remember meeting him and thinking he's exactly the sort of man Mom warned me about. And I remember not really caring what she might think . . . And then Mason sat down. *What if I had listened to* me *back then?* We'll never know.

He smiles, I think. I can only see one side of his face. "Yep. Somewhere around the time you did a trust fall off the bar, which turned into crowd surfing. I mean, I thought you were cute when we met, but that made me think you were probably a lot of fun."

"Pffft! Shows what you know," I mutter. "Until very recently, I thought you hated me. This is just a little hard to process." I'm still trying to figure out if he has a strange way of showing affection, or if I just misunderstood *everything* because . . . reasons. Like I was terrified of having my heart broken by another bad boy.

But Ryan isn't your average bad boy. *I wish I'd learned that sooner.* I didn't give him a chance. The person I was back then wouldn't have gone against Mom's wishes *that* much anyway.

His head jerks up and my way, and his gaze is *heavy*, pressing me into the couch as sure as his body would. *I wish he would.* "I never hated you. I was trying to protect you from all the bad things that could happen, including myself."

My throat tightens to hold back tears. *How can he count himself a bad thing?* He's so good, even when he's angry. I don't know why he said what he did to Amanda, but I have to agree with her. If he actually believes that shit, whoever convinced him of it should be in prison.

"You're far from a bad thing, Ryan," I say softly. I want to reach for him, but I'm not sure what's allowed right now. Our whole dynamic shifted with one kiss. *Three, actually.* And knowing how long he's held that kiss back has me revaluating a lot of things that have happened between us—especially the nights in his bed. *That must've been hard for him.* Not nearly as hard as me barging in here asking him to sleep with me, though. The man must be angling for sainthood.

"You heard what I told Amanda earlier. I wasn't lying to get her to leave." The despair in his voice has my hands itching to reach for him again.

I nod. I heard every word. And I believe exactly none of it. "So why did you kiss me?"

With a sigh, he drops his head into his hands, raking his fingers through his dark hair. "I shouldn't have. But I realized that you should get a say in the matter. I try so hard not to make choices for you unless I feel it's absolutely in your best interest—like the punching bag at Mason's. But that's exactly what I was doing by not telling you how I feel. I figured if there was any chance I could give you the happiness you want, even for a little while, you should get a say."

"*. . . Even for a little while . . .*" He's killing me. How does he have such a distorted opinion of himself? "Ryan, I'm no expert, but I don't think you go into a potential relationship with the attitude that it'll only be temporary . . ."

"You'll see—maybe, that is," he says flatly. "If you decide to . . . I'm really not a good boyfriend, Trista." *Who* hurt *him that bad—his mother or Selene?*

I close my eyes because I can't stop the roll and I don't want to hurt his feelings. I hate this. How is he so capable and confident in every other aspect of his life but this one? "How many exes do you have? Because I've never known you to date."

"Counting high school?"

I nod, but I brace myself for his answer. The depth of my jealousy for Fern surprised me. I don't know how I'll react to this information.

"Three."

So we're even. Not that it matters. It pleases me, but it also makes me sad to know he's been alone all these years. "Two in high school and Selene?" I ask, making a guess. His lips press tightly together, and he nods. "Ryan, again, I'm no expert, but I don't think anyone is really good at relationships in high school. That leaves you with one. You're basing a life-limiting decision on one trial." *And what were you doing, little miss hypocrite?* This isn't about me, though. I can unpack that later if I need to.

Scowling, he shakes his head at me. "You don't get it. I do the same things every time. I'm like my dad—I do what I want, when I want, with no regard for how it might affect others."

I don't try to hide my eye roll. "Do you hear yourself right now? You, the man who puts literally *everyone* else we know before himself, think you do what you want with no regard for anyone else?"

He looks at the floor and mutters, "That's different."

"How?"

He lunges to his feet to pace. "You're not going to like it when I get so wrapped up in a rebuild I don't come to bed until late three nights in a row. Or when I lose track of time at the bag, or planning my next class and I miss something special you have going on. Or when I go in to work early for a client who can't come at their normal time for some reason, or cover a class for Chris on my day off because something comes up with Keat."

I don't understand what he's getting at. Most of that is just him being a good person, but he obviously doesn't see it that way. I wait to make sure he's done ranting. "Really? That's it?" I ask when he doesn't continue.

None of those things seem all that horrible to me. It's not like they're everyday occurrences. If they were, no one would ever see Ryan outside of work or his shop. Still, he talks like all of that is as bad as being aggressive or abusive.

He turns quickly to stare at me, clearly frustrated that I don't understand. "What do you mean, 'that's it?'"

I stand up, causing Chevy to complain. I put her back where I got her and give her one last pat, then go to him. Stopping within arms reach, I look up into his eyes and hope he can see the truth on my face. "Ryan, those things happen. They're life. It doesn't mean it'll happen every time. At some point I'll end up doing the same to you. I'll get lost in a book or bring my work home because I don't know when to quit sometimes. But when you care about someone, you learn to compromise when it comes to the things that are important to them."

He holds his hands up at chest height, palms facing me in surrender. "I just want you to know what you're getting up front with me, Tris. I don't want to disappoint you. I don't want to *hurt* you. Ever."

"'Life is pain. Anyone who says any different is trying to sell you something.'" I've heard that recently, and not just in the movie *The Princess Bride*, but I can't remember where.

Angry as he is, one side of his mouth still quirks up into a half-smile. "Touché. So, about that date?"

That catches me a little off guard. I didn't expect him to give up that easily. And I don't know how to answer him. I was too focused on figuring out what just happened and why it took him so long to consider what I want. So what do I want?

I can say no, and things can go back to the way they were—maybe. Knowing he has any sort of feelings for me will change things. I'll worry about taking advantage of him anytime I come to him for something. Then, I'd stop because I'd worry I'm hurting him. I don't want that—to hurt him, or to lose him.

But if I say yes . . . I can spend time with him for the sake of spending time with him—because it makes me happy. I won't think twice about coming to visit or helping in the shop. And maybe there will be more sweet kisses that make my whole body tingle. And maybe they won't stop there . . . It's the easiest decision I've ever made in my life. "What did you have in mind?"

Hope comes alive in his eyes, lighting his whole face with a softness I've never seen in him before, but I want to see it again. Every day. "What's something you've always wanted to do but never did because your mother would disapprove. Something legal!" he adds quickly.

The first thing that comes to my mind makes me laugh. He raises an eyebrow and watches me, waiting patiently for me to share. "Well, cutting my hair is the first thing that pops into my head. That's not much of a date, though."

He smiles so big it has to hurt. "Let's do it."

My heart beats so loudly it's amazing he can't hear it, sending adrenaline racing through my veins. This can't be what he had in mind when he decided to ask me out; he was probably thinking along the lines of a movie or ice cream. But that *smile*. Is he really that excited just because it's something I want? *And he thinks he's selfish* . . .

Now that I've said it, I really *do* want to do it, though. And I know just what I want. But he's forgetting something. "It's nine o'clock on a Friday night! If there's anywhere open, I'm not getting in last minute."

He gives me a look, silencing my protests. "Give me two minutes." His phone comes out of his back pocket. A few taps, and he holds it between us. The person on the other end answers on the second ring and greets him by name. "Marie, I know it's late, but d'you think you could open a chair? I have a special case here."

"You get here. We'll make it work," Marie tells him.

***

Ryan steers the car into a parking garage. I should be excited, or apprehensive, but I'm still too dazed to feel anything. *Is this real?* One phone call and *voila!* He tried to explain that he has a network of small business owners who understand what it is to work long or odd hours. They do things like this for each other all the time.

I get it, but I don't. This Marie has to be tired and ready to go home, but she didn't even grumble. I'm not part of their group. Asking her to stay late for me when I don't contribute like the others do doesn't sit right with me. *Maybe I can pay her extra, or get her business mentioned in an article.* Heck, maybe at the end of my workout piece. I like that. It's about my transformation, after all.

On the walk to the salon, I catch Ryan glancing at me more than once like he's afraid I'll vanish into thin air. It's cute. I grab his hand to reassure him that I'm here, and I know what I'm choosing, and he squeezes it tightly. I could swear he's squeezing my heart because it disintegrates into a pile of goo in my chest. As sudden as it is, I'd make this choice again today and five times tomorrow.

This is just *right*. That's the reason holding his hand all those times wasn't weird. That's the reason I've always know deep down that I'm safe with him— even when I was afraid of him. I don't know if he's my one true love, but he's the happiness I've been searching for.

I catch a glimpse of my reflection in a window and do a double-take because I don't recognize the person looking back at me. There's something about my smile that wasn't there before, and I don't have to wonder why. The answer is walking beside me, smiling like life couldn't get any better.

How could he ever think he was bad for me?

"Here we are," he says, steering me to a door bearing the salon's name, Hair Works, in clean white script. It doesn't look like any sort of place Ryan would frequent, but if I've learned anything, it's that there's a lot more to him than meets the eye.

He opens the door for me, and I step inside to find exactly what I expected. The stylists all look tired. Every chair is full, and there are people in the waiting area too. I start to turn, already mumbling an apology, but Ryan's hand on my back stops me. Every eye in the shop is immediately drawn to him, and the exhaustion fades from the workers' polite smiles.

"Ryan!" they all cheer.

He laughs and slips the hand on my back around to my hip, squeezing gently. "Alright, what's broken this time?"

"Broken?" I ask softly.

"I fix things when I come in," he explains with a shrug. "I give discounts on memberships, and I will work hours that accommodate their schedules when someone needs me to. It's my end of the deal."

"Everything!" one woman cries. She's pretty and curvy, and her eyes fly to Ryan's hand on my hip when they're not trained on her client's hair. "It's all broken. Just burn it down and start over."

"Coffee shop out of blueberry bagels this morning, Genny?" Ryan asks her.

Genny pouts, her bottom lip poking out. "Yes."

"Sorry, sugar. Better luck tomorrow. Where's Marie?"

"It's her day off," another woman answers.

I take a step back, ready to bolt, but I bump into Ryan. "She must be on her way then. I called her. What is broken that I can fix?"

Several of the ladies' smiles become rather suggestive, but if Ryan notices he ignores it. Before anyone else can answer, a voice calls from the back of the shop. "I'm here! I'm here! Sorry, I got caught up talking to my neighbor."

"The cute one?" Ryan calls back.

The woman, who must be Marie, bustles out front. She's an older woman, well past curvy and verging on what Mom calls plump, but it looks good on her. "Not as cute as you, handsome, but he'll do in a pinch. Get over here and give me my hug! And oh, you brought a friend!" She's so excited she does a little dance on the spot. It makes me smile.

Ryan steps around me and obliges her with the demanded hug, but her eyes never leave me. "Honey, don't take this the wrong way, but that haircut doesn't suit you. You're in the right place, though. Mama Marie will get you all fixed up." Somehow, as anxious as I am, her confidence soothes me.

She releases Ryan and walks my way, hands extended in front of her. She takes my and holds me at arm's length to look me over. "What's your name, child?"

"Trista," I tell her, not even stumbling over it out of shyness. Marie just makes you feel welcome and loved—like family.

"Trista." She says it with a decisive nod and looks back at Ryan. "A *special* case, hmm?"

Ryan's cheeks turn red beneath his stubble. "Trista and her Mom have a complicated relationship, and, well . . . you tell her, Pixie Stix."

I fight a smile. He's called me that for years, but I can only think of one other time that he's used the moniker in front of other people. "My mother has firm opinions about what a lady should and should not be, so I've always let her decide how my hair should be cut," I tell her, my face hot enough to raise the temperature in the room by a couple degrees.

Marie gasps and is echoed by everyone else in the room except for Ryan and me. "Oh, child. A special case indeed. Come with Mama Marie. Tell me what you have in mind."

I do more than tell her. I open my phone and pull up a picture I saved years ago. The picture fills my screen, and I get a little choked up. *Is this really happening?* "This," I say, showing her the shaggy, A-line bob I've adored for as long as I can remember.

"Oh yes, this will be good. It's a big change, though. Are you ready?"

I'm a lot of things right now; excited, nervous, a little embarrassed, but hesitant isn't on the list. I need this. "I'm ready."

Ryan clears his throat. "Before you go work your magic, what can I fix?"

"Not a damn thing," Marie tells him. "Not today. You've already fixed it by bringing her in. You're coming with us."

"Uhh, yes, ma'am," he mutters, and he falls in step beside me. I reach over and grab his hand, squeezing it tightly and hoping it's enough to make him understand how happy I am to be here, and to have him with me, because I don't have words right now. Could I do this without him? Absolutely. But I want him with me because he's part of the reason I could.

Marie takes us to a room she explains is for people who are easily overstimulated by the hustle and bustle out front and do better in a quiet environment.

"Don't take it personally; it's just the only chair available right now," she tells me, patting my hand.

"It's fine," I say quickly. I kind of like the idea of privacy, but I'd just as happily stand on the sidewalk for this. "I'm just grateful you came in. I was sort of joking when I told Ryan I wanted my hair cut because it's so late and a Friday. And it's not really a . . . never mind."

"A date," he says, the words ringing with pride. *I wish we'd never left the couch.* Not that I don't want to be on a date with Ryan, but I'd rather get back to the business of that kiss, especially when he goes and says things like that—not what he said, but how he said it.

"Oh, good!" Marie gushes. "I hoped, but I didn't want to pry. You hop in that chair, and we'll get you sorted so you can go do something fun!"

"This is fun," Ryan tells her. "I always enjoy watching Trista do something *she* wants to do." *My heart can't take much more of this.*

I climb into the chair, and Marie throws the cape around me, fastening it securely around my neck. She goes through the familiar steps of spraying my hair with the water bottle, combing it smooth, and dividing it into manageable sections. Then, the shears come out. "Alright, honey child. Last chance to change your mind."

I take a deep breath and screw my eyes closed tightly. While it's nowhere near it, this feels like the first step toward becoming myself. It's definitely the most obvious one I've taken and the hardest to take back. The cape moves. My eyes fly open, and I find Ryan standing in front of me, searching under the cape for my hand. I grab onto his gratefully and squeeze.

I suck in a deep, shuddering breath and try not to panic. *I can't believe I'm doing this!* "I'm ready."

Chapter 27
Ryan

 he smile hasn't left Trista's lips since Marie turned her around and showed her the finished product in the mirror. She *should* smile, though. That was a huge step for her. The death grip she kept on my hand told me as much about how she felt as that smile does now.

She chose well. The cut suits her, transforming her from a childlike waif to a fierce woman with a mind of her own. The traffic signal ahead turns red, so I slow to a stop and take advantage of the opportunity to look at her again. I absolutely love her hair, but mine isn't the opinion that matters here. I'll tell her that later, though, when the double high of seeing it through and the reactions from everyone out front wear off. Some of the women in chairs when we came in waited to see her new style even though they were done. It's incredible how supportive women can be at times like that.

"What?" she asks from the passenger seat, having obviously caught me staring. I don't even care. I don't have to anymore.

"Just admiring the beauty here," I tell her, surprising myself. Compliments are something I am good with, but that cheesy, flirty stuff, not so much. I don't much care about that, either. I finally told the woman of my dreams that I have feelings for her, and she didn't run screaming. I'll be cheesy if I want to because it still *feels* like a dream.

She blushes, still managing to pull off a look of innocence with the new hair. *Good to know some things never change.* Like how much I want her in every way.

The thought of telling her good night and watching her drive away when we get to my place is turning me inside out. I need to dial back my crazy before I do something ridiculous and scare her off—like asking her to move in. But maybe just tonight isn't asking too much too soon.

"Stay with me tonight." I mean it as a question, but it doesn't come out that way. Still, she should know me well enough to know I'd never demand that of her.

I'm asking her a lot more than to crash at my place, and the heat in her eyes tells me she knows it. It leaves me a little breathless. It makes me want to pull her over the console and into my lap right here at this stoplight, and I'm not an exhibitionist. But I've seen that look on her face once before—when she came to the gym after her brunch date. I didn't understand it at the time, but I do now, and damn if it doesn't make me feel like a god. I'm so hard it hurts, and if she doesn't stay, there's a cold shower in my future.

"I'll make sure you don't miss class in the morning," I tease. That brings reality crashing down around my ears, though. Class tomorrow . . . I'm not sure I can pretend anymore—not after an entire evening of openly being hers—and she may not want to tell the others yet.

"What's wrong?" she asks. Something about my face must tip her off.

"Nothing," I say too quickly. I don't want her to worry about me. I'll be fine if she wants to keep things under wraps for a while. I have to be. I've made it this long.

The smile melts into a frown. "Ryan . . ."

I sigh, knowing that I'm busted. The light turns green, so I turn my attention back to the road. It gives me a little time to decide what to say. I won't lie to her, but how much should I reveal? "I was just thinking about how class tomorrow will go."

"What do you mean?" From the corner of my eye, I watch as she tucks her hair behind her ear and turns to look at me with those impossibly big, brown eyes, waiting patiently for an answer.

"All of your friends are in that class, Tris." Hopefully that reminder will be enough. I don't want to accidentally say something that will make her feel like she has to tell them if she isn't ready.

She continues to watch me like she's waiting for more. "And?" she finally asks.

Damnit, she's going to make me spell it out. I shift in my seat, more from the awkwardness of this conversation than physical discomfort. "And . . . I get it if you're not ready to arrive at the gym *together* . . ."

Her eyes go wide. "Oh!" She frowns again. "I hadn't thought about that . . . Is there a reason we *shouldn't?*"

I squirm some more. I can't think of any reason we shouldn't. Yeah, they'll tease—Dalton will be insufferable—but our shared friends will be supportive. I think. But this is *new* and *fast*. She might not be that sure yet. "Well, I mean, if you don't want them to know."

She shrugs and turns her body to face forward again. "They'll find out eventually."

My already weak resolve frays a little more. I don't *want* to hide from them, but I don't want to rush her. "Yeah but—"

She reaches over and lays her hand on mine on the gearshift. "I like you, and I don't care that they know if you don't."

I squeeze the steering wheel, trying to contain the thrill her words give me. It would freak her out to learn how happy I am knowing without a doubt that she has feelings beyond lust for me. I swallow the sigh of relief and force myself to stay upright when my body wants to sag forward. I can do that later when she's not watching. I don't want her seeing how her decisions affect me, not until she's more practiced at making up her mind for herself. Instead, I smile to let her know I'm okay with it. "So you'll stay?"

"I'll stay." The heat in her gaze practically sears my skin. She squirms a bit, but I don't think her discomfort has anything to do with the conversation. I'll be happy to help her out with it later. Keeping my mind on the road and off all the things I want to do to her is a chore.

Another problem occurs to me, thanks to a wayward thought about peeling that tight skirt of hers down her thighs. "Aw shit. Clothes . . ."

"Actually," she flushes scarlet. "I have a bag in my car. When I was over last time, I planned on staying with Tara, and I didn't. I decided to leave it in my car, so I didn't have to grab it if I changed my mind. It's still there because packing with Mom outside my door screeching at me is stressful."

"Thank God," I grumble to myself, knowing it won't carry to her over the roar of the 383 Super Commando big block powering my Barracuda. "No offense, but I wasn't looking forward to seeing your mom again. Especially not since you're leaving with me again, and my intentions aren't quite as pure this time."

Her cheeks turn pink, and she squirms some more. *I'll give you a reason to squirm, baby.*

My head swimming with need and thoughts of her skin under my hands, I turn onto my street and put my foot down. Those little wiggles have me eager to get home.

I park the car and hustle around to get her door. It's hard, but I keep my hands to myself while she climbs out. If I don't, we'll probably end up against the car, making out like we're in high school. Fun as that sounds, I have an entire house. We don't have to limit ourselves once the door is closed between us and the rest of the world.

Her car keys jingle when she pulls them from the depths of her purse. She quickly grabs her bag, locks her car, and takes my hand. I want to run, but I force myself to walk. There's no reason to rush. It's not the one-time thing she showed up here for. We can do this again tomorrow, and the next day, whenever the hell we want. But we only get this night once, and I don't want her memory of it to be dry humping against my car.

I lock the door behind us and turn to find her hesitating in the living room with her back to me. *Is she having second thoughts?* "Tris?"

"Hmm?" She looks back at me, a smile already in place. It fades when she sees me, though. "What's wrong?"

"Nothing." My voice cracks, betraying me. "You don't . . . We don't—" I take a deep breath, clear my throat, and try again. "It's okay if you need time."

Her eyebrows draw together, and little creases appear on her forehead. "Time for what?"

"To make sure this is what you want." It's going to hurt, but I'll give her all the time she needs.

The lines disappear, leaving her face smooth and calm. "I don't need time."

"But this . . . isn't what you expected when you came here tonight." *I'm* not what she expected when she came here tonight. She wanted a fling—a night to remember. I'm happy to give it to her if she still wants that, but there are strings attached now. Those strings are currently strangling me.

Shaking her head, she smiles again. Her bag lands on the floor with a muffled *thump* and a blink later, I'm in her arms, and she's hugging me tightly. "It's better."

This is a dream. That's the only explanation. If it is, I don't want to wake up.

This isn't just better than what she came for, but better than I ever dared to dream. "I'm not arguing, but I just want you to be sure. Nothing has to change yet, but if we do this . . . There's no going back. I'm yours until you're sick of me." And when that happens, I'll do my best to accept it with as much grace as I can muster so we can still be friends. Like it or not, our paths will continue to cross long after she's through with me.

Trista braces her hands on my chest and looks up at me. "Then you're mine for a very long time. Maybe it hasn't been five years for me, but I came to you tonight for a reason that had nothing to do with your preference for keeping things casual. I hope you know what you're getting yourself into. Don't worry, Mom will love you once she gets over herself."

As long as her mother is civil, I don't give two shits about her feelings toward me. Trista's happiness is my priority, not her mother's. "Have I told you lately that you're amazing?"

A slow smile spreads across her face. "Only six times a week for two weeks now."

"That's not enough. I think I need to show you." I grab her hips and pull her closer, giving her a preview of what I have in mind. I twitch in my jeans, straining to get to her, but I will myself to slow down. Take my time. This isn't some random woman who's only here for one thing. This is Trista. There's a long list of things I want to do with her, but I don't need to rush.

Her chest stills and a pink flush creeps up her neck to flood her cheeks.

"Helluva time to get shy," I whisper.

"I just . . ." She stops and swallows hard. "I'm nervous."

I love her honesty. Even now when other people would play it off—when *she* would play it off with other people—she's not afraid to tell me what she feels. "Nothing to be nervous about. Come with me."

I step around her and snag the strap of her bag. She's going to need it later, but first, I have a plan for those nerves of hers. All of them.

She follows me down the hall to the bathroom. Stepping inside ahead of her, I flip the light switch and turn the hot water in the shower on. I don't have the biggest tub in the world, but there's enough room for two.

"A shower?" she asks.

"Figured you'd want to wash up after that haircut." It's true enough, but I have multiple motives. This is just a reason for nudity that doesn't involve sex. It'll give her time to get comfortable. It'll be hell on my willpower, but I can do this for her.

She tips her head, watching me like I just sprouted another head or something, but smiles, and her shoulders relax a bit. "Actually, yes. Thank you."

Nodding, I grab the hem of my shirt and pull it over my head. All the heat from the car is back in her eyes when I'm free of it. *Damn, it's good to see her looking at* me *like that.* It's even better to know she means it.

Her eyes dart up to mine but sweep down to my torso just as quickly. "I know what you're doing," she whispers.

"And is it working?"

One side of her mouth turns up into a smile. "Yes, thank you." Her hands go to the top button on the collared blouse she paired with that skirt that drives me wild, trembling fingers fumbling with the small buttons. An eternity seems to pass while she works to unbutton them all, but I don't mind. Each new patch of skin revealed is exciting to me. The delayed gratification is kind of fun, even if I'm dying to kiss and taste the skin behind each button.

Her shirt falls to the floor. The bra she's wearing isn't sheer lace, but it's no less sexy, mostly because it's on her and I get to see it. I'm practically panting, anticipating the moment it joins her shirt, but she turns her back to me and looks over her shoulder. "Think you can help me with my zipper?"

Fuck yes! It takes me two steps to get to her. I'm not stupid. I know she can get that damn zipper by herself, but I'm also no fool. That's an invitation. "You bet."

My fingers brush the soft skin above her skirt, and she gasps. The soft little noise makes my dick strain painfully against my jeans, but I ignore it. The zipper slides down easily, but I don't stop there. *Fortune favors the bold.* I drop to my knees and work her skirt down her hips, leaving her standing in her bra and a tiny thong and the steam from the shower curling through the air.

Unable to help myself, I brush soft kisses across her back while I unclasp her bra. She trembles under my lips and moans but doesn't stop me. It's difficult to think, to remember why I'm not already balls deep inside her, but I somehow retain a shred of sense and limit myself to sliding her bra straps down her arms, letting it fall to the floor without touching her anywhere else. As much as it kills me, I leave the panties. She can take those off when she's ready. If I do it, we'll never make it to the shower.

"Your turn," she rasps. She turns, putting me up close and personal with the most perfect pair of tits I've ever seen.

I bite my lip to keep my mouth to myself. I can taste her later. All of her. Climbing to my feet, I reach for the button on my jeans.

"C-can I?" she asks, very carefully not looking at me.

I stop and consider her request. I'm holding onto my control by the skin of my teeth because I don't want this to be fast. If her hand so much as brushes my cock it might send me over the edge. "Next time, I would love that. If your hands go near my dick right now, I'm going to have you against the nearest wall before you can blink."

Her chest heaves, but she backs off, giving me space to strip. I hope to hell I don't regret that later because she's upset with me or something, but I'm not lying. Her hands near my dick is more than I can take. "Go ahead," I tell her. "I'll be right there."

She nods, but her eyes snare mine and hold them while she shimmies out of her thong. I take a step closer but catch myself before I get my hands on her. "You're killin' me, baby," I groan, watching her disappear behind the shower curtain. "But I'm gonna die a happy man."

The curtain moves enough for her to stick her face through. "Just don't die yet. I'm not through with you."

Fucking hell! That is so fucking sexy it's a wonder I don't blow my load in my pants.

"Yes, ma'am." With her watching, I yank off my jeans and boxers. It's not slow and sexy like she did for me, and maybe I should've returned that favor, but there's always next time. Right now, there's a wet, naked woman in my shower and it would be rude of me to leave her alone a second longer.

"Aw, sugar snaps!" she cries when I've got one foot in the tub. "I didn't grab my shampoo."

I could get it, but I like the idea of her walking around tomorrow smelling like my shampoo and body wash. "Use mine," I tell her, stepping fully into the tub with her and tugging the curtain closed behind me.

One of her shoulders lifts. "Okay."

Fuck, this tub is tiny. I've never had a woman in here. I don't mind one bit, but I'm afraid I'm crowding her, especially when we have to trade places for me to get my hair wet. She squashes that fear with a smile and my bottle of shampoo, which she turns upside down over her hand, letting some pour out into her palm. When she's satisfied, she bites her lip and looks up at me. "Turn around."

"Yes, ma'am," I murmur, already moving to obey. *She just stripped in front of me, but she's going to be shy about washing herself?* That's alright, though. We can—her hands in my hair kill that line of thought. *Damn, that feels good.* I've had my hair washed in a salon before, but this is something else. She has to stand close to reach, and her tits brush my back while she takes her time massaging my scalp. It is the most innocently erotic thing that has ever happened to me, and if it weren't for wanting to fuck her brains out soon, I'd never want her to stop.

When my hair is scrubbed to her satisfaction, the snap of my body wash opening bounces off the walls, and the scent of pine and citrus mixes with the mint of my shampoo. I hold my breath, waiting for the moment her skin is on mine again, and let it out with a groan when her fingers trail over my shoulder. Her hands are tentative on my back at first, but it doesn't last long. I love her hands on me and the little zings of pleasure that follow in their wake. She works fast with a light touch, smoothing suds over my shoulders and back, down my ass, and each leg. I didn't realize I was tense, but each muscle she touches melts.

"Turn around," she orders again. "I promise I'll behave."

I do as she orders once again, never doubting that she'll keep her word. I won't make her a similar promise when we trade places, though. "Oh, I don't *want* you to behave. I kind of need you to right now, though."

Her giggle echoes off the walls, surrounding me with her happiness. I love it. I love everything about this. Having her hands on me isn't the only part that's sexy as fuck; her confidence right now is mindblowing. She takes her time over my abs. It's probably not good for my ego or my vanity, but I enjoy it. So much so that I never want to shower any other way ever again. *Thank God for tankless water heaters.*

When she's done as much as she can without ending up against a wall, full of my dick and screaming my name, I grab the bottle. "Your turn."

I take my time just as she did, massaging her scalp and the muscles she's abused the last two weeks until she is plaint as putty under my hands. And fuck, it's a huge turn on. I'm so hard I'm not even sure I could come right now if I wanted to, but I love the intimacy of this. Her skin is so smooth and soft, and I know every ticklish place on her body.

"Are you trying to seduce me or knock me out?" she murmurs, sagging backward into me.

I reach around her and—finally—palm her tits. She gasps and arches into my hands. "Oh, I'm going to knock you out. I'm going to make you come until you can't keep your eyes open anymore. This is all to make sure you want me so bad you don't have time to be nervous."

"It's working!"

"Perfect." I circle her nipples with my thumbs, and she whimpers my name. "Mmm, you're easy. I like it. Let's find out if you come for me that easy too." I slide one hand down her abdomen, but she grabs my wrist. It's not like she could stop me, but I do because it's what she wants. *What's happening here?* Does she need more time, or did she change her mind? "Tris?"

She doesn't look at me. "Not yet, please."

"Okay?" I make it a question, concerned that there are more issues in play than shyness and nerves. "What's wrong?"

"Nothing," she says, shaking her head to emphasize it. "I just don't want to be done yet."

Done yet? That's cute. "Oh, Pixie Stix, we're just getting started."

"But I'd rather wait until . . ."

"Until?" What's going on here. No one *wants* to wait for an orgasm.

"Until you come too," she mumbles.

I almost laugh at the absurdity, but something she said earlier comes back to me. *"I just want a memory in case he's another guy who couldn't get me off if I came with instructions."* I thought she was exaggerating, but if she's never orgasmed during sex, I guess that could explain her hesitance. "You will then, too. And several times before then. Trust me, Tris. I don't need a map, a flashlight, and a compass to make you come for me."

"Okay," she whispers, releasing my wrist. *Fuck, that trust* . . . I'm not sure what I did to deserve it, but I hope I never lose it.

Teasing her until she comes on my fingers has lost some of its appeal now that I know it's likely the only way she's ever gotten off—assuming her exes were considerate enough to give her that much. But I have a point to prove.

I slip my hand lower, through the wet curls above her slit. My fingers brush her clit, and she jolts. "Oh my God!"

"Okay?" I ask over the water crashing against my back.

She nods, her chest heaving. I move lower, circling her entrance which is wet from more than the shower. Her hips buck, but she doesn't say anything. My dick twitches where it's pinned between us, as ready for her as she is for it. I press my palm to her clit and slide my finger into her. Our groans echo around us.

I keep going, applying pressure with my palm, and teasing that sweet spot inside her while her body slowly tightens. When she's close, her whole body trembles, so I loop my other arm around her, taking her weight so she doesn't fall.

"I'm . . . Stop! Please, stop!"

I freeze. "What's wrong? I'm not going to let you fall."

"Not like this. Please."

Her plea makes me angry, but not with her. I'm angry that anyone can be such an inconsiderate lover. "Tris, when we leave this shower, I'm going to lay you out on my bed and lick your pussy until you come all over my face. While you're still shaking from that one, I'm going to slide my dick so deep inside you, you can't tell where you end, and I begin, and I'm going to fuck you until you come again. Maybe twice if I can hold on that long. And then, while I'm recovering from mine, I'm going to start over on you and do it all again until you're too tired to keep going. And that's just tonight. So, come for me, baby, because this one is just a warmup."

Her pulse beats hard under my palm, and her body is rigid. I know she's still right on the edge. On little flick and she'll break for me. But I'm not going to force it on her. With a whimper, she rocks her hips, sliding herself on my fingers. *So fucking sexy. Take what you want, baby.*

Relief washes through me. *She'll never question me again after tonight.* "There we go. Don't stop, not until you feel good." I let her take over, grinding her clit against my palm while she rides my fingers until she cries out and her knees give.

Chapter 28
Trista

Ryan drops me on his bed, laughing at my startled yelp, and quickly covers my trembling body with his. I don't know if the shaking is anticipation or leftover from the best orgasm I've ever had. I didn't know they could be that good. *No wonder people love sex so much.* But all those things he said he was going to do . . . Of course, I *want* it all, especially if it's half as good, but I don't think I *can.*

Chevy's bell warns us before she enters the room and Ryan jumps up to grab her before she makes it to the bed. "Sorry, fuzzass. There's only room for one pussy in my bed tonight, and it's not you."

I cover my face with my hands, mortified by his plans and the picture in my head of the cat staring at me while it all happens. Possibly trying to cuddle with me while I lie here naked and he does unspeakable things to me with his mouth. In the shower, when he was growling his plans in my ear, it was sexy and exciting. But now we're here and it's about to happen . . . No one has ever done that to me, and I'm not sure if I can handle it.

Her bell chimes again, and his door closes. "Now, where were we? Ah! I know!" His warm, calloused hands close around my ankles, and he yanks me to the end of the bed, laughing at my squeal. "We were right here."

Oh shit. This is happening. I can't look. I can't let him see how uncertain I am. He'll think I'm afraid, or that I don't want it, and he'll be disappointed and maybe stop altogether, and that's not what I want.

His hands move to my knees, and he pushes them open, surging into the space he created between them. "Tris?"

"Yeah?" I ask though it's muffled by my hands.

"This is new for you."

It's not a question, but I answer anyway. There's no point in trying to hide it. He'll figure it out one way or another, then be upset I didn't tell the truth. "Yeah."

"Look at me." His voice is a soft rumble that sends shivers rippling through my body. His proximity and the promise in his voice makes my pussy throb, begging for him.

I shake my head, keeping my whole face covered with my hands so he can't see how freaked out I am right now. *Why won't he just do it?*

His stubble scratches against the sensitive skin on my inner thighs, a prelude to a gentle kiss that pulls a little whimper from my throat. "Look at me," he repeats.

I shake my head again. "I can't." It's too much. I don't know how to handle everything I'm thinking and feeling, plus the sensations he's giving me.

"Yes, you can. There's no reason to be shy. You're beautiful, every inch of you, and so sexy it fucking hurts. Look at me, baby."

He didn't say how long . . . I move my fingers to peek at him for a second but quickly cover my eyes again. He can't be mad. I did what he asked.

He growls something in French. Warm breath on the most sensitive parts of me is my only warning before he licks me there, swirling the tip of his tongue around my clit. A jolt of pure pleasure shoots through my body.

"Oh, shit!" I cry, my hips lifting off the bed to chase his tongue. It's so warm and soft, but still strong. Much better than his fingers, and those were . . . there are no words.

"You want more?" he asks. The air that forms the words hits me where his tongue just was, and it makes me tremble for want of more.

"Yes!" *I can't believe I said that!* I don't *do* that! But no one has ever done anything to me that feels like that, either.

He laughs just before his teeth close on the inside of my thigh. I jump. The bite wasn't hard enough to bruise, just enough to let me know he's there and he's in control, but that's new for me too. And, as shocking as it was, it only makes me want him more. "You know I have a reputation as a bit of an asshole, yeah? Well, here's the thing, Pixie Stix, it doesn't stop here. You do what I say; I'll make you feel good all night long. It's that simple. But when you don't listen, I don't deliver. So, are you going to look at me?"

I shake my head again, just to be contrary. I already know there isn't a whole lot I wouldn't do to feel that again, even if watching him do it might kill me. And, maybe, some little part of me is curious about how he'll punish my disobedience this time.

"Trista . . . Look at me . . ."

"Ask me nicely." *Oh, my God!* What is happening to me? He licks my pussy one time, and I turn into this . . . this . . . I don't even know!

He's silent so long I peek again to make sure he's there. He hasn't moved, and he's grinning at me. "I love the sass, but it has a time and a place."

He crawls up my body and straddles my waist to move my hands, treating me to an eyeful of his dick. I don't have much to compare it to, but it seems long and *thick.*

"Don't you go getting any ideas," he tells me, drawing my attention to his face again. "You can put your mouth on me later if you want to."

I clear my throat, embarrassed to be caught openly staring at him. Again. What he's suggested is something I've never done. I glance down again and bite my lip. What does he taste like? What would he *do?* I'll have to work up to that . . .

He grins. "But we're never going to get that far if you can't listen."

"Or you could just pretend I am?" I'm on board with trying this, especially after that teaser, but I'm not brave enough to do this without hiding. If he can see my face . . . He'll know everything I'm feeling. *And what if he doesn't like what he sees?*

"No." He shakes his head to drive it home. "I want all of you, baby. If you have to hide from me, then we're going to wait until you don't. Okay?"

I didn't know assholes could be romantic. That's probably not what he was aiming for, but it is. Because he won't be able to hide from me, either. And if he's not afraid, then why should I be? "Okay," I whisper.

He leans over and kisses me for the first time since I was on the couch earlier, only this time he doesn't run away. "Mmm, that was a mistake," he murmurs between kisses. "I don't want to stop."

"So don't?" I ask, the words slurring because my head is hazy with lust again. Kissing him is addictive. I get where he's coming from. His lips are so soft, but his kisses are anything but. I love everything about his lips on mine, the way our tongues tangle and dance, how he occasionally nips at my bottom lip before he dives back in for more. I could live here in this moment.

"I'm not going to, but I'm going to kiss you somewhere else, and you're going to watch me do it." Panic flutters in my chest while the throbbing in my center intensifies. There's an 'or else' in his tone that I have no doubt he means. *What if I can't?* His lips move to my chin, then down my neck, down, down, down to my chest, distracting me. It's hard to focus when his lips are leaving a path of sparks on my skin.

He grabs my breast with one hand, his callouses as rough as sandpaper but *oh,* they are an intriguing counterpoint to the softness of his mouth. His teeth threaten my nipple. I cover my mouth to hold back my groan, but he reaches up and moves my hand, shaking his head as he laves away the sting with his tongue. Practically purring, he moves to the other side. My hips rock, searching for relief for the throbbing that has become an ache.

His lips travel down my stomach and the closer he gets to that spot I want him to touch so much, the more I squirm under his kisses, anticipating the velvet touch of his tongue again. "Look at me," he says, whispering the reminder as he hovers just over my pussy, the puffs of air that form the words teasing me.

I know it's important to him; I just don't know if I can. And I don't want to ruin this.

Grinning, Ryan grabs my legs and pulls until my butt is off the edge of the bed. We lock eyes while he drapes my legs over his shoulders, and he grins at me, but I'm too anxious to smile back. He turns his head without breaking eye contact to kiss his way up my thigh. I tense more with each kiss, already so close, and he's barely touched me. My eyes drift shut, and he nips at me just hard enough to get my attention and make my eyes open again.

He continues to tease and torture me, kissing everywhere but where I desperately need him to, like he's testing me to see if I'll keep my eyes on him.

"Please!" I don't know what this feeling is, but I *need* him to do . . . something!

His eyes smile up at me, and he blows on my pussy. His breath should be warm, but I'm so hot for him it's cold as ice. My upper body jolts up off the bed until I'm propped up on my elbows like I can actually do something to get even when we both know he's in control here. *Funny how he never tries to control any other aspect of my life, but here he goes all macho.*

But I like it.

"Mmmm," he hums. "I like that view. Stay there as long as you can."

"Ryan, please," I whimper. I'm not above begging right now. I'm going to lose my mind if he doesn't—

His tongue delves into my opening and drags up to my clit, sending a tidal wave of bliss through my whole body. My head falls back, and my arms buckle from sheer pleasure.

Another quick nip to my thigh brings me upright again, and I'm rewarded with another swipe of his tongue. The surge of pleasure is just as intense this time. I'm ready for it, but my arms still threaten to give. "I'm trying here!"

He stops to laugh. "I know, but I'll remind you if you slip. I love watching what you feel in your eyes." *That's what I'm afraid of!*

His lips close around my clit, and my cares are muted by a haze of lust and pleasure. He sucks gently, sending that same pleasure rippling through me without overwhelming me with it. "Oh, that!" My head starts to fall again, but I catch myself. He hums his approval with my clit still in his mouth, and that somehow makes it even better. I'm so close, but he stops to tease me with his tongue again.

"Please!" I whine, begging him to return to what he was doing before. My hips rock against his mouth, and his eyes blaze up at me. *Oh!* He liked that, and knowing he liked that makes me want to do it again. *I get it now.* "Please!" I try again, hoping he can see how much I mean it.

His lips close around me once more. "Yes!" I say it over and over, unable to help myself because I'm lost in the heat in his eyes and the fire in my veins, until he hums again, sending me cartwheeling off the edge of oblivion.

"Damnit, that was too fast, but I couldn't deny you." Ryan moves my legs off his shoulders and pushes me up the bed so I don't fall off when he lets me go. "Wait right there," he says unnecessarily. I'm not moving anytime in the next millennia. "Gotta get a condom."

"Pill," I manage to find the breath to murmur. I've taken them since Mom found out about Tyler. Might as well put them to good use.

He stops in the act of reaching for the drawer on his nightstand, and his head falls back with a groan. "Don't tempt me. I'm clean, and I'm sure you are, but I'm also careful. I don't want any surprises."

"Your call," I tell him with a shrug. It doesn't matter to me either way.

"Better safe than sorry." He grabs a condom, tears it open, and rolls it on, then more or less dives onto the bed. "Come here, you. I want to feel you."

I grin at him, glad to know I'm not alone. I want that too. So bad. Despite the orgasms, there's an empty ache I need him to fill. I don't know how I can possibly take one more feeling after what he just did to me, but God, I want him inside me. "Just don't ask me to move."

"I'll move you if I need to." He parts my legs with a knee and settles between them. I slide my arms around him, holding him to me while my heart beats faster and faster. "Look at me," he whispers, already pressing against my opening. He sweeps my hair back where sweat has it plastered to my face and kisses me softly. My eyes close out of habit. "No, don't close your eyes," he murmurs against my lips. "Give me all of you."

The nagging fear that he won't like what he sees is a faint echo in the back of my mind now. He kisses me again, and I part my lips, inviting him in. He fills my mouth with the taste of my desire while he fills my body with his slowly, his body trembling over me. I clench around him, riding out a storm of sensation I only thought I was ready for. Stretching and filling, pleasure and pain. It's too much, and it's not enough. He holds there, as deep as he can go.

I was wrong. What just happened wasn't bliss. *This* is bliss. A piece I didn't even know I was missing is finally in place and I'm whole for the first time ever. His groan is an echo of mine.

"Sorry," he whispers. "I should've taken that slower but you feel so good."

I toss my head. It doesn't hurt; it's just so much. Not just physically. My body adjusts to accommodate him gladly, welcoming the fullness and the sunburst of pleasure that came with it. It's my head and my heart I'm struggling with. My heart says all I need to be happy is to stare into the fire in his eyes every day for the rest of my life. But my head says it's too soon to have feelings like that and the fire isn't what I want to believe it is. It worries me. Does he see something I'm not even sure I feel yet? Will that scare him?

If it does, he gives me no sign. "You good?" he whispers.

"Yes. Move, Ryan. Please!" I can't take the stillness. My hips rock to satisfy the primal urge that's pushing me to the brink of insanity. Trapped beneath him, I can't move much. It's not enough, but it will have to do until he decides to give me what I need.

"You feel too good. I'm not going to last long," he warns me.

I don't care. I don't know if another orgasm is even possible for me after that bone-melting, soul-searing pleasure he just gave me, but I *need* him to move. "That's okay."

He moves slowly as if worried I wasn't telling the truth, but there is no pain. Only an exquisite pleasure I've never experienced before, building and burning within me. I cling to him, terrified it will stop if I let go. I don't know what it is, but I know it's good and I want more. All too soon and not soon enough, it detonates. I hold him tighter, wrapping my legs around him too, desperate to hold onto that beautiful feeling as long as possible while it rushes through my body to sweep my worries away in a rush of sparks and stars.

"Fuck, that was good," Ryan pants. "I don't want to stop."

"Why would you stop?" I ask, gasping the words because I'm too breathless to speak. He's close, I can tell. Every muscle in his body is tense and ready, but he's holding himself back. That's not how this is supposed to work. Even I know that. He's holding out on me. I want him to explode for me the way I did for him. I want to feel him lose control and come undone.

"You feel so fucking good. But I need to pull out."

I grab his face and kiss him. "Come for me. I want to feel you too."

The fire in his eyes is gone, doused by anxiety that shows in every fleck of color and every line in his face. "I thought I could, but I can't. I always pull out."

"Ryan," I hesitate, unsure of what to say to fix this for him. If I'm doing something wrong he would tell me. The truth is in his eyes. "Look at me," I order because he squeezes his eyes shut. They snap open like I took a page out of his book and bit him. "You wanted all of me. I want all of you."

"Oh, fuck yes," he whispers. His body trembles, and he thrusts one last time, burying himself as deep inside me as he can go and holding. I rock against him, little twitches triggered by the pulsing of his cock while he empties himself into me.

He sighs and his body sags, too spent to hold himself up anymore.

Utterly content with life, I run my fingers through his hair while every inch of him slowly softens, his body pressing mine into the mattress. It doesn't hurt. I kind of like it. I feel safe here. And . . . treasured. It's too soon for the other word that keeps popping into my head. *It was the sex. That's all.*

"You gonna be mad if we delay the repeat an hour or two?" he murmurs into my hair.

"I'm gonna be mad if you don't." I might even be mad if he wakes me up in an hour or two, but for another round of *that* it would be hard to hold a grudge.

"Good. That one took a lot out of me."

"I could tell." It did a number on me too—not that I'm complaining—but I'm physically and emotionally wrung out after all that. Sex with Ryan was a whole new experience. I'm glad he's *mine* because I don't know how I could ever be with anyone else.

He picks up his head and kisses me. "I'll be right back." Another kiss. "In case you're asleep before I get back." Another kiss. "Good night." Another kiss. "I . . . will see you in the morning."

"Good night," I tell him, giggling as he kisses me yet again. *I could get used to this.*

He climbs out of bed and leaves the room. Chevy bolts inside as soon as he opens the door, triggering a stream of curses that make me laugh again. She jumps as high as she can and climbs the rest of the way as she's wont to do, but she can almost clear the top of the bed now. He's still cussing about 'that mangy cat,' just loudly enough for it to carry back to me when his phone rings on the nightstand.

"Ryan? You've got a call!"

"Who is it?" he asks.

I roll over to check the ID. "Tara," I answer, wondering why she's calling so late. *Oh, my gosh! The baby!*

"Answer it, please," Ryan calls, the urgency in his voice a match for my worry.

I swipe the screen to answer and raise the phone to my ear. "Hello?"

"I need Ryan!" she cries, her fear evident through the phone.

"He'll be right here. What's wrong, Tara?"

There's a pause. "Who is this?"

"Trista?"

"*Trista?* Oh, thank God. Your mom called me looking for you because you aren't home from your date yet, but you're not answering your phone. I called all the others, but none of them have seen you since class this morning, and Noel is at her apartment packing, so we knew you weren't there. I don't even know why I called Ryan, but Gabe said Chris told him you like to help with the car sometimes and I should try and . . . Why did you go to *Ryan's* after your date?"

That last question rings with hurt. She's not asking me why I came here; she's asking why I didn't come to her if I needed a friend. I'll never tell her that I feel like she's too busy for me between her business and the baby sometimes. It would crush her, and it's only part of the truth. I know she would make time for me, but right now, there are too many other things in her life that need her more than I do. Same with Noel now that she has Colton. But, in a way, I owe them both. I turned to Ryan when I couldn't go to them, and something beautiful came from that.

My mistake finally hits me. I meant what I said in the car; I don't care if our friends know, but I don't want to do this over the phone. I close my eyes and try to come up with something halfway believable to no avail. "Uh . . . I was in the neighborhood?"

"Trista," she says, a warning in her voice.

The bed dips under Ryan's weight. "What's wrong?" he asks.

"Put him on the phone right now!" Tara snaps.

"She wants to know why I'm here," I whisper. "She knows I had a date, and Mom called her when I didn't come home or answer my phone." The phone that I left in the purse I dropped on the floor in the front room when we got here. I should've thought to check in with her and let her know I was okay, but I had other things on my mind. *Damnit!* I didn't mean to make her worry. I'll call her when we get Tara calmed down.

Grinning, Ryan takes the phone from me and puts it on speaker. "Yes, T-bird?" he asks, his voice dripping with innocence.

"Trista sidestepped my question, so I'm asking you. What is Trista doing at your house at," there's a pause, "midnight on a Friday? I know you're not working on the car; you're not echoing like you would in the shop."

He looks at me and raises his eyebrows. "Damn, T-Bird. Were you a detective in another life? Your attention to detail is incredible."

"Ryan!"

"I'm going to take a page out of your book here and say, 'you can't handle the truth!'"

Tara gasps. "No way!"

The grin still hasn't left Ryan's face. "We'll see you at class tomorrow, T-Bird. You need to chill before you send yourself into labor. Everyone is fine here. Trista is calling her mother."

"Good. And tell Trista she better never lie to me again."

"What did you want me to say, Tara?" I ask, my voice pleading with her to understand.

"Oh, I dunno, that Ryan *was* your date? That you two finally gave in and humped like rabbits? Whatever happens to be *true.*"

"Well, Ryan wasn't supposed to be my date," I begin, but at the same time, Ryan shouts, "You *knew?*"

Tara scoffs and addresses Ryan, "Of course, I knew. But I also know you can't push a cart sideways and I had to let you reach the correct conclusion yourself. And Trista, if you're not going to see that guy again, don't leave him dangling on the hook."

"I didn't intend to," I murmur, the post-sex glow washed away in a wave of guilt. It doesn't matter that I've made him no promises; I should've cut ties with him before I went this far with anyone else.

"Good. Good night you two. Don't do anything I wouldn't do."

"Oh, *that* narrows it down," Ryan mutters. She ends the call. He leans over me to put the phone back on its charging cradle. "Well, I'm awake now."

"Yeah," I mutter, still drowning in guilt over the whole situation. "I need to call Mom before she tries to report me as a missing person or something."

He nods and rolls out of bed to go to his closet, pulling the first shirt he grabs off the hanger and tossing it to me. "I'm guessing you don't want to have this conversation naked?"

I don't think he's *trying* to be funny, but I laugh as I tug his shirt over my head. "I don't want to have this conversation at all. I don't know what to tell her. I don't want to lie to her, but she's not going to be okay with this," I say, swiveling a finger between us. It breaks my heart that I can't share my happiness with her, though.

He sits on the edge of the bed and pulls me close for a kiss. "So don't tell her that part yet. Not until you feel she's earned the right to know."

Why are you so great? What other guy would put up with this kind of drama? "Thanks," I tell him with a smile. "Don't wait up. She could yell for a while, and sometimes it's best to let her get it out of her system."

He kisses me again. "I'll be right here if you need me."

My phone shows twenty missed calls and twice as many texts from Mom alone. *Wow.* I'm surprised it didn't vibrate itself to pieces. But when I call her back, it goes straight to voicemail. I'm either getting the silent treatment or her phone died. I find it unlikely that she'd let her phone die if she's so worried she's called *that* many times *and* called my friends.

"Hey, Mom," I begin at the beep. "I'm so, *so* sorry. After dinner, I just had some things I needed to talk about. I ended up at Ryan's and forgot my phone was in my purse. Tara just called him, freaking out because no one knew where I was. I didn't realize it was so late, so I'm just going to crash here tonight. I'll see you tomorrow. Love you. Bye!"

There. Not a single lie. *Unless you count lies of omission.* But, as Ryan said, it's not her business. I'm a grown woman.

Ryan's nightlight is still on when I shuffle back to his room. "Hey, Pix. You alright?" he asks, moving Chevy so there's room for me beside him. I climb in from the foot of the bed and settle in as close to him as I can get, laying my head on his chest. I've woken up like this twice, but this is the first time I can remember getting here. Just like last time, I don't want to leave. There's something so comforting about being in Ryan's arms.

"I don't know what I am," I answer once I'm settled. "She didn't answer, so that's going to be fun tomorrow." The worst she can do is yell at me. And really, I don't have to tolerate that. I can leave. I don't *have* to stay there. I have options.

"I can take your mind off all that if you want." His hand trails up my ribcage to my breast, and he squeezes in case I missed his meaning. My pussy throbs its approval like he hasn't already wrecked me three times tonight.

"Yes, please." There's no sense in dwelling on what's coming. It's going to happen one way or another. I may as well enjoy right now.

The drawer on his nightstand opens and closes, then he flops onto his back and pulls me on top of him. His lips chase my worries right out of my head.

Chapter 29

Ryan

We're late. I'd be more upset if not for the reason. I refuse to regret anything that happened last night. *Except maybe not pulling out. . . .* Nah, not even that. Coming inside Trista was the best orgasm I've ever had in my life, bar none. The whole thing is my new favorite memory.

As long as our friends don't give us too much grief, everything will be great. The closer we get to the studio, the more my body coils, ready for . . . I don't even know. I don't care, either, so long as no one is too brutal to Trista.

I open the studio door, and Tara's smug smile is the first thing I see. I drop my arm across the door, blocking Trista's way, and push her behind me so I can take the brunt of the teasing.

"Well, well, well," she calls. "Look what the cat dragged in."

I scratch my temple with my middle finger, flipping her off on the sly.

She notices and cackles like a madwoman. "Come on now, the walk of shame looks good on you."

"Who said anything about shame?" I growl at her. "I'm just tired."

She makes a show of tapping her chin, thinking it over. "Gee, maybe you should've *slept* last night."

"I was about to, but someone *called* me. Since I was already awake, things happened. Again." And it was every bit as wonderful as the first time. I could live inside Trista, which is part of the reason my inner asshole is straining to get off his leash today. For once, this is not where I want to be.

"Secrets don't make friends!" Dalton shouts, pulling everyone's attention to himself. "Someone tell me what the hell is going on!"

Trista pokes me between the shoulder blades. "Might as well get it over with," she whispers.

I shake my head. Not yet. Let him get a shot or two in first, then he'll lose steam.

Noel smirks at me, then turns to him. "Well," she says slowly. "Ryan is late, and we all know that *never* happens unless he's picking up Chris. So is Trista. And we," he gestures to herself and the other ladies, "all received panicked phone calls around midnight last night looking for Trista. The math here is hard, *but . . .*"

Dalton points at me. "I knew it! I fucking—oops, sorry ladies—*knew* it! Come on, Boss Man, let me hear it!" He cups a hand around his ear and leans my way. "Say it with me now. Dalton, you were right."

"Burpees," I snarl at him, making half the team recoil in horror. I'm only joking, though. Today.

"I didn't hear you!" he says in a sing-song voice.

Trista sighs and shoves her way out from behind me. "Dalton, you were right," she says.

Dalton frowns at her and shakes his head. "Nope, sorry, Mighty Mouse, not working for me. Gotta hear it from the Asshole In Chief."

"Yeah, well, take it or leave it," she tells him, shrugging on her way to the weight rack. The whole team watches her go, amazed at the lack of give-a-damn she's displaying. Watching *them,* I realize none of their barbs were aimed at Trista. It's like they knew better, but I think we're all underestimating her.

"Trista!" Tara gasps, pointing after her friend. "Your *hair!*"

Trista drops the eight-pounder in her left hand back on the rack and reaches up to finger comb the longer bit in front. She beams at Tara. "Like it?"

"Looks good, Mighty Mouse!" Dalton cries. His thumb jerks my way. "You didn't let *him* pick, though, did you?"

I'm sure he's trying to goad me, but all I can do is smile. She didn't *need* me to help her decide. My girl already knew what she wanted.

Trista turns her smile on him. "Nope. This was all me."

A quick clap brings their attention back to me. I'm pleased with Trista's new confidence and the team's reception of us and her new look, but we're here for a reason. They can socialize later. "Alright, enough gossip. Let's work."

***

The stack of paperwork on my desk isn't shrinking, even after an hour of work. Grumbling at myself for putting some of it off this long, I pull another stapled form my way and read over it. This is normally Chris's thing, but he's been busy too. House hunting for a place with a yard his boy can play in. Last year on Keaton's birthday, during the height of his *Paw Patrol* mania, I promised him a puppy if they ever moved out of their apartment. I'll be able to make good on that soon.

But, for now, I'll do the stupid paperwork while Chris shops with Gabe.

A soft tap on my door surprises me. All of our employees know I don't close my door, and if I do, it's an *enter at your own risk* situation. "Yeah?" I call, hoping whoever is on the other side will make it quick. I don't want to get too off task, or I'll never get back on.

The handle turns slowly, squashing that hope. They take so long opening the door, my patience nearly snaps, but then Trista's sweet face appears in the gap, and all is forgiven. "Pixie Stix? What are you doing here still?" I glance at my watch and fight off the urge to beat my head on the desk. It hasn't been an hour since I sat down here, merely twenty minutes.

She comes in and closes the door behind her, then leans on it. Her skirt gives me a nice look at her legs, bare from about mid-thigh down. It's hard not to imagine them wrapped around my head like they were last night. The tiny top she's wearing does great things for her chest, but those legs . . . They're killing me. I'd like to take her home and show her what she does to me without trying, sink myself inside her and make her come for me again and again. "I got cleaned up in the locker room to put off dealing with Mom. I thought I'd pop in before I left to tell you goodbye."

Can't say no to that. I didn't think I'd see her again after a quick 'bye kiss in the studio, but I'm glad that's not the case. A shove against my desk sends my chair rolling back to make room for her. Grinning, she crosses my office and leans in for a kiss. She doesn't stop there, though. Bracing her hands against my shoulders, she climbs into my lap. It's unexpected but very fucking welcome. My dick is straining to get to her through my shorts before she's settled.

"Seems more like a hello," I murmur against her mouth between one kiss and the next. My arms go around her, hugging her to my chest, pinning her in place while I buck my hips to show her how much I appreciate her visit. I'm going to have to hide in here for a while once she's gone, but the paperwork provides me a perfect excuse.

One hand slides down her back, over her butt, and down to the hem of her skirt. It would be easy to slip my hand up that little skirt and send her out the door with a smile on her face. No one would be the wiser, and I'd have something else to smile about all day too. *But will she let me?*

There's only one way to find out. Ever so slowly, I work my fingers between the material and her soft skin. She smiles into our kisses but doesn't move to stop me. My hand travels upward, searching for her panties but only finding skin. I swallow hard, forcing down a groan. A thong, then. I'll think about that all day now, but . . . yay!

"I'm not wearing any panties," she whispers.

I exhale like someone just socked me in the gut. "Trista, are you *trying* to kill me? Actually, are you trying to get someone else killed? If the wind blows your skirt up, I'll have to kill every guy close enough to get a peek." I palm her bare ass and squeeze. "This is mine now. I don't share."

She sits back in my lap and smiles at me. "Oh, I'm not leaving here without panties on."

My dick catches on before my brain does. "Mère de Dieu! Here?" My eyes go to the door. No one should bother us, but I'll need to lock it.

Her sexy, *confident* smile wilts. "I just—"

I stop her with a kiss. "Oh no. No, no, no. You're not taking this back now."

"I can—"

Grabbing her by the waist, I kiss her to stop whatever she's about to say and stand, depositing her on my desk. "You can stay right there while I lock the door."

"It's locked," she whispers.

She thought of everything. That might be sexier than knowing she showed up in my office, on a whim, with no panties on, hoping for a quick fuck. I bury my face in the curve between her neck and shoulder and cover the sensitive skin there with kisses. "Mmm, you little sneak. I like it."

"You're not mad?" she asks. I look at her, actually looking, not just assessing the best ways to make her come. She's avoiding my eyes again, slouched over on my desk, hugging her middle with her shoulders up by her ears. However she interpreted my reaction, she took three giant steps back from all the progress she's made because of it.

"Trista, give me all of you." A shudder rocks her body, but her eyes snap to mine. "I will never be mad about you trying to seduce me. I'm yours. You can have me whenever you want me. You surprised me, though. And, really, we shouldn't do this here. This is my business, and we might lose members if they find out one of the owners makes a habit of fucking his girlfriend on his desk. But occasionally . . . I'm all for it."

Her lower lip disappears between her teeth for just a moment and pops free when she opens her mouth to speak. "You told me I wouldn't like it when you got so wrapped up in something and forgot to make time for me. So, I thought, maybe if I let you know when I *need* your time instead of getting mad when you don't give it—"

I cut her off with a kiss because I don't need to hear anymore. "Yes. Always. I'm *never* too busy for you. Sometimes, I just . . ."

"Get lost?"

"Yeah. I lose time, and then, I assume I lost my chance."

"Never. But this isn't one of those times when I *need* your attention. I figured if I maybe . . . practiced from time to time, I wouldn't second guess myself about interrupting you?"

Everything about this is so unexpected, but I love it. Something surges in my chest, making it hard to breathe for a moment, but it passes quickly. "Oh, baby, you practice all you want. But this is happening now. *I* need your time. I need *you.*"

"You have me," she whispers, leaning in for a kiss that I'm happy to give her.

This is really happening! Best Saturday morning ever. I'm so excited my hands shake while I unlock my desk drawer and get the condom out of my wallet, scanning the room for a place to make this happen because the desk is too short while my hands operate on autopilot. The options are limited.

Finally, I can't take one more second without feeling her slick heat squeezing my dick. I pick her up, settling her legs around my hips, and carry her to the door. *No one can get in if we're fucking against it.* It's not the smartest thing I've ever done in my life, but the only fuck I have to give right now belongs to Trista. Reaching between us, I slide my shorts and boxers down enough for my erection to spring free, roll on the condom, and bury myself in her wet, waiting pussy with one quick thrust.

Fuck yes! I don't know how, but this gets better every time. She's so damn tight I worry I might not fit, but I do. And fuck, the way she squeezes me, I have to take a second to get control of myself so I don't blow my load on entry.

"Hurry," she pants, bucking her hips to urge me on.

"No one is getting through that door." It's a promise I don't make lightly. No one gets to see Trista like this. Only me. And I'm not rushing for anyone. They can wait. I set a slow pace, but she tries to take over again.

"No," she gasps. "I was wrong. I need you. Please."

My control breaks. I pick up the pace and am rewarded by her body tightening around mine, squeezing me as I rock in and out of her.

"Yes!" she hisses, and it becomes a chant in my ear until she presses her face against my shoulder to muffle her cries of pleasure while her body pulses around me.

Maybe I'm the easy one. I follow her into bliss, smothering my groans in her hair while I thrust to bring us both down easy. She shivers and moans with each stroke.

This woman . . . I don't deserve her. Never in my life have I done anything to be worthy of her, but I'm too selfish to walk away now.

Trista

My grip on the steering wheel is so tight my hands hurt when I turn into Mom's drive. *Mom's . . .* My heart sinks. When did I start thinking of it that way? It's still my home too. Until later this week, at least. And maybe me moving out is the very thing we need. I won't hide things from her for the sake of keeping the peace. She'll be impossible to live with if I tell her about Ryan.

Tears blur my vision. All I want is to go inside and tell my mom about the best thing that's happened to me in a long time, but I can't because she won't be happy for me. It'll have to stay a secret for a little bit longer.

I'm petrified of moving out, but I'm more afraid of what will happen when I get out of the car and go inside, and that's not right. It used to be the other way around, which is how I got to this point.

A lot has changed in the last twenty-four hours, though. I climb out of the car and shut the door behind me. *Just get this over with.*

"Where the *hell* have you been?" Mom shrieks the second I walk through the door. *Hi, Mom. I missed you too.* She glares at me from the head of the kitchen table—her throne. "I *couldn't sleep.* I was so worried about you!"

She has the bags under her eyes to back her up. She's not just being dramatic; she really did lose sleep. Guilt stabs me in the heart.

"I called you," I tell her, struggling to control my voice. I don't care how angry I get; I don't want to yell. *How does Ryan do this?* "As soon as I talked to Tara. You didn't answer, so I left you a voice mail." I drape the handle of my overnight bag across the back of my seat at the kitchen table, but the lack of yelling stops me from sitting.

Looking up, I find her too-wide eyes fixed on my hair, and the color drains from her face. "What did you *do?*"

I shrug because the answer should be obvious, but I spell it out for her anyway. "I needed a haircut."

The legs of her chair squeal in protest when she surges to her feet, forcing the chair back. She marches around the table and grabs handfuls of the longer strands. "No, you needed a *trim!* Your beautiful hair!"

"Well, I like it." That won't mean anything to her, but I did it for me. Not her.

Mom looks up, entreating the heavens for help. "Where did I go wrong, Lord? I raised her to be a good girl, and she's staying out late, sneaking around, going against my wishes. What do I do?"

"Maybe try accepting that I'm my own person and I get a say in my life?" I ask, keeping my voice soft to cushion the blow. It takes every ounce of patience I possess, but I'm proud that I manage it. I don't want to be her. I don't want to yell. It will only make this worse.

Mom's eyes widen so far, her eyeballs are on the verge of popping out of her head. Her fingers catch in tangles leftover from telling Ryan goodbye when she withdraws her hands, taking some hair with her, but I don't think she did it on purpose. One hand draws back, and I cringe, afraid I've pushed her too far, and she's going to slap me like she did when she found out about Tyler. She promised she'd never do it again, and she keeps that promise. Her hand falls to her side.

"You think you do, but you *don't*, Trista Lorraine! The sooner you accept that, the happier you'll be. Good men don't want a woman who stays out late, drinks, and spends too much time alone with a man she's not married to. They want a quiet, pleasant, happy woman!"

"So, you're saying that none of my friends married good men?" Are the guys perfect? No. But who is? That doesn't mean that they're bad people. They might be a little too rowdy sometimes, but they all have good hearts.

She opens her mouth to yell at me and snaps it closed. "That may be. Look what happened to Tara. And that Austin boy is nothing but trouble. Don't get me started on that hellion that showed up here to take you *furniture shopping.*"

My eyes start to roll, but I stop myself. "*Ryan* is one of the sweetest guys you'll ever meet." *And he's mine!* I'd rather have a hellion who makes room for me in his life even when it's inconvenient than some perfectly proper guy who wants a woman to walk around pretending life is cupcakes and rainbows all the time, which is exactly what men like Peter and Nick wanted from me.

Mom rolls her eyes at me. *And they wonder where I get it?* "Listen to yourself! Do you want to end up like me?"

"Bitter, lonely, and controlling? No thanks, I'll pass. You let one guy who may have been a bad person or may have been a scared kid himself ruin your outlook on life, and you're punishing me for the things you did. I'm done. I don't have to live like this!" Reaching around her, I grab my bag, turn around and walk out the door, letting her screeching go in one ear and out the other until I slam the flimsy wood between us.

I'm done.

I'll come back to get my things later, and I'll bring backup, but I'm not spending another minute letting her tell me how to live my life when she's too hung up on the past to live her own.

The door slams behind me, but she's too late. I get in my car, turn the key over, and go. Ryan is working, but I'm sure he'd be happy to let me hang out at the gym all day. A warmth spreads through my chest just thinking about what he'd say right now. He'd be so proud of me for standing up for myself. But I need to be on my own for a bit.

Tara would tell me to eat chocolate. Noel would be all about wine. I know Fern, like Ryan, hits things when she's frustrated. Madi throws herself into her work and Jamaica into her studies. None of that hits quite right, though. Except for the chocolate, but it's only part of the equation.

I want to do something for *me*—like my haircut, but I can't do that again. While I think it over, I visit the drive-thru at my favorite ice cream joint and order the chocolatiest thing they have on their menu—chocolate ice cream blended with chocolate milk and hot fudge, with chunks of fresh-baked brownies, chocolate chips, and more hot fudge drizzled on top. It's *so* chocolaty I think I might choke, but it does make me smile.

I find a nice place to park in the shade to eat my chocolate fix. While I'm lighting bridges on fire, I may as well call Grant. And I already have the chocolate on hand if it goes badly.

It takes five rings—and I'm about to hang up—for him to answer. "Trista. This really isn't a good time."

His terse greeting sends my mind reeling. I guess I should've expected him to be working today, even though it's a weekend. I know he's a lawyer, and he's probably with a client, but I have a whole list of people who would make time if I called unexpectedly—at least a minute to hear me out. It really underscores the mistake I almost made with him. I don't need to be the center of a man's world, but I do want to be a priority. "I'm sorry, but I needed to tell you I've thought about what you said, and I don't think it's right for me. I need to cancel our plans . . . indefinitely."

The world seems to hold its breath while I wait for his response, and it's a long time coming. "You're breaking up with me over the phone?"

Seriously? Two dates and he thinks he owns me? My free hand fists around the steering wheel until my knuckles are white. "Can you call it breaking up when we've only had two dates?"

He chuckles, but it's more like he realized that he stepped over a line and is trying to save face than amusement. "That's fair, I suppose, but I really thought . . . It's Ryan, isn't it?"

I release the steering wheel to fidget with a thread hanging from the hem of my skirt. "Actually, yes. I wasn't lying—there was nothing between us before— but . . . Things changed."

"I knew it!"

Everyone did. Everyone but us. How were we so blind? "I'd say I'm sorry, but I'm really not. I'm happy."

"Good for you. I have work to do." And he ends the call.

And I really don't care. While my phone is out, I call Noel. I know she still has some things to pack, but I'll stay out of her way.

***

My phone rings, interrupting the mental pep talk I'm giving myself, hyping myself up for a little retail therapy. I *hate* shopping, but mostly because I never buy the things I like. I check the ID to make sure it's not Mom—again—and answer upon seeing Ryan's name. "Hey!"

From the noise in the background, I can tell he's still at the gym. "Hey. Where are you? Tara called looking for you."

I tap the button to put the phone on speaker and bring up my call log. The number of missed calls from Mom today is *ridiculous*, but I did miss one from Tara. "Oops. I'm ignoring Mom's calls and missed Tara's. Do I want to know why she's looking for me?" She's not far off the mark about where to look, though; I'm still working to convince myself that running to him is only supporting Mom's idea that I *need* a man. I don't *need* him, but I sure do want him. Especially right now.

"Your mom called her. Said you yelled, and I quote, 'childish, unfair, hurtful things at her and ran away.'"

Maybe I do need to go see Ryan. Ryan has a heavy bag. Heavy bags are good. "*I* yelled childish, unfair, and hurtful things? Hello pot, meet kettle!"

"Okay," Ryan says, drawing both syllables out. "So, you had a fight. You left—good for you, by the way. And now you are . . .?" He stops, waiting for me to fill in the blank.

"Shopping." I eye the mannequins in the display window of a store I've always wanted to check out but knew better than to suggest. There's not a dress to be seen.

"Shopping," he repeats, his voice quiet and curious. "Baby, are you okay?"

I love it when he calls me that. It's a funny decision to make so soon, especially since he rarely uses it. I'm still Trista or Pixie Stix—which I mind less now than I used to—but he seems to reserve baby for special circumstances. "Well . . . I'm still riding the high of telling her I don't have to live like that and walking out. So, for now, yes." I don't know if I'll be able to say that when reality kicks in, but that's a problem for later.

"That's great, Pix! I'm so proud of you." The warmth in my chest is so big I can't sit still, so I squirm in my seat. "So I can expect you shortly after I get home from work? We can work on the car. Shower . . ."

The mention of a shower gives me goosebumps. His hands in my hair, on my body, and the way his touch changed with his intentions, from gentle and soothing to rough and possessive . . . Showers will never be the same. "Well, when you put it that way . . ."

"Tell me all about it over dinner?"

"What time?" We both know I'm not saying no at this point. I don't care if it *is* all happening too fast; I can't get enough of him. I've missed him since I walked out of his office this morning.

"Six. I'll order. Ever had sushi?"

"No." It's never been high on my list of things to try, but he was right about the Chinese food, so I give it the benefit of the doubt.

"Trust me?" Translation: am I alright with letting him decide for me?

"Always," I say through a tangle of emotion. I'm not sure what I did to deserve someone like Ryan, but I'm so thankful he's mine.

"I'll see you then, Pixie Stix. And don't do anything I wouldn't do."

"That narrows it down," I mutter, smiling when he laughs before ending the call.

Talking with Ryan was exactly what I needed to bolster my confidence, even if there was no pep talk involved. Just hearing his voice makes me feel better about myself because I know he believes in me. I get out of the car, shoulder my purse, and walk into the store with my head held high, ready to expand my wardrobe choices. I've outgrown flowers.

Chapter 30

Trista

First thing Monday morning, I knock on Rachel's door and wait, resisting the urge to fidget with the notes I have tucked under my arm. Or worse, to run away. I need to do this, though.

"Come in," she calls. She looks up from her computer and smiles when I walk in. "Trista! What can I do for you? How's the class going? And the progress photos? I don't need them! I can already see the changes!"

I smile at her enthusiasm, but I'm not happy to be here because she's probably going to pull me from this piece. *My, how things have changed.* "The class is going great, thank you, but there's a problem."

She waves at the chair in front of her desk, inviting me to sit while I explain. "I should've considered this from the start, but I was so overwhelmed at first it never occurred to me. Personally, I feel that I can give a completely unbiased review, but you need to know that Ryan LeDoux, the instructor I'm working with and co-owner of the gym, is a personal friend of mine. And . . ."

She purses her lips. "And?"

"And we're involved now." I bite my lip, trying not to smile because she's my boss, not my best friend, and she's probably going to be pissed about this news and the impact it has on the article.

The slightly pinched scowl becomes a smile. "First, good for you! I don't know him, of course, but I've seen pictures, and . . ."

"And," I agree, unable to stop myself from grinning like a fool.

She giggles. "I'm happy for you. But about the article . . ." Frowning, she taps her nails on her desk. It gets a little harder to breathe with each tap until I'm holding my breath. I don't want to be pulled from this article, but I'll understand if she thinks it's the best move.

Finally, she nods to herself. "I don't think anyone will be able to look at your pictures and complain that your write-up is biased as long as you stick to the facts. Eddie is friends with half the people in the industry. He'd never be able to write a fitness piece again if we benched him every time he would have to work with someone he knows. We'll have him read over it and check for anything that might need to be reworded, though."

A sigh escapes me, and she smiles at my relief. "Thank you. I know I wasn't happy about it at first, but I'm really enjoying this assignment—and not only because of Ryan." *Would we be where we are right now if Rachel hadn't put me on this piece?* I don't want to think about it. "That's definitely a perk, but I feel like a whole new person, and this is just week three."

She smiles again. "I'm so glad! I knew it would be good for you. Let me know if you run into any problems."

"Thanks, Rachel."

I let myself out of her office and return to mine. At my desk, I check my phone for missed messages because Tara mentioned getting everyone together for lunch today, but she was still working on the details. There's a message waiting for me, so I respond, confirming that I'll be there, then put my phone on its cradle, so I don't call Ryan and tell him the good news. I hadn't mentioned it to him yet because I didn't want him to stew on it, so he doesn't even know it was an issue. I can tell him at dinner tonight.

Ryan

"I'm looking for Ryan LeDoux." The no-nonsense voice cuts through the noise on the gym floor. It's familiar, but I can't place it. Either way, whoever is working the front will send them my way or call for help soon, so I might as well go.

"Logan," I call out, motioning for him to come to take over for me, spotting for one of our regulars. He nods and quickly takes over. "Thanks, man," I tell him, clasping his shoulder as I pass him. I hustle to the front, already talking before I step through the double doors. "Someone looking for . . . me?"

That someone stands about four-foot-ten but packs all the menace of an angry mama grizzly bear into her small frame.

I quickly shift gears into customer service mode and flash her a smile. "Miss White," I say, remembering that she never married and seems bitter about it. She might not take kindly to being referred to as a missus. "What can I do for you?"

She plants her fists on her hips. "Where is my daughter?"

She knows. I don't know how because Trista wasn't going to tell her yet, but she figured that shit out fast. I need to be careful here. Trista's relationship with her is damaged enough. I don't want to make things worse. "Uhh, at work?" I ask, choosing to play stupid while I feel her out. It is the correct answer to her question, but I know it's not the one she wants.

Her lips press into a hard, colorless line. "Are you harboring my daughter?"

Mon Dieu, she makes Tris sound like a fugitive. "No?"

She narrows her eyes at me. "So if I show up at your house in the middle of the night, I will not find my daughter there?"

"Now that I can't promise. Trista likes to help me work on my project car. She kind of likes my cat, too."

Her eyes go crazy wide. "Is that some sort of euphemism?"

Years of practice at keeping a straight face serve me well. "No. I adopted a kitten. Her name is Chevy. Trista found her, actually. Wanted to keep her, but . . ." I let that one hang in the air. She knows the rest. "Look, let me simplify this. I know where Trista is staying, but I will not share this information with you. If there's something else you'd like to discuss, my office is this way," I extend my hand in the appropriate direction. "Otherwise, it's been nice talking to you, but I have a job to do. Have a fantastic day, ma'am."

She makes an honest-to-God harrumphing noise and marches in the direction I indicated like the Winter Soldier on his way to murder Captain America. Leslie, the college kid working the front desk, meets my eyes and widens hers slowly until I can see white all the way around her irises as if to say *what the fuck was that.*

I lower my voice so it won't carry to Miss White. "If she's not gone in fifteen, send someone in to rescue me. Hell, send them all in. I might need them."

Still wide-eyed, Leslie gives me a thumbs up. "Good luck, boss."

"Been nice knowin' ya. You're good help." I wink at her and walk away.

I'm really not scared of Miss White. I already know what she sees when she looks at me—a broke-ass, good-for-nothing lowlife who blows his money on tattoos and piercings and probably drugs to boot. What she doesn't know is that I could drop a couple-grand on tattoos every day for the rest of my life and not put a dent in my bank account. It's the car hobby she should worry about. I could maybe bankrupt myself there if I try really hard. I may not live like I have money, but I do.

I catch up to her quickly and escort her to my office. Only after I close the door behind her do I realize my mistake. She'll never know what her daughter and I did against that door, but I sure as hell do, and I'm going to have to talk to her with it as a backdrop.

"Can I get you a water?" I'm not asking to suck up. It's the standard operating procedure for me. Most of the people who end up in my office are either brand reps who have just arrived from a long drive or guys who just came in from sweating their asses off on the floor.

She looks up at me like I just offered her a severed head or something. "No, thank you."

"Alright, then what can I do for you, Miss White?" I take my seat and try my hardest not to look threatening. Most of the time, I don't *try* to; it just happens, or so I'm told. But, this is Trista's mother. Even if they are on the outs right now, I don't see that lasting forever. I don't want things between us to be rocky for whatever time I have with Trista.

She takes a deep breath and smiles at me. It's Trista's smile. *I am so fucked.* "Can I call you Ryan?"

"Uh, sure?" The sudden shift in demeanor sends my brain into a tailspin. It doesn't matter to me what she calls me, but Trista will care later. Maybe.

"Ryan," she smiles again. "Call me Susanne, please. I think maybe we got off on the wrong foot last time we spoke, and even now. I apologize. I'm just very concerned about Trista."

My bullshitometer is going crazy. Something is definitely up. "I saw Trista this morning, Susanne. She's fine."

She brings a hand to her heart and sighs in relief. "That's more than anyone else would tell me. Thank you, Ryan." She smiles again, but I'm not buying it. No one would keep that information from her. For whatever reason, she's lying through her teeth, but I let her go. "Let's not beat around the bush here. It's obvious you care about my daughter. I'm just trying to do what's right for her. Trista is . . . so impressionable. She's always been a follower, wanting to do what all the cool kids were doing. But I'm rambling." She pauses to smile at me again, and it kind of gives me the creeps. At first glance, yeah, it's Trista's smile. But it's not. There's no joy in it. No warmth. "I know about you and my daughter."

It's no more than I expected, so it's not hard to keep my face blank. But does she really know, or is she only guessing, hoping for a reaction? Either way, she looks way too happy for it to be a good thing. "What about us?" I ask, refusing to say anything that might incriminate myself yet.

"I know you're not just friends."

Denying it is only another wedge between me and her and her and Trista, but admitting it doesn't feel like I'm winning right now. I'm not sure there *is* a way to win since I don't know her angle. *Doubt she's here to give me her blessing.* "And?"

"And I want to know what your intentions are."

Oh, God, we're doing this. Does any man *ever* confess to intending to use the daughter for a quick piece and then bail when a better option becomes available? It's fucking ridiculous.

"I intend to make her happy." It's the truth. All of it. I will do my absolute best to make Trista happy every day of her life for as long as she wants to share it with me. But I don't think that's the answer Susanne is looking for.

She rolls her eyes at me. *Now I know where she gets it.* "Trista doesn't know what makes her happy."

I very pointedly arch an eyebrow, the pierced one. "Respectfully, I disagree." She is very good at telling me what makes her happy now, but that's not something I'm going to discuss with anyone.

The friendly smile disappears, and a cold, hard glare replaces it. "Please! You think you know her better than I do? I've spent the better part of thirty years ensuring she doesn't destroy herself by making the same mistakes I made!"

She can attack me all she wants, but my Pixie Stix is off-limits. I let a warning growl slip into my voice because she's doing line jumps with my patience. "That *mistake* gave the world your daughter's beautiful soul."

One of her little hands slams down on my desk so hard it hurts *me,* but she doesn't flinch. "Yes, it did! And I'm not about to let some punk kid who probably can't make ends meet because he spends all of his money on tattoos, booze, and drugs ruin her life!" *Oh, look! I was right!*

Her comment about me ruining Trista's life hits a little too hard and sends me reeling. But I'm not going to let her see it. I'm through playing nice. "Ma'am, I know you look at me and you think you know me, but you don't. Yes, I drink, but rarely to excess. I smoked a little pot in college, but that was nine years ago. Haven't touched it, or any other drugs, since.

"As for my tattoos," I glance at my arms and shrug. "I can afford them. I may not look like your standard trust fund baby, but I am one. Oil money on my mother's side, my father's people own casinos in France. So, you look at me and see someone beneath you, but I laugh because, on paper, I'm exactly the sort of man you keep setting your daughter up with. The only difference is I'm not some desk jockey in what you consider an acceptable, stable profession."

If she's surprised, she hides it well. Her beady-eyed glare doesn't slip a millimeter. *She probably Googled me.* I'm on more than one 'most eligible bachelors' list, but I pretend I don't know that. "Be that as it may, there is more than one way to ruin her life. Will you marry my daughter someday? Give her a family? Or is this all a bit of fun to you?"

I swallow the lump forming in my throat because I can't answer those questions in a way that will make her happy. I don't want children, and I don't believe that marriage should be a foregone conclusion. It's not a milestone in the game of life. Couples can stay together forever without an antiquated ritual that doesn't mean what it used to. I'm not opposed if it's what we both want someday, but it's not my endgame. "That's between Trista and me."

She rolls her eyes again. "If you won't give her the things that are important to her, you're only setting both of you up for heartbreak. Get out now, before she wastes more of her life with someone who doesn't want the same things."

The silence stretches on uncomfortably long. I don't know what to say. Trista doesn't speak wistfully of white dresses or the number of children she wants. But she spent like five minutes feeling Tara's baby kick a few weeks ago. And she was going to marry someone she had no real feelings for. What if her mother is right?

Either way, it's between Trista and me.

Susanne rises, steps aside, and pushes in her chair. With a knowing look and a sad smile, she tells me, "The wild ones like you, they never want to be tied down. Please, think on it. You'll only hurt her in the long run. Do you want her to end up like Selene Miller?"

Oh, fuck. My hands clench into fists until my nails dig into my palms. This bitch *did* look me up, and she dug *deep* to find my connection to Selene. It takes real effort to keep my ass in my chair when I want to leap to my feet and . . . And do nothing because there's nothing I can do. I don't hit women and yelling won't change anything. I squeeze my fists a little tighter, letting the physical pain cut through the hurt in my heart and the anger raging in my head until I can think rationally.

Trista isn't Selene. She is more cautious.

That doesn't mean I can't still ruin her life. Her mom was right there, at least.

One last nod and Susanne is gone, leaving me to wrestle with the demons she awakened in my head.

"Damnit, Ryan," Mom sighs, pinching the bridge of her nose to ward off the migraine she gets every time I displease her.

"But Mom, they were hurting him!" I couldn't sit by and watch my classmates bully that kid for being different. I'm different in a way. My anger, it takes over. I'm just along for the ride. It's the same for that kid, but anger isn't his problem. He has too much joy and doesn't know how to control it.

"That's not a you problem, Ryan. Why can't you be more like your brothers? They don't give me these problems. You're so selfish. Can't you ever think about someone other than yourself? You're just like your father! You live to make my life difficult."

I already knew I was no good for Trista, but I thought everything would be alright if I made her happy enough. What if I *can't* make her happy enough? What if this is just me being selfish again, and I only make her miserable so *I* can be satisfied?

Chapter 31

Trista

My call to Ryan rings through to voicemail—again. I know he's off work. He went in early, so he got off early. He's probably in the shop, lost track of time, and can't hear his phone over the music and the tools.

I make another call and place an order at his favorite Chinese takeout place—the one Matt delivers for—and run out the door. He's obviously distracted. I just need to remind him to give me a little of his time.

***

Noel's apartment is a little farther than Mom's is, so Matt beats me to Ryan's. He waves when I pull up to the curb. "Trista, right?" he calls when I open my door.

"Yep!" I hop out and hurry up the path to him. "Sorry, he's probably in the shop."

Matt frowns and shakes his head. "Nah. I checked there. I'm here enough I know the drill. But he's not here. The Barracuda is gone, shop is locked up, house is dark."

The excitement sustaining me since I hatched this plan evaporates. "Alright. Here, let me get your money, and I'll take that."

"Was he expecting you?"

I freeze in the act of reaching for my wallet to look at him. "No . . . He's not answering his phone. I thought he got wrapped up in the rebuild, but maybe something came up at work."

The look Matt gives me is pure pity. "I thought you'd last longer."

"Wh-what?" I ask around the knot of fear lodged in my throat. I know what he's saying, but . . . no! That's not possible!

"He's never let any of the other girls into the shop; that's why I thought you were family. When he's done with a girl, and she doesn't get the memo, he ghosts."

Tears flood my eyes, and I look down at my wallet before he can see them. I take a deep breath to center myself. There's no reason for me to cry. There's nothing to be afraid of. This is a misunderstanding. "It's not like that, Matt."

"Sure," he says. "Listen, if you don't want the food, it's okay."

"No, I'll take it." I grab enough money to cover the food and a tip from my wallet and trade him for the bag. "He must've got hung up at work. He'll be hungry when he gets home."

"Sure," Matt says again, like he's humoring a delusional idiot. *Maybe he is.* "Thanks, Trista. Hope to see you again."

"I'll see you next time," I tell him, infusing more confidence into the words than I feel right now.

I wave at Matt as he drives off, then climb back in my car and skirt the speed limit all the way to the gym.

His Barracuda is in the employee parking lot, along with Chris's Durango and a small handful of other vehicles. The customer lot is respectably busy, but the hours after work and dinner are the second rush hour—the first being the before-work crowd I usually encounter on my way in and out.

Logan is leaning over one side of the reception desk, and a girl I don't recognize is seated on the other side. They both look up when I walk in, and Logan visibly relaxes. "Oh, thank God. You're here."

"What's wrong?" I ask, my stomach clenching because I'm already conjuring up the scenarios—ones that have nothing to do with what Matt implied. Is Ryan not answering because he's in the hospital somewhere? Why wouldn't they call me?

"He's in a fucking *mood!*" Logan grumbles. "Most of the time, we're joking when we call him the Asshole In Chief, but he's earning it today. Maybe you can calm his ass down. Just get him out of here. He's pissing off the regulars."

"Where is he?" I ask, my heart in my throat. Maybe he needs my time more than I need his?

"Bags," they say together.

"Community or studio?"

Logan shrugs. "Whatever one is closest when he's done prowling."

A deep breath helped before, so I try again. It's *Ryan.* My Ryan. Yeah, he hasn't been mine very long, but he is. I can at least calm him down long enough to get him outside before he does something he regrets.

I walk through the double doors onto the gym floor, and my eyes find him. I could happily watch him square off with his anger all day long, but this isn't the time. I've seen him angry before, but his body isn't right for that today. Instead of facing off against something that can't hurt him—the bag and his anger—he's curled forward, protecting his body. It speaks of pain, and it echoes in my heart. I wish he'd called, but I'm here now.

I approach slowly so I don't startle him. As I draw closer, some guy I don't know grabs my arm to stop me and shakes his head. "You don't wanna go there, sweetheart. Whatever business you have with him can wait."

With a roar, Ryan whirls around on the balls of his feet. I knew he'd hear, but the other guy obviously didn't because he flinches. Ryan's eyes zero in on the guy's hand on my arm. He takes a quick step forward and stops, squeezing his eyes shut like he can block that image out of his mind.

"Ryan?" I speak softly, as if one loud noise is all it will take to make things worse. Can *things get worse?* His pain . . . It breaks my heart. What could hurt him so much?

"Studio," he barks, his chest heaving as he fights to catch his breath. He walks off without another word, leading the way.

"I'll be alright," I tell the guy trying to save me from the big, bad monster who is really as soft and gooey as an underbaked chocolate chip cookie when you get to know him. He would never hurt me. I have nothing to fear.

"Your funeral," he says, letting me go with a shrug. "Just shout. There should be enough of us here to hold him back."

As if Ryan would hurt a woman. I let it drop, though. Ryan needs me.

I follow him into the dark studio and reach for the light. "Leave it," he whispers.

Some of my anxiety melts away. He's already getting a handle on himself. Everything is going to be fine. Since he doesn't want the light on, I leave the door open. It doesn't let in enough light to see him, though.

"What's wrong?" I ask him.

"Everything."

"Well, if one of those things is you being hungry, I brought dinner!" I force some cheer into my voice, hoping to be the sunshine he needs to pull himself out of the darkness of his anger.

"You shouldn't have." His words, though whispered, echo in my ears with a bleakness that threatens to smother me.

"Ryan?" I whisper because my mouth is too dry from fear to speak normally. Not fear of him, but for him and whatever is happening.

"I'm just gonna say it." He pauses and blows out a breath before he continues, his voice as gruff and grim as ever. "This was a mistake. I'm not right for you. It's not you, alright? It's me. Thank you for these last few days. They've been . . . a dream. But I think we need to stop while we can still be friends."

My knees threaten to give, but I somehow manage to stay upright. *"It's not you."* *This isn't happening.* "What?"

"You heard me, Trista. I don't want to be your mistake, and that's all I ever could be. I'm sorry I was a selfish asshole and that I thought I could do this. But I can't. You need to go. I'll see you in class tomorrow." His dismissive tone brooks no argument. His mind is made up.

His words ring in my ears until it's all I can hear. They ping around my brain, leaving a swirl of confusion and hurt in their wake.

In a daze, I stumble backward out the door but stop when another roar from the studio cuts through the chaos in my head. The muffled thump of a strike landing on a heavy bag makes me jump. Into the silence, I swear I hear him whisper, "I'm sorry. I love you." But a flurry of strikes quickly drowns it out, and I'm not sure what I heard. I turn around and run—away from his pain and mine. He warned me. Mom warned me. But I didn't listen.

I collide with something warm and sturdy. "Easy, Tris," Chris murmurs. His arms surround me, and he hugs me tight. "I've got you. Don't listen to him when he's like this, hun. He's not himself. He doesn't know what he's saying. Tomorrow morning, he'll kick his own ass to hell and back for upsetting you. Just give him tonight."

You're wrong. Ryan knew exactly what he was saying. He knew just what to say to hurt me the most.

***

Gabe's lime green Charger turns into the parking lot. He turns our way, driving too fast, and slams on the breaks. The car is still rolling when Tara opens the door. I try to smile my thanks at Chris, knowing this is his doing, but a sob ruins it.

"Tris!" Tara cries, colliding with me in a bear hug that only makes me sob harder. "What happened?"

"Ryan," Chris murmurs.

"That's what you said on the phone, but what?" she asks, petting my hair and pushing it off my face where it's stuck in dried tears.

"He's in a mood. Went the fuck off and told her they're a mistake." Chris keeps his voice low, like he can shield me from the pain if he's quiet enough, but I can't hurt any more than I already do.

Tara gasps. "He did *what?*"

My head is heavy, but I lift it off her shoulder. "Tara, please let's just go." She'll go in there and cause a scene—another one—and it won't help anything.

"Yeah, that. Let's go, sweetie." With her arm around my waist, she leads me to the passenger side of my car.

The bag in the seat brings on a fresh wave of tears. I snatch it up and thrust it toward Chris. "I b-b-brought this for Ryan. Will you give it to him?" Somehow, I just know he'll forget to eat. I don't want that.

Chris sighs, shaking his head, but he takes the bag. "Yeah, I'll make sure he gets it, hun."

"Thank you."

Tara urges me into the car and closes the door. She runs around to the driver's side while I find where I stashed my keys.

"What happened?" she demands, slamming the door behind her.

"I don't know," I say between sniffles. "Everything was great this morning. Can we just not right now?"

"Yeah, but I'm here when you're ready," she says, reaching over to grab my hand.

Ryan

The studio door slams and the lights flick on. "Is she gone?" I ask, knowing Chris is behind me.

Someone must've called him and told him I was nuclear after Trista's mom left because it's supposed to be his day off. But he showed up to clean up my mess. It's the only thing that kept me from chasing Trista down and taking it all back—knowing he was out there for her.

"Yes, you motherfucking asshole!" he shouts. I'm not sure if he's shouting at me for himself or for the benefit of the members on the floor I've pissed the fuck off. They need to know I'm getting my ass put in my place if Trista leaving didn't do that for them. "How *could* you? To *Trista* of all people? You're fucking *crazy* about her, you dumbass! If you needed to take it out on someone, why not me? I'm used to your fucking shit! I know you don't mean what you say when you're pissed about something."

I cringe at his liberal—for him—use of expletives. It's something he avoids since Keaton learned to talk. For him to be throwing them around like confetti now, he's probably ready to go a few rounds. *And I deserve it.* My head falls forward, resting against the bag while I work to get my shit under control so I can walk out of here and drive home later. "Because I meant it, man. I'm no good for her. I'd rather we both accept that now than a year from now when we can't stand the sight of each other."

Chris's booming laughter echoes in the small space. "Oh, and you think she's going to want to see you again now?"

My hands shake, but I ignore the urge to swing. I need to calm down. My anger has never been *this* out of control—and it's all directed at myself. I'll be wrestling with it for years to come. "It'll take her a few days, but she'll bounce. It's what she does." *Now.* She'll show up tomorrow. She's too committed not to—and I'm so fucking proud of her for that. At least in that way, I can make her life better. It's going to hurt, but I deserve that.

Chris sighs. I don't have to turn around to know he's shaking his head at me—likely thinking I'm an optimistic bastard for believing that. "She brought you dinner. I almost kept it because you don't fucking deserve it after what you did, but it's in the fridge."

"Keep it." I *don't* deserve a single kindness from her. And I don't want it. It'll only hurt, and I can't take anymore today. I've never wanted anything as much as I want her. I tried hard to put the things her mother said out of my mind, but they dug in and wouldn't go away because there's some truth to them. Even if Trista *doesn't* want those things I can't give her, I'm still no good for her. I've always known it; I just seemed like the lesser of two evils at the time.

He scoffs. "Nope. I've instructed everyone not to even fucking look at it. She was fucking bawling because of you, but she still cared enough to make sure you eat tonight."

"Tell me you called her a ride?" She shouldn't drive if she's crying. She might cause an accident. *She didn't even cry when she left her Mom's.*

I wouldn't cry over getting away from that manipulative bitch *either.* It's like she read my mind. She knew just what to say to me to get the outcome she wanted. And I let it work because, deep down, I know she's right. Maybe not about what Trista wants, but about me fucking up her life.

"Tara and Gabe."

"Thank you." It won't stop me from worrying, but at least I know she'll get home safe.

"I didn't do it for you, you fucking prick."

For some reason, his response makes me smile. Which only makes me angrier. How can I smile right now? She's out there hurting because of me. I did the one thing I never wanted to do because I'm a pathetic, selfish, piss-poor excuse for a human being. "I know."

Footsteps on the floor warn me before Chris grabs my shoulder and tries to pull me around to face him. "Will you fucking *look* at me?"

I shake my head. I don't want anyone who actually cares about me to see me right now. It's why I told Trista to leave the lights off. She wouldn't have left. One look would've told her that, as much as I meant the words coming out of my mouth, I didn't want to say them. I didn't want to lose her.

"Lydia," Chris snaps.

I cringe. That one word says it all. He was a wreck after Lydia told him she was scheduling an abortion and told him he had to choose—the child or her. *In the end, I guess I'm not so different.* At least I didn't get Trista pregnant first.

It would almost be easier if I had. I might be scared as fuck, but none of this would've happened because I wouldn't leave her and our child. *Then you would've destroyed them both.*

Chris squeezes my shoulder. "I told you then that I'd repay you for all of it someday."

I shake my head without raising it from the bag. "Today's not that day, friend. I'm fine. Great. Never better." Even I can hear the bitterness of the lies in my voice.

His hand withdraws, and he shoves me between the shoulder blades. "Like hell you are. Your friends might be idiots—myself included—but we're not blind, Ryan. Just because we never said anything doesn't mean we don't all know. You love that woman and you just fucking *shredded* her."

Did everyone *know? Everyone but her?* I shove the bag aside and stomp my way to the chairs at the back of the room. I sit down and lean forward to hide my face in my hands like the coward I am. "If you love something, let it go."

Chris follows me. "Stop being stubborn!" he says, kicking my shoe hard enough to slide my foot to the side, knocking me off balance. He follows that with a swat to the same wrist, shoving my hand away from my face so he can see me. "You think she's going to come back to you after *that* without some heavy ass-kissing on your part?"

Sitting back in my chair, I work to stretch my shoulders in hopes of easing the ache there. I deserve to hurt, but the pain in my chest isn't going to go away with a little stretching. "Nope. Best if she doesn't. I'll ruin her life."

He crosses his arms. "You can't know that. But you just ruined yours."

Actually, I can. I ruined Mom's life—she told me so the day I told her I wasn't going to college for the MBA she wanted me to get. I ruined my sisters' lives—they told me so when I couldn't control my temper. And I ruined Selene's life, and she died. It's what I do best. It's also why I do this for a living—like the small, positive impact I have on the lives of our members can somehow balance out the bad things I do. "I'll live."

He scoffs at me and shakes his head. "I'll remind you of that in the morning. Get your ass out of here. Fern and Mase have Keaton. I'll stay."

Nodding, I stand and accept the hug he gives me without complaint. I'm almost out of the room when he calls after me. "But Ryan?"

I grunt to let him know I'm listening.

"Someday very soon, we need to have a talk about this picture you have of yourself in your head."

"What about it?" I ask, looking at him over my shoulder. He hasn't moved.

"It's wrong."

"Or you are," I mutter to myself.

Chapter 32

Ryan

The burgundy SUV parked in front of my house makes me groan. I consider driving on by, but the longer I put this off, the worse it'll be. Class aside, I've managed to dodge the ladies for two days now.

The first day was bad. Tris nearly burst into tears when she walked into the room, Tara would hardly speak to me, and the entire class was pissed at me by the end of the hour because I was such a dick.

The guys know something still isn't right, but they don't want to pull the pin on that grenade. It's a small miracle the ladies don't do more than shoot me the occasional glare. A few more days and things will be normal again. This conversation? It's inevitable, but *fuck*. I'm hurting enough today. Trista actually smiled in class this morning—at Logan.

I park my car in the drive and climb out, giving the little blonde on my front steps a tired smile. "What are you doing here, T-Bird?" I ask as if I don't already know.

"Don't play stupid with me, Ryan *Bartholomew* LeDoux," she snarls at me.

I hold my hands up in surrender. "Hey now. I know you're practicing for motherhood but don't three-name me. You know I *hate* my middle name."

She scowls at me. "Then don't be an ass and make me!"

"Fair enough." I close my car door and make my way to the steps to take my ass-chewing like a man. I stop at her feet and spread my arms out wide.

"What are you doing?" she asks, eyeing me up and down like I asked her to critique my outfit or something.

"One free shot—above the belt." I'd do the same for Trista's father or brother, but she has neither. She has Tara, so it's only fair to make her the same offer. *I'm just lucky it's not Fern sitting here.*

Tara's cute little nose wrinkles in disgust, and she shakes her head. "Eww, no!"

"Suit yourself," I tell her with a shrug. I motion for her to move and she scoots to the side, making room for me to collapse on the top step next to her. "Before you rip my ass, how is she?" I have no right to ask, but not knowing is eating me alive. Trista is too good at pretending everything is fine for me to gauge her accurately in class.

The fight bleeds out of Tara's face, giving way to a bottomless well of sadness. "Remarkably better than I expected, but not okay. Mostly, she acts like it never happened. She won't talk about it, and if I try, she changes the subject. She will *be* okay, but she's not there yet."

Better than I hoped for. It doesn't make me hate myself any less, though. "Get it over with, Tara."

She leans over, resting her head on my shoulder. "Just tell me why."

"Could you be more specific?" I ask to buy myself some time to come up with an explanation that doesn't require me to explain Selene.

She sits up and levels me with a look that says it all, but ruins it with a jump and a silly grin. "She's kicking," she tells me, holding out her hand for mine. I'm not in the mood for it, but I humor her and let her place my hand on her belly to feel the little flutters against my palm. Yeah, it's amazing, and I can't wait to meet the little person growing in there, but it only reminds me of the things Susanne said.

"I can't give her this, Tara," I whisper, withdrawing my hand. It's only a small part of the reason, but it works. The confession damn near turns me inside out, starting with my chest. The pain . . . it doesn't go away. *How can something so small have the power to bring me to my knees?*

"*Can't,* or *won't?*" she asks.

"Does it matter?"

She nods and holds out both hands as if weighing options. "Yes. *Can't* implies you lack the ability and you're selling yourself short by assuming that Trista would care about you any less. There are other avenues if it's something you both want. *Won't* is different. Won't means you have a choice in the matter and decided it's something you don't want—and there's nothing wrong with that—but you should still have an adult discussion with her before you assume that's a deal breaker for her."

"*Won't,*" I say, emphasizing it like she did. "I'm the last person who should raise children, Tara."

She shrugs one shoulder. "I beg to differ," she says, watching my neighbor reverse out of his drive. He sees us and waves, so we wave back. "You're great with Keaton and Ronni and Mason's nieces when they're around."

I love all those little shits. They're so fun. But . . . "Yeah, but that's different. I get to return them to their parents. That doesn't work when I *am* the parent."

When I'm the parent, they're stuck with me through good days and bad. They'll end up scared of me because of my anger or fucked up like I am because I don't know how to parent.

She sighs and shakes her head at me. "I'm not going to sit here and try to convince you that you should have children, Ryan. I'm just pointing out the flaw in your logic. You'd be a good dad; I know it. I have enough faith in you for both of us. While I support you in whatever decision you make, I want to know . . . did you ever ask Trista what she wants, or did you suddenly realize she might want something different than you and panic?"

The anger rises again. I clench my fists and take a deep breath, but it's like trying to extinguish a wildfire with a garden hose. "It doesn't matter. I knew this was temporary, but her mom said—"

"What?" she cries, shooting to her feet to pace back and forth in the little, fenced-in patch of grass that passes as my front yard. "When did you talk to her mother?"

"Monday." *The worst fucking day of my life.*

"Why did you talk to her mother?" Her voice gets a little higher with every question. If she doesn't knock it off, she's going to break windows.

It's not like I went looking for her. I rest my arms on my knees, letting my hands dangle between them because if I clench my fists any longer, I'm going to find something to hit. "She came to the gym wanting to know where Trista was. Before she left, she said some shit that hit a little too hard. I've always known I wasn't good enough for Trista, that I was bad for her. It's why I never tried. Her mom just reminded me how badly I can fuck up her life."

Quick as a striking snake, Tara draws back and socks me in the arm. The power behind the punch shouldn't be surprising, considering she grew up with four brothers—one of whom is a respected MMA fighter. The surprise is that she did it at all.

"What was that for?" I ask, rubbing my arm. It's a stupid question, but my brain is still glitched out from seeing Tara, who hates violence, hit me. I'm kind of proud of her . . .

"You *dumbass!* You listened to her *mother?"* she shouts, causing the guy who walks his dog around this time every evening to stop and stare.

"She made a lot of sense," I mutter. Though, after Tara's lecture about *can't* and *won't* and how Trista might not care, most of the things her mother said don't seem as relevant. Still, it is what it is.

Tara throws her hands into the air and sets off pacing again, following the picket fence this time instead of walking back and forth. "She *always* makes a lot of sense. It's a talent of hers. She makes you think that Trista is some flighty little woman-child who will walk out into traffic if not constantly monitored and sells you this poor-me story about how she sacrificed her life to make sure her daughter has a better future, and only she knows what Trista really wants! But when you think back on it later, things don't make sense.

"Trista *has* a good life. She's a little gullible at times and way too passive, but she has a good head on her shoulders. Trista knows what she wants, but she's lived with someone who manipulated her into believing otherwise her entire life. Trista's *mother* wants her to do all these stupid things—like have kids—because that's what *her mother* thinks she needs to have a better life than she did. But what does Trista want?"

That question cuts through the bullshit the voice in my head is whispering. The voice that sounds a lot like my mom. That I'm not good enough. That I'm selfish. That I'm going to ruin Trista's life. That I'm just like my dad, and Trista will grow to hate me.

Says who?

I knew I shouldn't listen to Susanne that day, but Tara is right. The woman is a talented manipulator. I don't know how she knew just what to say to play on my fears, but I was her fucking fiddle. Especially once she mentioned Selene.

My pulse thrums in my ears, blocking out the rest of Tara's tirade. It's hard to question shit you've had pounded into your head your whole life. After you hear it so many times, you just accept it as a truth. But what if it's not?

Maybe I'm not good enough for Trista, but that just means I have to work hard every day to be worthy in her eyes.

She is the one thing I want more than my next breath, but I kept my distance for five fucking years—until I thought she might want me too. How does that make me selfish?

I might be a little like my dad, but if Mom hadn't been so horrible to him all the time, maybe he would've spent more time at home?

And . . . maybe Tris was right, and I'm too hard on myself about Selene. I didn't make her decisions for her.

But I did make this decision for Trista because I assumed I knew best. Because *I* was afraid of hurting her and of getting hurt. We're both hurting now because of me. If Trista can find the courage to face her fears, then so the fuck can I. I'm on my feet so fast it's a wonder my head doesn't spin. "Where is she?"

Tara stops her restless walking to look at me. "She's living at Noel's, but she was having dinner with her mom tonight. Susanne convinced her to try and patch things up. She'll probably have her talked into moving back home before it's all said and done."

"Over my dead body." *This* is her home—here with Chevy and me. If she's moving anywhere other than Noel's old place, it will be here. If she wants, that is. She's worked too fucking hard to get away to go back now.

She smiles, and it lights her whole face, chasing away the sadness and worry. "There you are. Go get her."

"How?" I whisper, a new fear worming its way into my brain. What if she can't forgive me? "You weren't there, Tara. The things I said . . ."

She storms over to shove me toward my car. "The *truth* Ryan. The one you should've told her years ago! Get your ass in that car or I will call Colton to come kick it!"

The truth. The fist around my heart loosens its grip. The truth is that I love her. It might not be enough now, but if it's not, nothing is.

Trista

I let myself in the front door of the only home I've ever known and kick off the cute little sandals that go with the dress I wore because I don't need a lecture today. The dress is at least something I don't hate.

I find Mom in the kitchen at the sink, washing the pots and pans from cooking. "Hey, Mom."

She doesn't even look up. "So he left you too, hmm? I'm sorry. I know it hurts."

How does she know that? I haven't told her. I didn't even tell her I was seeing anyone. She's not above calling my friends, though. She probably tricked it out of Tara.

"I'm alright, Mom," I tell her, taking up the dish towel to dry while she washes. Yeah, it hurts, but I was happier in the weekend I had him than I've been my entire life. I have the memory to get me through whatever comes next. I wanted to crawl into a hole and die when he sent me away, but I realized something I already knew. I don't *need* him to be happy.

And he wasn't a mistake. Mistakes imply regret, and I have none—other than that it ended. I will survive this and, somehow, we will still be friends. Eventually.

But oh, it hurts. It all happened so fast, but I really thought we had something good. We had a foundation of friendship to build on, after all. It's not like we met at a bar and fell in . . . I can't even think the word without the memory of what I thought I heard flashing through my mind. *"I'm sorry. I love you."*

"You'll be wanting your room back then," she says, handing me a pan to dry.

The statement is no surprise to me. The shocker is that she didn't open with it if she already knows. And I already know she'll be mad about my answer, but I'm too excited to care. "Actually, no. I'll be by this weekend to get my things. Tara, Gabe, Fern, and Mason are going to help me pack."

"No."

I stop drying to look at her, but she continues to scrub. "Excuse me?"

"I said no. If you want your things, you can live here. This is ridiculous, Trista. This is your home, and it's time for you to get over your little temper tantrum."

The oven timer saves me from answering with the first thing that comes to mind, which is a resounding *fuck you.* Mom leaves the sink to turn it off and get the food out, giving me time to think of a more diplomatic answer.

She's my *mother.* I only get one, and I don't want to lose her. But those are *my* things. I paid for most of them—it was the only thing that gave me a sense of independence. I will take them with me. I've already looked into what I can do if she tries to stop me.

"I'm sorry you feel that way, Mom, but there's nothing you can do to stop me, and you've given me no reason to want to stay. I *will* be by this weekend to pack the rest of my belongings, and I *will* call the cops if you try to stop me."

She looks up to glare at me as she closes the oven door. "How many times does life have to kick you in the teeth before you give up?"

Does she expect me to crumble? I stand up a little straighter. Hold my head a little higher. I did get kicked again, and I'm still standing, ready to try again. "That's the difference between you and me, Mom. You quit trying after the first time. I learned from my mistakes and tried again."

Anger flares in her eyes, but the doorbell rings before she can unleash it on me. "We will continue this discussion in a moment," she snaps before she rushes out of the room to get the door.

Oh, joy. I grab the dishrag and a dirty cutting board to have something to distract myself while I wait.

"Oh, it's you," Mom's voice is heavily muffled by the door and the distance between us, but I hear every word. Whoever it is, she's definitely not happy to see them. "You did the right thing."

Curious, I creep to the window to see who is here. The car in the driveway is one I'd know anywhere. *Ryan.* I can't hear what he says, but the low rumble of his voice is angry.

"No, you can't see her. She's going to be fine. Just leave her be. Grant will take care of her. You can be happy knowing you did the best thing for her. Thank you for seeing reason."

What is she talking about? When would Ryan and Mom have talked? And what does it have to do with me? Or Grant? I haven't talked to him since the day I told him it wasn't going to work, and I haven't changed my mind. Ryan was right; I should hold out for the happiness I want.

Ryan's reply is sharp but still not loud enough for me to make it out.

"I don't care what you want. She doesn't want to see you."

Yes, I do. If nothing else, I want a chance to talk to him now that he's rational again. He's still my friend, after all. I run out of the kitchen, down the hall to the front door. "Ryan?"

Mom tries to step back inside and close the door behind her, but he grabs the door and holds it open. "Tris! I'm sorry!"

"Get off my property before I call the cops!" Mom screams.

"Call them," he tells her, but his eyes never leave me. "I don't care. I'll spend the night in a cell. Pix, just hear me out. Please."

All the harsh things he said that day fade away. Whatever he has to say, it's important. He wouldn't have come otherwise because he'll see me in the morning. "Mom, stop it!" I cry, interrupting her tirade.

"You will not speak to me that way!" she yells.

She might be my mother, but respect goes both ways, and I'm not feeling it. "You can stop this, or I will walk out that door, and you'll never see me again."

"Don't try to bluff me, young lady!" she yells, standing up straight and trying to look a lot bigger than she is. It used to scare me, but it doesn't anymore.

"Try me."

Mom hesitates, but her hand falls away from the door. Ryan pushes it all the way open and leaves a hand on it, holding it there, but doesn't come inside. "What did you mean by 'thank you for seeing reason?'" I ask her.

"She came by the gym on Monday," Ryan answers. "She was looking for you, but while she was there, she told me she knew about us and convinced me that I'd never make you happy and I'll just ruin your life."

My eyes sting, warning me that I'm on the verge of tears. *Since he was already worried about that, I'm sure it wasn't hard.* "But?" I ask him because there obviously is one, but I glare at Mom. How *dare* she go behind my back to meddle in my life like that! All because I wasn't following her plan?

"But nothing! It's the truth!" Mom snaps. "He'll never marry you! He'll never give you children! All he'll do is get you high and leave you to die somewhere!"

Why would she think that?

Ryan stares my mother into silence. "Can we do this elsewhere, Tris?"

Mom steps between us. It's kind of cute that she thinks she could stop me. He could pick me up and lift me over her head without breaking a sweat if I wanted him to. "You're not going to take my daughter away and manipulate her into accepting less than she wants!"

"Mom, shut up. Ryan, give me the short version?" I don't want to get my hopes up, or his, if these difference are something we can't work through. But I've lived my whole life letting someone else decide what I do and don't want, and that's over. I will hear him out if what he says now seems reasonable enough and make up my own mind.

He shifts his weight from one foot to the other and back again, rocking uncomfortably under Mom's glare, but his eyes are on me. "I'm not sure there is a short version, and we've already discussed most of it once," he says softly. "And I'm happy to do it again elsewhere. But since she brought it up . . . The things she said just made it feel like every second you spend with me is wasted because I don't believe marriage should be the goal in a relationship. If it happens, great. If not, that's great too. Skipping that step doesn't make the relationship any less valid. And I've never wanted children. I'm terrified of being like my parents. Or yours," he says, throwing another glare at my mother. "I know I should've asked before making assumptions, but it was too easy to believe her."

Oh, Ryan . . . If only he'd called me after she left. Even a text would've done the trick. But I get it. She's good at picking at someone's vulnerabilities, such as my fear of making another mistake like Tyler. He wasn't ready for her to hit him where it hurt.

I hold up my hand to stop Mom before she can start her squawking again. She's done enough damage. I can hardly stand to look at her right now. This conversation would probably be over already without her here to complicate things. No, we wouldn't even be having this conversation if not for her and her need to control my life.

But I don't want Ryan to think I'm upset with him for falling victim to her tricks, so I take a deep breath and ask, "So that's why?"

As questions go, it's not much. But he nods. "That's part of why. I'm sorry, Trista. I know I can't unsay those things, but I take it all back. It was my fear talking."

I breathe freely for the first time in days. There was only one mistake, and it wasn't us. "Let me get my purse." Just because he has different ideas about marriage doesn't mean he takes relationships lightly, and I've never said anything about wanting children. That's Mom's dream for me.

Without a word, Mom puts herself between me and the door to the rest of the house like I won't walk out without my purse.

I swear she thinks I'm five. I mentally count to ten and gather my patience so I don't yell at her. This situation is bad enough. "Mom, you can move so I can get my purse and we can talk about that later, or I can walk out that door, and I'll be back tomorrow to get my things with a nice officer in tow since I'm sure you'll try to withhold them. I'm a grown woman. You have to let me go someday."

"You'll always be my baby," Mom protests.

"Yes, but you can't treat me like one! This doesn't have to be an either-or situation! I'm twenty-seven, Mom. You got me this far. I'll take it from here, alright? You don't have to worry about me anymore. Yeah, I might fall on my ass from time to time, but *you* don't have to pick me up. I have good friends. I have Ryan. I'll always have you. But it's time for you to worry about *you* for a while. Take a vacation. Go on a date. Take up painting again. Do the things *you* want to do."

"But I don't know who I am without you," she whispers.

I choose to believe she genuinely means that and isn't saying it to manipulate me into staying. "You're whoever you want to be. Just like I am. The choice is yours, but either way, I'm leaving right now."

A small sob rocks her as tears well in her eyes, but she steps aside. I want to grab her and hug her for not forcing me to choose. It's not that I'm shying away from a decision, but because I don't want to lose her. But I need to get my bag before she changes her mind.

Tears cloud my sight, but I rush by her and grab my purse. On my way back by, I kiss her tear-streaked cheek. "I love you. Everything is going to be fine. I'll talk to you tomorrow."

Sniffling, she nods and turns to shuffle back into the house.

The door closes behind her, and I turn to Ryan. He's watching with that fire burning in his eyes again. "Pixie Stix, I'm sorry."

"Stop that. You've said it once. Do you think that I don't know how my mom can twist your thoughts up like a pretzel until everything she says seems like the only option?" Even knowing she does it, it's hard to break away from. Especially when she's right a lot of the time. But she was wrong this time.

He shakes his head. "Just, hear me out, please? I know we're leaving here separately and I don't want to walk away from you until I say this." On my nod, he takes my hand and leads me away from the house and prying ears.

"Can I?" he asks, holding out his arms. I answer by stepping into him, and he wraps me up in my favorite place to be. "Tara was waiting for me when I got home. She . . . I . . . I couldn't tell her the real reason I lost my shit. All she knows is your mom came by the gym and fucked with my head. But she brought up Selene."

I suck in a breath. How the hell does she know about Selene? "I swear I didn't—"

He squeezes me and cuts me off. "I know, baby. She probably looked me up or something. It would take some digging, but it's out there."

I sag into him, but it still bothers me that Mom would stoop to that. We can talk about it later, though. "I'm sorry, Ry."

He takes a deep breath and lets it out slowly. "I'm not, actually. I did some soul searching while Tara was ripping me a new one for listening to your mother. And I'm not scared anymore."

"Scared?"

"Of hurting you, or of ruining your life, assuming you really are okay with—"

I reach up and stop him with a finger against his lips. "We can talk about that more later. Get on with the part about you not being afraid." It's the part that's most important right now.

He raises one shoulder. "I'm just not. I realized a lot of things before I got in my car to come over here, and we can talk about them all when we get wherever we're going. I just wanted to make sure you know that I'm sorry, I'm not scared anymore, and I'll do better."

"Alright," I agree, nodding slowly. "I'm hungry. We never got to dinner. How about you order something, and we go back to your place and eat and work on the car while we figure this out?"

His smile is brighter than the sun sinking toward the horizon behind him. "Have I told you how amazing you are lately?"

"Only a time or two." I lower my voice in case Mom is listening. "But I liked it best when you showed me."

Ryan's eyes flutter closed, and he groans. "Careful, or I'll take you to my car and show you now."

I grin, enjoying how I get to him with such simple words. It's only fair since it only takes him a look to make me burn for him. "I need a shower first."

He groans again. "We'll add that to the agenda."

Chapter 33

Trista

Dinner is Thai. It's a little thing, but I think we both enjoy this arrangement. He's sharing things he likes with me, and I'm trying something new. Like the first time we did this, he plates the food and gets drinks, but I get Chevy's dinner ready. It's difficult for me, though. I can't get the trick of opening the can one-handed, and I don't want her to treat my dress like a tree.

Ryan watches me take my first bite, and smiles when my eyes widen in delight. I chew quickly and swallow so I can say, "This is amazing."

"I'm glad you like it." He clears his throat and does that thing where he shifts around in his chair. "So . . ."

"So."

"Where do we start?"

"How about I go first?" I know there are still things he wants to say, but I want to clear a few things up first. He cringes, but nods. "I don't have strong feelings either way about children."

He inhales sharply and chokes on a piece of food. I'm on my feet before I'm conscious of making the decision to stand. What I'm going to do to help is a mystery to me, but he waves me off. "I'm okay," he says between coughs, his voice tight. He takes a drink, then asks, "You really don't care about kids?"

Fingers drumming against my thigh, I sit down and try to put my feelings into words. "I wouldn't say I don't care. I do like kids. But I never saw myself as a mother. It was something I was told would happen, like going to college, getting a job, getting married. It's just a rung on the ladder of life. My opinion didn't matter, so I never really formed one, I guess."

I hate how many things I can say that about, but I'm well on my way to remedying that problem with the help of Ryan and my friends.

"Alright," he says, accepting my explanation with a nod. "But . . . married?"

"I want to hear your side of it." I scoop up some of the noodles on my plate and pop the bite into my mouth.

He shrugs and clears his throat again. "Well, I mean, to me, marriage should be this special thing, but everyone treats it like a rung on the ladder of life," he says, borrowing my phrase with a nod. "It's the endgame of every relationship, and no one seems to know what the hell they're supposed to do after they get there. It's just the thing they do because it comes next, not because it means something to them. Then, those marriages fall apart. They either stay together and make each other miserable, or they split; either way, the marriage meant nothing. And I don't want that. I'm perfectly content to dedicate my life to one person, with or without marriage. A relationship doesn't need that commercialized bullshit to thrive."

That does make sense. I nod to let him know I hear him and eat a few more bites while I think it over. He didn't seem to mind weddings when he was in Fern and Mason's, but I suppose they're not one of the couples he was referring to. Their wedding wasn't just a milestone for them; it was important.

What is marriage, after all? A piece of paper that says that two people promise to love each other forever. And, Ryan is right; a lot of those end in divorce. That promise meant nothing. So why do I need it? We could promise each other right here and now that we'll always be together and it can be just as binding. And, maybe, years from now, if that sticks, we'll get married. But we'll make that decision together.

"Trista! You're killin' me over here!"

His outburst startles me out of my rabbit hole. "Sorry," I giggle, but the anxiety written all over his face sobers me. "I was thinking about it."

"And?" He leans his arms on the table and hunches over like he's preparing for a blow.

I shrug. "And I kind of see your point."

"*And?*" he repeats, making a 'get on with it' motion with the hand holding his fork.

I shrug again. "And I can live with that."

The weight of his stare makes me antsy. I grab my napkin and begin to wipe up imaginary messes, but he reaches across the table to stop me with a hand on mine. "So, you're okay with maybe never getting married?"

I freeze as the reality of what he's asking hits me. For as long as I can remember, I was told I'd get married someday. Not asked, told. It wasn't a decision I made for myself. This is.

I get choices! I made a choice about children, too. I'm on a roll!

But this one is easy because I already chose.

I'm okay with whatever the future brings, as long as Ryan is beside me for it. "Well, the way I figure it, if we're happy together, it's the likely outcome anyway, so why worry about it?"

He blows out a sigh and sits back in his chair. "I'm sorry I didn't talk to you after she left. You have no idea how sorry . . . Those things I said, I thought I was going to die, baby."

"I know how she is," I whisper. Maybe I'm an idiot, but I blame Mom more than him. Yeah, he made the decision, but if she hadn't meddled . . .

"I'm not scared anymore," he says again. "I'm not afraid of ruining your life. I'm willing to admit that I can't blame myself for what happened with Selene. And being like my dad isn't such a bad thing. If Mom wasn't so hard to live with, he would've been around more."

I reach across the table and take his hand. I'd love to do more, but I'm not sure if he's ready for it yet. "I'm sorry it took this for you to come to those conclusions."

"Me, too," he says with a little nod. "But I realized that if you can face your fears, I can too. That is, if I still get to call you mine."

It's impossible not to smile. I am absolutely his. I think I have been since the day we met; it just took us all this time to figure it out. "Yes, but . . ." Before this goes anywhere else, some things need to be said, and agreements need to be made. There's no time like the present.

Both eyebrows climb his forehead. "But?"

I smile, hoping to convey that it's nothing bad. "I need some promises."

He nods. "Hit me."

I point my fork at him. "First, you never again make decisions for us out of fear. Us decisions are made by us."

Ryan winces. "Deal," he agrees quickly.

"Second," I say slowly, giving myself more time to think. "There will always be another project car, and you will teach me to fix them with you." I don't want him to give up something he loves because it might interfere with us.

He laughs so loud, Chevy spazzes out and runs out of the room, her little claws scratching for purchase on the worn linoleum. "Deal."

The next one is easy. I smile as I say it. "Third, we do this once a week."

"This?" he asks.

"Dinner right here, and talking about problems if there are any. Neither of us really had great relationship role models growing up, but I'm kind of looking at it as a job. If we make a point to talk about little issues before they're big problems, everything works smoothly."

He grins, but holds up a finger. "Deal, if I get to pick dinner."

"Deal." It's an easy promise to make. I adore how excited he gets about sharing things he loves with me. As unconventional as it is, I love everything about this relationship with him.

"Anything else?" He laces his fingers behind his head and watches me while I think it over.

"Yes." A blush creeps across my cheeks because it feels wrong to include it like it's essential, but it kind of is. "Forth, you have to show me how amazing I am, like, a lot." I can't count the number of articles I've edited that revolve around improving a relationship by improving your sex life. If people write about it *that* much—and I understand why now—it must be a big thing.

He gives me a grin that sets my blood on fire. "Define 'a lot.'"

"I dunno . . ." Just thinking about it makes me squirm. Or maybe it's that look he's giving me. *Or both. Both is good.* I'm not exactly well versed in how often most couples have sex. I don't want to aim too low and offend him, or too high and . . . wear him out? *Is that a thing?* The articles all talk about doing it *more*. They don't touch on that.

His grin spreads into a hungry smile that sends a rush of molten lava straight to my core. "How about you let me be the judge of that, and if I'm not meeting your expectations, you can let me know like you did in my office Saturday?"

"Deal." That seems reasonable enough—assuming he doesn't get frustrated if I remind him too often.

"Deal, then." He leans forward, crossing his arms on the table. His eyes are so intense, it's hard to look into them. "Now, I have some conditions."

I swallow hard, but it's only fair. "Fire away."

"Your clothes—"

"What about them?" I ask, already getting angry with this condition. I didn't make any demands that would change him, not really. Why is he trying to change me?

He arches an eyebrow at my impatience. "Replace everything you don't like."

I frown. "Well, I'm working on that, but, I mean, I have bills now so . . ."

I trail off because he leans forward and grabs his wallet from his pocket. He thumbs out a credit card and slaps it down on the table between us. "Not an issue."

"Ry—"

"Not. An. Issue. I told your mother that I intended to spend the rest of my life making you happy. I'm don't care what you keep and what you replace, or what you buy, but no more *anything* that doesn't make you happy. Deal?"

He's missing the point! It's not about the clothes. All the pink, flowery stuff will go to the nearest donation bin eventually. It's the funding. "I can't spend your money!"

"Fine!" He rolls his eyes. "I'll write you a check. Then, it's your money."

"Ryan! Be reasonable!"

"Trista! I am," he says, grinning across the table at me. "Do you think Noel would tell Colton no? Or Fern would argue with Mason?"

"Yes," I say to the last one. Fern will argue with Mason just to argue until he finds a way to make his request more reasonable.

His grin becomes a real smile. "Bad example. But Noel would be all over that, and you know it."

"She'd say it's her prerogative to be spoiled," I agree. She's kind of a diva like that.

"Trista." I look over into brown eyes that glow with a fire so intense, it's amazing I'm not sweating. "I just want to spoil you too."

My mouth goes dry. I don't know how to argue with that. I don't expect him to spoil me, but he knows that. "Well, when you put it like that . . ." I leave the credit card where it is, though. "Next?"

"The Camaro is yours when it's done."

"Ryan! No!" I looked up pictures of what it's supposed to look like. It'll be beautiful, and I adore it, but I can't just *take* it. He's put so much time and money into it!

"Yes. Your car is a piece of shit anyway. I cringe every time I see you get in the damn thing. And this way, I can sort of keep it without feeling greedy."

"I'll buy it from you," I say, making what I view as an acceptable counter offer. It might take me the rest of my life, but I'll feel better about it if I pay him.

"Hmm . . ." He scratches at the stubble on his cheek. "You pay for the next project," he counters.

That's probably as close as I'm going to get to anything reasonable from him. The man just gave me a credit card and told me to go shopping. He has a different idea of reasonable when it comes to money. "Deal. What else?"

He uses his fork to toy with the food on his plate, his eyes tracking every movement like he might discover something important there. "Whenever you're ready, this is your home."

"What?" I swear the world freezes around us. Living together isn't anything that crossed my mind. It would be *nice,* but this is his home. His space. And we haven't been together that long. He can't really mean that the way it sounded.

"You heard me," he rumbles, going all authoritative and sexy on me.

"Ryan, I—"

He holds up his hand, asking me to stop, so I do. He reaches across the table and laces his fingers through mine. "I get that you need to stand on your own for a little while. I applaud that. I'm so. Fucking. *Proud* of you, baby. But when you're ready, I'm right there to help you pack your shit. Today, tomorrow, next year, whenever."

"Ryan," I say, melting even though he's the freaking marshmallow here. "There's no need to rush."

"I know." One shoulder hitches up a fraction of an inch and drops. "That's why I'm leaving it up to you. I've been in love with you for damn near five years now. I'm not rushing, Tris."

"I—You—what?" *Am I hearing things again?* I have to be. I'm hallucinating because I *want* it to be true. I want to know I'm not the only one.

He leans over the table to kiss the back of my hand. "I love you."

I stare at him, waiting for him to laugh or *something.* I know he said he's liked me for a while, but how do you love someone for that long and never tell them? *"I'm sorry. I love you."*

He smiles and settles back into his seat, but he keeps my hand. "It's okay, baby. I can wait for you to catch up. But I wanted you to know."

Mom would say it's crazy—that there's no way I could feel the same after a few days and the things he said. But it *hasn't* been a few days. It's been years. He was always there, a helping hand, a kind word, a smile on a bad day, someone to catch me when I fell, someone to *save* me when I made a stupid decision. And, more recently, the person I turned to when I didn't know where else to go. He's seen me at my worst, and he was there through it all without asking anything of me.

And he thinks he's selfish.

I stand up and take the two steps to the other side of the table. "Baby?" he asks, quickly sitting up and scooting his chair back, ready to jump up and do whatever I need.

But I don't need him to do anything. I throw a leg over him and climb into his lap, straddling him like I did in his office and kiss him, clinging to him like it's been *years* since his lips last touched mine instead of just days. But those days were too long. Any amount of time apart is too long. "I love you too," I whisper.

His breath leaves his lungs in a shuddering rush. "Say it again, please?" he whispers, but he kisses me before I can.

I pull back, breaking our kiss though it should be a crime. "You first."

His smile is slow and easy and takes no prisoners. It leaves me wiggling in his lap, anxious to skip the rest of our plans for the evening and go straight to bed. "I love you."

Who knew three little words could pack so much punch. I shudder in his arms and whisper, "I love you too."

His hands slide down to my hips, and he uses his grip on me to press me firmly against the bulge in his jeans. "The car will be there tomorrow."

"Yeah. Let's skip to the last thing on the to-do list." I want his hands on me and him inside me so badly I could cry.

"You are *never* the last thing on my to-do list, Pixie Stix. I just save the best for last." He adjusts his grip so his hands are holding my ass and stands up. "But I am happy to clear my schedule for you."

"Yes, please." He carries me down the hall, his lips ceaselessly roaming, kissing my neck, my ear, my lips. Chevy runs in behind us, but he throws me down on the bed and quickly catches her, locking her out again.

"She'll learn," he grumbles, reaching for the button on his jeans. I knock his hands aside, wanting to do it myself, but he shakes his head and takes over. "Can't wait." He yanks his jeans and boxers down his hips so quickly it's amazing they don't rip.

He shoves the skirt of my dress up to my hips, yanks my panties off, and plunges home without a condom. Groaning, he thrusts his hips while he finishes removing my clothes. "I thought I'd never do this again," he says, the words coming in quick bursts with his panted breaths. "Fuck, you feel amazing. I never want to leave."

His urgency is contagious. I cling to him, digging my nails into his back as every quick, short thrust hits that spot inside of me, and every frantic word pushes me closer and closer until I come undone, quivering around him and shaking in his arms. He moves faster then, driving harder until he's pulsing within me and muttering nonsense again. And the world is right. This is where I'm supposed to be.

We stay like that, him halfway on the bed, and me wrapped around him until our bodies cool and our breathing slows. I'm close to sleep when Ryan tenses. "I forgot a condom," he whispers into my hair.

"Pill." I remind him, tracing patterns on his back with my fingertips until he shudders.

"I know, but I've never . . .I'm cautious. Birth control fails all of the time. That's why I wear a condom and pull out."

"It'll be alright," I promise. "And, even if it's not, we'll figure it out together." The future can bring it. I've got Ryan.

He sighs and his body melts like the weight of the world just rolled off his shoulders. "Together. I'm yours. Always."

There's no talk of *until you don't want me anymore* this time. I smile against his shoulder. "And I'm yours. Always. I love you."

"Love you too."

Epilogue
Ryan

"How did you know?" I ask Mason, looking over to where he sits next to me, watching our ladies chat. There's a party going on all around us; everyone turned up to celebrate Austin proposing to Jamaica—or to offer her their condolences once she accepted.

Trista keeps smiling down at the baby in her arms, and some small part of me acknowledges it would be alright for that to be a daily occurrence—without borrowing someone else's baby.

He looks my way. "Know what?"

I swallow hard and give voice to the question that's pinged around my brain for a week now. I expected this to take a lot longer than eighteen months to come up. "That you were ready to get married?"

It's been a year now since I told others about Selene at Trista's insistence. Turns out, I don't need a therapist. I have her.

Gabe threw an eighty-dollar bottle of whiskey at a tree in a fit of anger, but that's better than him drinking it, which is probably why he threw it.

Austin shut his mouth for a change.

Chris just watched, smiling his approval.

The ladies gasped and swarmed me, babbling apologies.

But Mason, he knew there aren't enough words on the planet to fix that loss. He just hugged me. He cried. I cried. We all cried before it was over, and we walked away with a better understanding of each other.

"Well, I mean, I kind of felt like I didn't have a choice," Mason tells me.

I roll my eyes at him. "I don't mean the contract bullshit."

"Ah," he intones, nodding. "How did I know I wanted it to be real?"

"Yeah."

"It wasn't any one thing, really. A bunch of different things that culminated in me waking up before her one morning," I snort, and he raises his drink to me, "I know, rarely happens, but it was just before Thanksgiving. I was already planning how I was going to propose. I had the ring, her family had their plane tickets. And laying there watching her sleep, the first thing that went through my head was, 'I'm so glad I get to marry her.' It didn't really dawn on me what it was at that time. It wasn't until a few days later, when I was laying in the grass struggling to breathe, afraid if I closed my eyes I'd never see her smile again, that I knew what that feeling was and that I was so fucking gone for her."

I guess almost dying would make a man figure some shit out real fast. There has to be an easier way, though. "I don't feel like having a near-death event to figure out if I'm ready or not."

Mason laughs, the happy sound booming out over the noise around us, drawing some looks. "I don't recommend it. Ask yourself this, if you were to wake up tomorrow and she wasn't next to you, and it's all because you were too afraid to promise her forever, how would you feel?"

I close my eyes and paint that picture in my mind, waking up to empty arms and her side of the bed cold. Realizing she slipped away in the night because I didn't step the fuck up and admit that my feelings for her have reached the point we talked about before, where marriage is something I'm ready to consider. And it fucking hurts.

Trista wouldn't do that. I brush the thought aside because it's not the point. She wouldn't. I know as sure as I know the sun will rise in the east in the morning that she won't leave over something like that. As long as I love her and am someone she can love, she'll stay. But if she wants to marry me, I want to marry her.

"Thanks, Mase." As hard as it was to ask, I'm glad I did. I knew he could put into perspective better than the others.

His glass touches mine with a *tink*. "Anytime."

"What if I end up like *them*?" The question nearly chokes me, but I have to know. How do I stop it from happening? How do I make sure that things never change?

"Your parents?" he shrugs. "You won't because you decide every day to be different. You should know that. You, more than anyone else, are the one who helped Trista figure out who she is. It's as simple as that. But if it helps, I promise to have my wife kick your ass if you start making the wrong choices."

My eyes burn with tears I refuse to let fall. "Thanks, man."

***

Trista is in the shop when I get home from work, singing along to the song on the radio by her favorite band—Three Days Grace—while draining the oil from our next project. A Carousel Red '69 GTO Judge that belonged to her father. *I'm glad he wasn't the rat bastard her mother made him out to be.* I already know he's not here, but I glance around to make sure he didn't change his mind.

Now that I'm here, I can't believe this is happening. My talk with Mason feels like a forever ago, but it was only last week, and his words are with me every day. But I'm ready.

"Hey," I call to her, but Chevy's excited meows are probably all the warning she needs. Chevy loves her servants.

"One sec," she calls back. "Almost—there! Oh!"

I smile and put a boot on the creeper to roll her out from under the car. There's a greasy rust stain on her forehead where I'm guessing the oil plug landed when she broke it loose.

"Grease looks good on you." *Everything* looks good on her. The torn jeans, combat boots, Mopar shirt from a car show we went to last year, and red bandana tied around her hair are a far cry from the flowers and frills she used to wear, but she's still my Pixie Stix no matter what her clothes look like.

"I prefer it on you," she says, smiling up at me. I hold out a hand and pull her to her feet when she takes it, then grab her for a kiss. I never get tired of being able to do that.

"Hey," she says, her eyes more than a little dazed.

"Hey," I repeat. "We need to talk."

"Alright?"

It's mean of me to leave her hanging like that but I don't know what to say to put her mind at ease. I don't know what to say at all!

Ignoring the rust and grease on her hands, I thread my fingers through hers and lead the way to the old bench seat I made into a couch for us. While she settles in, I work the ring out of my pocket and palm it so I'm ready.

She curls her legs underneath her and pats the seat, inviting Chevy to join us, which she does without care for where she puts a foot or claw until she's comfortable. "What's up?" Tris asks while she stops Chevy's attempts to tenderize her thigh.

I don't know where to begin. Trista and I talk about anything and everything without reservation or hesitation now. We have no secrets anymore. But this seems like something I should ease into. After all, I'm the one who said marriage wasn't a priority for me. "I've thought about this a lot lately, and I know my answer, so it's time to get yours." It's not the most romantic setting in the world. There's no grand gesture involved. I probably could've planned this better, but this is us. "Do you want to get married?"

She springs to her feet like the couch bit her ass, dumping Chevy off onto the floor. Her feelings hurt, the cat slinks off to pout like the little diva she is. *"What?"*

Oh, fuck. She's not ready. Slowly, I stand up to tower over her. We were at least closer to being eye-to-eye as we were before. I don't believe a man should get down on a knee like he's begging his woman to be his wife. They should be on equal footing then, as they should be in all things. "Have you ever thought about it?"

Her eyes get even wider. "Yes, but . . . Are you proposing right now?"

Hand shaking, I hold out the ring. It's a simple thing, a solitaire diamond mounted on intertwined platinum bands fused together, but something about it spoke to me. "Yes, I am. But—"

"Oh, Ryan." A tear drifts down her cheek and drops to the floor.

What the hell does that mean? I don't know what to do here. I expected a yes and joy, or a no and a discussion about our future together, because no doesn't mean the end of us. It just means we're taking a different path together through life. Either is fine, so long as we're on the same page.

"Yes!" she cries.

My heart stops, but then takes off like it's gotta make up for that lost time. "Yes?" I shout, caught up in the excitement of the moment. I never dreamed I'd want this, but with Trista, I want everything. All of her. Every day for the rest of my life.

I reach to wipe at a tear suspended in her eyelashes. "Yes! I was just thinking . . ."

"What?" I ask, but I have a feeling I know where her mind went.

She shakes her head and grabs the collar of my shirt, tugging me down for a quick kiss. "It's nothing, really, but I wish—"

"I asked your dad," I cut in, anticipating her words. The ol' man bawled so hard, all he could do for a while was hug me and shake his head. Said it meant the world to him that I thought to ask since he hasn't been part of her life long. "And your mom . . ."

Susanne wasn't as enthusiastic as Dale was, but she did get a little teary and hug me. That's a huge step up. I really don't care that she approves of me, but I knew it would be important to Trista. Their relationship is still strained, but slowly improving. And I'd be lying to myself if I said I'm not happy about her blessing.

"You did!" She jumps up and down and throws herself at me. I catch her and give her a real kiss.

Helping Trista find her father was the most rewarding thing I've ever done. It wasn't easy convincing Susanne to give me his name, and calling him once I found him was terrifying. What if he denied knowing Susanne or anything about a baby? But it took seven words to change their lives for the better. *I'm calling on behalf of your daughter.*

"Um . . . There's more," I say, hoping she still has some enthusiasm. "I'm . . . ready to talk about a family."

If it weren't for me holding her, she'd probably be on the floor right now. "Fam—what?"

"Not like right away or anything," I say before she gets too excited. I mean, if she wants to go practice, I'm all for it. But we need to talk about this before it happens. I'm still scared. "Just . . . soon."

"Soon," she repeats.

"Are you okay with that?" I ask, second-guessing myself. I don't want her to feel like I'll only marry her if she agrees to have my babies. She already said yes to that. She's mine either way. "It's okay if you aren't."

"Yes," she says again, and it might be my new favorite word. "I know you're scared," she whispers, reading my mind, "but a baby will be the best of both of us because that's what we'll give it."

That doesn't sound so bad. A child who is the best of both of us will be a force to be reckoned with. The world better watch out.

Thank you for reading *It's Not You*! If you enjoyed reading it as much as I enjoyed writing it, I hope you'll consider taking a moment to leave a review and share your thoughts. Reviews are magic fairy dust readers use to help good books fly. Your review could help other readers decide to read this and the other stories in the Tarnished Hearts series.

My newsletter is a great way to stay up-to-date with the newest releases. If you haven't already signed up, you can do so on my website, caradsmith.com. You'll get a free short story about the day Ronni, Fern, and Mason from *I Kinda Do* met when you sign up, and there are sure to be more short stories made available to subscribers along the way!

It's Not You ran away with me. I quickly fell in love with Trista and Ryan and their simple acceptance of each other. The story evolved well beyond my plans for it, and I'm so glad it did. It may be my new favorite, but don't tell *I Kinda Do*!

Acknowledgements

As always, thank you to my little family. We made it through another one, boys! Lesson learned. Deadlines aren't a challenge and writing during summer break is *not* a good idea!

Kelsey, thank you for helping me realize that word count limits shouldn't be a thing. Katie for all those typos you caught that no one else did. And Shannon for supporting my general craziness. There's so much more I should thank you three for, but if I get started I'll end up writing another whole book about it.

Thanks to Nancy, Dawn, and May for doing their best to make this the best! You all three faced different challenges during your part in this project, and I want you to know how much I appreciate you and all you do for me.

And thanks to my mom and dad for their unquestioning support, even though their daughter writes *those* books.

Follow Cara

My website:
www.caradsmith.com

Facebook:
www.facebook.com/CaraSmithAuthor

Instagram:
www.instagram.com/caradsmith

Pinterest:
www.pinterest.com/CaraDSmithAuthor